The House of Trembling Leaves

The conjuring of period and culture is impressive. The novel conducts its narrative historical and geographical, from ... and from pre-war Cambridge through ... pivotal moments in those countries' respe... Through it all are woven the compelling stories ... women and a friendship which transcends time and separation, and which survives through war, personal suffering and political division. Their enduring friendship is beautifully depicted – as are their family relationships – and gives the novel a warmth and humour at its core which makes a great counterpoint to the external horrors and hardships of war and hostile occupation.

Rosy Thornton, author of *Ninepins* and
The Tapestry of Love

The Fan Tan Players

'Satisfaction, even joy, accompanies the discovery of a new author, one previously unfamiliar, who proves his ability within a few pages and then tells an exciting tale. Without hesitation, Lees flexes his impressive storytelling muscles, giving readers and undeniable tingle of anticipation that he may have many more tales to tell.'

Cairns Media Magazine

'Romance, action, suspense.'

O Veu Pintado

'Engaging.'

The Bookbag

A Winter Beauty

'Opulent family saga, love story and lavish feast for the senses.'

Neues Deutschland (New Germany)

'A great novel. Colourful and vibrant.'

Altmuhlbote

'The story seems so realistic, exciting, tragic and rich in imagery.'

Sandammeer.at

'The debut of a born storyteller.'

Freis Wort

'His novels are set in a world where East meets West, a cross-cultural paradigm that he captures bewitchingly and dramatically in his fiction.'

Nick Walker, the *Star* (Malaysia)

Julian Lees was born and raised in Hong Kong. After attending Cambridge University he returned to live in Asia. He has written two previous novels: A Winter Beauty and The Fan Tan Players, which has been sold into four languages. Julian currently lives in Malaysia with his wife, Ming, and his three young children, Augustus, Amber, and Aisha.

Also by Julian Lees

The Fan Tan Players
A Winter Beauty (German publication only)

THE HOUSE OF TREMBLING LEAVES

Julian Lees

SANDSTONEPRESS
HIGHLAND | SCOTLAND

First published in Great Britain by
Sandstone Press Ltd
One High Street
Dingwall
Ross-shire
IV15 9WJ
Scotland.

www.sandstonepress.com

The publisher acknowledges subsidy from Creative Scotland
towards publication of this volume.

 Scottish
Arts Council

ISBN: 978-1-908737-17-5
ISBN e: 978-1-908737-18-2

Cover design by River Design, Edinburgh
Typeset by Iolaire Typesetting, Newtonmore
Printed and bound by TOTEM, Poland

Dedication:

For my brother Adrian.
For what we shared then and
for what we share now.

Acknowledgements:

I would like to thank my wife Ming and my children Gus, Amber and Aisha for inspiring me to write this book and for putting up with my frequent bouts of grumpiness along the way.

I am also indebted to Ben and Nelly Thomas for their humour and pep. And to Andrew Stephens and Matt Cross for their ceaseless flow of lewd yet inciteful tales.

This novel would not be possible without my agent Kate Hordern. Thank you for your foresight and for giving me the right advice whenever I needed it.

Thanks also to Richenda Todd for putting her invaluable time and expertise into this story.

Lastly, special thanks must go to Jasmine Oh, David and Katherine Lim, Yang Riches, Eddie Chew and Jeremy Cheam for sharing their stories of childhood in Malaysia.

PROLOGUE

Seen from high ground, amongst the coconut groves and flames-of-the-forests, the Juru River on the Malayan peninsula swelled and rolled through the jungle. The tawny length of water ran for seventy uninterrupted miles from the timber dam to the mouth of the sea, passing monkey colonies, palm frond tangles and longhouses made of cane and thatch.

Despite the Penang to Juru train chugging in from the north once a day, bringing supplies from the world outside, the tributaries remained the main roads through the forest. On the sandy banks splay-footed men with strips of cloth wrapped loosely about their heads traded pineapples. Hens with bold red flashes of feather scuttled about as bare-shouldered women in sarongs pounded *belacan* paste. Old women with white powder on their faces to block out the sun sat on their haunches winnowing rice.

To the people of the riverbank the Juru was a wellspring, giving life as a mother gives life; a fount of shrimps and fish, clean clothes and mud-free hair. It irrigated their rubber trees and moistened their cabbage crops; it doused their fires and swept away their night soil. For centuries these people had worshipped its might and treasured its bounty.

And so each year, near the river's crown, the villagers gathered to celebrate.

The stringy line of dragon boats bobbed about on the black water, knocking hulls and bumping paddles. Eight boats, made from jungle teak, each representing a nearby village, slowly manoeuvred into position for the start of the race – a two-mile sprint through an artery of the Juru River.

Sinewy, bare-chested oarsmen, sitting two abreast, flexed their muscles. They chatted and waved to the gathered crowd. *"Mm ho dam sum!"* they cried. "For the honour of the kampong! *Gaa dai lik! Gaa dai lik!"* their supporters bellowed back.

As soon as the *bomoh*, armed with his yellow bag of sparrow nests and animal bones, chanted his blessing, the headman from the local Chinese Association climbed onto a stilted dais and clasped a hornbill's tail feather at arm's length. Two hundred sets of hands drew their paddles out.

In the centre of each boat stood a canopied shrine housing a giant drum, a gong-beater and a cymbal-clanger. With a pair of bamboo sticks poised, the drummer of the closest vessel, the heartbeat of the crew, raised both fists and watched with a sideways squint.

The boats held a line against the current. Their multi-coloured banners fluttered from the sterns as village dogs pursued each other along the banks.

Schoolgirls with hibiscus blossoms behind their ears held their breath. The Association headman paused, looked about him and tilted his head. He let the hornbill feather fall.

With a roar all eight dragon boats lurched forward; wooden dragon heads, elaborately carved and painted with red and yellow scales, cut through the water. Firecrackers popped. "They're off!" yelled little boys perched on their fathers' shoulders. The schoolgirls squealed and tossed coconut shavings high into the air. "Come on Po On Village!" Drums thrummed, gongs sang out and cymbals crashed. Giddy-brained children cheered and stretched their arms. Chickens and geese scattered as bicycles gave chase with sisters riding pillion behind their brothers.

Po On Village was a rural settlement, some ninety miles to the northwest of Kuala Lumpur, made up of mainly rubber tree tappers and timber workers and the odd fisherman.

With a population of eight hundred – a lucky number for the Chinese, symbolizing wealth, balance and symmetry – the Chinese and Malays lived side by side in houses made from *attap* thatch and wood. The homes had kitchen gardens at the back and vast communal areas where children could play. There was a noodle vendor, a satay man and for those after a hint of sophistication, a chicken cutlet shop that cooked food 'Western style'. The kampong had a provision shop, a pith wood store, a toddy shop as well as a small mosque, a Chinese Temple and an Anglican Church built by an Invernesian expatriate in the 1890s. The church was perched on the river's edge, made from local wood and stone, and looked as if it had been transported from the Scottish Highlands.

The Teohs were the principal members of the church. They raised money for its upkeep, they maintained the slate roof, and they financed the installation of the prized pipe organ. Whenever the choir announced itself, Mrs Teoh, sat in the front pew and dressed in the floppy flowered number she wore every Sunday, smiled with reassurance, beaming with pride at the sound of her children's voices, at the roar of the copper pipes. This organ, this 'king of instruments', was as important to the Teohs as the stretch of prime agricultural land on their doorstep. There were only three other pipe organs in the whole of Malaya and to them it stood for civility, affluence and respectability.

"Come on Po On Village!" The boats, fronted with ferocious dragon heads, swept along.

In the crowd a young Chinese woman distributed small parcels of glutinous rice and salted chestnuts from a basket. She had an oval face, a high, intelligent forehead and dark, lush hair that jumped along her shoulders as she laughed. "Happy Dumpling Festival!" she said, smiling, offering the food to the local fisherfolk and rubber tappers. Each parcel was bound with bamboo leaves and raffia. "Eat them while they're still warm," she insisted. "Compliments of the Teoh family."

"Thank you, First-daughter Teoh!" a tree tapper replied. "Your family's kindness overwhelms us. And good luck to your brothers. I hope they win today's race."

The young woman thought of her brothers, James and Peter Teoh, frantically paddling, eyes out on stalks; the image made her smile.

Not far behind her, a maidservant dressed in a white tunic and loose dark trousers, traced her every step. The servant girl carried a Kodak Retina in her hands and every once in a while she paused, thrust her elbows out like chicken wings and took a photograph.

"Hurry up, pumpkin-head," urged her mistress, "and whatever you do don't drop the camera. Ah Ba will kill us if we damage it." Ignoring her, the maidservant wound the film with the crank pin and took another shot of the crowd, snapping images of Woos and Teohs together.

The annual Dumpling Festival was one of only a handful of days in the year when the settlement of debts took place amongst the villagers. It was also one of the few occasions when the Teohs and the Woos intermingled peaceably. There'd been a feud going on between the two families for as long as anyone could remember.

Mud-slinging, territorial conflicts and threats were common; sometimes a roadside scuffle broke out, sometimes a *parang* was wielded; only occasionally did bloodshed raise the stakes to such a degree that the council of kampong elders were called in to resolve the issue. And it all stemmed from a dispute over water. The great Juru River was their lifeblood and it ran through their individual lands. The Teohs owned 27,000 acres on the upper reaches of the river; the Woos controlled 30,000 acres along the valley floor. If a Teoh got the opportunity to cheat a Woo he would; if a Woo could outsmart and trounce a Teoh the whole of the lower valley rejoiced.

One would have imagined that such sworn enemies might choose to live as far away as possible from each other, yet their compounds stood a mere mile and a half apart, on the peripheries of their respective estates, separated by the watercourse and near enough to observe one another through a spyglass. It was as though they needed to keep a close eye for fear of attack.

The Teohs named their house Tamarind Hill after the massive trees that flanked their drive; the Woos called their property Swettenham Lodge in honour of Malaya's first Resident General. Both buildings scrutinized their rival with snake-eyed suspicion. Like twin jousters in some grim medieval fable, they kept sullen watch, monitoring every movement through the armoured slits of their helmets.

"Come get your rice dumplings while they're hot!" the girl sang. "Compliments of the Teoh clan!" She glanced towards the Woo camp where a troop of men were busy spit-roasting suckling pigs over hot coals. The rich caramelized glaze of the pork skin made her mouth water. "Much tastier than the rubbish those people are trying to peddle!"

She felt a hand on her shoulder. "Who are you calling rubbish?"

The girl spun around and looked the Chinese man sharply in the eyes. He was dressed in white linen, his hair was oiled and neatly parted to the left and he smelled as crisp and clean as sandalwood. "Well, well, if it isn't Number One Son Woo," she said. "*Dai-yee-jee*. Old egghead, look-how-important-I-am, Mr Brainbox from Cambridge University, himself!"

"I asked you a question. Who are you calling rubbish?"

"Who do you *think*?"

The maidservant took a picture of them quarrelling.

"I'd prefer it if you didn't refer to my family that way, especially on such a festive occasion."

The girl pursed her lips. "Oh dear, I am sorry. What was I thinking? Let me rephrase. How about thickheaded good-for-nothing halfwits instead? Is that more polite? Or gormless monkey-face."

The man grasped her by the wrist. "You're coming with me!"

She dropped her basket and felt herself being dragged through the throng, through a line of chickens scratching the ground, away from the river's edge. She glanced about for her maidservant but she was nowhere to be seen. They swept through the village square, past the toddy sugar shop, the pith wood store and the mosquito-net maker, and rushed towards the hillside path. The old men playing Chinese dominoes by the walls of the village temple, shaded by its overhanging eaves, looked up, as did widow Ping, kneeling in prayer by a tin of joss sticks and an offering of fruit.

"Let me go!" the girl hissed.

"No," he said. "You're coming with me!"

A train of firecrackers exploded, crackling the air and making people gasp and stare into the sky. "You're hurting!" she warned.

The sounds of the crowd receded as he pulled her into the bush, climbing the steep hillside path fringed with tall weeds and elephant grass. Surrounded by tropical foliage they stopped to catch their breath. Looking over his shoulder, he checked they weren't being followed and then pressed her against the trunk of a rambutan tree. His eyes shone like wet bronze. "Thickheaded, good-for-nothing halfwits?"

"Don't talk. Don't say anything." She clasped his face and kissed him hard on the mouth. His lips tasted like sweetened tea. She ran her fingers though his hair and down along his back, hitching up one thigh to allow his hand to move freely between her legs.

"Not here," he said, catching his breath. "Not in this undergrowth. There might be centipedes."

"Where then?

He looked up.

At first she didn't see a thing, but then as the wind shifted and sunshine poured through the canopy she saw a tiny bamboo and rattan tree house with a palm frond sunshade. "When did that come from?'

"It took me all of last week to finish. I swept it clean of cobwebs this morning. There's a rope tucked away . . ." He reached behind her. ". . . just here."

She whispered a series of curses. "You know I hate climbing."

"Nonsense, it'll be fun. Besides, if us Woos and Teohs are going to get up to a bit of clandestine" – he slewed his eyes left and right comically – "*sooky-sooky*, we better do it in complete privacy, don't you think?"

"Are you sure we weren't seen?"

"Yes." He gripped her by the waist and guided her up the tree.

Five miles upstream, amongst a wasteland of dead trees, dark shapes materialized from out of the jungle; their outlines silhouetted against the fading evening light; their clothes the colour of ash. The brush and timber dam appeared before them, entombed in shadow. As they approached they saw that the logs, piled up high, lay lengthwise side by side; some as thick as three feet in diameter, they extended from one bank to the other.

The men exchanged looks and nodded to one another.

Splitting up into pairs they reached the crest of the dam and knelt against the upper tier of logs. With hand axes they hacked half-moons into the wood and inserted the red sticks of dynamite. As they worked, wiping the sweat out of their eyes, a hornbill heckled and squawked from the coconut groves further up the river. They placed the explosives at nine strategic points, inserted the detonating caps and lit the thirty-minute fuses. The small flames sparkled in the grey dusk.

Seconds later, like ghosts in the night, their silhouettes vanished into the rainforest.

The tree house took on an amber hue from the sunset.

Their torsos were ringed with sweat. As she lay on her

back, sliding against the dry weave of rattan flooring, prickling her bare bottom, he worked his way down her body. He kissed her throat and the tips of her breasts. She felt his lips skate along her navel, felt the softness of his mouth edge lower, flicking the flesh rhythmically until his breath warmed the spot between her thighs. She threw her head back and stared at the sky. The clouds seemed to wobble and crumble.

She pulled at his hair, thirsting for him to enter her. *Please*, she mouthed, breathing fast, *now* . . .

She crushed herself against him, arching her hips. A ripple of pressure raced through her just as he raised her knees to her chest and slid into her.

The world shrank in that instant.

Legs entwined, they rocked in unison.

The maidservant edged her way up the hillside to get a panoramic shot of the river, stepping through grass so high it tickled her fingertips as she walked. The land around her was lush and green and full of bugs. She spotted an old tree trunk and decided to use it as a resting place. It was hot work. The perspiration made her dark hair shine. With arms cocked like chicken wings, she adjusted the rangefinder and saw the ornate boats in the near distance, snaking along the river like a varicose vein.

She took a couple of snaps before turning abruptly. Someone was walking through the forest behind her. She heard a tree branch snap, followed by a series of low whistles. Twenty feet away, a man emerged from the thicket. He was dressed all in grey and had a mole on his left cheek. One of his shoulders was lower than the other. Instinctively, she took a photograph of him. Through the frame she noticed he carried a red tin in his hand. He extracted whatever was within the tin and tossed the container into the brush; she made a note to retrieve it later.

She shifted, rustling dry grass. Her eyes met his eyes, black and gleaming. His lips curled into a sneer.

When she saw the gun in his hand she began to run.

There was a low boom, followed by the screech of birds and the barking of every dog in the village. The ground shook, startling the leaves from the trees. At the dam face, water began to spray out from tiny chinks appearing all along the log wall, bursting through the gaps like needles of light through black *Peranakan* lace.

The timber dam began to tremble. It began to groan. And then with a deafening *CRACK* it gave way.

The torrent gushed forth, tossing logs about as if they were toothpicks. Like a ravenous sea monster, it came barrelling onto the banks, flattening all that stood in its path. It consumed a drove of bullocks in a giant cloud of spray. It smashed against a lone fisherman, devouring him in one like Leviathan swallowing Jonah. It gobbled up a small house and carried away its contents, including a child who was still inside. It obliterated everything in its path, growing higher and higher with each passing second and it was heading towards the main village.

She reclined on her front, his face resting on the small of her back.

It was a beautiful and clear evening. The mosquitoes stayed in the tall grass and the low sun hung in the sky like a copper penny. She could hear the laughter and sigh of the festival crowd not far away. Through the canopy she saw the lines of rubber trees reaching out for miles beyond. "I remember when my father first took me down to the plantation," she said in a wistful tone. "I must have been five or six. We made a cutting in the bark of a tree and teased a dribble of milky sap into a bowl. I used to do lots of things with Ah Ba."

"But not any more."

9

"Not any more. The business has taken over his life."

She draped her head over the edge of the tree house to listen to the sounds of the forest and to allow the breeze from a distant sea to tingle her skin. She heard a swish of leaves. At that instant she thought she saw a human figure at the fringe of her vision – a faceless man looming momentarily out of the elephant grass. A knot in her stomach tightened. Her eyes scanned the forest floor. She tensed. Was that a silhouette plunging into the darkness? She couldn't be sure. There was a snap of twigs and a quick, sharp whistling, a call to someone, followed immediately by a whistled reply.

She sat up straight and reached for her clothes. She wanted to flee.

"What's wrong?" he asked.

"I want to go."

"You're trembling."

"Someone may have seen us."

They dressed and climbed down from the tree house. A chill went through her bones. And that's when she heard it – a rumbling, crashing noise, like rocks shifting under the weight of a hundred waterfalls. There was no way of knowing what it was but the vibrations could be felt through the soles of her feet. At first she guessed it was an earthquake or a thunderclap; then she thought of cannon fire. Running was the only way she knew to ward off the fear.

She ran downhill towards the village, tearing through the tall weeds and lalang thickets, towards the growing mass of sound. Her cotton shoes squelched with every step. She couldn't understand why there was water rising up above her ankles. Each stride she took the water got deeper. The cold crept higher up her legs and then to her bewilderment she found dozens of silver-scaled fish sprawled out on their sides, gasping in the marshy shallows.

She rushed through the elephant grass and stopped dead at the perimeter of the village square. The river was overflowing, unloading cargoes of mud. Everything was swamped. Staring in disbelief, trying to catch her breath, she watched the torrent sweep past her at a ferocious speed, carrying flotsam and stubble, bullock carcasses and uprooted trees. Choking, goggle-eyed people clung to walls and windowsills and knolls with the current tearing at them; hands ripped fistfuls of grass from the earth before vanishing. Someone was screaming to get the children to higher ground. A woman searching for her baby bawled with frenzied panic.

She thought of the schoolgirls with the hibiscus flowers in their hair, wondered if they'd been drowned. A tree came crashing down to her left, throwing clouds of spray into her eyes just as a young boy's face, her cousin's she was sure, appeared abruptly out of the water and disappeared just as suddenly. "I'm going to die too," she told herself.

Confusion was everywhere; she heard a desperate shout and watched as the Association headman, with his body pinned to a tall pine, raise his voice in terror. An upturned bullock, hocks stiff as glass and breaking the water surface, speared towards him. With a sickening thud the half-ton animal slammed into the headman, ripping his neck from his shoulders. A handkerchief of blood fluttered the air. The water turned fleetingly from black to red.

A moment later the Anglican Church began to shake. Slate tiles fell from its roof, lashing the water like mortar shells. She saw her Second-aunty Doris hobble in her direction, she was shouting at her, telling her to run for it. The church organ twisted and crumpled as the torrent swept it away. And then the entire structure collapsed.

PART ONE

January 1936

1

"*Aiyoo*, you know she's gone completely cuckoo-clocks, don't you?" Sum Sum said to a passing bird as it landed quietly on the boat's gunwale. "Ever since she tripped over on lawn and struck her head on a stone she spending hours writing letters to herself, growing out her armpit hairs and speaking fancy-fancy English to imaginary sausage rolls. And now she's running away from home to marry Big Ben."

"I can hear you," said Lu See wrinkling her nose.

"Oh good," Sum Sum replied. "I thought you fallen asleep standing up, lah."

"Will you please be quiet? I want to enjoy the sunset."

Emerging from deep shadow, the low-slung *tongkang* followed a flock of bulbuls as they took to the air. On its teak deck, Lu See sipped water from a coconut husk and gazed into the tropical forest, at the filigrees of late afternoon sunlight filtering through the mist. The tongue of land wrinkled and folded before her eyes as the river mist rolled in, damp and thick. Lu See bounced the coconut husk in her hand a few times and then flipped it overboard; her eyes followed the bulbuls.

"My God, I've done it," she said to herself quietly. For days a heavy thread of anxiety had sewn itself into her chest, ravelled and intertwined like the Iban sleeping mats of Sarawak. But now, slowly, the stitches were coming undone. As they drifted further and further away from her family's rural retreat in Juru, Lu See felt the unease subside and in its place a sense of hope and excitement emerged. She was still frightened, terrified even, that her father or Uncle Big Jowl would snatch her away, but now she had made the first step she felt her spirits leap. Her future was now in the hands of the Gods.

Earlier in the day, just before dawn, Lu See and Sum Sum snuck away from Tamarind Hill via the servants' quarters. Using a wheelbarrow to transport Lu See's trunk, they carefully and quietly made their way across the back lawn. At first Lu See could not see the garden from the trees as it was so black, but when her eyes adjusted to the darkness, she half turned her head and made out the row of massive tamarinds lining the drive. *That way* she whispered, finding it hard to breathe, sensing her nerves getting the better of her.

Sum Sum shuffled up beside her and they exchanged uneasy glances. Together they pushed the wheelbarrow along the dirt road. When the moon appeared from behind some clouds, they knew they would be visible against the surrounding forest so they increased their pace. Gradually, Lu See lost track of time; her world was restricted to the audible crunch of the wheelbarrow against the road, the ache in her hands and arms against the handlebars, the suffocating fear of being caught. She was so absorbed that when they reached the river's edge she did not hear Sum Sum speaking to her. "We take small row boat now and catch *tongkang* later on. Maybe one mile away. I arrange everything already." She watched her maidservant squat low to plunge a hand into the Juru's current and pull at a thick rope. Lu See was aware of the silence all about her – it was as if the night animals had stopped what they were doing to watch them.

The moonlight shone on the smooth black water. Sum Sum climbed aboard the small rowing boat and, by touch, shipped the oars. Lu See loaded the trunk into the stern and then stepped into the little vessel, trying to hold the craft steady with one hand. The boat was light and shallow-bottomed; it wobbled side-to-side under her weight so she sat down quickly.

"You ready, meh?" asked Sum Sum.

Lu See nodded. She looked behind her, wondering if they'd left muddied footprints in the ground.

Sum Sum untied the rope from its moorings and pushed them away from the earthen bank. Lu See felt droplets of water on her forearms as the little craft, unstable now it was laden, bobbed downriver. In the distance, up on the hill, she made out her home at the top of the drive – granules of light sparked on, indicating that the other servants were now awake. A rooster began to crow as they melted into the darkness. It would only be a matter of time before the household sent out a search party.

The trauma caused by the dam burst scarred the entire village. For weeks sobs of despair filled the night like fireflies released from a jar and one could not walk into the village square without embers from holy paper fanned by the temple monks catching in your hair.

Half a year had passed since the disaster. It had taken months to repair the damage and almost as long to recover the dead; for weeks decaying bodies, all bloated and white, were fished out of the river miles downstream, most of them unidentifiable. The official death toll was put at 32, but Lu See was sure that the number was more like twice that. And of course the feuding between the two clans intensified – each blaming the other for sabotaging the dam. She also remembered Sum Sum talking about seeing a man with a gun on the day of the tragedy. Who was this man? Why did he point the weapon at her? Nobody seemed to know.

Lu See and her family attended every funeral – Muslim, Christian and Taoist. Some affected Lu See more than others. The dead baby, tightly swaddled in a white shawl, haunted her, as did the sight of Mr See, the grandfather who owned the pith wood store, with his wispy Chinese beard, so long it had to be tucked into his waistband. And at each one the grief was visible wherever she looked. Women clasped and unclasped their hands, swaying their bodies and shaking their heads. Men slouched over and stared at the floor, round-mouthed with despair.

But it was her cousin Tak Ming's burial that cut her up the most. Tak Ming was Second-aunty Doris' only son. He was twenty. Lu See's brothers, James and Peter, had been particularly close to him.

When they lowered his coffin, Lu See let out a whimper like a strangled animal. Even Lu See's father, who had taken off his hat and placed it over his heart, was bawling.

Only Uncle Big Jowl stood without tears in his eyes.

Later, she found her father, Ah Ba, in their garden. He was kneeling, resting his head on the root of a fig tree and when he saw Lu See he hugged her so hard it hurt her ribs. He reached into his pocket and took out his wallet. He opened it to reveal a photograph of a five-year-old Lu See and her two brothers sitting at the steps of the gazebo, a bowl of lychees beside them. Lu See wiped her hand on her skirt before taking the photograph, realizing without having to be told how important it was to him. "I look at this picture every morning after I wake up," he said. She studied the small movements of his face. "I cannot imagine what I would do if anything happened to you. If it was my daughter I had to put in the ground rather than Tak Ming."

It was then that she'd decided to build a new pipe organ in her cousin's memory.

She tried not to think about this now.

She also tried not to think about what they'd be saying about her back home, but the thoughts came nonetheless. Like a bullhorn blast, she heard her mother's blaming tones – *how can such a girl, so pretty with such shapely-shapely mouth and bright complexion do such a thing! So much going for her, you know. Clever student, good with numbers. Cha! And athletic, aiyoo, so athletic, played field hockey for the English-stream Bing Hua Upper Sixth, to boots.*

Enough, Lu See said to herself. She shook off her mother's

voice with a twitch of the head. I'm free now. I'm Teoh Lu See, I'm nineteen and I'm off to start a new life. I may be suffering from a god-awful head cold, but I'm feeling great! Oh God, I'm really doing this, aren't I . . . I'm actually eloping.

She took a deep breath. She had never slept outside her parents' house.

Eloping. To Lu See it was a deliciously secret word, rich in taboo and mystery and adventure. The idea of running away both thrilled and terrified her, as did the thought of the huge passenger liner she was going to board in Penang and the trip across the oceans. But at least on ship, nobody would pass judgement, nobody would chastise. There would be no marriage to the One-eyed Giant, no more tongue-lashings about seeing that 'dreaded Woo boy'. On ship she would be free.

Eloping. Elope. From the Middle Dutch *ontlopen*, to scurry away. From the Anglo-Norman French *aloper*: to run off with one's lover; possibly related to the word to leap. She had looked it up in her father's dictionary. In her mind, however, she wasn't simply eloping – she was pursuing a dream; inspired by Adrian she was going to apply for a place at Cambridge. Truth was she was more excited by the prospect of studying at Girton College than marrying Adrian Woo.

Lu See closed her eyes and felt the last dabs of evening sunshine warm her face.

A few steps behind her stood Sum Sum, her best friend, confidante and maidservant of seven years. Her black cloth shoes shuffled beside a shining eel skin trunk. Sum Sum was Darjeeling tea in colour with a moon face and stringy hair that she wore tied into a bun. Whilst Lu See was willowy legged, Sum Sum was pleasantly round. She had a compact hour-glass figure and held her back imperiously straight, clutching a small red onion which she held, arm extended, towards Lu See.

"For your cold," she said.

Lu See shot Sum Sum a hurried look. "Are you serious? You expect me to chew on a raw onion?" As she spoke she could feel something trickle from a nostril. She blew hard into a handkerchief.

"For sure, lah. My mother was tip-top Tibetan medicine woman, lah. She gave me onion all the time."

The *tongkang* drifted on towards Butterworth. The flag of the Malay Federation billowed in the wind – horizontal stripes of white, red, yellow and black with a prancing tiger at its centre. One of the crew, a Malaccan in a short sarong, with arms bitten black from the sun, moved cautiously to the poop, kneeling. He unfurled a thick rope with a slab of rotting mutton attached to a fist-sized hook. With one end secured to a capstan, he tossed the rope astern. The crewmen were trawling for crocodiles, hoping to sell their flesh for medicinal broths and their skins for leather. Palm fronds flowed past. A breath of wind shifted a fringe of scrub by the riverbed, exposing the nostrils and shimmering, wet marble eyes of a partially submerged beast.

"An onion?" Lu See repeated belligerently.

"*Ayo Sami*, don't argue, lah, I'm older than you."

"By eleven bloody days!"

Sum Sum held the onion at arm's length. "Well? You going to eat or not? Come, before I get damn powerful angry."

Lu See made a face, as if something sharp and vinegary had crawled into her mouth. She took a bite and almost at once her eyes began to tear. She felt the spasm of a sneeze building, jellyfish tentacles tickling her sinuses, and held her breath for several moments to allow the sensation to pass.

"See?" said Sum Sum, stifling a laugh. "Just like biting into a sour guava, no? Now, when you're ready, rub some of this lemongrass oil on your skin, lah, before the mosquitoes find you."

When Lu See's vision cleared, she stared into the hushed gloom within the rainforest. Bats pinged in and out of the darkness. Downriver she could make out a cloistered village perched on the banks of the Juru – row after row of cane longhouses held up by stilts on the water's edge, rising eight to ten feet above the jungle floor. Their broad-leaved thatch roofs looked frayed from the recent great storms. Each home had a raised verandah in front where children sat on mats eating rice from banana leafs. Feet dangling, they all waved at the approaching vessel. Lu See and Sum Sum waved back.

A little while later, with nearly all of the sun seeping out from the sky and the fireflies beginning to show, there came a squawking high-pitched cry from one of the crew. The thick rope was straining at the capstan. And that's when she saw it, both hook and mutton in its maw. The long snout slicing through the water, the pale cresting underbelly, the sinuous tail; interlocking teeth snatched and twisted, churning the spinach-green water into a milky froth. The crocodile's thick globular eyes seemed to stare at her for an instant, following her, and then, with the boat listing precariously, it was lifted off the surface of the water and hauled aboard.

She watched the men, all dark faces and hard seafaring hands, gather quickly around in a huddle, each carrying a club or a sharpened *parang*. The seven-foot crocodile hissed. Someone lit a lantern and held it up on the end of a pole as the men swung their weapons. The huge muscular tail thrashed and thumped the deck and soon the blood sludge was being smeared across the deck by bare human feet. With a fierce thrust one of the machetes pierced the crinkled flesh between the animal's eyes. Black blood spewed. Then, like a piece of heavy driftwood, the crocodile went still.

The crewmen hacked away, whooping and shouting, separating reptilian head from body. Their sarongs became streaked with red. Lu See, white-faced, felt compelled to watch. The commotion shook the bulbuls from the trees and set off a cacophony of squabbling, until all of a sudden there was another shout, more panicked than the ones before. And the men stopped. One or two of them dropped their tools.

"What's happening?" said Lu See. "What have they seen?"

Sum Sum crept along the starboard railing and listened to the salvo of chatter and stop-start quarrelling. She saw the front feet of the reptile, black and murky and pointed with no webbing between the toes. She snatched a look at its hind leg – webbed and amphibious like the horror hands in the wax museums. "They're saying that the thing was missing a limb. They are saying that to catch a river dragon with only three legs is a curse. The fourth leg will appear in your dreams and snatch away your firstborn child."

"Do you think it's true?"

"How in Dharmakaya heaven would I know? I grew up in the buckwheat fields of Lhasa."

"And the way you're dressed it looks like you still work in one." Lu See flicked the catches of one of the eel skin bags. "Here," she said pressing a folded clutch of blue cotton into Sum Sum's hands.

"What's this?"

"What do you think it is, pumpkin-head? It's a sundress."

"What do you want me to do with it?"

"I want you to wear it, of course."

Sum Sum positioned her hands firmly on her hips and looked down at her white amah's tunic. "Why?"

"Because we've run away from home and my mother's going to try and track us down. We sail first thing tomorrow."

"I bet this is what it feels like when you've robbed a bank."

"I've booked our tickets on the *Jutlandia* under an assumed name but Father and Third-uncle Big Jowl will be asking round for a young Chinese woman and her pumpkin-headed maid."

"An assumed name? *Ayo*, damn-powerful exciting, lah! What did you call yourself?"

"Lucy Apricot."

"Crazy crackpot idea. Going to England is like fairy tale story. I love it!"

"I know. And if you wear this we'll be less conspicuous. Big Jowl Uncle will never find us."

"In which case, maybe you give me some of your jewellery too? How about the jade earrings with the tigers, lah. I should wear those as well, no?"

"Sometimes I wonder why I didn't just leave you behind." Lu See looked out into the stillness and shook her head slowly.

The *tongkang* drifted. Everything around them grew still. A forest bird shrieked.

Sum Sum gave a little shudder. "I'm scared of the jungle at night. Scared of the Pontianak." She meant the vampire of Malay folklore.

"Nonsense, there's no such thing."

"Its eyeballs roll up into its head."

"Quiet, will you?"

Lu See stood beside the metal railings, gripping them. She listened to the night fall in around her and heard in her head the juvenile refrain her brothers would sing when she lay in her mother's bed sick with the flu: *Naughty girl, naughty girl pretending to be sick, Big Jowl uncle is coming with his stick.*

And she knew, instinctively, that he was already hot on her trail.

2

Following the early morning rains, the sun threw its heat slantwise over Penang port; an unyielding tropical blanket that tore the moisture from your skin like a furnace. All along the dock the Lascars sat on their haunches, chewing bhang and sucking on hand-rolled *bidis* to get them going, blowing the smoke downwind. And whilst the dogs barked and the roosters crowed, hawkers set up their stalls by the quay from one end of Chulia Street to the other, busily grilling stingrays and skewering satays over charcoal and cracking eggs to make oyster omelettes on cast-iron woks. Tamil, Hokkien, Bahasa, pidgin English and Cantonese pinged back and forth like flies in the tall grass.

Standing on the deck of the MS *Jutlandia* where the life rafts were stowed, Lu See had long ago resolved to sketch every detail of her crossing. She knew Sum Sum would be elsewhere on ship snapping photographs with the Kodak Retina, but it didn't stop her. This, she decided, was a journey of a lifetime, especially for a girl who'd never ventured beyond the Straits of Malacca. She unclipped a pencil from her sketchbook and began folding back pages, scribbling notes and making quick outline observations – every tint of cloud and sea shimmer, each scent whether it was perfumed or putrid, every sound from the piston blast of the ship's horn to the calls of the Mullah citing his morning prayers. Hastily she outlined a sketch of a linen-suited European, sporting a sola topi, having his shoes blackened by a bald-headed Malay.

Jim-dandy, she said to herself, adopting an American

expression she'd heard at the movies, *everything's all jim-dandy now*. Thrilled at the prospect of flight, a sense of liberation coursed through her. She often marvelled at what she was like before she knew Adrian, how her life had lacked adventure and meaning, how she'd lived so long without passion.

She was seventeen when she met him at the New Year's Dance at the Selangor Club. Dressed in white tie and tails, he approached her about twenty minutes after the Royal toasts with a ceramic bowl of dried fruit in his hand. The band started playing a Count Basie number. "Did you hear the story about the man who drowned in a bowl of dried fruit? A strong currant dragged him in. Fancy a raisin?" he asked, proffering the bowl. She shook her head. "What about a date then?"

"That's one of the worst chat-up lines I've ever heard."

"Lime sorry, but I couldn't give a fig."

He was five years her senior and attached to the Royal Anthropological Institute, one of the few Chinese in their employ. "I've been studying the Sea Dyaks of Borneo, spent the last seven weeks in the forests of Kuching. Most of the women I meet walk around in nothing but a grass skirt." He looked her up and down and grinned. "My name's Adrian. Adrian Woo."

"I know who you are, Number One Son Woo. We're not meant to talk to each other."

Lu See noticed that he had big, strong hands and there was this lustrous timbre to his voice. "So as an anthropologist I suppose you use your hands to dig up old bones and bits of broken crockery."

"That's more an archaeologist's job. I'm more of a voyeur."

"Sounds . . ."

"Naughty?"

"A little. So, Adrian Woo, as an anthropologist, can you tell me *one* fascinating fact about the rain forest?"

"Hmm, well let me see." He thought for a second. "How about this: the male proboscis monkey can maintain an erection for over twenty-four hours."

Smiling, "Okay, I'll grant you that that is quite interesting."

"Only quite?"

"Only quite."

"You're hard to satisfy."

She bit her lip. "Not always."

"Well, I like a challenge."

The way he spoke to her, so directly and openly, was irresistible. But it was when he buffed her dancing shoes that she fell for him.

"Look," he said. "They're all muddy from the rain."

He sat her down, propped her feet on his lap and polished them with his handkerchief, using champagne froth to get the proper sheen. Watching his fingers make little circles, she felt something ignite in her chest like a bush fire. She wanted to lose herself in him, surrender to his wild, reckless, free spirit.

Later, on the drive home, her mother said. "*Cheee-cheee-cheee*. Why were you speaking so long to that Woo boy, *hnn*? What were you thinking, you thinking he wants to steal you away, is it? Have nice Teoh girl like you in his love hut shack in Borneo jungle, *hnn*?"

"Isn't it time that this stupid Woo-Teoh feud ended?"

"Please," her father, C. M. Teoh, said. "Let's not talk about this now." He slewed his eyes toward the chauffeur. "Lu See was only making polite conversation with him. Whole world knows she's promised to somebody else."

Indeed, her parents had entered into a marriage agreement with the Chow family as long ago as 1930, promised to a boy at the age of thirteen; a young man with money and connections called Cheam Chow. They'd set an auspicious date for the end of May. And every weekend or so her mother said she should start preparing the wedding plans.

There was so much to do. Even the dress was fitted months in advance: after dinner Lu See would stand on top of the tea table with her arms held out to her sides as the tailor took her measurements and pulled the silk material tightly to the small of her back. "You no become pig-blubber-fatty bom bom now, ok?" the tailor warned. "Otherwhy you make me look bad on wedding day when people say you spilling out everywhere and everyone say tailor Pang made a dress for Terengganu elephant."

"I won't go through with this, Mother!" Lu See hissed as tailor Pang went to gather some more pins from his store-room. "Forcing me to marry this way. It's barbaric and outdated."

"I don't care what you're thinking."

"You know damn well I don't want to marry him."

"You do as your father says."

"Ah-Ba never talks things through with me. I can never reason with him."

"What, you don't want to bring wealth to our family, *hnn*? The day you join with the Chow family will be a proud day for us all."

"I'm stagnating here. I have to take control of my life."

"*Cha!*"

"I need intellectual freedom. I'm going to be a modern woman and enrol as a student at Cambridge."

"*Cambeech University?* Don't be silly."

"I'm being serious."

"This is because of Second-aunty Doris, is it? Filling your head with nonsense."

"It's not nonsense."

"How many Chinese you think they take?"

"Adrian Woo for one – "

"And how many *female* Chinese, *hnn*? Cambeech University indeed . . . what next, you want to raise the *Titanic*, is it?"

"Abdul Rahman, the son of the Sultan of Kedah, was at Cambridge."

"What, you think you're daughter of a sultan now, is it?"

"And the poetess Sarojini Naidu went to Girton."

"I never heard of her."

"She was the first woman ever to be elected President of the Indian National Congress. And then there's this fellow Nehru, the Indian statesman, he went to Trinity."

"Look, you can do what you want after you are married."

"You should be helping me to foster my talent not squander it. The only person in this family who appreciates my academic record is Second-aunty Doris."

"*Cha!* Don't mention that woman's name! Always she encourage your foolish academic pretensions."

"It's true."

"The thing is to find a good husband first. Afterwards you can go join the French Foreign Legion for all I care. You marry Chow Cheam, no more talk."

"I won't do it!"

Her father entered the room. "What is all this commotion?"

"I refuse to marry him, Ah-Ba!"

"You do as you are told."

"If you won't listen to me I'll be forced to do something drastic."

Irked, his face darkened. "Your heart is young and impetuous. Go to sleep. In the morning you will realise how rash your words are. By the morning your soul will know the truth."

But in her soul Lu See knew that day would never come. She knew she would never marry the One-eyed Giant.

Turning to the front of her sketchbook her gaze fell on a square of newsprint that had been glued to the endpapers. Five months ago, days before his return to Cambridge, she'd been photographed with Adrian at the Swettenham Ball. The picture of them together appeared in the society pages of the *Malay Mail*. Their respective parents had been livid. As if in prayer she would piously bend over the hazy image and study his face, thinking how lucky she was. He was every-thing she wanted: intelligent, funny, fluent in three languages and so handsome that his smile lit up the darkest room.

Instinctively, she knew he was somebody to admire; a person with strong political beliefs; someone who was as adept at talking to the old dowagers at ambassadorial parties as he was to Communist Party leaders. He had the authority and dignity that other men seemed to look for. And now, as he studied for a doctorate at Jesus College, Cambridge, he commanded respect wherever he went. Five weeks, she assured herself, five weeks before I see him again. Giddy with expectation she kissed the picture lightly and pressed the book to her chest.

"You know he spends far too much time on his hair, don't you?" said Sum Sum, her cloth shoes making *shlip-shlap* noises on the deck.

Lu See sighed and shook her head.

"I'm sure he keeps a hairbrush in his back pocket, lah."

"Shouldn't you be unpacking or something?"

"Cannot, lah. The cabin boy says he will show us to our room after the boat has launched."

Minutes later a thin glaze of sea spray salted Lu See's lips. Some people tossed fragrant rice into the water, others threw flowers, or paper streamers, or bits of coconut. Amongst the cries of excitement, she watched the ship loose its moorings, watched the backwash leave the port of Penang in its wake as the tug pulled the ship out of the harbour.

And that was when she saw Uncle Big Jowl, pushing through the crowd of coolies on the dock. He was shouting and waving a stick in the air. The coolies turned from their work to gawp at him; some put down their sweat-towels and gunnysacks full of spice and peppers. Uncle Big Jowl shouted at the *Jutlandia* as it crept away, shouted at it to stop, his face pulled tight like a drawstring bag, flesh bulging under his shirt like mattress stuffing. He had spotted her. A fist inside Lu See clenched. She watched him smash his cane against the wooden jetty in anger, splintering it into match-wood. His face grew smaller and smaller as the ship pulled away. The fist inside her relaxed, yet she kept thinking that a hole had now formed in her middle.

Everything – the shophouses, the colonial two-storey buildings, the Indian women in yellow saris, the Muslim men in their *songkok* skullcaps, the Chinese children playing with paper lanterns, Uncle Big Jowl – became tiny grey specks, washed into the sea. *That's me right now*, she thought, *– unmoored and free. No turning back. No regrets. Hungry for adventure.* She had never rebelled against anything before: this was the turning point in her life. She had crossed the Rubicon.

Having carried the guilt around in her chest for days like an undigested egg, she now felt an indisputable freedom taking hold, a self-reliance that hadn't been there before. Her heart felt lighter, her eyes brighter; satisfaction at having defied her family stole over her.

She returned to her sketchbook and tore out a page from its middle. It was a pencil drawing she'd done weeks before of her home, Tamarind Hill. Turning away from the wind, she pulled a matchbox from her pocket and set the sketch alight.

She felt like a bird in the open sky.

Sum Sum removed her black cloth shoes at the threshold, as was the Malay custom. She stood barefoot, breasts squashed into Lu See's tight blue sundress, feeling the cool sea air slide around her legs. With her tribal toe rings contrasting against the dark carpeting, she assessed the first-class suite. She marvelled at the luxurious sheer sea-green curtains, the marble-topped tables and the vases of pale pink coral.

"Welcome aboard the MS *Jutlandia*. We will be calling at the Nicobar Islands, Colombo, Bombay, Aden, Tobruk, Lisbon and Felixstowe before heading for our final destination Copenhagen. And if you come this way, Miss Apricot," said the Chinese cabin boy, "your bedroom adjoins your cousin's room. Queen beds as requested."

"*Cousin?*" Sum Sum exclaimed, looking directly at the cabin boy. "I'm not her-"

"Yes, thank you!" Lu See interjected, pressing a Straits dollar into the young man's hand. "Just leave the trunk by the window. We'll sort it out later."

"Enjoy the rest of your journey," the cabin boy said, shutting the door with a soft click.

When they were alone Lu See fluttered her eyelashes at Sum Sum – little moth wings of amusement. "What? You actually expected me to stick you in steerage, sharing bathrooms and breathing space with all those pimply-arsed men? You should be so lucky."

Sum Sum did a little victory jig across the carpeted floor. She felt the air escape her lungs in a wheeze of laughter and instinctively she reached out and touched Lu See's face, whose cheekbones were so high and angular they often threatened to break free from beneath the skin. "Seven years! Seven years and you never surprised me like this before!"

Lu See smiled. "Has it really been seven years?"

"Almost, lah. March 1929. Same year my father died." Sum Sum recalled the first day they'd met, when they were both only twelve years old. "Your mother shepherded me into breakfast room and announced that I was to be the new laundry amah, remember?"

"You avoided everybody's eyes and turned your face away."

"Towards the door, to hide my tears." She nodded. "I was so homesick. I felt like an imposter in your house. Fresh off the train, lah. I remember the long journey in that iron coffin. I came via Assam, Mandalay and Siam. *Tickety-tak, tickety-tak*, all night long. And you, I remember this skinny, cheeky little girl with your hair cut above the collar."

"School regulations. All hair had to be cut above the collar."

"Your mother said, *Sit up straight, Lu See!* You were always being warned by your parents, no? Always same thing: no more biting your nails, stop slouching at dinner table, never forget to wash hands after pee-peeing."

"Which I never did!"

"And then you took me by the hand, no?"

"And I led you through the house."

"*Aiyoo!* So many dark corridors! It was still gas-lit in those days."

They tripped over each other's words, laughing.

"We both sat down in the back, at the servants' table to share a bowl of *mee hoon* noodles."

"And you told me not to chew with my mouth open!"

"Did I really?"

"Yes, lah."

"We played a round of Chinese chequers. Then I went to throw small stones on to the roof to chase the monkeys away, but all you wanted to do was read your letter."

"You know, for weeks and weeks I carried that letter from my mother in my tunic pocket."

There was a long pause. Sum Sum remembered every word of the letter. It said now that she was a fatherless daughter she had to be respectful and clean, to live a decent life, to honour the memory of my ancestors and to not be scared of the thunder. She remembered, too, the Himalayan sun breaking through the clouds; the deer hides used as groundsheets for sleeping; her mother warming her pink, stiff fingers over the teepee of flames as Sum Sum threw more kindling and bark resin on the fire. The horse and yak caravan had taken them to within sight of the Indian border. The journey across the mountains had taken sixteen days. It was here that they would say their final goodbyes. Sum Sum felt the prayer box amulet being secured around her neck and the shoulder bags being hitched in place. She was crying so hard that when she looked at her mother her image blurred and wavered. They pressed the palms of their hands

32

to each others' cheeks. Then her mother pulled her into her arms before Sum Sum could see the tears streak down her face. Sum Sum tried to speak but could say nothing; it was as if someone had placed stones in her mouth. When they pulled away, her mother's eyes shot towards the distant hills to the south and she tipped her head. It was time to go.

At the time she never thought about whether Malaya would be different to Tibet. She did not know that there might be another way to live, unfamiliar foods to eat, outlandish customs and habits and languages to comprehend. Nobody told her anything. All she wanted to do was make her mother proud.

Sum Sum shook her head forcefully at the memory. Her teeth bit into her lower lip. Seconds later she was busying herself with the unpacking, putting things away, fastening cocktail dresses and cheongsams on to padded wooden hangers, arranging toiletries, unwrapping this and unfolding that. She retrieved Lu See's brass statuette of Ganesha, the Hindu elephant-headed god, and positioned it by the bed.

Lu See went over and rubbed his pot belly. "We'll need all the help we can get from this fellow - God of new ventures and remover of obstacles."

"Remover of obstacles? *Aiyo*, you sound like you're constipated."

Lu See cracked open the window. The distant sounds of the swing band on the promenade deck floated down from above. Springboarding into a yoga headstand, she closed her eyes and waited for the enjoyable rush of blood to her cheeks. She glanced at her watch, upside down. "I fancy a walk. You want something to eat?"

"Can, lah." Sum Sum sighed, coiling her prayer beads round her wrist. "But I still think we should have bought some coconut candy at the quayside. I miss my tongue-touchers already."

"Yes and we would have been collared by Uncle Big Jowl if you had done."

They strolled along the Lido deck under parasols, watching a group of people play an impromptu game of shuffleboard. Three stewards with braiding on their shoulders cruised the deckchairs with pitchers of iced lime juice. Both Lu See and Sum Sum accepted a glass and sipped the cool drinks, relishing the cold against their lips.

A little further on, they came across a tall European man holding a filbert brush. He stood by his easel wearing a blue blazer with gold buttons over a white shirt and white linen trousers. His teeth looked too large for his mouth. To his left a muscular, well-groomed Indian in a khaki safari suit was holding up a holland umbrella, shielding the canvas from the sun.

Lu See stood behind the European for a while and then cleared her throat.

"God, Christ! You scared me half to death."

She asked, "Are you the captain?"

"Do I *look* like the captain?"

"Yes, actually, you do."

"Well, I'm not."

"Where is the captain?"

"Hell if I know."

Her head tilted to one side to look at the canvas. She made out some curvy blue and white lines that resembled waves with a blue purple blob in the middle. "It's obviously a boat on the sea."

"No, it's a picture of Edinburgh."

"It is not."

"Why would I lie?"

"So you're telling me that's not a boat?"

"No, it's a bus travelling down Princes Street."

"Where are the buildings?"

34

"I haven't done them yet, have I?"

"Why are you staring out to sea but painting pictures of Edinburgh?"

"It's a free world." He paused. "All right if you must know, my family's originally from Scotland."

At which point Sum Sum came forward and belted out a repertoire of Scottish sounding phrases she'd picked up from the Glaswegian chaplain who called on the Teohs each month: "Och, aye, the kirk roof still needs ah-mending. Milk no sugar if ye will. Thy Kingdom come, thy will be done, Amen. I'll see ye in a wee while, lassie."

"For the love of Rita! Bit of a fruitcake, isn't she? Perhaps your friend could do with a hat. The hot sun, you know. Those paper parasols don't do much good."

"Oh, don't mind her. She's very excitable. My name's Lucy, by the way. Lucy Apricot."

"Stan Farrell," he said, extending a hand. Lu See took it and felt his fingers close around hers.

"We're off for lunch," Lu See said.

"I don't eat lunch."

"Everybody eats lunch."

"I had a big breakfast." He removed a sweet from his pocket. "Fancy a gumdrop?"

"You're a very odd man, Mr Stan Farrell. Are you getting off at Felixstowe?"

Stan sucked his oversized teeth, disappointed. "'Fraid I get off in Bombay. I'm finishing my senior police officer training in Colaba."

"So you're a bobby."

"Probationary Inspector at your service, marm." He clicked his heels.

Lu See glanced at the well-groomed Indian. "And who is he?"

"This is Aziz Humzaal, my orderly."

"Hello, Aziz."

Aziz wiggled his head and pressed his right hand to his heart.

"Well, it was nice meeting you, Mr Farrell. Sum Sum and I are off to find some food." She twirled her parasol. "See you later, no doubt."

As she turned to leave, Stan said, "I do, however, always partake of a midday meal on Fridays. I skip lunch every day of the week except for Friday. I saw on the bulletin board that tomorrow's curry day. Want to join me?"

Lu See looked at Sum Sum and shrugged. "Yes, all right. That sounds jim-dandy."

"Jim who?"

"Jim-dandy, oh never mind. We'll see you Friday."

The girls made their way towards the main dining room. Lu See smiled to herself.

Sum Sum glanced over her shoulder and pinched her nose. "He smelled of boiled prawns."

"No, he did not."

"I'm telling you he *did*, lah. Made me want to fry him in ginger and sesame oil."

"He was quite handsome all the same."

"Handsome? He looked like he was trying to eat a corncob through a tennis racquet. Teeth spilling out like prison escapees."

"Aziz was nice-looking though, don't you think?"

"No."

"Oh really? Well if you don't find him handsome why are you blushing?" she teased.

"I'm not blushing. Just hot, lah."

"Hot to trot for Mr Aziz. I can see you like him."

"*Aiyoo!* Don't put words in my mouth, lah!"

Amused, Lu See scratched her nose to cover her smile. Sum Sum always spoke of men's looks in this vague sort of way, as if to imply that they made no impression on her; it was something Lu See always saw through.

When they returned from lunch, Lu See found a note slid under her door. Laughing, she read it aloud to Sum Sum:

Started, Farted,
Stumbled, Fell,
See you Friday,
Stan Farrell

Later, still in her cabin, Lu See dipped her pen into the inkstand and wrote:

Dear Second-aunty Doris – well I've done it! I'm aboard ship and on my way to Europe. The money you gave me, all 2,000 Straits dollars, is safely locked up in the Captain's personal strongbox and as soon as I reach Cambridge I will open a bank account to receive the monthly allowance you so kindly offered to wire over. Once I get settled I will begin to look into sourcing a pipe organ for the new church to be built in Po On Village. I did some research and came up with a number of firms that may be able to help us: Conrad P. Hughes in London, Brinkley & Fosler of Yorkshire, and Harrison & Harrison who were responsible for the King's Chapel organ. Let us pray that I can find something suitable (and within budget) and have it shipped to Malaya in time for the memorial service planned for Christmas. Donating an organ to the church and dedicating it in Tak Ming's memory is an admirable idea – I know that he would have approved.

As for my own situation, how can I thank you enough for helping me? How can I ever repay you? Thank you for believing in me when nobody else in the family did.

Wish me luck with my Girton interview. My old headmaster at Bing Hua has already received a reply from the college and I am due to meet with the Mistress and the tutors on March 2nd so fingers and toes crossed!

I will write again soon.

God bless you.

Your loving niece – Lu See

She replaced the pen on the writing table and looked around to find Sum Sum sitting cross-legged on the floor going through a set of photographs. "What are those?" she asked.

"Pictures taken from dragon boat day. We so busy with funerals and everything I forgot all about them. Only had Mr Quek develop last week."

Lu See sat by her side. "Who's that one of?" she asked when Sum Sum paused at the man with the mole on his cheek.

"Remember I told you? Up on the hill I saw man come out of the trees with a gun."

Lu See peered at the man's face. "I've seen him before."

"Meh?"

"He's a Woo. Adrian's cousin. What was he doing up in the hills with a gun?"

The girls looked at each other. "You think he has something to do with dam explosion?"

"Wait," said Sum Sum. She got to her feet and returned with a red tin. "Look, meh, I keep my beads in this now. It is the same tin he has in his hand. He threw away but I go back to find it."

Lu See reached for the tin. On it were the words 'DuPont No. 6 Blasting Caps'. She stared at the photograph; the container was clearly visible in his hand. "Adrian's talked about him before. They call him the Black-headed Sheep. They say he is connected to one of the Penang secret societies, one of the Dragon Heads." She looked at Sum Sum again. "Did he see you take this picture? Did he see you with a camera?"

Sum Sum shrugged.

"This is serious, pumpkin-head. If he had something to do with the dam and he knows you took a picture of him that day, there's no telling what he might do. He might think there are more photographs, of him setting the charges perhaps."

Sum Sum laced her fingers together and stretched her arms. "*Aiyoo!* Stop worrying, lah. What you think, he going to follow us? Cut out throats in our sleep? Silly, lah."

"Mr Quek developed these photographs, right? Did you talk to him about us? Did you tell him we were going abroad?"

Sum Sum looked affronted. "Of course not. I'm not stupid."

"Quek works for the Woos. Has done for years. I bet you when he saw this picture he went and told mole-face about it straight away."

"But why would mole-face blow up dam?"

"I don't know."

"You really think he maybe come after us?"

"The people he is involved with go to any lengths to achieve their aims. If you have any evidence that might convict him of the dam sabotage he'll find you and kill you."

"Next you going to tell me he is already here, on this ship."

"Perhaps he is. If Uncle Big Jowl found us then he could too." The girls felt their mouths go dry as they stared at one another.

Sum Sum got to her feet to lock the cabin door. "Should we tell anyone?"

"Who are we going to tell? And what are we going to say? That there might be a saboteur on board? A man who killed over thirty people and almost destroyed an entire village? Someone who might be planning to kill us because you took his photo? Lord, we'd start a panic and before you know it we'd be on the first boat home. No, I think we should just stick close to our new policeman friends Mr Farrell and Mr Aziz."

Sum Sum groaned. "*Aiyo*, not smelly boiled-prawns-man."

"Yes, smelly-boiled-prawns man."

"You only doing this to torture me, I know you, lah."

"Well now," said Stan Farrell at Friday tiffin, "let's see what's on the menu." He peered at the carte du jour. Owing to Aziz's ethnicity they were in the salon rather than the main restaurant, seated at a table for four. A string quartet played in the corner as potted palms swayed in the sea breeze. The other diners were mostly English, colonial civil servants in pale linen suits, holding up their newspapers, smoking their pipes and sipping their whisky *stengahs* – all very white and restrained.

"Isn't it odd for a sahib to mix so freely with his orderly and two Chinese women, Mr Farrell?" asked Lu See. "Aren't you concerned how others might view you?"

"Well, as you said earlier, Miss Apricot, I'm a very odd man. I actually like mixing with Chinese."

Lu See smiled at him. "Have you, by any chance, come across any other Chinese passengers on board?" she probed.

"Any with mole on face?" Sum Sum added, pressing.

"A mole?"

"Yes, lah, mole." She prodded her left cheek with an index finger.

"Why?"

"Oh, it's nothing," said Lu See with an embarrassed flourish of her hand.

Stan returned to the menu and a deep line appeared between his eyebrows. He clearly had no idea what they were on about. "So then, Sum Sum," he asked, "how hot do you take your curries?"

Sum Sum beamed. "Volcano hot!"

"Glad to hear it. Let's get four portions of basmati rice, some mutton randang to share, chicken Madras, Bengali potatoes, and poppadum with lime chutney. Sound good to you?"

"Sound tip-top to me, lah."

When the condiments arrived in a lazy Susan, Lu See noticed how distracted Sum Sum appeared. Her friend seemed transfixed by Aziz, staring quite unabashedly at the delicate way he manipulated his food, guiding curry into his mouth, working the fingers of his right hand gracefully through the basmati, shaping the long-grain rice into balls and using his thumb to flip the fragrant portion through his parted lips.

"You eat like a swan," Sum Sum declared with delight.

He smiled, waggled his head and dipped his hand in a fingerbowl before drying it with his napkin.

Stan cleared his throat. "So, tell me, what's your story? What are you both running away from?"

"What makes you say that?" Lu See said indignantly.

"You're either running away from somebody or you're running to someone. Which one is it?"

"I don't know what you mean." Lu See folded her own napkin. "Why on earth do you think we're running?"

"Instinct. I'm a policeman, remember." He tapped the side of his nose. "And my pal here rarely lets me down."

"Why can't we just be travelling, off on a European grand tour?"

"At your age, without a chaperone – unlikely."

"Well, you're wrong."

"Am I?"

"Yes."

"Ha!"

Lu See felt Sum Sum give her a kick under the table. "Well, all right, if you must know I'm running from someone my family wants me to marry."

"Heading for?"

"England."

"To Picalilli Circus," Sum Sum added.

"Where I hope to get engaged to the man I love."

"You *hope* to get engaged." Stan tilted his head.

"Yes. I also HOPE to win a place at a top university."

"University, eh? Well . . . good luck. And how about your cousin? Sum Sum, what about you? Are you in love with a man too?"

Sum Sum smiled, blushed, and smiled once more. "*Aiyo*, nobody to fall in love with. I'm not pretty like Lu See."

"Begging your pardon, for it is here that you are grossly mistaken, young *bibi*." It was Aziz speaking. His head was dancing on his shoulders. "You are vastly pleasing to the eye and if I may be so bold to saying you remind me of the village cows in Hyderabad."

"Cows, lah?"

"Most engaging creatures. Strong udders and noble facets, *bibi*." He held his palms upwards towards the ceiling, tilting his face to one side in appeasement. "We have very pretty cattle in my home village. Their eyes are like sparkling Indus river water flowing over pebbles from an enchanted mountain stream."

Sum Sum's mouth broke into a wide grin. She looked at the well-groomed Indian and coloured.

Stan shifted uncomfortably in his chair. "A man of fine taste is Aziz. Rarely says much, but when he does he sounds quite poetic, don't you think?"

"Your skin is very pale for an Indian man," observed Sum Sum.

"My grandfather had Pathan blood." Aziz wobbled his head and grinned boyishly.

"Why do Indian men do that shaky-shaky with head, lah?" asked Sum Sum.

Aziz raised a finger in the manner of a professor. "It is a quiet way of saying you may trust me, that I meaning you no harm. That I am your trusted friend." The finger brushed the skin of Sum Sum's hand and from some place deep inside her she felt a warm tingling, first inside her tummy and then spreading gradually to her chest.

"*Aiyo Sami!*" She squirmed. "You speaking like a snake in

the grass now. Quit talking and eat, lah. Too much talk-talk causes hindi-gestion!"

Time drifted like the sea. During the day, full of repressed mischief, the girls occasionally slipped grapes into the shoes left outside of cabin doors and told tall stories to the Chinese cabin boys, declaring that they were Siamese princesses, running off to join a Catholic convent, becoming postulants, trainee nuns. In the afternoons they took part in shuffleboard contests and attended tea dances while at night, sipping from tall glasses of lemonade along the Lido deck, Aziz showed Sum Sum the constellations, pointing out the stars whilst singing Urdu folk songs to the moon. "If only, *bibi*, we had Galileo's tube I could show you the furthest-away planets."

Sum Sum didn't have a clue what he meant. *A telescope maybe?* She didn't really care. They sat in the darkness for hours until Lu See, playing canasta with Stan in the salon, came in search of her.

The boat left Colombo. With Sum Sum so distracted Lu See borrowed some paints and brushes from Stan Farrell and drew nautical scenes and portraits of the stewards. When Stan craned his neck to sneak a peek at her pictures he said, "Y'know, Lucy, you're pretty good. Have you ever painted before?"

"Only garden furniture!" she replied with a giggle in her voice, before admitting that she'd had some lessons. She looked about her. "Any idea where Sum Sum's got to?"

"She went off with Aziz."

"They've been gone for ages."

"He's probably teaching her a few more of his Urdu folk songs."

Lu See dropped her brushes into a jar of water and then cleaned the paint off the bristles with a square of newspaper. She had just finished drying them with a rag when she saw a man standing by some deck chairs about twenty yards away, looking in her direction. He was wearing a hat that shadowed his face entirely. How strange, she thought, as she put her brushes away, one of his shoulders is higher than the other.

Nine days later the yellow basalt of the Gateway of India swept into view as a white-throated cormorant rose into the drizzling sky, wet post-monsoon rains rippling its wings.

Lu See and Sum Sum leaned against the ship's railings, waving. They threw paper streamers overboard and shouted their goodbyes to Stan and Aziz. The men waved back. Sum Sum cocked her arms like chicken wings and took several snaps with the Kodak Retina. Stan blew a kiss and smiled like a donkey as Aziz pressed his right hand to his heart and mouthed Sum Sum's name. They paused for a moment. And then they were gone. As Lu See turned and moved her hand up to her eyes to shield them from the sun, she saw the same man she'd spotted several days earlier. He was standing by the deck chairs again. His face was still hidden by his hat, but she recognized the irregular slope of his shoulders. She wheeled around and tugged at Sum Sum's sleeve. When they looked back he was gone.

Later, in her cabin, Lu See stretched into a yoga asana, into an Upward Facing Dog pose. After several minutes she relaxed, slipped into her pink terrycloth bathrobe, and picked up her book of Cambridge poetry. Then she put it back down again.

"Do you really think it could be him?"

"Was there mole on his cheek?"

"I couldn't see his face."

"But his shoulder was same-same like this, meh?" Sum Sum demonstrated by allowing her left side to drop away like a caved-in roof.

"Yes, just like that. Do you think it really could be him? I bet he's been hiding in his cabin all this time. Maybe he's been waiting for Stan and Aziz to leave and now he'll come after us."

"Or maybe you only imagining, lah. How come I never see him?"

"Well, just to be safe, I think we should stay in our cabin and take our meals here."

As the rain sluiced down the window, she pictured Stan Farrell standing outside, his blue blazer with gold buttons drenched from the earlier downpour, his white linen trousers clinging tight to his thighs. How she'd love him to be here now. She turned to Sum Sum, who was reclining on the floor, in a lotus pose, inspecting her brass toe rings and mouthing the bars to 'Night and Day', a melodious song she'd heard the band play.

"You're going to miss him, aren't you?"

"Who?"

"Aziz."

She looked crestfallen. "*Aiyo*, too much, lah."

"I'll miss Stan too." Lu See peered out the cabin window at the waterfront jammed with rickshaws and donkey carts and beggars with their begging bowls. The rickshaw wallahs were wreathed in waterproof capes made from palm leaves. She could already hear the vendors gathered at the gates of the Taj Mahal Hotel shrieking and shouting as bare-chested porters rushed about with bags hoisted on their heads. Lu See pictured Stan confronted by this landslide of humanity as he left the ship, and then plunging into the slow clumsy sway of the crowd, until his blue blazer was subsumed, out of reach.

As she stared into the rain, through the glass, she questioned not for the first time why she was doing this – running from her family, repudiating everything that was sacred and secure. She thought about her mother and father sitting at the dining table; their wilting, forced conversation followed by the inevitable brooding silence. Ah Ba, the esteemed banker C. M. Teoh, stabbing at his food, wondering what his employees at the bank would be thinking, what the Turf Club members would be saying about his errant daughter. And her mother, obdurate and wounded, looking more and more like a wide-eyed fruit bat; nervously scratching at her palms; blaming Lu See's brothers, James and Peter, the servants, the school, everybody but herself, for Lu See's desertion.

"Do you think what I'm doing, turning my back on my parents, is defying nature?" she asked Sum Sum.

"*Ayo Sami!* Having sex with a goat is defying nature. Being born with three ears instead of two is defying nature. All you're doing is following your dreams, lah. You always complaining how much your parents control your life and how they're forcing you to marry One-eyed Giant, it only natural you rebel, no? By Dharmakaya heaven, I'd run like hell too from him if he wanted to marry me!"

"They're still precious to me. I'm abandoning them, throwing my past away with a wave of a handkerchief."

"*Aiyoo!* Why you being so mego-dramatic, lah!"

"I wonder if Sarojini Naidu went through all this when she told her parents she wanted to go to Cambridge."

"Did she run away too?"

"No, her father wanted her to become a mathematician, but she was only interested in poetry. When she was 16 the Nizam of Hyderabad was so impressed by her poems he arranged a scholarship for her to study in England. Now she's known as 'The Nightingale of India'."

"And you'll be known as the 'Mego-dramatist of Malaya', is it?"

Lu See paused, feeling a slither of regret. "Do you think Mama's furious?"

"I'm sure she's damn-powerful bloody livid." Sum Sum clicked her tongue just to show how livid.

Lu See stretched her willowy legs. "I still can't believe they wanted me to marry the One-eyed Giant."

The One-eyed Giant was their nickname for Chow Cheam.

He lived five miles away and was the sole heir to the Chow Titt Municipal Bank. At the age of eleven he'd been blinded in his left eye whilst playing badminton. The shuttlecock had struck him before he could blink. Now, aged twenty-three, he was a squinting, arrogant, flat-footed brute, with dog-fart breath and a face studded with pockmarks.

"Your father believed it was good for the family business. But deep down Mama probably understands, lah. She was in love once too, you know – she married your father after all, even though the fortune teller said he was unsuitable. Besides," she puckered her lips, "it's not the first time you've run away."

Momentarily bewildered, Lu See frowned. Then, raising her eyebrows, she tilted her head at the memory: it was the day her aunty Mimi was getting married. She was playing in the garden and heard her mother calling for her. "Come on now, we're late! Where you gone, *hnn*?" But Lu See didn't want to be a flower girl, standing in front of all those people, with everyone staring at her. Even then she'd yearned to be free, to be like the village children – running shoeless through the fields, hunting butterflies, climbing trees and picking mangoes. So she went and hid under the hibiscus bush. "Where are you, Lu See? Lu See!" Later, much later, she went and took cover down by the river. Mr Bala, the gardener, eventually found her and brought her home. It was dark by then.

"I've disgraced them," she sighed.

"Could be worse, lah." Sum Sum's tone was gently teasing. "You could've gotten pregnant."

3

7.45 a.m. Mid-February. The Customs officer in Felixstowe took his stick of yellow chalk and marked her eel-skin trunk with an X before ushering the girls on their way.

Instinctively, Sum Sum looked over her shoulder to see if anyone was following, but she saw no sign of the 'mole man'. In fact, there had been no further sightings of him since Bombay.

A porter took the luggage and, choking with anticipation, they hurried past the bookstand and into the greeting enclosure. A group of about twenty people had gathered. One woman held up a banner saying 'Welcome Home Albert.'

"Can you see him? Is Adrian here?" asked Lu See.

"*Aiyo!* I don't see him. He's probably still in front of the mirror doing his hair, lah."

"He must be somewhere. He wrote to say he would be here to meet us. I sent word giving him our arrival date." They looked at every face but there was no sign of Adrian. "Come, he must be waiting outside." They hurried through the main doors to stand on the street outside the wharf buildings. From high up the sounds of seagulls floated down. By the docks a crowd of labourers gathered by a hut, thrusting their black books forward, baying for a job as the stevedore yelled "Call off –" and chose his men for the day.

"*Wahhh!* So cold, lah! Like sticking your face in an ice-cube!"

The roads were grey and wet. Unlike the succulent

pigments of the tropics, Felixstowe looked sucked dry of colour, as if coated in an eczema of dust blown from an old book.

"There he is!" Sum Sum yelled.

Lu See felt a rush of liquid weakness in her knees.

Tossing his silk-lined trilby high into the sky, Adrian rushed up to Lu See and lifted her up by the waist, swinging her around and around. "You look beautiful," he said into her hair.

She had missed him so much that the bones in her chest ached for him

She clung to his neck and they only separated when a horse-drawn Express Dairy cart trundled by stacked tall with 10-gallon steel cans.

Adrian led them to a scruffy looking Austin Chummy with tall, thin wheels parked across the square.

"New motor-car?" she joked, draping a tartan blanket across her lap.

He shrugged, tipping the porter who touched his cap with thanks.

Adrian slipped on a pair of string-backed driving gloves. "Who are you looking for?" he asked, noticing both Lu See and Sum Sum were watching people coming through the crowd.

"I think your cousin, the one known as the Black-headed Sheep, was on the ship."

"Lu See thinks he is following us," blurted Sum Sum.

"Why would he do that?" Sum Sum explained why, keeping her story short. With a dubious frown, Adrian climbed into the driver's seat. "Well, the less you have to do with him the better."

The car clattered down a narrow lane passing a horse-cart laden with straw.

In the back seat Sum Sum sang snatches from an Urdu folk song.

"Enough room back there?" asked Adrian.

"Plenty," replied Sum Sum. "Enough to fit six people and a goat, lah."

Minutes later they were racing through the village of Little Piddle, leaving behind sleepy pubs and hedgerows and thatched cottages, heading northwest towards Ipswich. Theirs was the only car on the road. Lu See saw cows in the fields, horses in their paddocks, sweeping pastureland that stretched on and on over the hills. It was a picture of tranquillity; a collage of winter greens and browns. Two hours later, she caught a signpost that said they were a mile from the Corn Exchange. She'd already been impressed by the panorama of wheat and grasslands at the town's perimeter, but as soon as she entered Cambridge proper her eyes lit up with animation. Although she had never been to Cambridge before, had not seen King's Chapel, nor its river and punt boats and the newly erected University Library, it was all strangely familiar to her from Adrian's letters.

As they rolled down Castle Street, leaning back as they descended the steep slope, crossing Chesterton Lane, and passing Magdalene College on the left, Lu See noticed how the town's cobbled streets were lined with bookshops and antique stores and every thirty feet or so she came across another sculpted-stone façade. "St. John's on your right, Divinity School on your left," exclaimed Adrian. "Here's Trinity College, and over there," he said, pointing, "behind that massive horse chestnut tree, is King's Parade." Everywhere she looked she saw Gothic spires, Tudor arches, gargoyles, steeples, turrets and towers. Here and there she spotted students clad in black college gowns and squares; some sat on wooden benches reading, others stood about chatting, warming their faces in the wan afternoon sun.

Lu See turned to Sum Sum. "What do you think?" she asked.

Sum Sum gazed up at the turrets and towers and gables. "Everywhere looks like Dracula's castle."

The jalopy coughed just as Adrian spoke again. "I found you some digs on Portugal Place. I told the landlady, Mrs Slackford, all about you and your plans for Girton. You and Sum Sum can live there until we get married."

"And when will that be?"

"In the summer. Let's get you settled into Cambridge life first."

At the entrance to Park Parade, Adrian left the Austin Chummy near the Laurel Tea Rooms and, travelling trunk in hand, steered the girls up a crooked cobbled pedestrian street to a blue painted door with the number 23 trimmed in red. "Now remember," he said in a stage whisper. "There are different formalities in England. Discretion and restraint is the hallmark of class. We're the only Chinese people your landlady, Mrs Slackford, has ever met so–"

"Yes, yes, don't worry. We'll be on our best behaviour. I'll try not to spit on the rug and belch noisily after each course."

He rolled his eyes. Looking eager, Lu See lifted the heavy brass knocker and let it fall.

A hunched, silver-haired lady appeared at the door, squinting at her as though she was peering through a pall of cigarette smoke. She was dressed in a brown housedress and thick woollen stockings. "Yew must be Miss Teoh."

"Hello, Mrs Slackford." They shook hands. "Please call me Lu See."

"Well come on in. No need to remove yer shoes. We're not in Japan now, yew know. Four basic rules for yew to follow – no food of any kind in yer bedrooms, no gentlem'n callers." She raised her eyebrows at Adrian accusingly. "No pets and we have a nightly curfew of 10 p.m. Is that clear?"

"Yes, very."

"It's two pounds a week, an extra five bob if yew want breakfast and supper."

"No problem."

"And oi'll expect two weeks in advance. The whole of the top floor is occupied by me. Yew and yer cousin have the two bedrooms on the first floor. Bath nights are Tuesday and Saturday when the hot water boiler's turned on. "

"Fine."

Mrs Slackford smiled. "Well, now that that's all sorted, come and have a look round, won't yew? Yer friend Mr Woo will have to wait here."

Lu See walked into a bright little living room decorated with tapestries, chintz sofas and a leather armchair covered in lace antimacassars. A little further in, she found a dining room filled with walnut furniture and a large 19th century refectory table. There was an old stone fireplace in the far end of the room and the walls were lined with Victorian oil paintings depicting bucolic scenes of English village life. Everything smelt of wood polish. On the refectory table was an Emerson 5 tube phonograph, gently playing a swing band number.

"I usually don't enjoy any of this modern music," Mrs Slackford said, stopping to turn up the volume. "But I do like this new fellow, Benny Goodman."

"The house is very nice," Lu See declared, taking in her surroundings.

"Mr Slackford was a furniture restorer. He loved nothing better than sourcing damaged pieces and fixing them up."

"How nice," said Lu See. "And Mr Slackford is . . ." She craned her neck towards the kitchen expectantly.

"Dead. Killed in the war. The Boer War."

Boer War? God, she must be ancient, thought Lu See. *Now, don't say anything silly. Remember to respect the elderly.* "I'm so sorry to hear that, Mrs Slackford."

The landlady took in a sharp breath. "Nothing to be sorry about, dear, he's been dead, oh, 35 years now. His pension keeps me in tea bags but not much else. Well then, how about a cuppa tea? Let me show yew the kitchen. We got sausages in the meat safe and oi get fresh eggs each morning from across the way." Lu See and Sum Sum followed her down the corridor into a small room with a stove, a meat safe and a three-door cupboard filled with tins of tea, Horlicks and odd bits of crockery. There was also a shelf stacked with white-and-blue teacups.

"My cousin Sum Sum can help."

Removing four cups and a teapot from the shelf, Mrs Slackford filled the kettle with water from the tap. "If yew take sugar yew'll find it in the cupboard."

Sum Sum rummaged about and found a bowl of salt, a jar of flour and a black sock held tight with a clothes peg. When she looked into the black sock she found it filled with birdseed.

"Oi often feed the pigeons in the park," Mrs Slackford conceded.

"*Aiyo*, good idea, lah. Fatten them up for a roast, is it?" The landlady didn't reply.

Once Lu See and Sum Sum returned from their tour of the house Adrian announced that he was leaving. "I'm returning to my college. I've a lecture at noon. Mrs Slackford, why don't you show the girls the market square, I'm sure they'd like to see a bit of the town." He gave Lu See a wink and saw himself out. "I'll see you later."

"I . . . I think I'll stay behind and unpack my things." Lu See concluded, passing Sum Sum her purse. "Sum Sum, please can you buy a packet of Bee Bee brandy snap biscuits, a few metal hangers for the closet, a tin of drinking chocolate, a bar of Cashmere Bouquet soap and a pair of woollen socks." She turned to Mrs Slackford. "I never expected it to be so cold. I think I'm going to have to wear two or three layers. And perhaps you can buy Mrs Slackford some flowers for her bedroom."

Within minutes Mrs Slackford had her headscarf and coat on. "Be back in half an hour or so. Yew sure yew'll be all right on yer own?"

"Yes, thanks," Lu See replied. "Bye, Sum Sum."

*

In the park, hidden behind a tree, Adrian watched Sum Sum and her landlady head down Park Street. As soon as they were out of sight he sprinted along Portugal Place and rapped on the door of number 23.

Seconds later he and Lu See were racing up the stairs to the first floor. "My bedroom is in here," she said feeling his hand on the small of her back. "We don't have much time."

Inside, the damask curtains were drawn and the bedside lamp was on. Adrian shut the door behind him and they rolled onto the large iron bed, pulling away the crisp white sheets and pillows, tossing the neatly folded horsehair blanket to one side.

He kissed her throat and her neck. "God, can you imagine if we get caught?" she interrupted him.

"We won't. I bolted the front door. If Mrs S returns early I'll climb out the back window." Easing her clothes over her head, he laid her gently on the bed and caressed her smooth calves and ankles, bronzed from sunbathing on the deck of the MS *Jutlandia*.

He knelt on the bed and removed his yellow waistcoat and bow tie and began unbuttoning his shirt as she ran her bare leg up the inside of his thigh. The prickly horsehair blanket tickled her naked bottom as she pressed herself against him. They both giggled as they kissed. "God, you feel good," he said.

Tossing his trousers over the lampshade, he threw shadows across the room.

She smiled wickedly at him. "What was all that talk about discretion and restraint?"

"Quiet, you." He ran his fingers under her hair, flicked his tongue along her breasts, feeling the nipples swell in his palms. She traced her fingertips along his ribs and could feel his heart drumming against his chest.

She felt him smooth his hands over her hips. His fingers reached down and caressed the skin along her thighs, rubbing the thin material between her legs, touching the moist fold beneath the silk. Weakened by his touch she pulled him onto her, opening her legs to him. Their movements quickened in the cold.

Her lips sucked at the flesh of his shoulder. Tenderly, he slid into her. Arching her spine, she gasped. She clenched her fists and wrapped her calves around the small of his back. She bit her lip as a warm rushing sensation raced though her body, blinding her head with stars. Never had she acted this wantonly. Never had she felt such release. The muscles along the back of her legs quivered as she came. She laughed out loud. If this was selfishness, she thought, then she found her selfishness incredibly liberating.

The tears of happiness hung on her face. Suspended like berries on a string.

The following morning, after a breakfast of grilled tomato halves, bacon and soggy sausages, Lu See glanced through the newspaper. Nestled among the inside pages, she came across a photograph taken in Germany, at the Nuremberg Rally of 1935. Two pretty young women were posing amid a group of storm troopers in black, with eagle cap badges. The headline read: 'Mitford girls to be guest of Hitler at Berlin Olympic Games.'

She was about to ask Mrs Slackford about the relationship between the British aristocracy and the German Third Reich when there came a knock on the front door.

"Morning, loosey-goosey," Adrian said as he leaned on the doorframe, tracing his knuckles along her cheek. She loved the sound of his lilting voice, the way he said loosey-goosey. "Sleep well?"

"Very."

"And Sum Sum?"

"Incense sticks are burning by the windowsill and my statue of Ganesha is on the hall table. She's made herself at home."

"Come on then, grab Sum Sum and your coats, we're going out."

"Are we? Where to?"

"You'll see."

As they walked to the end of Portugal Place, passing the Round Church, Lu See watched a soot-smeared chimneys-weep heave his brushes up a ladder. "You still haven't told me where we're going?"

"Don't be so impatient, goosey."

The sky was grey and grim. A shire pony hauling beer barrels cut across them. As they passed St. John's, avoiding the steaming horse shit, an undergraduate in a college scarf and black robes and stomping his feet from the cold, handed him a sheet of paper.

"What's that he gave you?" Lu See craned her neck to see.

Adrian read aloud: " 'The Cambridge Union Society debated and carried the motion by 312 votes to 113 'That this House will under no circumstances fight for its King and Country.' "

"Fight? Fight who?" asked Sum Sum.

Adrian furrowed his forehead. "The Fascists."

They entered Trinity College via the Great Gate and made their way to a set of rooms near the Wren Library. Inside, a group of about fifty undergraduates mingled. Some were dressed in Oxford bags, others in six-guinea suits.

Someone had pinned up a red flag with the hammer-and-sickle crest. Adrian led the girls to a row of seats and sat down to listen to the debate.

"What's going on?" asked Lu See.

"Everyone in this room is committed to fighting fascism. We've got Bohemians, socialists, communists here, from all the different classes of society. It's really become quite fashionable to dabble in Communism."

A young man struck the hall table with a gavel and called for order. "In Marx and Engels," he began, "we see how everyone can share the benefits of industrialization. Socialism is liberal. Through Socialism more people will have a say in how our country functions. But that ideal is now coming under increasing threat!

"Germany and Italy are led by dictators and the risk of a fascist uprising in Spain is upon us. We must act. And we must act now!"

Another young man stood up. "That's all very well, but first we must halt the fascists' march on Britain."

Adrian leaned over the girls and explained, "We have extreme political polarization in England at the moment. Oswald Mosley and his bigots on the far right of the spectrum and Willie Gallacher, the Scottish Communist MP, on the far left."

The young man continued: "We therefore urge the Prime Minister, Stanley Baldwin, to pass the Public Order Act without delay!"

"Hear, hear!" came the cry.

"The Public Order Act will ban the wearing of political uniforms in public. This will, in our mind, play a major role in keeping Mosley's blackshirts off the streets of London."

"Who are these blackshirts?" asked Lu See.

"Mosley's pro-Nazi fascists," replied Adrian. "Bunch of hoodlums."

A sheet of paper was passed around, demanding the signatures of all attendees.

Lu See looked at Adrian. He'd obviously become more radical since leaving Malaya. She realized he had socialist leanings but she never thought of him as a full-blown communist. He hated fascism and all it stood for; that she knew. But what else did being a communist entail? Perhaps he believed that all wealth should be equally shared. She thought about the substantial amount of money Second-aunty Doris had given her to pay for a pipe organ and suddenly felt guilty. Think of how many struggling families that could help, she reflected.

And didn't communists have no religious beliefs? Weren't they also anti-imperialists? If so, that meant he would move to oppose the British in the Far East. Was he looking towards an independent Malaya?

"Are you hoping for a revolution back home?" she challenged him, whispering.

"I'm fed up with seeing our people getting trampled on."

"What if we're not ready for self-governance?"

"Marx once said that revolution is the midwife by which a new society is born," he replied. She stared at him. "The great man said that communism is the riddle of history solved, and it knows itself to be the solution."

"Don't even think about trying to convert me."

She turned away and then looked back at him. He was now nodding at the speaker, nodding in sync with every point like a presidential candidate's wife. Was this why he was at Cambridge, to gain a political education? Was this why he had encouraged her to travel all the way from Malaya? Surely, he wasn't going to attempt to brainwash her.

The questions came at a pace, rattling through Lu See's head. She could feel them tying her insides in a knot.

A little later, Lu See insisted on visiting King's College Chapel. She wanted to see the famous pipe organ, keen to learn anything that might help with Aunty Doris's commission. But she also wanted to see if Adrian's heightened radical views meant he opposed visiting a church. She hadn't enjoyed sitting through the political gathering and wondered if Adrian was intellectualizing his creed. Did he truly understand the reality of Communism? Did she? Had he ever seen it in action?

She entered King's College Chapel and was pleased to find him tagging along without complaint.

As soon as they entered Lu See could smell the musty history within its walls. Looking up at the stained and painted-glass windows, she was stunned into silence. *Wonderful*, she thought. *It turns sunlight into rainbows.* They spent several minutes admiring the lower lights on the north side portraying the life of Jesus and the upper lights that depicted Old Testament scenes. Afterwards they moved across to the altar to view *The Adoration of the Magi* by Rubens. Finally, Lu See remembered why she had come in the first place and sat in the choir to admire the Open Diapason of the organ. For several minutes she studied the pipes and tubes that rose like a copper citadel.

"Can't we go and get a closer look at it?" she asked Adrian. "I'd like to see the console."

"No, I'm afraid it's closed off to the public."

They sat in the choir stalls for a while in silence before Adrian shepherded them through the massive Gothic fan vault, their heels ringing out on the stone floor, and out onto the lawns of the Front Court.

"I read somewhere that it took over a century to build this," he said, peering up into the blue sky. "Just look at that buttressing. It's over 150 feet high. You can't imagine what the view is like from up there."

Sum Sum wasn't interested in Gothic fan vaults or buttressing of any sort.

Talk about reckless, lah! Having an affair with a stranger, a man I'd known for only nine days, someone I'd never see again. What was I thinking?

Allowing a naughty smile to creep across her face, Sum Sum cursed and congratulated herself with equal gusto. She was both thrilled and contrite that it had happened, thrilled because she had thoroughly enjoyed the experience, the furtive lovemaking, the intimacy, yet contrite because she definitely wasn't that sort of girl and hated keeping any secrets from Lu See. She hadn't confided in Lu See because she wasn't sure how she would react. She believed Lu See was still a virgin.

All right, so he said I had beautiful eyes, made him think of his beloved cows (!) did that mean I had to sleep with him? Aiyo Sami! But it felt so good; so much better than the only other time I ever did it – that messy thirty-second episode spent with Haram Yaakub the vendor of pickled delights. Sum Sum shivered at the memory.

Up until now she'd stubbornly avoided telling Lu See anything about Aziz. One half of her wanted to confide in Lu See, bursting to share the precious thrill, the fillips of excitement; the other half just wanted to enjoy it for herself, to savour it. And somehow every time she tried to casually bring up the subject her throat underwent a kind of paralysis. The words would not come; her mouth simply would not form the sentences.

Because there was so little she could call her own in the world she longed to keep this secret pure, out of sight, hidden away. Her little indiscretion was hers to cherish. And more than anything it made her feel independent; for the first time in her life she felt like a woman.

When she thought of Aziz Humzaal her mind drifted someplace else, where time progressed at an unfamiliar pace – slower, more elongated, like a rope of honey trickling from a spoon.

Hnnn . . . if only I had a few more nights with him – she pictured in her head Aziz's muscular brown arms, his trim waist, the concentrated tautness of his body and the smoothness of his skin. A curious warmth filled her insides.

She heard her name. ". . . you okay, pumpkin-head?"

The question snapped Sum Sum from her dream. They were still in the First Court of King's College. Sum Sum had no idea how long she'd been standing there. "Me? I'm fine, lah." Her face felt hot.

Lu See raised an eyebrow. There was humour in her voice. "You know, ever since Bombay you've had this expression on your face."

"What expression?"

"Like a woman whose won the lottery but has nobody to tell."

"You silly, lah." Sum Sum's laugh sounded hollow. She wanted to run to the cloakroom and splash cold water on her face. *Wash my thoughts clean.* Instead, she stood there and felt the warmth of memories ease across her shoulders.

4

At two in the afternoon Adrian, Lu See and Sum Sum entered the Pickerel on Magdalene Street. The low-ceilinged pub was oak-panelled and the tables carried the smell of beer and pipe tobacco. There were college oars mounted on the walls. Apart from the two old men sat by the dartboard the place was empty.

They stood at the bar under the oak beams.

"What'll it be?" asked the pudding-faced man who had a drying-up cloth draped over one shoulder.

"Pint of Adnams for me," said Adrian. He turned to the girls. "And two ginger ales."

"We never 'ad no Chinese in here before."

"Are you serving lunch?" asked Adrian.

The publican slewed his eyes at Lu See, more in curiosity than anything else, before grabbing a dimpled glass. His Cambridgeshire accent was slow-paced. "Oi got me a choice of ploughman's platter – Stilt'n or cheddar – shepherd's pie and cold bangers with grey-vee."

"What do you want to eat, goosey?"

Both Lu See and Sum Sum looked bewildered.

"How about we order three Stilton ploughmen's," Adrian offered.

They sat at a table by the window.

Lu See wanted to bring up her forthcoming interview at Girton. "So tell me, what kind of questions will they ask? My interview is next week, on March 2nd."

Adrian sipped his beer. "They'll start with your academic record."

"I received a high pass in my Cambridge Senior School Certificate. They even printed my name in the *Malay Mail*. I was on a list with about thirty other pupils."

"Then they'll want to know what you intend to read."

"Theology. The church back home has always been important to me. Perhaps more than ever now that I'm looking to replace the pipe organ."

"What about fees?"

"I have money from my aunt. She's made a deal with me. If I can find her a suitable pipe organ for the new church at Po On Village by the autumn, she will support me. I just have to get the organ shipped in time for Christmas."

As they chatted, an angular man dressed in a buff waistcoat and cream jacket minced through the door. His face was smooth and long and very pale. He stopped to admire his blond coiffure in a mirror and then swung his shoulder round theatrically to face the room.

"Adie!" he cried.

"Hello, Pietro."

"I was just on my way to Heffers to grab the new book about Stalin's reforms. You really have to applaud the man. The Webbs are all for what Russia's trying to achieve." He touched his hair and grinned at Lu See, showing her his left profile. "And who might you be?"

"Me? I'm Teoh Lu See."

"Tea-oh loo seat, Tea-oh loo seat . . ." He stuck a finger to his chin, trying to place her. "Brah-haaa! Of course!" He laughed a hyena laugh. "The girl you told me about, Adie. Oh, what a beautiful face you have. And you?" He flipped the same finger at Sum Sum. "Who are you?"

"My name is Sum Sum."

"Samson! What a delightful name! Jawbone of an ass and all that! You look more like a Delilah if you ask me. Lovely hands, beautiful fingernails, dahling. Anyway, I must dash." He capered out the door.

"Who on earth was that?" asked Lu See with a giggle in her voice.

"*That* was Pietro. He's a second year at Christ's studying political science. Half-Italian, but hates Mussolini and the fascists. We share similar world views. He's deaf in his right ear and asks everyone to stand on his left."

"*Adie?*" Lu See regarded him.

He shrugged. "That's what he likes to call me."

"His head's a bit of a funny shape."

"It's what we like to call an intelligent forehead."

"It looks like a milk bottle."

"You have a high forehead."

"Nonsense."

When their lunch appeared Sum Sum's eyes widened in disbelief. She studied the objects on the plate: four large pickled onions, a droopy spring onion, a dollop of brown chutney, a bread roll and a sweaty slab of veined cheese that smelled of feet.

"What do I do with this?" she asked Adrian.

"What do you mean?"

"Is it supposed to smell this way, lah, like rotting shoes?"

"Have you never had Stilton before?"

Sum Sum shook her head, blinking at the stinky, sweaty triangle. "My grandmother's legs used to look just like this."

"Break off some bread and have a slice of the cheese with the chutney. It's nice once you get used to the odour, a bit like eating durian." He pushed her plate closer, almost teasingly.

She took a bite and almost gagged. "*Aiyo!* No wonder we only people eating here! They trying to poison us." She washed her mouth out with a swig of ginger ale.

Adrian speared a bit of crumbly Stilton with a fork and stuck it in his mouth. "It's actually very nice with a pickled onion. What do you think, goosey?"

"To be honest I feel a bit nauseous."

"Funny you should say that, my sociology lecturer this

morning was talking about the many herbal treatments for nausea. Things found in the jungle and in the Tibetan plains. Arrowroot works best. Also good for infants with urinary complaints."

"*Aiyo!* What are blue things in the cheese?"

"Mould."

She lifted her eyes and stared at him. "You joking now, meh? I smash you if you're joking." He wasn't. "Mould? Do people in this country always eat like this?"

Adrian dabbed his mouth with a paper napkin, trying to hide his smile.

The publican thumped his hand on the bar counter. "Time! Drink up please."

Adrian looked at his watch. It was 2.40 p.m. "Right, I suggest you girls go home and take a nap. I have a surprise for you tonight, after supper. Remember to wear your most comfortable shoes."

That night Adrian met the girls outside their door at Portugal Place at 8 p.m. He lit a cigarette and tossed the matchbox on to the cobbled ground. "Listen," he said, almost in a hush. "I'd like you both to squeeze my hand. I want to see how strong your fingers are."

"Why?"

"Just do it, goosey."

Lu See gripped his hand as tight as she could and then came Sum Sum's turn.

"Good. Finger strength is vital. There's something I want to do. Something I want to show you."

"What?"

He caressed the nape of Lu See's neck. "See that matchbox on the floor? That's what other buildings look like from the top of King's Chapel."

"I don't follow."

"From that high up you feel like an eagle, like a God even. We're going climbing."

Five minutes later Lu See, Sum Sum and Adrian were standing by the horse chestnut tree on King's Parade, staring up at the stars. They were wrapped in warm coats and scarves and Adrian had a knapsack slung over his shoulders. Lights lit up the nearby Gibbs Building and the Old Lodge but where they stood it was pitch-black.

"First we have to climb this tree and get over the wall into King's College. Then we're going to climb to the top of the chapel," said Adrian.

Was he serious? Lu See took a step back. She grew as stiff as a stone gargoyle. "You're pulling my leg, right?"

"*Wahh*! Fantastic exciting, lah!"

"No, it's not, Sum Sum! It's bloody madness!"

"*Shh!*" Adrian pressed a finger to Lu See's lips. "We don't want to attract the college bulldogs."

"How high is the chapel?" Lu See whispered, trembling a little with a mixture of nerves and the cold.

"Not sure, over a hundred and fifty feet maybe. See the lightning conductor? That'll help us get all the way to the main roof."

Sum Sum was beaming. "In Tibet I was damn-powerful good climber. Many rocks and mountains in Tibet."

"I've scaled nearly every college. Trinity is pretty hard. Peterhouse is the easiest."

"But it's so dangerous," said Lu See.

"Of course it's dangerous. That's half the fun." He smiled.

"How often do you do this?"

"If it's not raining and there's no snow on the buttresses, once a week, more in the warmer months. I was inspired in Borneo watching the Dyaks climbing coconut trees, then later by the Sabah cave raiders who scaled these massive cliffs for bird's nests. Are you going to give it a go? Trust me, you'll love it."

Lu See shook her head. "I'm not going up there, no bloody way!"

Adrian rubbed his chin. "Perhaps you're right. It's a bit

ambitious of me to start you off with King's. Let's go with something less challenging. Come on, follow me."

"Can't we just go home?"

"No, goosey. Follow me."

They cut across the road and headed down Trinity Street.

As they walked past Trinity Lane, Lu See said, "You want to climb hundred-foot buildings. In the dark! At midnight! In this weather!"

"In Tibet when I was nine years old my brudder and I, we climbed Jade Dragon Mountain and jumped down into Tiger Leaping Gorge."

"Climbing a mountain, maybe. But a bloody chapel roof!"

"You're scared of heights."

"You know I am."

"Well, this is one of the best lessons you'll learn in life. How to overcome your fears. Here we are," said Adrian.

"Here we are what?" asked Lu See.

He lifted his hand and pointed upwards. "The Divinity School. It's got good sturdy drainpipes and the stonework's not at all crumbly. You can cling to the window bars on the second floor if you get tired." He looked around to confirm that the streets were deserted. "Right, who's going up with me?"

"Me!" Sum Sum raised her hand.

"We have to be back at Mrs Slackford's. There's a 10 p.m. curfew."

"Plenty of time. It's not even gone half eight." Adrian extracted a long coil of rope and three short slings of cord from his knapsack. There was a noose at either end of the cords, which made them resemble rawhide handcuffs.

"What on earth are they for?" asked Lu See, reaching out and touching one of the slings.

"In winter the drainpipes are a little too cold to hang on to for very long. Each time you stop to rest, you can slip one end of cord behind the piping and loop it over your wrists and lean back." He passed one each to Sum Sum and Lu See.

"It's much less tiring than hanging onto the wall-jams with your fingertips. Right, take off your coats and scarves and put them in the knapsack. You don't want to be overburdened with clothes. No gloves either. With gloves you can't feel for the grooves in the finger-holds." He wound the long coil of rope around his left arm as he said this. "I'll go up first with this top-rope. I'll secure it to one of the chimneys and drop it down from the roof. Remember to get your fingers behind the drainpipes and bend your knees. Use your toes for climbing and your heels for securing your position."

"God, I don't believe this is happening."

"We go now?" asked Sum Sum.

"Just try to follow the route I take. If you lose your footing and think you might fall reach out and grab the top-rope." He gave Lu See a coaxing kiss on her forehead. "Don't worry, you'll be fine. See you on the roof."

"I don't want to do it."

"Remember what I told you about overcoming your fears. You'll be fizzing with excitement when it's all over."

Adrian shimmied up the drainpipe, using footholds wherever he could. Then about five minutes later, once he paid out the rope, Sum Sum began her ascent.

After a few seconds Lu See looked up and crossed herself. *One hand over the other*, she said to herself. She grabbed hold of the metal pipe and immediately felt the strain in her arms and back. When she felt her fingers lock, she pushed out with her knees and shinned up a few inches, then slipped left hand over right as her shoes found something to wedge into. Each time she did this, she transferred her weight from one hand to the other, creeping skywards like a crab, forcing her feet into the slippery holds of the ribbed stonework.

She edged heavenwards. All the time the long top-rope dangled by her side. *Ignore the rope*, she told herself. *Use it only as a last resort, otherwise you'll overbalance and topple sideways. Use it only if you fall*. Her fingers and forearms began to burn. *One, two, three . . . up!* She kept on going. But then the drainpipe made an odd moaning sound, as if the metal was beginning to strain. *God, what if one of the brackets gives way?*

Her heart started to pound but she refused to panic. Without her coat, the air was bracing but Lu See soon found herself perspiring. She could feel the sweat prickling her skin beneath her sweater.

Eventually she reached a small ledge and rested. Puffing hard, she drew in great gulps of air. With one hand clutching the drainpipe and another gripping the mossy wall, she hugged the building for all she was worth. *I can do this*, she told herself. *Actually, it's quite good fun. Just take your time.*

Some of the green moss came away in her fingertips as she pressed her face to the icy parapet and panted for breath. Her eyes darted about. *Bloody hell! This is pretty high up!* She felt precariously exposed.

Suddenly she felt something strike her hand. Lu See screamed.

THRUP! THRUP! THRUP!

A foot from her face a bird burst out of one of the deep crevices, beating its wings and scattering feathers.

THRUP! THRUP! THRUP!

"It's okay, goosey!" Adrian yelled down. "It's just a pigeon. It's flown off now."

Despite herself, Lu See began to laugh. She was alight with excitement.

Peering upwards she saw Sum Sum's bottom and thighs in shadow as she scrambled over a ridge.

Lu See flexed her fingers and thumbs. The joints of her hands were killing her. Suddenly, from below, a car drove by. A wide beam of headlights illuminated the length of the street. Lu See gasped as she looked down. The car was the size of a packet of cigarettes. With renewed energy, she dug her feet into a slanting ledge and hauled herself onto a flange to grasp hold of an overhanging shelf. Pulling herself up, she came face to face with her own reflection. She'd reached the second-floor windows. Crouching and positioning her feet sideways on the frame, she seized the iron bars of the window. They were icy cold.

"How are you doing?" It was Adrian. He'd shinned down to check on her.

"Oh, I'm just fine," she replied with a laugh. "A surprise attack by a killer pigeon when you're dangling on the edge of a building is really fantastic fun."

"You're doing a brilliant job." He smiled. "The next part is a bit tricky, however, so I thought I'd lend you a hand. Ready?"

"Onward and upward." Lu See snatched at the sides of a narrow chimney, wrenching herself up, jamming the tips of her shoes into little recesses for leverage and hauling her body higher.

When she reached the next level, she swivelled her hips to face him, grinning. "I'm going to kill you for this, Adrian Woo."

Just then she slipped. One of her footholds came loose as tiny bits of masonry crumbled and fell away. *"Oh God!"*

Her hands groped for something to grab onto and she seemed to hang there, suspended for a second. Clutching at air, she missed the rope and felt herself dropping backwards, away from the wall.

Her heart was in her mouth. She began to fall.

D
O
W
N

"I've got you!" said Adrian. He seized her by the waist. He drew her close to him. Lu See's eyes were swimming.

"I think from here on you should use the rope and I'll support you from below with your feet on my shoulders," he said.

Her knees were shaking now. She felt weak and jelly-limbed.

"Just take your time, goosey."

A few minutes later they were at the top, leaning back against the slanting roof. The muscles all along Lu See's arms were twitching. Her heart was thumping. But she was laughing, bubbling over the views of the river and the spire and lanterns of Trinity College nearby.

Sum Sum pushed the hair back from Lu See's face. "Look at the lights over there, so far away, lah. Look like fireflies!"

"Quite an adrenaline rush, isn't it?" exclaimed Adrian.

Lu See plunged her head between her knees and continued to laugh. "I don't think I've ever felt so alive," she said, panting. "My hands are torn and sore, my elbow's bleeding and my back aches." She raised her head. The river looked purple in the moonlight. The tips of the college buildings resembled ornate wedding cakes. She let out a cry of exhilaration.

"You cuckoo-clocks crazy!" Sum Sum said, giggling.

"Did you see how I almost broke my neck? That pigeon was huge!"

"As big as ostrich, lah!"

"I thought your eyes were going to pop out of your skull," said Adrian.

"I think I peed my pants!"

All three of them were roaring with laughter now.

"Next time I'll bring a thermos of hot chocolate." Adrian said, lighting a cigarette and inhaling deeply.

"Next time?" cried Lu See.

Adrian pressed a finger to her lips, grazing her cheek lightly with his thumb. "*Shhshh!* That's fear number one put to bed. You're now an official nightcrawler. You've had your climbing cherry broken. Enjoy the moment."

5

Monday, March 2nd 1936. The day of the interview and Mrs Slackford was up before sunrise to fire up the stove.

As Sum Sum worried her prayer beads, Lu See sat with a cup of tea and read the newspapers, circling with a pen all the bits she thought would be relevant to her evaluation. They were sure to ask her about current affairs, she decided, yet most of the headlines were of Edward VIII's doublespeak and rumours of his relationship with Wallis Simpson. She reached across and rubbed Ganesha's tummy for luck.

An hour later she rode her rented bicycle up Castle Street, passing through the avenues of cedars and oaks and poplars on Huntington Road, arriving at Girton College a full thirty minutes early for her 9 a.m. appointment.

She waited in the cold, bicycle propped against the Porter's Lodge.

Cloister Court, Room 11. With a steadying breath, Lu See knocked on the door. Entering, she found herself in a small, dark study lined with books.

Dr Mildred Coutts, the Mistress of Girton, wearing a blue cardigan with pearl buttons, was the first to come forward. "Miss Teoh, allow me to introduce you to Dr Agnes Brooks, director of studies." Dr Brooks clamped her pipe between her teeth and shook Lu See's hand. "And this is Miss Watts-Thynne, lecturer in Theology and tutor."

They all sat down in stiff-backed chairs with Lu See facing the three ladies. "We're delighted you could join us today, Miss Teoh," said Dr Coutts. "I received excellent references from your former headmaster at Bing Hua School and I note that academically you excelled in your Senior School Certificates but I'd like you to please tell us a bit about yourself."

Lu See started to elaborate about Malaya, her schooling and why she felt Girton was the right place for her. As she spoke, her shoulders sloped forward. *No slouching!* Her mother's voice yelled in her head. *Sit up straight!* Immediately, Lu See's back grew as straight as a number-2 pencil.

"Why have you set your heart on Girton?' Dr Brooks asked. "Why not Newnham College?"

Miss Watts-Thynne added, "Or the Oxford establishments – St. Hilda's or Somerville or Lady Margaret Hall?"

"The history of the college attracted me, being the country's first residential college for women."

"Indeed, and do you know what the first intake of students were known as?" asked the Mistress.

She nodded. "The Pioneers."

Miss Watts-Thynne interrupted. "But you do realize we are not officially recognized as a fully-fledged member of the University, at least not yet. We're still regarded as an institution for the higher education for women." Lu See said she was aware of that.

"Male-chauvinist poppy-cock of course," Dr Brooks bit down on her pipe. "Any other reason for choosing Girton?"

Lu See smiled a half-smile. "Well, I must confess that I'm a fan of Sarojini Naidu. I love her poems."

"And you want to follow in her footsteps."

"Not into politics, no, but as an example to women around the world? Yes, I do."

"And you wish to read Theology," Miss Watts-Thynne said.

"Yes. Living in Malaya has exposed me to Islam, Hinduism, Buddhism, even Sikhism. I think it would be fascinating to take it further."

*

After seeing to the breakfast dishes, Sum Sum and Mrs Slackford walked together into town. Bulrush basket in hand, the landlady headed along Sidney Street with Sum Sum following close behind. As they turned down Petty Cury, Sum Sum stopped to take a snap of a street scene with the Kodak Retina. A barrow boy was selling cod and herring at 8d per lb. The fish flopped about in the barrels of water. "Straight out of Southwold 'Aarbour! Get your fresh 'erring!"

The morning sun was in Sum Sum's eyes. She was a good ten yards behind Mrs Slackford when she felt as if somebody was watching her. Ever since arriving in England she'd felt more aware and suspicious of her surroundings. For a moment she thought she was simply imagining things but then she saw a man standing in front of a set of bakers' stalls; a dark figure against the glare. Smiling self-consciously, she shielded her eyes with a hand to try and make out his features, but the sunshine flashed red against her eyelids. When he began to move towards her, something inside her tightened and she took a step back. She looked again for Mrs Slackford but the landlady was nowhere to be seen.

The sun disappeared behind a cloud and she saw his face. The mole on his left cheek appeared as dark and slippery as black onyx.

She ran.

"Whom do Buddhists worship?" asked Miss Watts-Thynne.

Lu See took a deep breath. *A trick question.* "Nobody. Because Buddha is not considered a God, at least not in the supreme creator sense. The word 'Buddha' means 'the enlightened one'. Siddhartha Gautama by all accounts was a spiritual teacher, not a God."

"So why do Buddhists idolize Buddha? There are statues of him in Buddhist temples and monasteries across the Orient. Surely it's a form of iconography."

"They're not worshipping him. I believe you'll find that they are paying respect to his image and to his teachings. The statues help to focus the mind for meditation. Buddhism should be seen more as a philosophy than a religion; it doesn't share any hallmarks of the other faiths."

The ancient road marker read *Falcon Yard* but as Sum Sum ran down the lane turning left into what she thought was the market square, the lane narrowed and dimmed under the dark mass of a derelict pub.

She was lost.

And she was trapped.

Behind her, the thud of shoes echoed against stone. Sum Sum's eyes flickered back and forth, struggling to find an opening.

She tried to get in through the door of the pub, but it was locked. "Help me!" she screamed. "Can anyone hear me?" Slowly, the pressure in her chest increased.

The silence told her she was the only person in the abandoned lot. The surrounding buildings were deserted too. Looking over her shoulder, she prayed that he had gone. Perhaps, she thought, she had lost him. But no. He was still there, in full view now, visibly panting from the chase, the shadows emphasizing the deformity of his shoulders.

"Go away!" she screamed. A flash of metal caught her eye. There was a knife in his hand.

Sum Sum edged up against the wall.

He moved in close. A vulgar smell of camphor filled her nostrils. His clothing and skin stank of rubbing liniment.

Suddenly his face was just in front of hers. She placed her hand on the flat of the blade as it pressed against her stomach.

"You want camera? Here, take. I give you negatives and all photographs." Sum Sum removed a paper packet from her coat. "There is only one photograph of you."

"That is what Mr Quek said when he developed the negatives." His eyes never left her. "If it wasn't for him I would never have tracked you down."

She felt the first brush of his fingers on the back of her neck. And then in her hair. The blade pressed slowly harder.

"I should kill you for what you saw," he said, his tone deliberate.

"I saw nothing."

He shook his head, measuredly. "You know that I dynamited the dam."

Sum Sum hesitated before nodding.

"There was another village girl who saw me besides you. I drowned her and threw her in the river before she could talk. Are you going to talk?"

Sum Sum shook her head.

"I could have slit your throat on the *Jutlandia* but you were with a policeman and killing you would only have drawn attention to me. And then I would have had to kill your mistress."

"She has nothing to do with this!"

"Did you mention me to the policeman?"

"No."

"I have been watching you, making sure the fat man Big Jowl is not around. I hear he is on your trail. I would prefer not to have to deal with him too." He snatched the camera from her together with the negatives. "You tell your mistress that if she says a word I will come back and hurt her, the same way I am about to hurt you. Only worse."

He motioned with his eyes and she got down on her knees. The tip of the blade scraped her chin. His hands went to her breasts.

"It is my experience that a terrified victim is more useful than a dead one."

Sum Sum closed her eyes. She understood. She had to do this to protect Lu See.

"You say Buddhism doesn't share the hallmarks of other faiths; perhaps you could elaborate."

Lu See thought for a minute, her spine rigid as an ironing

board. "Well, to start with Zen Buddhists don't believe in a transcendent God or Gods. Nor is there a concept of heaven or hell. Instead they focus on reincarnation and the attainment of nirvana."

"But nirvana is heaven is it not?"

"If you ask a Muslim or a Christian, heaven is a *place*, somewhere you hope to go when you die. Even for Hindus, in the Mahabharata it is written that the Pandavas go to heaven and the Kauravas descend to hell."

"So if nirvana is not a place, what would you classify it as . . .?"

"It's a state of mind."

Miss Watts-Thynne nodded. "How strong are you on the Christian teachings?"

"Not terribly. I can't quote long tracts from the gospels. Should have paid more attention in Church."

They all smiled politely. Dr Brooks took a hit from her pipe and showed off her yellow teeth. Lu See smiled back. *This is going quite well*, she heard herself think.

"The Passion of Christ," Miss Watts-Thynne continued. "Tell me why in theological terms the word 'passion' is significant. Doesn't passion imply sexual love, or a strong emotion towards something?"

Hell! I ought to know this. The Passion always refers to the crucifixion and death of Jesus. *Accounts of the Passion are found in all four canonical gospels, but from where do the doctrinal roots to the word originate?* She was in a bind here. She racked her brains.

"Let me give you nudge. You do know, by the end of year one you'll be asked to master one of the Scriptural languages, either Hebrew, Sanskrit or Ancient Greek."

Lu See looked down at her hands. *The answer must lie in the etymological origins of the word. God, how I wish I had Ah-Ba's dictionary here. Passion: from the Greek word . . .?* She drew another blank. She tried not to panic. She made another attempt. *Passion: from the Latin word 'passio' meaning suffering.*

77

That's it! The relationship between holiness and suffering.

She gave them her answer. There was much nodding of heads all round.

Next, they talked about the current vogue for cubist painting and atonal music, wanted to know her views on Stalin, the Moscow show trials and the recent Japanese incursions in China. After this, they discussed college life and the syllabus and then Dr Coutts asked Lu See whether she was available to sit a special entrance examination in early September.

"Yes, of course, I'd be honoured to."

"There'll be a general paper and one on comparative religions." As she stood up to leave Miss Watts-Thynne handed her a long reading list of theological texts as well as a card that allowed her the use of the Divinity School library. "Do your very best and we hope to see you here at the start of Michaelmas term in October."

Moments later Lu See emerged from the dark study into the bright mid-morning sunlight. Before the interview she might as well have had lead weights clamped to her feet. Now her tread was much lighter, as though wings had been sewn to her ankles. Feeling as if she'd been dismantled and put back together again, she rode her bicycle down Huntington Road with her head abuzz with thoughts: *That went well, I think. I hope they liked me. A general paper and one on comparative religions. See you here Michaelmas term.* She stopped cycling after five minutes and retrieved the list of theological books from her basket. She counted sixty-eight titles and immediately broke into a prickly sweat. *Hell . . . ! Sixty-eight bloody textbooks! September's less than . . She counted out April, May, June, July on her fingers. Less than six months away! That's almost twelve textbooks a month!*

When she returned to Portugal Place, she saw red, and blue and white tea towels twitching in the breeze on a long pole; laundry aired from the first floor window, swaying in the wind high above like Tibetan prayer flags.

"What's all this?" she asked Sum Sum when she came to the door.

"For luck and happiness. My way of appeasing the gods. Mrs Slackford not home yet, still at market. How was interview?" Sum Sum's bloodshot eyes flickered up and down the cobbled street.

Lu See gasped hard when she saw Sum Sum's face. "What happened to you?"

Sum Sum touched the side of her nose lightly, wincing in anticipation of the lancing pain. "*Aiyoo!* I so stupid, lah. I was taking picture of one of the big colleges and climbed on to a bridge to get tip-top shot, but then my foot slip and I fall and hit head on floor. Camera smash on ground and then fall into river."

"Do you want me to take you to a doctor?"

"No, lah!" Sum Sum sounded offended. "Only small accident. I'm sorry for the camera." Just then a fat string of blood seeped from her nose and down her chin.

"Never mind the camera. Take this tissue and keep your head up. Let me get you some ice to put on it."

Sum Sum set her head back and blinked away the pain. She wouldn't be aware of her scraped hands and elbows until much later.

6

The following week, to celebrate Lu See's success, Adrian promised to take the girls to London as a treat. *A day at the zoo followed by a trip to the Natural History Museum!* – Lu See could hardly contain her excitement. "It'll be fun, don't you think, pumpkin-head? You might even see your Picalilli Circus. And while in London I can call on the organ maker, Conrad P. Hughes." Pietro decided to tag along too.

They lingered in the waiting room at Cambridge station before catching the 09.45 for King's Cross. The conductor, leaning from a carriage door, blew his whistle and a great gout of locomotive steam engulfed the railway.

Adrian wore a plaid, Windsor double-breasted suit and a Cagney-style homburg. He carried his overcoat draped over his arm. Lu See thought he must have dressed in a hurry that morning because his back collar stud was missing. "Love the outfit, Adie," mewed Pietro. "Do you like my hat? It's by Elsa Schiaparelli. It's a woman's hat, I know," he sighed, "but I simply had to have it."

When Lu See watched Sum Sum settle into her compartment seat she noticed something she hadn't seen before – she looked morose. Sum Sum had always been feisty, sometimes touchy, but never ever morose. *It must be this grey weather and stodgy English food*, she decided. *All those pork pies! Still, that's no reason for her to be acting like a cursed princess in a fairy tale.*

Ignoring the scrutiny, Sum Sum pretended to read a copy of *Modern Screen* magazine with a picture of Marlene Dietrich on its cover. Meanwhile, Adrian buried his nose in the *Manchester Guardian*. After a while he muttered something about German troops crossing into the west bank of the Rhine. "It's a flagrant violation of the Versailles Treaty," he said to nobody in particular, shaking his head. "Bloody fascists!"

Outside, beyond the window, a steady drizzle of rain hit the glass.

Pietro clapped his hands to cheer everyone up. "When we get back to Cambridge tonight you're all invited to supper at Christ's College Hall. I've asked chefy to prepare something gorgeous – I've even offered to lend him a hand."

"You? Cook? No, lah." Sum Sum proclaimed, momentarily sparked by the news.

Offended, Pietro removed his hat and patted his blond coiffure. "I'll have you know, Samson, the maternal side of my family is Italian. Cooking is part of my heritage. And speaking of heritage, are we museuming it as soon as we get to London?"

Adrian shook his head. "First stop will be Lu See's organ man. Then we'll head for the zoo."

On arrival at King's Cross they pushed past the red-coated porters and jumped into a taxi. Sum Sum had a vague notion of where London was, but no idea where to find it on a map, or how big or small it was. As she stared out the taxi window she couldn't help but feel a little disappointed. *This*, she thought, *is the heart of the Empire?* "Everything so grey and dirty. Nothing like pictures of Big Ben and Buck-and-Ham Palace."

The taxi dropped them at a store front near the Angel tube station. There was a black Vitrolite fascia hung above the main entrance with the legend *Conrad P. Hughes – Pipe Organ Specialists* in crimson raised letters. Once inside, Lu See was greeted by a delicate, worried-looking man in a six-guinea suit and two-tone shoes.

"Conrad P. Hughes at your service," he said. "Miss Teoh, is it? Yes, I received your letter last week." He looked at Adrian, Sum Sum and Pietro in turn. "A project you have in mind for Malaya, if memory serves correctly. Yes, we would be more than happy to take on the commission." He took a few moments to show them to a low-level glass-fronted display case with an array of miniature pipe organs. "All built to scale," he said. "Now if you'll come through here and take a seat . . ."

He spent the next few minutes presenting himself and his designs to the four who sat in judgement of his work.

"How long have you been in this industry, Mr Hughes, if you don't mind me asking?"

"Not at all, Miss Teoh," he replied, proudly fingering the lapel of his six-guinea suit. "All of sixteen years. We've had some ups and downs but overall the business has done me proud. Now, shall we move on to the mechanics of the beast?"

"Please do."

For almost half an hour he pieced together the many features, explaining how the sound was produced via the workings of the air reservoir, the reed and flue pipes and the stop-action sliders, and how each pipe equalled one pitch. "It's not like a flute or a clarinet which produces multiple pitches depending on the instrument keys. No, the organ pipe's pitch is determined by the pipe's length."

"How many pipes will we require?" asked Lu See.

"Typically, a church organ would have a keyboard span of five octaves, from C2 to C7. And each octave has twelve semitones, hence a rank of 61 pipes."

"That's a lot of pipe," said Pietro.

"Our pipes are made from only the finest copper and aluminium. No cutting corners here. But what we'll require from your people in Malaya are specifics for the Great and Swell divisions. Here you are," he said, handing Lu See a tiny manual. "You'll find everything explained in this pamphlet. It's all to do with the range of sound you want. Once we have an idea, then we can get things rolling with some drawings and sketches."

Much pleased, Lu See shook hands with Conrad P. Hughes and said her goodbyes.

With that over, they flagged down a cab and headed for Regent's Park Zoo.

"In sum, a good meeting, wouldn't you say, goosey?"

"Yes," replied Lu See, who was already drafting a letter to Second-aunty Doris in her head.

"Lot of roads seem to be closed, guv," said the taxi driver.

The taxi turned into Eversholt Street and headed north. A few seconds later they were greeted by a mass of people gathered by Camden High Street.

"Labour strikes," Adrian said in a subdued tone. Sum Sum clasped her throat.

Further along, they encountered a full-blown crush along the Oval Road. *'Jobless Men Keep Going!'* came the cry through a brass megaphone. *'Workers of the world unite!'* Demonstrators in scruffy trousers and long john tops held up banners and placards and marched up and down the street. Moving in shoals of six or seven, thrusting past women and children standing in the sidelines, they sang and whistled between chants. As Pietro pointed out "a ducky with deliciously muscular arms", Lu See watched with wonder. Her instincts told her she was in no danger here; these people had no quarrel with anyone but the establishment. "In Malaya such a public show of dissent would see the army being called in," she heard herself say.

A little distance ahead there was a protest by the NUWM. "Hunger Rally," informed Adrian. "I wanted you to see this," he continued.

Marchers banged their drums and held out tin buckets for collections, picketers cried out to abolish the Means Test. 'Sack the Unemployment Assistance Board!' they yelled. 'Down with the National Government!' came the reply. Police constables on horseback rode next to the throng, keeping the peace.

Lu See looked at him. "Did you know there was going to be a protest?"

Adrian admitted as much. "I think it's vital you witness this first hand. To enhance your political education."

"If you're planning on turning me into a communist, don't bother. I believe in religion. I believe in capitalism."

Immediately Lu See felt the atmosphere in the taxi crackle. It was often like this when the subject of politics came up. She stiffened in apprehension about what they would argue about next. "But then there's fascism," he continued. "And what about imperialism? Do you believe in that? Don't you want a free Malaya?"

"Yes, but only when the country is ready for it."

"But who gets to decide when we are ready? Our colonial masters or the people of Malaya?"

Lu See grew irritated. "Look, what's happening here, are you trying to convert me, to radicalize me?"

"No, I simply want you to see the world as it truly is. I don't think you should fear change. Haven't I taught you to confront your fears?"

"How can you accuse me of fearing change? I left my family. I'm here, aren't I?"

"I meant political change."

Lu See shook her head and turned to look at Sum Sum.

Sum Sum raised an eyebrow and pretended to read her copy of *Modern Screen* magazine.

At the zoo they visited the Reptile House, the Aquarium and the monkey enclosure where Pietro scolded a male chimpanzee for masturbating. In the Mappin Terraces they saw polar bears and snow leopards and even got to feed the penguins. A light drizzle of rain fell. It suited the penguins more than the people. Adrian clung to his homburg.

Afterwards they went for lunch at a restaurant in Marylebone where a waitress with a frilly cap and a rustling black satin uniform served them lamb cutlets and boiled potatoes. They all ate heartily, except for Sum Sum, who merely picked at her food.

"Are you feeling unwell, pumpkin-head?" asked Lu See.

Sum Sum shrugged. "I'm okay, lah."

"Saving room for supper tonight," Pietro said, approvingly. "Sensible girl." He flicked ash from his slender cigarette holder into a brass smoking stand. "Naturally, it'll be a four-course meal; three-course meals are so awfully middle-class."

Lu See noted how stylishly London ladies were dressed. Women here wore their pearls long and their hair short, in finger waves and soft curls. Some sported bell-shaped cloche hats; others donned velvet turbans worn at an angle. Their dresses were sleeker, more fitted, with wider shoulders compared to the styles worn in Cambridge.

With lunch over they tipped the hat-check girl and took a taxi to the Natural History Museum. As they drove down the Marylebone Road, Pietro and the girls tried not to gawk at the strings of men in oversized flat caps queuing up for jobs at Grimble's Vinegar Factory. In parts of the Edgware Road they saw tenants being evicted from their homes with their furniture laid out on the roadside. A little further on children with grimy knees kicked a ball made out of rolled-up newspapers, running beneath crumbling brick walls crazed with Communist Party posters and anti-Jewish slogans and bills promoting Fry's Pure Breakfast Cocoa (4 d per lb).

They spent four hours at the museum. As early evening fell they hailed a cab. The taxi driver wound his window down as they approached. "Aw wite?"

"King's Cross Station, please," instructed Adrian.

"You're 'avin' a laugh! Daan't you know there's a bleedin' rally on? The plods closed off most of Euston and 'alf the roads northeast of Hyde Park."

"What sort of rally?"

"Marches against mass unemployment. Also a load of lefties 're rallyin' against the fascists."

"Our train's at 6 p.m."

"For an extra two bob I can swing you through Kensington and Piccadilly then up through Farringdon, 'a is that?"

"Good man."

The taxi headed south.

"Those dinosaur bones were quite something, don't you think?" beamed Adrian.

Pietro patted his coiffure. "A trip to the museum is a bit like playing hide the thimble, don't you think? Wonderful fun as long as it doesn't go on for too long."

As they skirted Hyde Park and passed Queen's Gate, Lu See started to notice more and more people gathering. Many streets became impassable. Near Kensington Gore one of the roads was blocked off by an abandoned double-decker bus advertising Schweppes Sparkling Lime.

"What's that up ahead?" she asked, grasping Adrian's arm. "Who are all these people?"

"Mosley's fascists," Adrian spat from under his homburg.

"Ask him to turn the car around."

"Don't be silly, goosey."

The mood on the streets was different to the scenes they'd witnessed earlier on. This wasn't a controlled demonstration; this was more like a rebellion. The streets were suddenly filled with hard ugly faces, about thirty men dressed in matching black shirts and black caps; some handing out copies of *Fascist Week*.

Sum Sum stared, bewildered. "Why do they have Hindu swastikas on their arms?"

"Tell the driver to turn around, Adrian," insisted Lu See. "We'll be fine."

The taxi driver peered into his mirror. "It's aw gone pear-shaped, guv. The bloomin' right wing's accusin' the Jews of tryin' ter push Britain inter war with Germany. The lefties 're callin' Baldwin an 'itler stooge. And naa you 'ave the Trade Unions causin' grief. Lawd above, the world's gone barmy. You lot better keep your 'eads daan."

As the taxi passed the Albert Hall, Lu See saw more hardened faces. "I have a bad feeling about this, Adrian."

"*Ayo Sami*, that man there in trouble!" cried Sum Sum.

Lu See pressed her face to the window. From a distance she saw a crush of people milling about and as their car drew nearer her anxiety grew stronger. "I don't want to continue any further, Adrian."

A carthorse reared, kicking and neighing.

"Yes, let's go back, Adie!"

Twenty yards away, down a narrow side street, she saw three blackshirts shouting at an old man, pushing him to the ground, pulling at his beard and curly sideburns and spitting on his yarmulke.

"Stop the taxi," Adrian ordered.

"You wot?"

"I said stop the car!"

Adrian threw off his homburg, jumped out of the door and sprinted towards the trouble.

He grabbed one of the black-clad men by the collar and shoved him aside. Pointing his finger at the others he told them to back away as he helped the old man to his feet. At first the blackshirts appeared dazed by his courage but slowly their expressions turned nasty.

"Fuck off, you yid lover!" one yelled. He had a mop of blond hair and a sawtooth scar across his chin. "And a fuckin' Chink one at that!" Lu See watched in horror as the blond man's fist flew at Adrian. Flinching, Adrian raised an arm as a shield as another kicked him in the knee, buckling it. They circled Adrian like a bask of crocodiles.

"Do something!" Lu See screamed to the cab driver.

"Not on your porridge knife! Your Chinese bloke's on 'is own!"

The three men surrounded Adrian now. They held on to his hair and overcoat trying to wrestle him to the floor. Struggling from the clinch, Adrian's arm swung in a wide arc as they swayed.

If they get him on the floor, they'll kick him in the head, thought Lu See. She heard them grunt as their limbs entwined like a knot of snakes.

"Sum Sum, Pietro!" Lu See bawled. "We have to do help him!"

"*Lai-lah, lai-lah!*" Sum Sum removed a hatpin from her bag. At the same time Lu See grabbed the taxi driver's umbrella. They leapt from the car just as a fist smashed into Adrian's face.

7

The three blackshirts jeered as Adrian went down. The punch caused dark stars to appear behind his eyes. The crack of the blow resounded in his head. There was blood in his hair and scalp too; he could feel it trail and pool in his ear. He collapsed on to one knee but as soon as he saw Lu See, Sum Sum and Pietro rushing from the taxi Adrian held up his free hand and ordered them to stay back.

"Get away!" he yelled.

Thick arms grappled with him, pulling his overcoat sleeves behind his back, catching him in a wrestling lock. He felt a claw of fingers snatch at his hair, yanking his head from side to side. From the corner of his eye Adrian spotted the girls still advancing. Panic surged through him. "No! Get back!"

Ashen faced, the girls stopped.

"Not so brave now, eh, my Chinky-chink friend." The blond-haired man in front kicked Adrian in the stomach. His belly ripped hot with pain and a gasp escaped his throat.

Adrian swung his head round and stared hard at the girls. The last thing he wanted was to get them involved in this. "Stay away," he mouthed. His teeth were crimson with blood.

The blond slapped his face and sneered. "Fucking yid lover. Now see what you've done. Our Jew friend's gone and run off. Sprinted home to count his shekels."

The others laughed.

"No matter, a Chink's as good as a Jew when it comes to the end of my boot!"

People stared out of windows. A pack of onlookers gathered, keeping their distance; clustered ravens in greasy clothes. "Leave him alone!" someone shouted from afar.

The man holding Adrian in a wrestling lock relaxed his grip slightly as he peered around.

Still on one knee, Adrian sensed his moment. This was the chance he'd been waiting for. He squared his shoulders and threw his head backward. The reverse head-butt clattered into the face of the man behind. At the same moment he stomped on his assailant's foot. Stunned, the man released his hold completely and Adrian pulled free. Stepping to one side, Adrian wrenched off his overcoat and raised his hands like a boxer.

"Feisty little cunt, aren't you?"

"You have no idea."

The blond blackshirt swung at him. A clenched whoosh of flesh and knuckle skimmed past Adrian's cheek, grazing his shoulder. Bobbing and weaving, Adrian searched for a gap and then let fly with two swift whiplash jabs – *Snak-smaack! Snak-smaack!* – followed by a thumping uppercut. There was a crunch of teeth. When the mop of blond hair hit the ground Adrian drove his boot into his chest, but the man was already out cold.

"You fucker!" wailed the second blackshirt as he grabbed Adrian from behind. Whirling round, Adrian caught hold of his wrist and snapped it as he would a chicken neck. Then Adrian hooked his thumb into the blackshirt's eye and swung his right elbow hard, catching him on the point of the chin. He collapsed with a cry of agony.

With two men down, Adrian stepped forward, ducked his head, and took aim at the last man. He skimmed a jab at the base of his throat and then with a roundhouse right drove his fist into his opponent's face, following up with a hard left. There was a horrible *crack* of bone against cartilage. The man's nose blew apart and blood sprayed up and doused the street like a squirt gun.

At that point Adrian heard a clear high-pitched sound. Up the street a constable sprinted their way; whistle clasped between his lips; he had one hand on his bobby's helmet as he ran so that it wouldn't fall.

A covered lorry pulled up fifty yards back. Adrian ran toward Lu See and Sum Sum, seizing them by the arms as a fresh load of blackshirts poured out of the lorry. More policemen arrived. A roar of noise erupted as the two sides clashed.

Seconds later Adrian bundled the girls and Pietro into the taxi, sprang into the back seat and slammed the door. "Go, go, go!" he yelled.

The taxi sped off, leaving the bobby with the whistle in its wake.

"Cor, you 'eaven and 'ell clocked that last bloke, guv. I bet they could even 'ear his nose breakin' over in Timbuktu."

"Are you okay?" asked Lu See.

"You're ever so brave, Adie!"

"*Wahh!* You just like Gary Cooper! *Bing, bang, bang!*"

Adrian didn't say a word. He simply rubbed his right hand where a patch of red glazed his knuckles and breathed uneasily, in swallows. Blood pulsed behind his eyes. His head felt light, the ends of his fingers twitched – it was the same sensation as when he'd almost lost his footing at the top of Trinity spire last August. When he looked down he saw his heart thumping so hard it was shaking the torn fabric of his blood-splattered shirt.

"Are you okay?" Lu See asked once more.

"I'm fine. Did that old man get away safely?"

"Yes."

"Good," he said with a smile, pulling a comb from his trouser pocket.

"How . . .?" Lu See's voice shook. "How did you learn to . . .?"

His throat, dry as scorched hay, felt constricted. "Kung-fu lessons at Chung Ling High School when I was a bit younger," he shrugged.

"You could've been killed."

"And I could have lost my Schiaparelli hat!" cried Pietro.

"I was trying to save that man from being killed, goosey," he insisted, quietly. "Anyway, those fascists had it coming."

"You scared the hell out of me."

Adrian touched the small gash on his lower lip. "Oh hell, I left my overcoat behind. I loved that overcoat. Do you think we can go back and get it?"

Lu See pinched him hard on the leg.

Adrian grinned and calmly ran a comb through his blood-stiffened hair.

"Dear, dear, oh-dear, all this has made me ever so faint." Pietro brushed a hand across his eyes theatrically. "Would you mind if I called off our supper tonight. I'm simply drowning here with exhaustion." He swooned. "Too much exhaustion."

8

Midway through April, when the last traces of the winter which had chilled Lu See to the bone had dissipated, the postman shoved an envelope through the letter flap.

Lu See was standing on her head, nibbling on a biscuit as Sum Sum scooped the mail off the floor.

"For you, lah."

Lu See's heart lifted when she saw the postmark. "It's from Malaya."

Tearing open the envelope and settled into one of the suede armchairs. She recognized her mother's hand-writing immediately. Her mother explained how she had tracked her down by writing to the Admissions Office at Girton.

I had hoped that nobody would have to learn the truth. That we could say that you had gone abroad simply to study, but it was not to be. The Chows have learned the truth and are livid. Their son openly brands you a strumpet. The loss of face you have caused us is great. Your Ah-Ba naturally is most upset, the raw betrayal stings him, as does all the unavoidable talk and gossip of our neighbours and friends. He calls you a black sheep, says he should have thrown you out when he had the chance, instead of letting you pour humiliation on the family. His words pain me too, of course, but the truth is that neither of us can come to terms with what you have done – slipping out of the house the way you did, like a thief in the night . . . the ultimate rejection. And with a Woo! Chee-chee! I rub my fingers together and say shame on you.

The angry tone of her mother's words upset Lu See. Despite the warmer temperatures, Mrs Slackford still lit a fire every morning to soothe her old bones. Lu See strode over to the stone fireplace and threw the letter into the flames. With a mutinous expression, she watched the paper burn.

She spent the next hour drafting a response, punching out her reply on her new Smith & Corona typewriter. Lu See decided to keep her response civil: she apologized for embarrassing the family, explained how she was now happy and settled, and also stressed that her interview at Girton College was a success. She made no mention of her arrangement with Second-aunty Doris nor the search for a pipe organ. She signed the letter with a flourish and ran a blotter over the ink.

Pushing back the drapes and seeing that it was one of those glorious glimmering spring mornings she decided to walk to the post office for some stamps. By now she was a loyal customer of the Royal Mail (with letters to Second-aunty Doris and Conrad P. Hughes of London), a regular at Fitzbillies cake shop and a fixture at Heffers booksellers.

Shrugging on her coat she made her way down the crooked cobbled street and immediately came across Adrian who was on his way to the library.

"Morning, goosey."

"Fancy seeing you here." She glanced at his shock of a hairdo. "Don't tell me you've been jamming your fingers in electric sockets again."

"My hair looks fine." He gave it a stroke.

Lu See could always tell if Adrian had been out climbing the night before. The state of his hair invariably gave it away. Whipped up by the wind and rain it stood up on its own and being rebellious he refused to oil it down with lacquer like everyone else. He once claimed that the look gave him a

'Marxist air'. Today he resembled someone who was falling down a mineshaft.

"Where are you off to?"

"Sending a letter to my mother."

"Meet you for lunch?"

"The Pickerel at one?"

"I'll have your Stilton Ploughman's ready and waiting for you."

"Ha! See you later."

With Lu See out of the house, Sum Sum perched on the edge of her bed and stared at her hands. *Release the anxiety. Breathe. Fill the abdomen. Balance the chakra points.* She placed the middle finger of her right hand between her eyes. With her thumb she closed her right nostril and breathed slowly through her left. She inhaled and exhaled several times then, closing her left nostril with her ring finger, she breathed though her right.

I know, I know I must tell Lu See. The distress grew inside of her. The yogic breathing wasn't working. Her anxiety threatened to swallow her up.

What do I do? What can I say? I've let everyone down, no? But I did it to help Lu See. To protect her. Sum Sum felt a hard, prickly heat in her chest.

Hot like a secret.

A secret that made her feel fragile, a secret she knew that soon she would have to share with Lu See. And the more she thought about it, the more she wanted to return to Tibet.

She crinkled her nose. Was she imagining it, or was there a stink of camphor in the air? She peered out of the window and her sense of panic returned. A dark figure stood at the end of the cobbled street, hiding in the shade. The shock made her dart behind the curtains. When she looked again, he was gone.

On her return from the post office Lu See edged past the phalanx of people that had gathered on Regent Street. Up and down the junction, nannies pushed perambulators, barrowmen offered pipe tobacco and shag to passing gentlemen, carthorses crapped and knife-grinders whetted knives using wheels and a leather strops.

When she reached Park Parade, passing the soot-smeared chimneysweep who was hauling brushes up a ladder, she came across Mrs Slackford on her way to market. "There's a scary man come to visit yew."

"A scary man?"

"Oi let him in just as oi was leaving. Usually oi don't allow gentlem'n callers. Cor blast me if he's not the size of a bus, like Fatty Arbuckle, all dressed in black and foreign-looking!"

Dressed in black? Like a blackshirt?

Lu See stomped up to the entrance of number 23; the colour high in her cheeks. As soon as she was inside the front door, she hesitated. The smell of a lit cigarette drifted across from the living room. She flinched at the sound of a chair scraping the floor.

A man's dark form was silhouetted against the window behind. Seated in one of the suede armchairs, clutching his hat in his hand, the figure's blimpish bulk shifted on hearing footsteps.

Thinking a blackshirt had stormed the house, Lu See plucked an umbrella from the stand and cocked her arm threateningly. "Don't you dare come any closer!" she warned.

"You damn-fierce rude, girl," came the low-throated reply. "I travel all day searching for you-lah and this is the greeting I receive? And nothing to read in this house but this old copy of the *Modern Screen* magazine, aahh!"

The voice was unmistakable.

The thick Buddha-like body rose slowly to its feet and turned to catch the mid-morning light. His greying hair was oiled and parted to the left. His eyebrows were formidably hairy. In profile he resembled a giant panda wearing a life preserver ring.

"Uncle Big Jowl!" Lu See cried. Lu See rushed across the room.

She embraced the man with the enormous belly, folding herself into his big open arms. "I never thought I'd be this happy to see you!"

Round shoulders hunched, cigarette in hand, the old uncle beamed with pleasure. "Now, you see, lah, this is more like the reception I was expecting."

Lu See brushed a knuckle to wipe a tear from her cheek. "How are you, uncle?" she asked as they drew apart.

"I'm top-class, lah! *Ai-yooo*, my little niece is crying, lah! So happy to see me, is it?" He chuckled, brushing the front of his trousers with the flat of his palm. "I remember your eyes would get all red like this when I used to take you swimming as a young girl. You remember too? It was me that taught you to swim in the river. I used to watch over you like a lifeguard."

He wore a dark navy three-piece suit with a matching striped tie, an outfit Lu See suspected his Penang tailor had put together especially for this trip.

She looked at his face, noticed he had aged a little about the eyes. "When did you arrive in England?"

He loosened his tie, plopped his hat on the coffee table, and sank into the chair. "As soon as your mother learned you were heading for Cambridge I got on the next boat. I arrived London on Tuesday. Everywhere protests, protests. Arrived here last night. Staying at the University Arms Hotel. *Ai-yooo*, this town is so bloody-hell expensive! London full of poor people now, not like this place, *hnn*? In London I can get discount at Grosvenor House, but not at University Arms – I pay tip-top rate."

He swept a hand across the room to take in the entire house. "Nice home you have here, aahh!" He cocked his head, toying with an earlobe.

"Mrs Slackford makes us feel very welcome."

"Tell me. Little niece, what you have been doing?"

Lu See compressed weeks of activity into minutes, describing in turn the interview at Girton, the trip to London, the appearance of the awful blue cheese at the Pickerel pub. She decided to leave out the climbing episode.

"You married yet, aahh!" he went again, cocking his head. "To this Woo fellow?"

"No." She waited a few beats. "I came to England to win a place at Girton not get married. But we have plans to wed some time in June, after summer term breaks up . . ." She allowed the words to hang in the air.

Uncle Big Jowl's mouth remained stolid, as straight a line as a stingray's tail. "So, you are determined to be with him."

Sum Sum appeared, standing dignifiedly in the hallway, fingering her prayer beads, alert and attentive in the presence of an elder.

"Yes, uncle."

"Well, you are at a good age to be married, but who am I, an old man, to judge, eh? But are you settled here? Are you content?" he asked.

Lu See considered the question. "I'll be content when I get into Girton," she replied, sitting down opposite him on the dark settee.

Big Jowl Uncle nodded sagely. He fetched a handkerchief from his pocket and dabbed at his forehead, gazing out of the window, following the rooflines of the adjoining buildings, listening to the voices floating up from the street. A pigeon cooed on the building ledge. "No lifeguard watching over you anymore, girl. You're now swimming all by yourself."

Before too long Uncle Big Jowl looked at his fob watch, "Where is Mr Woo?"

"He is at the library." They both sipped cups of tea which Sum Sum prepared.

"Is he good to you?" asked the big man.

"Yes, he is," she said softly. She removed a metal clip from her hair and held it in her lap.

"I ask this because you ran away from home for love."

"No, I ran away to further my education. And I didn't want to marry the One-eyed Giant."

"*Ai-yoo*, big scandal, lah. Have you heard from your mother?"

"I received an angry letter this morning."

"Your father too is as angry as wild tiger, aahh! Not sure what makes him lose more face – you jilting Cheam Chow or you running off with a Woo!"

"How is he?" she asked after a time.

"Under a lot of strain. The police keep coming back and asking him questions about the dam."

"Have the police decided who was responsible for the sabotage?"

"No, bunch of useless boneheads."

Lu See suddenly remembered Sum Sum's photograph of the man with the mole. She looked at Sum Sum as she spoke. "You know, Sum Sum took a photograph of a man with a gun and explo–"

Sum Sum turned pale. She butted in quickly. "I saw a man with a monkey. He was organ grinder and his monkey made me think of Malaya." She made a gesture to Lu See with her hands, zipping them across her lips.

The big man sighed. "Your father under too much strain. He is suing the Woos for sabotaging the dam. The Woos in turn are suing him for the same reason. And both are being sued by Hip Sing Rubber Processing Co. because neither could deliver the promised amount of rubber due to the flooding.

"If this carries on we will all go bust from the lawyers' fees." He straightened his shoulders. "But he is also under strain because he is concerned for you. This is the reason why I am here. Your Ah-Ba wanted to come himself but with all the legal procedures and everything . . ."

"He couldn't spare the time."

"*Nah*, don't put words in my mouth. He only wants the

best for you. But he does admit now that he misjudged you. He should have listened to you when you refused to marry Cheam Chow. You are stronger than you look. I always knew you to be the solid type underneath. But Ah-Ba thought you were just going through a temperamental phase. I think he has not forgiven himself for what has happened."

"Really?" she added with a hint of sarcasm, "I didn't know he cared so much."

"Would I be here if it were not so? Now, I ask you again, lah. Three straightforward questions: Are you happy? Do you need anything? Do you wish to return to Malaya? No pulling wool on eyes now, tell the truth! There is no room in life for counterfeit happiness."

Lu See looked down and smiled at her hands. "Uncle, everything is sweeties and sunshine."

"*Ai-yooo!*" He guffawed. "You used to use that expression when you were a little girl, lah!"

Sum Sum appeared at his side with a plate of digestives. Uncle Big Jowl took a biscuit and patted his stomach, proud of his girth. He raised a hirsute eyebrow and finger-combed his hair, cocking his head. "So, you are happy here. Aahh!"

She leaned forward in her chair. "We are happy," she said, smiling. "Sum Sum and I are fine."

Uncle Big Jowl grew solemn. "There is a Malayan folk-tale," he said, "about an old fisherman living on the pirate coast. When this fellow was young, his daily haul of sea perch and moonfish brought him much respect in the market. But now, with his arms weak and his back stiff, his day-to-day catch dwindled to the extent that there were some evenings he took nothing home to his poor wife but the odd mackerel. One morning he woke before dawn and saw a large star in the sky. He prayed to the star and asked that he be granted much luck. Galvanized, next morning he took his skiff out further than he'd been before, to a hidden cove along the coastline, and came across a long-abandoned stone hut he'd not seen before. Drawn by curiosity he knocked on the heavy door of the hut but there came no reply."

"Does this story have a point to it?"

"Quiet, aahh! I am getting there. So when the fisherman tried the handle it would not budge, lah. He looked through the keyhole and was struck by a heavenly yellow glow. 'Pirate gold inside!' he cried, picking up a rock to smash the lock. But his weak arms hardly made a dent. Disconsolate, he returned to his boat. That night the star appeared once more to him. He dropped to his knees and prayed for a key to fall from the skies. A key that would open the stone door.

"The following day he caught only one miserable fish in his net. A curious looking thing he had never seen the likes of which before. As he handled it, he gave it a squeeze. It coughed up a key. 'My prayers are answered!' he exclaimed and sure enough when he got back to shore and pressed the key to the stone door of the hut it opened. 'Gold!' he cried damn-fiercely. But as soon as he was inside he saw not pirate gold but only super-bright sunlight pouring through the cracks in the roof, reflecting off the copper-toned shingles. And when he tried to leave he found the door had shut and locked itself from the outside. There was no way out. He was trapped forever."

"And the point being?"

"Be careful what you wish for, lah."

"I still don't understand."

"Sometimes love is not what it pretends to be."

She got to her feet. "I don't have to listen to this."

"Okay, okay," he said, gesturing apologetically. "Sit down, sit down."

After several moments he stretched out his legs and cracked an ugly face. "*Ai-yooo!* Bloody arthritic knees! This fifty-year-old body's no good, lah!"

He glanced at his fob watch and sighed. "Now that I've seen you, I'll be off to London tomorrow. I'll sail back east next week." From somewhere inside his jacket he pulled out an *ang pow*, a red envelope. "In case you need help," he said, bulging his eyes for emphasis. "Two boat tickets to Penang. For you and Sum Sum when you need it. I have also put some money in here. Only use for emergency." His knees crackled as he got up to leave.

"Uncle, please, I have ample money." She tried to hand the *ang pow* back.

"You dare refuse my goodwill?" His eyes continued to bulge.

She decided to keep her association with Second-aunty Doris quiet. She dipped her head. "Thank you, Uncle, for your generosity."

He straightened his tie, glanced at his watch chain and cocked his head. "Tickets valid for one year."

9

It was still dark. The night air remained ice cold. And there was a succubus in the room.

Provided that Sum Sum remained hidden beneath her quilt and kept completely motionless for long enough, the demon might think she was part of the bedding and take flight. If only her head wasn't left so exposed; she would be all right if she covered it with the eiderdown. But she didn't dare move.

The bubble of nausea climbed to the back of her throat again.

The dark spirit edged closer. Was it the man with the mole? Had he come back to hurt her? Or was it the devil himself?

The *tap-tap* of its cloven hooves crept up slow and even. Shadows closed round. Sum Sum squeezed her eyes shut, too scared to scream, too scared to chant her sutras. Too terrified to breathe even.

Sum Sum set her jaw and clamped her nostrils shut. *Is it a ghost? Or a devil? Aiyo, must be the Pontianak – the vampire of Malay folklore?* She heard a hiss. *Keep absolutely still. Otherwise it will disembowel me. Scream! Scream for help! No! The incense from the joss sticks will act like a shield.* The floorboards creaked as the succubus took a step forward. Sum Sum imagined the whites of the demon's eyes bulging as it approached, the beast's wild straggly hair, the tail with the spaded tip, the mouth half-filled with muddy brown blood.

"*Sssssssssssssummmmm-summmmm!*"

It was a barely audible hiss, but she heard it. A ghostly voice calling her. The floorboards groaned once again. Muscles tightening in her stomach, she pictured an emaciated arm reaching out to grab her. For an instant she was aware of its presence warming the back of her neck.

Sum Sum stifled a gasp.

When she felt its touch on her shoulder she sprang upright from her bed, flinging the quilt aside and spilling her prayer beads onto the floor. *"Wahhhhh!"*

"Aaargghhh!" yelled Lu See.

"Wahhhh!" cried Sum Sum.

"You scared the life out of my bones! Are you crazy-lah, creeping up on me in the middle of the night? I thought you were a demon!"

"I thought you turned into a zombie, sleeping with your eyes wide open!"

Hushing each other to keep their voices down, the two women glared at one another, panting, hands on throats.

Lu See, swaddled in her pink dressing gown, had to catch her breath. "I came to check on you. I heard you vomiting in the bathroom. This is the second morning in a row now. And last week you were sick too. Are you ill?"

"Aiyo, what was that tap-tapping noise? I thought it was the devil's hooves."

"My house slippers of course. Look, what's the matter? Is it something you ate? You've been acting odd for ages."

In the stillness of the house the clock in the nearby church struck the quarter hour. An incense stick, stuffed into a jam pot, smouldered on the windowsill. Lu See's concerned stare made the ensuing silence all the more uncomfortable.

"Do you need to see a doctor?"

Sum Sum didn't know what to say. She was exhausted, she felt stripped bare, like a tree torn up by a storm, dead yet not quite dead. After a while Lu See's hand came to rest softly on the back of her neck; stroking her hair as she would a child's.

"What's going on, pumpkin-head?" Her voice was soft. "Do you want me to take you to Addenbrooke's?"

Sum Sum felt her heart pitch over, tumbling like the prayer beads that now danced across the floor. Both girls regarded one another through the grey light.

Lu See thought the face watching her looked lost, as stunned and innocent as a calf that had just discovered where veal came from. The muscles around Sum Sum's mouth remained rigid. Eventually Lu See said, "We can't go on like this."

"Like what?" said Sum Sum in a subdued voice.

"Both with faces as long as a grasshopper's back leg. Tell me what's wrong. I can't help you if you don't tell me where it hurts."

Looking like a child swallowing a spoonful of cod liver oil, Sum Sum skated a hand back and forth across her tummy. Her heart burned. *You are my sister. I cannot keep secrets from you. Two thick tears coursed down her face.* "I been hiding this from you for weeks, vomiting every morning for the last month. Lu See, I am *mengandung*. I'm carrying a baby."

Retreating to the kitchen, the girls sat at a table before a pot of tea and a dish of biscuits. Their shoulders sagged. Lu See, shocked by the news, sieved the floating tea leaves from the surface of her cup. Smoothing her kerchief, Sum Sum contemplated her broken string of prayer beads.

"I thought you were still a virgin," said Lu See.

Sum Sum shrugged.

"Is it Aziz's baby?" asked Lu See.

Sum Sum hesitated. "Are you angry with me? I don't want you to be angry, lah."

"Angry? No, of course I'm not angry."

Sum Sum shook her head. *I should have told her much earlier. Could have saved myself so much heartache.* She felt sick with relief. "But do I keep the baby?"

"Well, that's something only you can answer. It's not going to be easy being an unmarried mother, especially in this country. And I don't know how Mrs Slackford will react to us raising a child under her roof. But if you want to know how I feel about it, well, I'm surprised of course. Surprised yet happy. Happy because if you choose to keep the baby I think you'll make a fantastic mother. I'm behind you whatever you decide to do."

Sum Sum nodded. A tiny smile crept across her taut, broad face. "I've been carrying this news about like a wicker basket on my back."

"Why didn't you tell me before?"

"I don't know." She sighed. "Scared."

"Scared to tell me I was going to become an aunty?"

Sum Sum offered a sheepish smile again. "I would like to keep the baby."

"Good. That's settled. Now, will you write to inform Aziz?"

Again Sum Sum hesitated.

"What?" Lu See prompted.

"Nothing. It's nothing." Sum Sum saw Aziz's face loom before her then everything flowed backwards to the days spent onboard ship. The images returned hurriedly, clear and firm – his muscular arms, his trim waist, the concentrated tautness of his body.

Bracing herself, Sum Sum shook her head. "The child will be raised fatherless, lah. I do not want Aziz to know about this. I do not want to shame him. Anyway, he never passed me his address."

Lu See's mind worked fast. "Never mind. We'll tell Mrs Slackford you're already married. We'll say that your husband is in the Gurkha Rifles, stationed in India. She'll be none the wiser and nor will any of the neighbours."

Lu See counted out the months on her fingers since they last saw Aziz. "The baby's due in early October, so that's almost six months away." She told Sum Sum she had to be brave. She thought back to when she was seven years old, of swimming in the river with Uncle Big Jowl. How he coaxed her into the fast-moving water. How she rose on her tiptoes, trying to keep her thighs and bottom dry as the oxen-voiced man called her name. She remembered the way she'd held her breath and plunged in headfirst, arms outstretched. She told Sum Sum now that she had to be just as brave.

"Are we going to be okay?" Sum Sum asked.

Lu See nodded. She felt a twinge in her heart. "We're going to be more than okay." She held her friend's hand, palm-on-palm. "We're going to bring up this child together. It will grow up to be strong and healthy and happy. And I promise you, we are going to be all right."

Lu See saw the emptiness in her friend's expression fade as her eyes turned bright against the semi-darkness. Each raised a teacup. Sum Sum's shoulders straightened. "To us!" The cups knocked against one another with a *plink!*

They sat in the kitchen until it got light and then, changing out of their nightgowns, they walked into the fresh new day, to Fitzbillies cake shop on Trumpington Street and bought themselves four Chelsea buns to celebrate. They stood in the long shadow of the morning sun, sticky cinnamon glazing their mouths.

10

But whatever optimism Sum Sum felt about the baby didn't last. Raising a child without a father was always going to be hard, she realized. Raising it in a country where people already looked at her askance was going to be nigh impossible. Is it my fault, she asked herself, that I do not speak the King's English, that my upbringing was so different, that my skin is unfamiliar? I am only a village girl from Tibet. These English people are funny-funny, meh? Some stare at me on the street, so curious; others refuse to look at me as if I am a witch that will make them go *ploof* and disappear.

She grew increasingly homesick. She also grew a tiny bit resentful toward Lu See, yet for the life of her she couldn't understand why. *Maybe I'm angry with her because she does not see my pain. If she was such a good friend she would sense what happened to me, she would feel it in her bones, no?*

One day two letters from Malaya appeared. Sum Sum placed them in front of Lu See. The first was from her mother. Her tone had mellowed.

My daughter, even though you have shamed us I still worry about you. You are my child. You live inside me. I will always worry about you, no matter how old you are.

It was Ah-Ba's birthday yesterday. His ankles have grown very swollen. The doctor says that he must cut all salt from his food. I blame the stress caused by the dam explosion. We are suing the Woos for sabotage, though we have no evidence. Cha! The bloody swindlers.

Other troubling news - your brother James has become a

Jehovah's Witness! He spends his days preaching about paradise on earth. He has taken to handing out pamphlets to strangers and telling them that Jesus is in fact Michael the Archangel and that blood transfusions and the wearing of beards are evil.

What terrible sin did I commit in my past life to deserve such children?

As the youngest you always hated being left behind. You hated being left out, and it made you headstrong and stubborn. And now it is your family that has been left behind.

On a positive note, your elder brother Peter has met a girl from the Ting clan. Her name is Irene. If the courtship is successful this would make for a favourable union. The same way you marrying into the Chow family would have been favourable.

I pray that you are safe. I pray that you return home.

Please write to tell us how you are – it is not so very much to ask.

The second letter was from Second-aunty Doris.

Dearest niece Lu See,

Your letter of March 29th received yesterday. I am thrilled about the Girton news. Be strong and be confident and always remember it doesn't matter what you do with your life so long as you push to better yourself. Stand out from the crowd! Never be a wallflower! Weather here is stifling. Frangipanis in the garden are thriving.

Tomorrow Po On Village celebrates Wesak, Lord Buddha's birthday. The Chinese Clan Association has erected a new shrine. The temple is already thick with incense smoke and full of flowers and statues of the baby Buddha. Needless to say, the Juru Diocesan Trustees Association is anxious to complete the building of the new Anglican church in the village in response. I agree with you that constructing a brand new organ will take too long to complete and that we should opt for a ready-made console. And, like you, I am sure Conrad P. Hughes of London will do us proud. I like their drawings you sent to me and think the casing is both elegant and practical. I enclose below the specifications as agreed by the Trustees:

GREAT	SWELL	PEDAL
Open Diapason 8'	Violin Diapason 8'	Bourdan 8'
Claribel 8'	Principal 4'	
Octave 4'	Rohrflute 4'	
Flute 2'	Nazard 2'	
Oboe 8'		

Time is of the essence now. Get Mr Hughes to have the pipes cast as soon as possible. The new church will be completed in November. We must have the organ and its full rank shipped here by early December for Tak Ming's memorial service.

How is your friend Mr Adrian Woo? I am so relieved you never formed a union with the Chow family. Remember, keep a green tree in your heart and perhaps the trembling leaves will stay away.

You are constantly in my thoughts.

Second-aunty Doris

As soon as Lu See read the second letter she and Sum Sum took a train to London to meet with Conrad P. Hughes.

Sum Sum and Lu See hardly said a word to each other on the train. By now both were deep in thought. Lu See reflected on Tak Ming – pictured singing with him in the church choir and tried to remember the way he laughed when he deliberately warbled out of tune.

All Sum Sum could think about were the mountains of Tibet, the beards of mist drifting across the plains, and the soft lullabies her mother would sing to her as a child. She closed her eyes and tried to distract herself with the thrump of the train wheels, the chatter of the other passengers, the talk of Hitler and the price of a loaf of bread and Noel Coward's new play. What was she doing here? It all seemed suddenly implausible. As implausible as running from a man with a mole through the streets of a foreign city where nobody stopped to help. She felt a lurching panic and opened her eyes. The face of the man recoiled to the dark corners of her mind.

Even in London she kept her silence. She sat in a wooden chair and watched the organ maker discuss his plans at length with Lu See. Sum Sum stared at his lips as they moved but hardly registered a word.

He said the flue and reed pipes would have to be made to order, cast from 'only the finest' copper and aluminium and insisted on collecting a deposit before proceeding.

Lu See handed over half of her funds as a down payment. If Sum Sum had been paying attention she might have stopped her.

11

Towards the end of May the grey days became less common. In their place came the intense dark blue skies of late spring and on the Backs the flowers threatened an ocean of yellows and violets.

Sum Sum enjoyed the fresh smells of summer, the sounds of the seasonal chirping and croaking. She felt the changes in her tummy too. *My little char siu bao is growing stronger. Swimming inside me like a fish.*

She tried to keep an open mind about the future of her child, tried to remain optimistic, but whenever she thought about the baby she grew overwhelmed. Freedom; that was what she wanted for her unborn child; a different kind of freedom than hers; not a maidservant's freedom.

She massaged her temples with the tips of her fingers. There were so many questions, questions with no answers.

Where would the child go to school? And who would pay for the schooling? If the baby was a boy would the Teohs sponsor him? They sponsored the wash-amah's son and helped him get an apprentice job in Penang. A boy, she thought, tapping her tummy. There might be a smiling little boy in me. For a while she imagined what he might look like.

Then she wondered about his nationality. If he is born in England will he be an Englishman? Can he not be a Tibetan? What if government here says he is neither? Maybe they say he is a stateless person, like a refugee. Not from here, not from there. What then?

They could put her on boat and tell her not to come back.

They could also send someone to take her baby away. Someone bad. Someone like the man with the mole.

Thinking about the man with the mole made her shiver. It made something within her turn black, darkening her insides like a stain.

In her bedroom, she watched herself in the mirror, looking for some physical sign of her ordeal. No extra lines around the eyes. No new wrinkles by the mouth. Her face registered nothing. It was as blank as a flag of surrender.

Was she ever going to tell Lu See, she wondered, or would she keep on denying it, deny what had happened in that deserted lot all those weeks ago. Can a memory be banished, she asked herself. Perhaps in time she'd bury it in the far regions of her mind. Or freeze it dead, as a fly is suspended in ice. She felt her hands turn to fists. What she really wanted was to leave, to get away from here, where it happened. Why couldn't her brain let it go?

Sum Sum cupped her hands over her eyes.

Just then, Lu See appeared at the door with a mug of tea for her. "Is anything wrong?" she asked.

Sum Sum shrugged.

"You've been so quiet. Have you been crying?"

Sum Sum looked away.

"Has something happened?"

"No." But she blushed.

Lu See placed the tea by the side of the bed. "I know it's not easy for you in England. You feel isolated here. We both do. We're outsiders. And I'm sure you're worried about the baby. Maybe you're missing Malaya too. I know I am."

Sum Sum said nothing.

"I've been thinking," Lu See continued. "Do you want to go home? Once the baby's born, do you want to return to Juru?"

Sum Sum took a careful sip of her tea.

"You mean the world to me, peanut-head. But if you're unhappy in Cambridge I can understand. You've no friends here. I've at least got Adrian and I've got my books to keep me occupied. I can arrange for you to return to Malaya. You can work for Second-aunty Doris. And don't worry. I'll be back once I've got my degree."

Sum Sum turned and looked at her friend. She wanted to tell her then and there about the man with the mole. She wanted to tell her everything but the words were crushed in her throat. The hand that held the tea trembled. Her chest trembled with it.

"Please don't look so sad." Lu See pulled Sum Sum close. "We cannot be sad, not us. Especially not us. And do you know why? Because you have me, pumpkin-head, you'll always have me, and I love you."

Sum Sum forced a smile. "Do I look sad now?"

"You cannot fool me."

"I am tired," Sum Sum said, eventually. "Nothing wrong. I am just tired with the baby inside me."

"You will tell me if anything's bothering you, won't you?"

Sum Sum could not find any more words. She simply looked at the floor and nodded her head once, gripping the mug in her hand, as though fearing she would be dragged away if she failed to hold on tight. Dragged away into a deserted lot.

June. With Lu See deep into her studies, lost in her textbooks within the Divinity library, Sum Sum grew increasingly morose. Lu See was right. She had nobody to talk to. Her world here was so constricted. And often, when she stepped out alone, she was scared she might see the man with the mole again. She still hadn't told Lu See about him. In fact she avoided thinking about him full stop.

One morning Sum Sum looked up from her copy of *Modern Screen* and was overcome by a powerful craving. *Noodles! I need a bowl of Pietro's delicious Italian noodles.*

She strode down Sydney Street and headed straight into Christ's College, past the Great Gate Tower and the porter's lodge with its bowler-hatted porters, into First Court and up staircase C.

She rapped twice on Pietro's outer oak door.

"Ennnnn-tarrr!"

With the bedder's permission, she let herself into his set. The walls were plastered with operatic posters and lobby cards from Tosca and Madama Butterfly. Pietro was reclined on a chaise-longue, fanning himself with an oriental paper fan. There was a hint of rouge on his cheeks.

"Morning, lah. I need that recipe," she demanded.

"Well, well, if it's not my favourite Oriental Samson, slayer of the Philistines. The girl with the beautiful hands." He shut the paper fan with a *clack* and looked down at his own fingernails. "If only mine could be as well maintained."

"Do you remember last week we all had dinner in college hall, no? I want you teach me how to cook that noodle dish, lah!"

"My dear old sausage, I have a lecture to attend in twenty minutes and the college kitchens are still shut. Besides we don't call it 'noodles', we call it 'pasta'."

"Please."

He showed her his left profile. "I'm taking luncheon at the Pitt Club. I couldn't possibly."

"It is emergency!"

An awkward pause.

"I'm pregnant, with no husband and I lost my flower to a vendor of pickled delights!"

Pietro's eyes widened to the size of tulip bulbs. "Well, why didn't you say so in the first place, sausage?" He sprang to his feet, grabbing his college gown from behind the door. "Come with me!"

Ten minutes later, down in the bowels of the college kitchen, Pietro posed in a pair of Greta Garbo sunglasses. Sum Sum, as instructed, stood on his left side so that she could be heard.

"Here, slip this apron on."

"Are you sure the cook doesn't mind you being in here, lah?"

"Strictly speaking only staff's allowed in the kitchens, but don't you worry yourself about Illingworth." He winked. "We, how should I put it delicately, we understand one another."

"I not following . . ."

"No, you wouldn't, darling." He laughed his hyena laugh. "You're what my mother would call *un pesce fuor d'acqua*, a fish out of water. A bit like me really . . . we're both on the periphery of conventional society. Outcasts almost."

"I like being outcast," she replied. "I am different to everyone here. I am Tibetan. I am a servant and not a student. And soon I will be a single mother."

Not afraid of the direct question, Pietro asked, "Tell me, so the father of your child, he sells pickled onions?"

"No, lah. I only say that to get your attention."

"Spill the beans then." He lowered his voice conspiratorially. "Is it Adie? Oh, please tell me it's Adie. I need a bit of juicy gossip."

She hesitated. "I do not want to talk about the father."

"Scheming Eros! Thou art such a tease! Love at our age can be so fickle. By the way, did I mention I met this pretty second year Botanist from Caius? He's got a fantastic body, slim at the hips, broad at the top. Problem is I keep staring at this V of curly black hair tufting from beneath his throat. It's so distracting, sausage, I really should ask him to shave . . ."

"You cuckoo-clocks crazy."

The tomato and meat sauce bubbled in a pot as the spaghetti noodles steamed on a plate. "How did Loo-seat react to the baby news?"

"Very supporting, lah. At first she not notice my throwing up because she's so busy studying. Even now she doesn't notice my tummy, but I can feel it getting bigger."

"You never had much of a waist, dahling."

"*Aiyoo!* Your mouth so rude, lah. Next time I see you I knock you on the head with a chestnut pan!"

Pietro twisted off a knot of herbs. "Smell this. Recognize it?"

Sum Sum cupped his hand in hers and took in the aroma. "No, but it's damn-powerful wonderful. What is it?"

"Rosemary. You won't find it in Malaya. I grow it on my windowsill. I give some to Illingworth in exchange for certain favours."

Sum Sum gave him a look.

"Don't ask."

Sum Sum ogled the pot of sauce. "Can I take rosemary back with me tonight?"

"First you steal my recipe, then you raid dear Illingworth's glamorous kitchen of all its ingredients . . ." He placed the back of his hand on his forehead. "Oh, the price of culinary genius."

"I bet I can cook something like this in no time, no?"

He shot her a look. "Let me assure you, dear sausage, that any fool can make a sauce, but to make it right you" – he touched his nose – "you need Pietro magic."

"How you learn to cook?"

"I started at eight years old. I trailed my mother whenever she was in the kitchen. Her hands were always covered in parsley or batter. When she let me wear her pink apron I was hooked!"

That night Sum Sum prepared dinner for Lu See and Mrs Slackford. With the smell of marinating meat in the air, she lit some candles and set the table with Mrs Slackford's finest silver.

"What have we here?" the landlady asked, surprised to see something on her plate prepared by Sum Sum. She balanced a pair of horn-rimmed spectacles on the end of her nose.

"This? This called spaghetti alla Portugal Place."

"It sure don't resemble jugged hare or suet pudding," said

117

Mrs Slackford with sarcasm so thick you could spread it like marmite. "Won't see this being served in the Blue Boar." She dipped her fork in and tried it. "It's tasty."

"Of course it tasty, lah."

"Well, Oi am very impressed. Yew *are* a dark horse. Oi expect yew'll cook up a storm for yer husband when he's back from his tour of duty. Lu See told me he's in the Gurkha Rifles. Oi bet he's ever so pleased yer expecting a baby."

Sum Sum pressed her lips together politely. She glanced at Lu See who was looking pensive. "You okay?" she asked.

Lu See made a face and shrugged.

"Aiyoo, what wrong, lah?"

"It's the organ. I've written several letters to Conrad P. Hughes and received no reply. All I'm asking for is a progress report."

"Maybe he busy."

"Too busy to acknowledge a customer who has left him with half her money?"

"How long since yew last heard from him?" asked Mrs Slackford.

"Several weeks."

"Cor blast me!" Mrs Slackford laughed.

Lu See felt the skin stiffen on her arms. Now that she thought about it, there was something very odd about Conrad P. Hughes and his insistence on a fifty percent deposit. Just how much did she know about his reputation and reliability?

"I'll go and see him personally next Saturday," said Lu See, gulping down a forkful of spaghetti. "Don't worry, I'll get to the bottom of this and give him a piece of my mind."

The following Saturday, with Lu See in London, Pietro and Sum Sum hired a flat-bottomed punt and spent a leisurely hour on the Cam.

Pietro, wearing a straw boater with a flower tucked in its band, handed Sum Sum the long pole and reclined across the pillows he'd brought from his room. Dressed in cream linen, he looked as though he was straight out of an E. M. Forster novel. "Beautiful day, sausage, it must remind you of Malaya."

"Small bit, lah."

"You're talking into the wrong ear, sausage! My left ear not my right."

"Ai-yoo! Wear ear-trumpet, lah!"

Theatrically, Pietro rolled his eyes. "No need to shout. Tell me, what language do you all speak at home?"

"Back in Juru? *Aiyo*, a jumble-mix of everything." She stood three-quarters of the way toward the stern and pushed the pole through the water, shifting her balance from foot to foot. The slap of water against the side of the boat was comforting.

"Like a bouillabaisse."

Sum Sum wrinkled her nose. A whispering vulgar scent was drifting across the water. It took her a moment to realize what it was. The smell of camphor. She looked about her urgently. Not far away an old lady was feeding bread to the ducks. *Mothballs*, she said to herself, relieved. *Old lady smells of mothballs*

"Bouillabaisse," Pietro added helpfully, "is a type of soup with all sorts of fish thrown in."

Sum Sum smiled and prodded her toe at a passing mallard. "I suppose so, yes, like soup. Malay people speak *Bahasa*. The Chinese speak Cantonese and Hokkien." She ducked her head as they went under a bridge. Her voice echoed as she spoke. "And the Indians speak Tamil."

"A tropical Tower of Babel."

"But almost everybody speaks mix-match of kitchen English."

Pietro trailed his fingers in the water. "Sounds chaotic to me."

"*Aiyooo!* No, lah." She gripped the pole under her arm and made a bowl out of one hand. "Say this cup of tea is

Malaya." She pretended to spoon something into the cup. "Add one sugar you have Chinese, second sugar Indian, third is Malay people. All put into cup of tea, mix it up, then everything blended."

They stopped and watched the ducks drift on the lazy current. A magical dappled tranquility descended. Later, as Pietro read the newspaper, he jabbed her in the ribs. "Listen to these headlines. *'Civil war in Spain looming!'* Oh what tommyrot, that Franco's such an ugly, louche man, let's see what's next – *'Edward VIII and American divorcee Wallis Simpson vacationing in Biarritz on a yacht!'* – naughty Eddie's playing hide the popsicle again, terrible way for the King of England to behave, and, oh, *brah-haa* look here, you'll like this one – 'Tibet willing to accept Chinese sovereignty? Yes, according to Wu Chung-hsin.'

"That man is a liar! Tibetans will never give up their independence."

"Who's this Wu fellow? Any relation to Adie?"

"Chinese director of Tibetan Affairs. I'd like to shove a pair of chopsticks up his fat nose."

"But reading the article, he sounds like he has such charm, dahling!" Pietro teased.

"Charm? This man, lah, he has same charm as open air shithouse in downtown Penang."

Pietro laughed, which in turn brought a smile to Sum Sum's face.

When their hour was up they moored the punt by the Anchor pub and hopped on to dry land. Pietro took Sum Sum by the arm and together they capered and pranced like children playing hopscotch back to his rooms in Christ's. "Feeling peckish, dear sausage?"

"Small bit, lah."

"I was going to take you to luncheon at a little place in Huntington, but the gorgon behind the bar took a dislike to me last time I went. Let's pop into the college kitchen. Illingworth and I will whip something up in no time."

"You remind me of my younger brudder. His name is Hesha. I used to play a game with him when he was nine years old. We pull five ingredients out my mother's market basket and he had to prepare a meal in the time that it took A-Ma to finish her small pouch of snuff. Hesha always win."

"Where's he now?"

"Hesha still in Tibet. He seventeen years old now. He say he wants to go over to Nepal and join Gurkha Army and fight for the British."

Sum Sum stopped dead in her tracks. There it was again, the same sly breath of camphor. She caught in on the breeze. But where had it come from? She couldn't trace it.

She grabbed Pietro's elbow. "Can you smell it?"

"Smell what?"

She sniffed the air. "Liniment, camphor." The fine little hairs on the back of her neck lifted.

She kept her eyes doggedly fixed on the road behind.

Pietro turned to see what she was looking at.

For a second she thought she saw a figure in the shade. When she looked again the shadow was gone. She shook her head in frustration. Her mind was playing tricks on her. "No, it's nothing, sorry."

They entered the gates of Christ's and headed into the court toward the Buttery where they sat in comfortable leather armchairs.

"Are you feeling unwell, sausage?"

"I'm fine, Pietro. Not worry."

Sum Sum took a deep breath and felt her shoulders relax. *Only my imagination.*

She repeated the words in her head several times. The eight syllables echoed softly inside her brain, sounding like waves lapping the shore.

"Perhaps what you need is a spot of refreshment," said Pietro. With a delicate *tinkle-tinkle* he rang a silver hand bell and a college servant appeared.

"Two lime drinkees, Hargreaves, and a plate of your

thrilling biscuits please." He waited for Hargreaves to leave the room. "Did you see the look on his face? Not sure he likes me bringing you here. Hargreaves is like everyone else in college. They frown at me for what I am. Only Illingworth understands. But we outsiders have to stick together, right?"

Sum Sum said nothing. Instead, she ran her eyes along the walls, admiring the elegant walnut panelling.

A few minutes later, as he sipped his lime cordial, Pietro said, "You must miss them."

"Who?"

"Your family in Tibet."

"Yes. Yes I do. I am thinking maybe I will go back to Tibet one day. I have to speak to Lu See about this."

Pietro shook his head. "I would never leave my family."

"Well you are here in Cambridge, which means you left your mother, no?"

"My parents died when I was twelve."

Silence.

Pietro set his delicate jaw.

"This is the point in the conversation when you should look mortified and apologize profusely."

"I'm . . . I'm sorry, Pietro."

He leaned across and took her hand. "You weren't to know, sausage. It's all so terribly macabre. Why do you think I stay here in Cambridge when term's broken up during the Long Vac? No, I go back to Italy once a year, at Christmas to see my surviving relatives. The Italians say that leaving your family is a little like dying." He lifted a finger to his chin as if remembering something important. "Speaking of dying and going to heaven, dear Samson, you simply must try this recipe of mine. Let's go have a poke in Illingworth's larder, shall we?"

From Illingworth's pantry cupboard he retrieved a bar of Rowntree chocolate, a can of sweet condensed milk and a fistful of fresh rosemary from the windowsill. He placed them on the kitchen counter. "Now this culinary triumvirate will serve you well for the rest of your life, sausage. Prepare to be dazzled!"

Clad in aprons, they mixed sugar with flour and tossed in an egg. "This will make the shortbread," he said. Then they combined a cup of condensed milk with some golden syrup and whisked in the rosemary, melting it with a dollop of butter until it turned to toffee, after which they spread it onto the shortbread and left it to set. "Finally break the chocolate into a bowl and heat it over a pan of boiling water. Now let it cool and pour it over the shortbread. And abracadabra, my boyfriend's an actor: rosemary and chocolate *frollino*."

Two minutes later they tried it. Sum Sum had never tasted anything so delicious in her life.

"Now I bet your Hesha would struggle to come up with something better than that."

Sum Sum had to concede. She scribbled down the recipe in a brand new blue exercise book. When she put her pen down Pietro asked her what she wrote. She wiped her hands on her apron and squared her shoulders proudly. "One day, maybe ten or twenty years from now, I open a damn-powerful restaurant."

"Where?"

"Perhaps in Malaya. The Malays and Chinese love noodles. Maybe even in Tibet."

Pietro struck his palm on his milk-bottle white forehead. "A Tibetan girl cooking pasta in a jungle trattoria? Whatever next, Mussolini addressing the nation in a tutu?"

When the London taxi dropped Lu See at the store front near the Angel tube station she saw immediately that something wasn't right. The black Vitrolite fascia, hung above the main entrance with the legend *Conrad P. Hughes – Pipe Organ Specialists* in crimson raised letters, was gone. Furthermore, the windows and main entrance were boarded up tight. She entered the grocer's next door and asked the frowning, lined face of an old man what happened. "They moved," he said.

"Moved where?"

He gave her the address of a warehouse near the river.

The same taxi took her through a series of wretched streets, past large unkempt depots without rails or fences. At the said address she stood in front of an abandoned warehouse. Nearby chimney smoke rose in slow suspended scrawls. There was a smell of old fish.

Lu See stood and stared at the 'In Receivership' sign. She clenched and unclenched her fists several times. A sense of emptiness and gullibility and failure spread up her arms and legs.

At least there was no one around to see her cry.

12

Lu See covered her face with a web of fingers.

The reality of the matter was almost too painful to be digested. Conrad P. Hughes, aware he was on the brink of insolvency, must have taken her money and absconded. Earlier, she'd filed a report at the Islington police station, but the duty sergeant said there wasn't much he could do, especially if Mr Hughes had fled the country. It was the first time she'd ever been in an English police station, or any police station for that matter. "Where would he have gone?" she asked the duty sergeant. "Perhaps to one of the lesser colonies," he replied. "Tanganyika's quite popular these days."

Lu See pulled her fingers from her eyes. "What the hell am I going to do now?" she exclaimed.

Adrian and Sum Sum shrugged their shoulders. They were in the Pickerel on Magdalene Street. The low-ceilinged pub still carried the smell of old beer and pipe tobacco.

Lu See stabbed a fork into her square of Stilton.

"I thought you said you'd never touch a Stilton Ploughman's again," said Adrian.

"I'm punishing myself."

Adrian sipped from his pint of Adnams. "You'll just have to write to Second-aunty Doris and get her to send more money."

Her face filled with colour. "I can't do that."

"Why, meh?" asked Sum Sum. "Too proud to say to her you make a mistake?"

Lu See covered her eyes and sighed. "Don't try to get inside my head."

"True, lah. Nothing in there anyway."

Lu See turned to Adrian. "How much do you have in the bank?"

"Not much. Ever since my father discovered I was a communist he's been keeping the purse strings tight. My allowance barely covers my food and lodging."

"What am I going to do? If I can't pay for the pipe organ then Second-aunty Doris will refuse to support me. Girton, all my hard work, all my dreams . . . I'll have to go home with my tail between my legs . . ." She left the words trailing.

"Look, I tell you what, goosey, I'll sell my car. It's a bit of a wreck but I'm sure it'll get us something."

"And I can start selling rosemary shortbreads on street," said Sum Sum. "Pietro has tip-top recipe."

Lu See forced a laugh. "Well, I hope it won't come to that."

"So what will you do?" asked Adrian.

"I'll arrange to head up to Yorkshire and meet with another organ maker. Brinkley & Fosler was one of the other names on the list I made. I'll plead my case, and see if I can get a ready-made console at a knock-down price."

"And if you can't?"

"Then I suppose pumpkin-head and I might just as well take the next boat back to Malaya."

When Adrian left them outside the pub, Lu See's mouth drooped. She'd been half-smiling up until that moment, but she couldn't keep up the pretence of lighthearted unconcern any longer. "What the hell am I going to do?" There were tears in her eyes.

Sum Sum immediately enveloped her in a hug. She put her hand in Lu See's and together they wiped the teardrops from her face.

"I shouldn't be crying," said Lu See.

"Don't be scared to cry. But be scared of giving up. You must not give up. You know that, meh?"

"I'm sorry."

"Don't be sorry, lah, be strong." Lu See nodded. "We will get through this together," continued Sum Sum, fiercely. "Yes?"

"Yes." Now it was Lu See's turn to hug Sum Sum. "I love you, pumpkin-head. I don't know what I'd do without you."

The following day Lu See received another one of her mother's letters.

. . . there are times when I cease to comprehend who you are. Ever since you turned 17 you have been uncontrollable with passions. Passions I cannot even begin to understand. I have been in contact with Uncle Big Jowl. He says you are determined to stay in England. Your Ah-Ba is threatening to hire a private detective to come and claim you, stick you in a burlap sack and carry you home. Which of the Gods did I upset to deserve such a daughter?

More calamitous news – your brother Peter has joined James as a Jehovah's Witness and has been rebuffed by his fiancée. Irene Ting now refuses to marry him due to his extreme religious views. First you damage our social standing by turning your back on the Chows, now Peter causes huge loss of face with the Tings. Cha! What sins did I commit to warrant such children? Sometimes I wonder if you were all secretly reared by jackals.

Ah-Ba is forced to shun the weekly mahjong games at the turf club for fear of ridicule. His ankles remain swollen because of too much salt in his diet – I think he is sneaking prawn crackers into his mouth at nighttime when I sleep.

The lawsuit with the Woos continues. They sue us, we sue them – only happy people are the lawyers.

Our rubber plantation continues to suffer. Prices are being squeezed like the last mango in the shop. Hip Sing Rubber Processing Co. wants to buy us out on the cheap. I think the Woos are behind this.

It hurts me more knowing you are in league with one of them.

With an exasperated puff of her cheeks, Lu See scrunched the paper between her fingers. She went over to the stone fireplace, struck a match and set it alight.

"Ai-yoo, what is it with you and fire," observed Sum Sum. "You always burning things."

Lu See gave a wintry smile. "Like I'm always covering my tracks, in order to keep moving safely."

Her mother infuriated and frustrated Lu See. Hadn't she tried to explain how she felt before running away? Sometimes Lu See wondered if her mother could suck the insides of her ears shut so that she wouldn't listen.

Lu See pictured her now, pulling her lips over her teeth and shaking her head this way and that with disappointment. She could almost hear the tut-tutting going on inside her skull.

Resentful, Lu See went for a stroll along the Backs, skirting the expanse of lawns and willow that curved along the river behind the colleges. She took in several deep breaths to clear her head. Okay, she said to herself, I'm ready.

She planned to catch the 09.45 train to King's Cross; from there she would connect to St. Pancras and catch the 13.20 to Sheffield. The meeting with Brindley & Fosler would decide her fate.

The next evening, as Adrian returned to his rooms in Jesus, he was confronted by Stevens his bedder. "Hullo Mr Woo. A young Oriental lady came callin' for you. But seein' that you were sportin' your oak, I informed her you were out. She signed the register and said she'd be back later."

"Thank you Stevens."

When he heard a knock on his door he was met by Lu See who kissed him hard on the mouth.

"I take it your overnight trip to Sheffield was a success?"

"It was," she beamed. The people at Brinkley & Fosler were wonderful. They even had someone meet me at the station and take me to a bed and breakfast."

"And what did they say about the organ?"

"Well, I started off by telling them about that swine Conrad P. Hughes. Of course, that brought about a great deal of head-shaking and pipe-chewing on their part."

"Did you tell them how you were swindled? What did they say?"

"They said I was daft not to have made the trip up to see them first, saying all those southerners were 'a law unto themselves' and that everything those Londoners did was 'wi' a lick and a promise.'"

"Did you mention you only had half the amount to spend?"

"I did."

"And?"

"They said 'ti'n't a problem.'" Lu See adopted a gruff male Yorkshire accent. "That for the amount I had they'd make me 'as 'appy as a pig in muck' by building me 'a reet proper' pipe organ. And they'd be working until they're completely 'paggered' to get it finished in time."

"Amazing."

"They were very taken by the fact that the pipe organ was heading for Malaya. One of the Mr Fosler's nephews lives in Penang. A fellow called Charlie Fosler. He runs a rubber plantation there."

"What a small world. I assume you left a deposit."

"They didn't want one." Adrian's eyebrows rose in surprise. "But I left them a token amount to give them face." She leaned across to kiss him on the cheek. "They said I could pay the balance on completion, on the condition I take out a full page announcement in the Yorkshire Gazette praising Brinkley & Fosler's dependability, integrity and craftsmanship. Naturally, I agreed."

Adrian opened a bottle of beer and drank a toast to her.

"I'm thinking we should go away," he said, out of the blue. "To celebrate."

"Away? Where?"

"It's the Long Vac, term's about to end and poor Stevens and the other gyps are due a break."

"But you said you received permission to study through the summer and finish your research paper?"

"I've been granted excess residence yes, but I'd still like to get away."

"How long for?"

He shrugged unapologetically. "I don't know, three weeks, maybe a month. Term ends on 15th June."

"I'm studying for my exams, or have you forgotten?"

"What's that got to do with anything? Bring your books. We can go to the seaside. The sea air, a nice restful journey and some sightseeing will do you good."

As a distraction, he turned on the radio. The voice of a sports announcer spilled through the room; he was expounding on Jesse Owens' gold medal prospects in the forthcoming Olympic Games in Berlin.

"I'm sitting for my entrance papers in late September. I can't rest now." She snapped the radio off.

He held his hands out like a peace offering.

His tone turned carefree, agile even. "All this studying has sapped your spirit. So has this whole business of the pipe organ. Trust me, a break will do you good, goosey, you need a rest to think and reflect. You've been at your books for months."

"A break, Adrian Woo, will ruin my chances of getting into Girton!"

He took her hand. "Goosey, you've been working non-stop. Take it from me, you'll go stale. We can bring all of your books with us. Have you seen the size of my trunk? Hell, we can take the whole damn Divinity library with us."

"Do you really think a break will do me good?

"Trust me."

A small smile came to her lips. "You're not going to lure me into taking part in a communist rally, are you?"

"No, I promise. By the seaside you can work all morning. Then we can have a nice long lunch, sip a cordial or two, and after that you can spend another three hours swotting. You know it makes sense. Goosey, I believe in you. I'm your greatest supporter. I have the utmost confidence that you'll sail through your entrance exams. The last thing I want to do is jeopardize your chances, but a trip away will refresh and reinvigorate you."

"All right, I'll come."

"Tell you what." His voice grew in pitch as a liberated expression filled his eyes. "Why don't we head for the beaches up north? Find a boarding house somewhere within a couple of hours from Sheffield. That way we can call in on Brinkley & Fosler once in a while and check on their progress."

"You promise I'll be able to study? You won't be a nuisance, trying to break into my room and have your way with me every hour?"

"More like every half-hour. And surely you mean *our* room?"

"What on earth are you talking about? We can't share. Think of the scandal if people find out."

"We'll be married by then." He dropped to one knee and removed a small gold band from his pocket. "Or at least I hope we'll be." He looked up at her, at the quivering muscles about her mouth. "I've already booked the register office for June 14th. Goosey, will you do me the honour . . .?"

She pulled him to his feet and jumped into his arms, wrapping her legs around his waist.

"For God's sake, woman . . ." He tried to hush her. "Stevens is nearby."

"What, you want him to come in and join us?" She giggled, kissing him hard on the mouth again. Stifling their laughter, they rolled about on the hardwood floor until their knees and elbows hurt.

"Wait!" said Lu See. "If we get married we can't live with Mrs Slackford. She won't allow men in the house."

"We could find some digs to rent in Jesus Lane."

"And Sum Sum?"

"She can remain at Portugal Place, can't she?"

"I don't want to abandon her."

"I love you, Lu See. And I want you to be my wife, but if you think Sum Sum should live with us, that's fine."

"Let me talk to her."

"I just think that we should be together for a while. Just you and me."

At noon, on June 14th Lu See and Adrian arrived at the register office. They stood in the white-boned reception room before the registrar, a thickly moustached man whose eyes swam with sherry. Pietro, sporting an absurdly oversized bowtie and Sum Sum were the witnesses. Adrian wore a morning suit and a silk top hat; Lu See wore an auspicious red dress and a pageboy's hat tilted at an angle. Earlier she'd purchased a pair of elegant brown flats with gilded snaffles. As the registrar spoke, Adrian draped his arm protectively around Lu See. "You happy?" he whispered into her ear.

"I'm exactly where I want to be," she replied.

Second-aunty Doris had once told her that life was not made up of days or weeks or years but of moments. This was one of those happy, memorable, fantastic moments.

Seconds later he slid a thin gold band on her finger. *Husband and wife!* She took Adrian's face in her hands and kissed him deeply. In the distance a bell tower struck. Lu See threw a sideways glance at Sum Sum who responded by crossing her eyes like a village idiot. Lu See guffawed. *Damn fool pumpkin-head!*

The two friends exchanged hugs. "Any advice for my wedding night?" asked Lu See.

"Yes, lah. When in bed, don't point at his pencil and laugh!"

Lu See was happy to see Sum Sum smiling again.

Adrian broke open a whisky bottle and handed it to the registrar who took a swig and wiped his moustache with the back of a hand. At which point Pietro cranked up his portable gramophone. Louis Armstrong's swinging trumpet came *toot-tooting* through the room. Clutching her bouquet, Lu See grabbed Sum Sum by the arm. *Come on and swing those hips!* Toot-toot toodly toot-toot! Laughing breathlessly, they lifted their legs to the beat, eyes shut with the music in their hair. Pietro bounced up and down on his toes and then did the monkey-knees. Beside him Adrian did an impromptu Charleston pumping his arms like a jogger. *Toodly-toot-toot!*

After a while Lu See collapsed in a fit of giggles, exhausted, hands folded on the mound of Sum Sum's tummy.

"How's the old sow's belly?"

"Feels like watermelon, no? So, when and where will you go on honeymoon?"

"Adrian is still looking into all the seaside resorts up north. He thinks a place called Cleethorpes in Lincolnshire might be nice. We'll be gone from next week for about a month. Will you be all right by yourself here?"

"Me? I be fine, lah." Sum Sum hugged Lu See. "*Aiyo*, stop focusing on me, lor, this is your wedding day. Go spend time with your new husband. And when you get back I insist you have privacy. You go live together."

Sum Sum went outside to get some fresh air. She stood on the cracked stone steps of the register office and shivered. The thought of being alone in this strange place scared her. She folded her arms. She would have to make a decision soon.

13

As the weeks progressed they grew increasingly stifling. Sum Sum, puffed up like a pastry, burst into Pietro's rooms one day and announced: "I'm in love."

"What do you mean, you're in love?" Pietro replied.

"His name is Cluck."

"*Cluck?* Like in chicken?"

"Dark hair, strong jaw, *aiyo* and shoulders like a Tibetan yak."

"Have you been at the whisky again, sausage?"

"I spent two magic-fantastic hours at Cosmo Cinema." Sum Sum shuddered.

"*Ayo*, this Captain Bligh one scary, crazy-crackpot man. Skin-crawling good film, lah. And this Cluck Gable damn-powerful handsome."

A Hawker Hurricane buzzed by overhead en route to RAF Upwood.

Sum Sum reached into a punnet of wild raspberries and popped one into her mouth. Pietro eyed her. "When is Lu See back?"

"In two days' time."

"You must have been lonely without her."

"She tell me she'd be gone for four weeks. It's now five."

"Oh, what treachery."

"Coming to England, I imagined it would be like fairy tale story, like Cinderella." Sum Sum patted her bump. "But look what happened to my fairy tale! I end up as Humpy Dumpy. Maybe I will go back to Tibet soon." A determined look swept across her face. "There is someone I want to see again.

This baby is making me see my life through different eyes."
Pietro knew she was talking about her mother; it was clear
even without having to mention her name.

"I always wanted to be Cinderella too," Pietro sighed,
showing Sum Sum his left profile. "You'd think glass slippers would cause bunions, wouldn't you?"

Sum Sum smiled politely. She was exhausted. *My breasts
are tender, I need to pee all the time and I feel this constant mild
aching inside my lower abdomen.* She felt rung out. *Like Mrs
Slackford's washing.* Scrunched and squeezed dry of her
contents. *Oh for goodness' sake, lah, stop feeling sorry for
yourself!*

Pietro took a dramatic puff from his cigarette. "You never
speak much of Tibet, do you? Tell me, how did you get to
know Lu See and her family? Lhasa's a long way from
Malaya."

"When I was twelve my A-Pha died. A-Ma and I rode on
mules to the Nepal border where she put me on train for the
south. She handed me a medal and a letter. She tell me to
contact Master Teoh, Lu See's father, in Penang. I had to look
for Penang on the British army map she gave me."

"Is Lu See's father a sort of grand pooh-bah or something?"

"I don't understand your fancy talk, but her father is
important man, yes. My A-Pha, you see, worked for British
in Nepal, number-one Sherpa, he saved many lives of British
officers, was awarded a medal, King Albert Medal, by
Viceroy.

"Master Teoh owned bank where many British officers
keep their money. Officers say to A-Pha, if you ever have
problem you contact this man. He can help you. So when
A-Pha died, A-Ma sent me to get work and get education, to
learn to cook and clean in a stranger's house. I came with one
set of clothing and shoes with holes outside."

"You seem quite well schooled, forgive me, sausage, for a
maid-servant."

"That is because Master Teoh insisted I go to local school twice a week. I also shared a private tutor with Lu See. Matty-matics every Friday afternoon. She had him for one hour, then my turn for half-hour. They also taught me how to sit at table and to use knife and fork rather than my hands."

"Do you think you will go back to Tibet then?"

Sum Sum shrugged. "Only if God wills it. For many years my karma, my life, was tied to Lu See. Now she is married, maybe my life rests elsewhere. And recently my karma has changed for the worse."

On the day Jesse Owens won his fourth Olympic gold, Lu See and Adrian returned from their honeymoon.

They moved straight into their new home on Jesus Lane, a two-storey terraced house with views of the park and the river.

Lu See purchased new sheets and pillowcases for the double bed, fresh soap and towels for the bathroom, and bread, milk and teabags for the kitchen. She installed a telephone line and had a wireless set up in the living room. She laid down a tastefully frayed Persian rug and hung Adrian's collection of watercolours in harmonious groups. In the tiny back garden she pruned the holly hedge and deadheaded the roses; she also cleared a small weed bed and planted rosemary plants, beans and onions. Within a week they'd turned the place into a home. Every night they dined by candlelight and each morning they breakfasted by the front window, bathed in sunshine. And always they found time to immerse themselves in little distractions.

And then one morning, she squeezed her stomach until she turned purple in the face.

She got a piece of her ankle between her nails and pinched.

"What are you doing?" asked Adrian.

"It's finished. It's all over. Months of studying wasted."

She pinched the tender, underside of her knee and winced.

"What the hell are you talking about?"

"All my plans are ruined. There's no way Girton will take me now."

"Will you please tell me what's going on?"

"Adrian," she said. "I think I'm pregnant."

14

Mid-September and the arrival of autumn brought a carnival of browning leaves to mop up the rain.

It was five o'clock in the morning and there had been a steady two hours of drizzle. Adrian, dressed in black to make him less conspicuous in the darkness, dug his fingertips into the cracks in the stone and made certain of his footing. He still couldn't believe he was going to be a father – the idea thrilled him, sent a warm surge through his bones. "A baby," he called out, his voice deep and solid. "We're going to have a baby." If it was a boy he was going to call him Vladimir – or maybe Vlad – after Lenin. His eyes brimmed with pride. He reached a hand to his face and felt one smooth warm tear sneak down his cheek. He stared straight out towards the Cam, the king of all he surveyed.

He was over a hundred feet up.

Advancing he gave a quick questioning glance at the coarse cloth in his grasp and suddenly was angry with himself. What he'd intended to do was drape the banner across two of the chapel roof turrets and then secure them with thick string, but he'd miscalculated. Its weight was becoming too hard to handle.

This was a two-man job – he needed a second person to take hold of one end of the strip of canvas as he held the other. The gusts of wind and rain weren't helping either; the gale blowing in from the coast turned the stone slippery, making him wish he'd worn a different pair of shoes, the ones with the scuffed leather soles. Instead he had to get by in his plimsolls, which made each step feel as if he was being forced to walk atop a slick rubber gangplank. Bracing himself, he pulled on the cord with all his strength.

Clouds wheeled overhead, blotting out the moon. Adrian was perspiring from having to heave and control the weight of it. Huffing and straining he fought to raise it like a sail against the wind. The cold rain stole through his clothes and into his body. His forearms and shoulder muscles ached.

Finally, it looked as if he'd done it. The long strip of canvas was in place, the string secure, the knots tight, the elevation as level to the ground as possible. Swaying in the breeze, tied with string to several steeples, the banner furled and un-furled, swaying like a pendulum, hanging on by a single knot. Its message was hand-painted in red. 'HAPPY BIRTH-DAY GOOSEY!' The canvas snapped in the wind.

Upside down.

He'd hung it the wrong way up and would have to start all over again.

Effing and blinding, he wiped his wet hands against his jacket to dry them, breathed on them for warmth and after that began to work the knots loose.

Using his thumbs and teeth, he undid the gnarls, pulling on the parallel strands, making certain they were free of kinks and kept well away from his legs. The string tasted bitter and smelled of dank earth. Reaching up he stretched to grab hold of more of the splice. The string came loose with a tug. The canvas buckled and billowed as one end broke free from its lashings. Adrian took a step to the side to avoid the tangle of string.

And then his foot slipped.

15

In the kitchen, with dark circles under her eyes, Sum Sum plopped a pair of eggs in boiling water and grilled several slices of bread. Having suffered through three straight weeks of interrupted sleep she was exhausted. She mumbled an oath and rubbed her engorged tummy.

As she buttered her toast, she heard a knock on the door, polite yet urgent.

With Mrs Slackford at market, she opened the door herself.

It was Lu See.

The cool air nipped at Sum Sum's knees. "You want breakfast? I'm cooking eggs."

Lu See shook her head no. She felt nauseous and a little dizzy. She sat at the kitchen table. "Well, the good news is the pipe organ was shipped yesterday. It's on its way to Malaya. Brinkley & Fosler kept their promise. The organ will be in Po On Village by Christmas, in time for Tak Ming's memorial."

"And bad news?"

Lu See rubbed her eyes. "Well, I wouldn't call it bad news but I haven't seen much of Adrian recently."

"Meh?"

"He's busy with his thesis. He came to bed at ten but was up again at midnight. I heard him moving about, working in his study but when I woke this morning he was gone."

"What, he out already?" Sum Sum eyed her friend. "Are you feeling all right, lah?"

The smell of Sum Sum's buttery toast made her feel sick.

She nodded without conviction. "By seven, he'd already left the house, but I didn't hear him go. He must be at the library."

"Pietro says library not open until nine o'clock."

Lu See's face was smiling before her mouth could shape the words. "I just received a call from my doctor with my results. Adrian's going to be a father."

Sum Sum's eyes almost burst from her face. "You are pregnant with baby?"

"The doctor confirmed I'm two months in."

Sum Sum almost fell off her chair as she rushed to embrace Lu See, throwing her arms around her neck. After a while Sum Sum asked, "But what will happen with studybooks?"

Lu See shrugged, trying to sound upbeat. "I'm not sure what Girton will say. I haven't been accepted yet . . . hell, I haven't even sat for the exams."

"This man better start spending more time with you and less on his books or I give him one hell of a earboxing."

"I'm sure he will."

"Well, tomorrow your birthday. He will spend all day with you for sure, lah. No more of this–" Sum Sum opened her mouth to say more but stopped herself.

Lu See stared at her friend. "What were you about to say?"

"Me? Nothing."

"Say it."

"I have nothing to say, lah."

"You think he's doing his nightcrawling again, is that it?"

"Maybe, lah."

"He promised me."

"Sounds like he break promise. Either that or he goes and visits floozy-woozy woman after you fall asleep."

"Don't."

"Sorry." Sum Sum raised an apologetic hand. "Only joking, lah."

A minute's silence.

"Do you really think he has a floozy woman?"

"*Aiyo*, I was only joking."

"Or maybe you were right the first time, maybe he's scaling rooftops again."

"Maybe."

"God, I hope not."

"*Aiyo*, don't worry," Sum Sum said, appeasing, "Adrian not stupid. And when he knows you are having his baby, no more climbing for sure, lah."

Lu See strummed her fingers on the table, pensive. A moment later there was another knock on the door. "That must be Adrian. I'll get it," said Lu See, watching Sum Sum bite into a square of toast.

She checked her face in the hall mirror before reaching for the doorknob.

A stranger in uniform confronted her. "Mrs Woo?" Lu See hesitated before nodding her head. She still wasn't used to being addressed as Adrian's wife. The police constable removed his helmet and tucked it under his arm. He was a young man, nineteen at most. It was his turn to hesitate now. "It's about your husband."

"Is something wrong?"

"Yes, I'm afraid so . . ."

"Has he got into some kind of trouble? If he's gone and got himself arrested for climbing, I'll be livid."

"It happened early this morning."

"I told him he'd get into trouble."

His face was hard. His voice was gentle. "There's been an accident. Your husband . . ."

That was when she spotted Adrian's library card in his hands. She blinked at him, bewildered, and then slowly turned to look at Sum Sum. Beyond her, the eggs kept boiling, bubbling on the stove, the white albumen coagulating, seeping out of the cracked shells like bleached blood from broken skulls.

"He fell from a great height, Mrs Woo." Lu See took a

small backward step. There was a sudden snatch at her heart. "I'm afraid he's dead."

She heard her mouth repeat those unbelievable words. She turned away and stumbled against the wall. The light went out in her eyes.

PART TWO

1945

1

Before the invasion of Malaya in 1941 there had been anti-Japanese demonstrations in George Town, Penang. Fueled by news reports of Japanese barbarity in Nanking, the local Chinese grew increasingly worried that the Imperial Army would extend their savagery into Malaya.

Lu See signed a petition drafted by the Chinese Chamber of Commerce calling for the deportation of Japanese expatriates. It was presented to the Resident Councillor who politely had it filed away in a bottom drawer.

Nobody suspected Tokyo of employing spies disguised as rubber buyers, barbers or timber merchants. No one guessed that they might be recruiting locals to flash secret signals out to distant ships. Few people thought a full-scale invasion was on the cards at all. The Governor of Singapore had assured everyone in Malaya that the allied troop build-up was nothing to be alarmed about, that the increase in Australian and Welsh and Scottish soldiers was purely to protect the supply of rubber and tin.

"Singapore is impregnable," the British said. The naval batteries and thirty-inch guns aiming out to sea were testament to that. "The Japs would be mad to attack us. You'll be better off here than anywhere else."

On hearing this, hundreds of British families crowded Penang harbour to board ships sailing for Singapore. There was a sense of relief when they climbed aboard. But the Chinese knew better. Many believed that the Japanese wouldn't meet the might of Singapore full on, but would attack from the east coast, nullifying the British guns pointing the wrong way. They would come overland.

As soon as Lu See heard rumours that the Japanese had beached on the north-eastern shores of the Malayan Peninsula, she got to work. She began dismantling the organ pipes at the new Anglican church, carefully disassembling them one by one.

"Why are you doing this?" asked Uncle Big Jowl. "Shouldn't we be hoarding rice or filling baths with water to combat fires instead?"

"It's the copper," she said, watching the heat of the sun crawl across the church floor. "The Japs will have it melted down and used for their war effort. I'm not going to let that happen. This organ means too much to me."

"What will you do with them? Aahh! There are how many pipes?"

"There are five ranks. Sixty-one pipes per rank." The veins of her neck strained as she prised a pipe from its neighbour by loosening the slotted screws. "We're going to bury them in the jungle and mark the spot with a gravestone."

Together with her uncle's help she marked each pipe, indicating where it belonged, and wrapped it in lengths of oiled canvas.

Lu See lost track of time. The sweat thickened on Uncle Big Jowl's shirt like moss on a temple wall.

"*Ai-yoo!*" he complained, cocking his head and flexing his sausage fingers. "Who are you and what have you done to my niece? Who turned her into this pucker-mouthed do-gooder, nah?"

"Almost done, now," she said, kissing him on the cheek. "Almost done."

Afterwards, she drove one of the estate trucks to transport the load to the periphery of the jungle. They took turns digging a ten-foot trench. Whilst Lu See worked the shovel Uncle Big Jowl kept watch.

"Who am I supposed to be looking out for?" he asked.

"I don't know: Japanese spies, opportunists, the Woos."

Two hours later Lu See turned around and gazed into the distance to take her mind off her aching back and arms. Perspiration left pink lines on her dusty face. Her hands were raw with painful sores. "Whole body feels like hell," she exclaimed.

The horizon was obscured by mist. In the darkened forest to her left the trees cast mottled shadows across the ground. All of a sudden she saw something stir. She rose on tiptoes to peer out of the ditch. "What the hell is that?" She pointed.

"Hnn?"

"There, in the clearing."

Where the jungle emptied on to an expanse of elephant grass she was sure she caught a wrinkle of movement.

Blinking, she strained her eyes and thought she saw the figure of a man. A man with one shoulder higher than the other. She remained very still. It was like being in the presence of a snake. She didn't dare move. When she blinked again he was gone.

"I don't see anything, aahh!"

"I'm sure I saw somebody."

Uncle Big Jowl regarded her sideways, registering the fear that was written in her face. Had she imagined it? She shuddered; a tremor emanating from some primitive part of her. Her eyes raked the elephant grass once more. She started to feel stupid. Hurriedly, she laid the pipes to rest.

Two months later, on 16th February 1942, Lu See picked up a copy of the Straits Times and saw a photograph of General Arthur Percival signing surrender documents and presenting them to General Tomoyuki at the Ford Motor Factory in Singapore.

Word arrived from KL that the Japanese had looted from banks, churches, mosques and temples.

The capitulation was complete.

*

"*Jo-san*, Miss Lu See." The shopkeeper set his palms on the counter and leaned forward. "And *jo-san* to you, my little friend. What should I call you?"

Lu See placed her hands on her daughter's shoulders. "Tell him your name."

The little girl bit her top lip and mumbled, "Mabel."

The shopkeeper smiled. "*Gwai-lah!* She so pretty, same-same her mother. Now, what are you looking for today?"

Lu See eyed the bare shelves. "Do you have any white sugar, Mr Ko?"

The shopkeeper wagged his head. "No have, sorry."

She looked over her shoulder. "I'm prepared to pay."

He wagged his head again. "Even if you can pay me in diamonds, I still have no sugar. Our Dai Nippon brothers are holding everything back."

"Look, please." Her voice hissed. "There are no government agents about. Anyway, this is for the Colonel. His weekly supply truck seems to temporarily have run out of sugar. I'll pay whatever price."

"*Aiya*, Miss Lu See." Mr Ko made a face, feigning hurt. "If I have, of course I sell to you, but I have none." He then twitched his chin toward the door and lowered his voice. "But I know this man, a friend, hnn?" He looked sideways at her. "He can get for you."

"How much?"

"*Aiya*, this man a swindler. He charge way too much."

"How much?"

He clicked the beads of his abacus. "This swindler, he wants something like $35 per katty."

"That's absurd. Last year you were selling tins of sugar at $6 a katty."

"This man, he is a swindler I tell you. I advise you not to buy."

She extracted a fistful of Japanese Military scrip from her purse but he threw up his hands. "No, do not pay now. I cannot guarantee he can deliver. You come back tomorrow."

Lu See returned the next day. "This fellow, he a true devil. He says sugar now $37 a katty. I advise you better not buy."

She knew shopkeeper Ko's friend didn't exist, that his hidden loot of sugar was stored under the floorboards. "Look, stop playing games. If it's $37 a katty then so be it, but I'll need a receipt for the Colonel."

He laughed and shook his head. "This fellow a real swindler."

She paid him and left with a tin of sugar tucked under her arm.

Once outside Lu See cupped a hand and shielded her eyes from the glare. She looked up and saw the Hinomaru waving in the breeze, the flag of the rising sun unfurling like a shroud over the village square.

She hated having to buy goods over the black market, but she no longer had any choice. She'd got used to it; just as she'd got used to everything else brought about by the occupation.

In an effort to wipe away the last traces of British power, the Japanese printed a new military currency, issued postage stamps announcing the 'Rebirth of Malaya' and even pushed the clocks forward to conform to Tokyo-time. There was also an attempt to make Nippon-go the common language of the region – Japanese was taught in schools and the *'Aikoku Koushinkyoku'*, a military marching song, blared across the airwaves at all hours of the day.

She crossed the street, into the main square of Po On Village, scattering a clutch of chickens scratching the ground for grubs. All about Lu See the shop signboards were in Katakana; the hawker stalls, too, advertised in Japanese script; and every road sign and traffic marker saw Katakana superimposed over the English original.

A pair of Mitsubishi Zeros flew by overhead, resulting in an *onk-onk* complaint from the village goose.

Not long now, you bastards, she muttered, staring at the retreating fighter planes. For months she'd heard whispers of the American successes in Iwo Jima; the retaking of Rangoon; the liberating of Manila; the air raids over Osaka and Yokohama. Each time someone dared speak of an Allied victory her heart jumped and sang. Now, as she moved through the town, she heard talk of the RAF dropping arms and radio equipment into the Johor jungle. *Not long before the British take back control,* she thought. *But in the meantime keep your head down and your mouth shut. Stick to your own business.*

She walked past the old pith wood store and drew the usual hostile looks from the people inside. She realized some of the villagers resented her working for Tozawa. *In the circumstances they'd do exactly the same. At any rate I don't see them turning away Japanese customers. Bloody hypocrites!* Just then she collided with an infantryman as he strolled out through the entrance of the toddy shop.

"*Rei!*" he yelled.

Lu See bowed.

The soldier drew himself up to his full height. She bowed again, glared at his trousers gathered at the knees into webbing gaiters, and offered the soldier polite salutations.

He slapped her across the top of the head and stuck out his hand. He wanted to see her papers.

Lu See bowed once more and proffered her Special Protection Certificate. The infantryman looked at the official Imperial Seal and thrust the papers back at her. Lu See bowed for a fourth time. When she looked up he had gone.

For the past three years that little scroll of paper in Lu See's hands had kept her family alive. In exchange for the 'gift' of the family car, a 1935 Bentley Saloon, the Special Protection Certificate issued by Colonel Tozawa, the Provincial Garrison Commander, had ensured their safety.

She trekked toward the limestone boundary wall and up the driveway that led to Tamarind Hill, over frangipani blossoms scattered in her path, ready to sacrifice another tiny piece of her soul. The road shimmered with heat haze and the chatter of birdsong and the scratch of cicadas filled the air. As she approached the sentry box a guard marched out of the shadows and into the ferociously hot sun. She offered a bow and handed him her papers. He waved her through.

Colonel Tozawa stood at the front verandah of the big house dressed in a satin kimono. In the shadows behind him Lu See saw a Malay servant-boy poised with his arms outstretched, holding a tray of tea.

Tozawa had a bald head and a stubbly toothbrush moustache. His eyes were jet black and unyielding; Lu See found them awkward to look at, as though they could see into her soul and read her thoughts. She could feel his fondling gaze on her as she made her way past the row of tamarind trees towards the servants' quarters.

"My dear Teoh-san," he said, sucking air loudly between his teeth, "you are being most foolish."

Lu See bowed deeply. "I apologise if I have offended you somehow."

"You are foolish to walk in such heat without cover."

Lu See glanced away. She knew he was right of course; she just did not want to acknowledge it. "Thank you for your concern, o-colonel-sama, but I am used to the sun."

"In future please, you are to carry a parasol."

"*Hai*, o-colonel-sama."

"Also, I would like you to wear these hair grips when you make your appearance after dinner." He dropped several ornate hair clips into her hand. "I cannot have hairs falling in my food, do you understand?"

"*Hai*, o-colonel-sama."

His eyes fell on the tin of sugar tucked under her arm. "I am most looking forward to your English bread-and-butter pudding. I will dine at the usual hour. Please leave the receipt for foods with my attendant. He will reimburse you accordingly."

Once more she bent from her waist with her hands on her thighs. She waited for him to move off before lifting her chin.

153

The Imperial Army had requisitioned Tamarind Hill in 1942. At first they planned to turn the building into a retreat for convalescing Hikotai pilots but then Colonel Tozawa viewed the site and chose it for himself. It galled her that he was living in her house, but at least she knew the Colonel treated her home with respect. With his fleet of servant-boys, he ensured all the rooms were well looked after and the gardens maintained.

Lu See had been hired to cook for Colonel Tozawa at the big house. Originally Ah Gwei, the Teohs' cookboy, had prepared meals for the Colonel, but he was beheaded in the summer of 1943 for spitting at a Seicho representative during a drunken rage. With nobody else to call on, Tozawa sent for Lu See. The first dish she knocked up for him was a noodle recipe from Sum Sum's little blue exercise book, but he hadn't liked it. "This is not British!" he screamed. "Nowhere in the *Katei-no-Tomo* magazine did they say noodles are British." From then on Lu See relied on the recipes she found in her father's old copy of *Mrs Beeton's Book of Household Management*.

Despite the Nipponisation of the country many of the top brass craved British food – it gave them a feeling of authority and social status; they loved English roast beef dinners, pork chops, HP brown sauce, Baxters tomato soup, shepherd's pie and canned ox-tail. They drank Johnnie Walker and Dewar's. They smoked Capstan and Raleighs. And they breakfasted on Earl Grey tea and marmalade on cold toast.

All week long she worked at Tozawa's, arriving mid-morning and leaving only when the last of the scoured pots and dishes were set away, returning to her little house to put Mabel to bed, scrub her clothes clean, hang them up, tidy up the mess, then to wake at seven to prepare breakfast for her daughter before walking her to the village school and going to Ko's shop for supplies.

"There is an elegance to the British colonial lifestyle, no?" said Colonel Tozawa as he took his seat at the dinner table.

The table was laid out with sterling silver cutlery, crystal glasses and fine Blue & White china with a pair of silver candelabra anchored in the centre. As usual there was only the one place setting. "It is one of the things we envy you for." Tozawa spread his napkin on his lap. Apart from his wooden sandals, he was dressed smartly, in a white shirt and green single-breasted tunic and trousers.

"May I remind o-colonel-sama that my family is not British nor are we colonials."

"Yet you chose to mimic a country house thousands of miles away."

Lu See struck a respectful pose beside the mahogany sideboard as his meal was served, ready to receive his compliments or complaints. She wore the ornamental hair clips he had given her. He smiled a thin smile. She watched as a servant-boy poured him three fingers of whisky into one of her father's crystal tumblers.

"Very good flavour," he said of the shepherd's pie, taking a mouthful.

She bowed and with a geisha's glide took her leave. She felt his fondling gaze on her back. Just as she reached the door he said, "One more thing, please."

She stopped and turned to face him. "Yes?"

"Why is it that you never speak about the Woos?"

"Excuse me, o-colonel-sama?"

"Your neighbours, the Woos. They are supporters of Chiang Kai-shek, no?"

Lu See's blood quickened. She could almost feel his dark eyes boring into her skull, trying to read her. "Not to my knowledge."

He picked up the pepper pot and shook it, contemplated the pepper powder fall on to the palm of his hand. "You do not think they are Chinese Nationalists?"

"No, o-colonel-sama."

"In which case they must be communists." He watched her watching him.

She swallowed. "As far as I am aware the Woos are loyal supporters of the Emperor, Tenno Heika."

"You are saying they are not communists?"

"No," she said without hesitation, keeping her voice as steady as she could. "They are not communists."

"There is something you are not telling me." He kept his unyielding gaze fixed on her face, her throat, her hair. "I find your answer curious."

"Oh?" She swallowed again. "How so, o-colonel-sama?"

"The Woos were your father's sworn enemies, or so I have learned. Your father would have used a gun on them, no?" The words had barely left his lips before the serving-boys perked up. She didn't know what they expected her to say. *But he didn't use a gun on them. He used it on himself and blew his own head off.*

"Surely you must have heard something to connect them with communists?"

"The Kempeitai military police have already questioned me on this issue, o-colonel-sama."

"I am aware of that. But I find it strange you have not accused them of anything. Some rumours that they are involved in political crime?"

Lu See blinked. She knew what type of game was being played here. She had to be careful. "My family's issues with the Woos are all in the past. My late husband was from the Woo clan. We have no axe to grind now. As I said, the Woos are loyal supporters of Tenno Heika."

"Your late husband? Is that so?"

"Yes, o-colonel-sama."

"You are on friendly terms with them."

"Ever since my child was born we have been on cordial terms."

"They see your daughter often?"

Lu See smiled through unsmiling eyes. "No."

"Because they still cannot trust you, even though she has Woo blood. How do you know they have not said anything against you? Surely, there have been times when you have complained about the high cost of living or the worthlessness of our military scrip, or joked about *Nippon-go*? It is only a matter of time before they say such things of you."

"If they accuse me of such things then I shall deny it."

He took a sip of whisky. His bald head shone in the candle light. "If you tell me the Woos are helping to finance the communist hill-people you will be rewarded. In fact any information you can supply of the *genjumin* would be whole-heartedly appreciated. I can provide new clothes for your daughter. I can give her English Canterbury biscuits. She must like Canterbury biscuits, no?"

Lu See felt something quiver within her. The only sweet things Mabel had eaten since the outbreak of war were rambutans and mangoes filched from the forest floor and a coconut sugar birthday cake once a year. She would dearly love to give her a tin of Canterbury biscuits. "I'm afraid I have nothing to tell you, o-colonel-sama."

He placed his crystal tumbler down carefully. The tip of his black toothbrush moustache glistened with whisky. For several moments he watched her, studied her mouth and eyes.

Then with a loud suck of his teeth he slapped the air and waved her away. She'd been dismissed for the night.

From the day Colonel Tozawa took possession of Tamarind Hill, Lu See was forced to live in a small Chinese-style house by the river which once belonged to the rubber estate's overseer before he was arrested by the Kempeitai. Allowed to take only what she could carry, she stuffed her old eel-skin trunk with anything she thought she could barter and made her way down the hill. The small house had a tiny stone courtyard and a neat roof made of clay tiles, with two bedrooms, a wet kitchen and a teetering porch, which was home to a family of yellow geckos. And because it wasn't connected to the electricity board, candles were used after dark.

It was a pleasant little place, surrounded by shady trees and the call of birds, and there was always a cleansing breeze which cooled the air at night.

Her mother slept in one bedroom and Uncle Big Jowl in the other, which meant that Peter and James claimed the settees in the main room whilst Lu See and Mabel shared a mattress and a conical mosquito net in the wet kitchen. Before the war Uncle Big Jowl lived in Penang but his home was bombed from the air by the Japanese.

There were two wicker chairs on the porch, a large worn one reserved for Uncle Big Jowl's cheroot smoking and a smaller one with a bright red cushion nestled at its heart. Each evening Mabel settled on the red cushion with both hands clasped in her lap waiting for her mother to return home.

Sometimes she ate her stale-rice supper propped high on the red cushion, rice bowl in hand, eyes fixed on the dirt road that led up to Tamarind Hill. Sometimes she ate by the window of the wet kitchen, heaping grains into her mouth with a pair of chopsticks, never allowing her attention to waver. She watched the beaten earth path like a hawk.

"*Chee-chee-chee!* Staring at the road will not make your mother return any faster, little one."

"I know, Grandma."

"So why not come inside and relax. You will wear out eyes otherwise."

"I'm fine."

"Come, I'll light fresh candles and make banana bread." Mabel shook her head no.

As the darkness thickened and the smell of kerosene lamps soured the air Uncle Big Jowl beached himself in the chair by her side. He lit a cheroot and smoked, cupping the cigar in his hand, hiding the crimson glow within his palm. Mabel wondered whether he did this to protect it from the breeze or to conceal it from sight; he was forever telling Mabel that smoking was bad for you. She glanced at him momentarily then continued her vigil.

"*Ai-yooo!*" he wheezed, half-slumbering with his arms hung slack. "I used to have a dog like you. She used to hunt for squirrels, watching every tree branch like it contained a bar of gold. Speaking of gold, next week is end of durian season. Remember never to mix durian with alcoholic drink, can cause bad reaction you know."

"What time is it, Uncle?"

Uncle Big Jowl rubbed the top of his head with cheroot ash to ward off the mosquitoes. His short grey hair was unevenly pruned as if cropped by a goat. With a languid lift of his wrist he checked his watch and then replaced his hands on his melon-bellied gut. "Two minutes later than when you last asked me, aahh."

Mabel blinked into the darkness, listening to the sounds of the jungle. Straining to hear footfalls amongst the sounds of the tree frogs, she stared beyond the tangle of vines dangling from the mass of trees. And then, craning forward like a chipmunk spotting a stray nut, her back flinched and her throat tensed and before you could call her name she was bounding from the porch and along the road. "Mama, Mama, Mama!" Running with her arms outstretched she hopped over a pothole and threw herself into her mother's embrace.

Since the start of the occupation both Peter and James worked as Post Office inspectors at the former De La Rue printing press in Butterworth, reporting to a Mr Miyagi. Each day they cycled to Juru station and boarded a train, returning each night in time for supper.

As Lu See entered the candle-lit kitchen she heard Peter say, "Today, on my way back from the presses, this Japanese lorry almost ran me off the road. I was lucky not to lose control of my bicycle and end up in a ditch."

Lu See saw them sitting with her mother, in the centre of the room, around a table laid with a bowl of bananas. Mother plucked one free and waggled it at her son like a pistol. "You a mouse or man! There's plenty of room on the roads. Where's your backbone?" Lu See half expected her to reach over and twist his earlobe.

"You should have seen how close he was," he exclaimed. "Jehovah be my witness, it brushed my sleeve."

"*Cha!*" said Mother.

"It's true," challenged Peter.

Mother shot him one of her looks. James rose to do the dirty dishes, moving cautiously as if there was a sleeping tiger sprawled across the floor.

Removing a deck of withered playing cards from a drawer, Mother gave her thumb a lick. "Gin Rummy?"

"We're not allowed to gamble!" her sons replied in unison. Both men looked almost identical with boyish clean-shaven features and slightly protruding eyes, which gave them an air of perpetual bewilderment.

Mother gave an exhausted sigh. "What did I do to deserve sons like you? No matter how many years go by I never-never get used to this Jehovah's Witnesses business. And both unmarried to boots."

James rolled his bulbous eyes. "Not this again."

"I mean, take you for example, Peter, you always hated going to church as a child," she continued. "You had tantrum in the pews. The whole congregation turned and stared."

"That was James."

"I was four," argued James, cradling a bible in his lap.

"You were seven and you wet your front side," Mother counteracted.

"He was scared of the priest," said Peter. "Something about his red hair, wasn't it?"

James shut his eyes as though to block out the memory.

"Now you turn into religious fanatics," huffed Mother.

In unison: "We are not religious fanatics!"

"I'm relieved," said Mother, sounding not the least bit relieved.

In the ensuing silence a variety of winged insects knocked and pinged against the bare ceiling bulb. Lu See cleared her throat.

Mother looked up from her deck of cards, which she'd fanned across the kitchen table. "What the matter? What is wrong?"

"Nothing's wrong."

"You only clear your throat like tree frog when something is wrong."

"Nothing's wrong. I just put Mabel to bed."

Mother rose from her chair and moved to replace the kettle on the stove, bare feet padding across the floor. "You want tea?"

Lu See declined the offer.

"A slice of banana bread maybe? Or peanuts, nah, we have plenty of peanuts." Mother nodded her head encouragingly. "Come, eat." This, Lu See knew, was her way of showing love – showering food on her children.

Lu See shook her head and drew a hand over her face. She still had the smells of cooking under her fingernails. "There was some rice left over at the colonel's."

"But you didn't eat," said Mother.

"How can you tell?"

"You loitering and nobody loiters on full stomach. Whole country starving and you don't eat his leftover food." Mother brought out a large basin of peanuts. "Come, help me shell these, will you?"

Lu See took a chair. "For the record I wasn't loitering."

"Just skulking," said Peter.

"Precisely," said James.

Peter pressed a finger to the sky like Moses. "For they are called labourers and should not be loiterers!"

James smiled. "Thessalonians?"

"Precisely."

James began to flick through the pages of the bible on his lap. "Let me guess. Chapter 15, verse – "

"*Cha!* Will you two be quiet for once!" cried Mother. "Every other minute it's the bible say this, the bible say that, Jehovah said this, Jehovah said that, knick-knick, knack-knack. Can't we have one nice evening together without preachings and bickerings! Why can't you have the quiet grace of your sister?"

Peter frowned.

"You've upset him now," said James.

Mother shelled a nut and tossed it in her mouth. "One harsh word and he fall into a sulk."

"No, I've not."

"Peter, you cannot act like a cissy-cissy all your life, especially now that Ah-Ba has gone to walk a new path. *Cha!* Look at you, face like basket of crabs."

"Colonel Tozawa says he wants me to prepare peppered crab for him next week," said Lu See.

"Why must you mention his name?" challenged Mother. She was forever fearful that her daughter might be sleeping with this non-Chinese, barbarian invader. "Whatever you do, withstand his advances."

"Mother, really . . ."

"They are all rapists."

"He is a gentleman," Lu See said, unsure why she needed to defend him.

Her mother's furrowed brow promised to engulf her entire face.

Sensibly, Lu See changed the subject. "What are you preparing?"

"Satay dip-dip sauce." Lu See felt her mouth moisten at the image of grilled meat skewers and the puddle of peanut sauce she dunked them in. "But we're using squirrel again instead of chicken, so don't tell Mabel. Come, nah, grab me that bottle of soy, then chop up a half inch piece of galangal with some ginger." Mother began pounding peanuts. "We finish this before bed, no more talk."

Lu See worked her knife into a gnarl of ginger. She had

never been much of a chef before the war, and was far less experienced than the Colonel imagined. But she persevered. With the house and money gone she needed the work – it was a long fall from her earlier intellectual aspirations. Cambridge seemed a lifetime ago. Sometimes she had the sense that she was living in a dream, that her past was made up of imaginary seductions rather than real memories. She looked at the slivers of ginger and felt a sudden punitive urge to slice into her own flesh. A clench of guilt and regret pressed against her chest. It was simply a reflex, an instinct. She winced and waited. Seconds later the urge had waned.

The following night, up in the big house, as Lu See stood beside the mahogany sideboard watching Tozawa spoon bubble and squeak into his mouth, he turned to her and smiled.

Nonplussed, she smiled back.

"How old are you, Teoh-san?" he asked, dabbing cabbage remnants from his moustache.

"Excuse me, o-colonel-sama?"

"Your age. I gather since your husband died you have not remarried, and I am curious about your age."

Lu See felt herself colour. "Forgive me, o-colonel-sama, but in all the time I have worked here, you have never asked me about my life." Indeed, it was the first personal question he had ever put to her. She was unsure how to respond.

He sucked air through his teeth and grinned. "Perhaps with this dreaded war drawing to a close I am throwing caution to the wind."

"I don't understand." His words lingered with her. She wanted to ask him exactly what he meant by the war drawing to a close. Were the Japanese on the verge of surrendering? Were they about to withdraw from Malaya? She'd heard rumours that the Allies were closing in, that submarines bringing Gurkhas had reached Malayan shores, but she hadn't dared dream.

A silken smile. "It is a simple question, Teoh-san. I wish to know when you were born."

Lu See hesitated. She felt her heart expand in her chest and her breath pull tight. The blood in her veins turned cold. "I have an eight-year-old daughter."

"Quite." He looked at her, encouraging her to go on. "But I asked you your age, not hers."

"I am 28."

"*Ahhh-so*." His dark eyes narrowed and shimmered with moisture. "Very young still, very young."

He took a sip of whisky and watched her over the rim of his glass.

Lu See could sense his eyes painting patterns across her body. In the months she had worked for the Colonel, apart from the odd fondling gaze, he never once made advances towards her and for this she was grateful, but suddenly she felt a shift in him. Her face became tangled with dread. She made to change the subject. "H-how is your meal tonight, o-colonel-sama?"

"Very fine, as usual." He placed the crystal tumbler down carefully. "So, you are 28 and you have an 8-year-old daughter."

Silence.

"You have been very protective of her since the New Order took control of Malaya."

Lu See swallowed. "I've done what any mother would do."

"A mother's will is like iron when her child is in danger, no?" His lips twitched, an odd secret smile.

Panic ignited in her and spread like sparks on kindling.

"She will make all sorts of sacrifices, no?"

Lu See could not hold his gaze. Her eyes fell to the floor. Outside, the sultry hiss of rain fizzed the air. She thought of Tozawa's stubbly toothbrush moustache brushing her skin and shuddered.

"I make you feel discomforted, Teoh-san?"

Again, she said nothing.

"It was not my intention to do so. Forgive me. The reason I ask you such questions is because you are a beautiful woman. And in times like this beautiful women such as you can become very ugly so very quickly. They need protecting, you see." His moustache twitched with his smile. "Otherwise they might disappear. And I would not want to see you disappear."

Lu See made a tiny pleading gesture with her hands. "Your Special Protection Certificate has helped me on numerous occasions, o-colonel-sama."

"I am certain it has. But I have not done enough personally to ensure your safety. You work for me. You are my responsibility. Tell me, how do you return to your family at night when you finish here?"

"I walk down the hill."

"That must take you many minutes to reach the village." Involuntarily Lu See glanced at her wristwatch – Adrian's old wristwatch. It had stopped working years before, but habit dictated she keep it close to her skin. "And the road is unlit," he continued. "Are you not afraid of bandits?"

Lu See wanted to say that she was more scared of the Japanese patrols and the sentry who searched her person each night for pilfered food. "I am used to it, o-colonel-sama."

"And what if it is raining, like tonight?" Tozawa stroked his toothbrush moustache with his thumb knuckle. He made a little motion with his head. "No longer will you walk down the hill. From now on I will tell one of the servant-boys to take you directly to your home. He can drive the scout car."

Lu See blinked a few times before bowing, her hands on her thighs. "You are too kind, o-colonel-sama, but I really cannot accept."

"You must accept. I will instruct the sentry guards of the new arrangement. Now, clear my plate and bring me your sweet dish. I have waited all day to taste this pie of yours and can wait no longer."

2

Tuesday evening, three days later. Lu See pulled the toad-in-the-hole from the oven and plated it up. It was hot in the kitchen and the warm breeze coming in through the open, mosquito-mesh window did not cool anything. Earlier in the day, she was told to lay out the dinner settings for two; Colonel Tozawa was having a guest for supper.

"Do you know who the guest is?" she asked the servant-boy.

He shrugged.

She placed the two Blue and White china plates on a tray together with a large bowl of boiled peas, and told the servant-boy to serve the colonel.

A moment later, as soon as the servant-boy left with the tray, Lu See adjusted her ornamental hair clips and made her way into the dining room.

She struck a respectful pose beside the mahogany side-board as his meal was presented, ready to receive his compliments or complaints. The guest was a man, dressed in a white linen suit. He was seated with his back to Lu See. She could tell by the colour of his hair that he was either Japanese or Chinese. From the moment that she entered the room she smelled the liniment on his skin; the vulgar scent of camphor.

When he turned to look at her, she obediently lowered her eyes.

"What do you think of our Teoh-san?" asked Tozawa in English.

"Pretty, but a little on the old side," the man answered, returning to his food.

"Old? She is only 28," retorted Tozawa. They spoke as if Lu See wasn't in the same room.

"Does she have children?"

"One only."

The man in the white suit tutted.

Lu See raised her eyes a fraction. Tozawa looked at her and smiled a thin smile. She watched the servant-boy pour three fingers of whisky into the colonel's crystal tumbler. As he shuffled across to replenish the guest's glass, the man in the white suit placed a flat hand over his glass and shook his head.

Something about him was vaguely familiar.

Lu See did not move. She watched him eat. She was silent. And then she recognized the slope of his shoulders.

The man turned his head a fraction. She tried to hide her eyes from him. Too late. "Why are you looking at me?" he said.

She gasped. Recognition made her mouth pull taut. No, it couldn't be! Not after all this time. It couldn't be him.

"You!" she yelled, making no attempt to hide her shock. The man in the white suit dropped his fork. There was no mistaking the mole on his left cheek. It was the Black-headed Sheep.

Tozawa jumped to his feet. "What are you doing! How dare you act so disrespectfully to my guest!" He stepped up to her and raised his hand, threatening to slap her across the mouth. "*Boujakubujin!*" He ordered her to go out into the corridor and kneel.

She left the room and knelt in silence on the tatami mat, head bowed. She tried to listen to the conversation taking place in the dining room, but heard nothing. The silence scared her. Eventually, Tozawa appeared with a crystal tumbler of whisky in one hand. He held a *Katana* sword in the other. He was swaying a little bit. She could smell the alcohol on him.

He stood staring at her, dressed in his wooden slippers and green trousers.

"Explain," he said in a soft yet menacing voice.

"He is a Woo."

"You told me the other day, Teoh-san, that you had no problems with the Woos."

"I don't. I only have a problem with that man."

"*That man* is a very important friend to the Imperial Army."

"Years ago he did something terrible."

"We have all done something terrible in this war."

"He will cause me harm."

"I assure you, he will not. Whatever went on between you in the past is no longer his concern."

"How do you know?"

"He told me."

"And now he is an informer."

"He is a loyal servant to the Emperor."

Silence.

"Just as you, Teoh-san, are a loyal servant to the Emperor, no?" He smiled a thin smile.

Tozawa at this point might have expected Lu See to turn her eyes away timidly, or lower them to the floor. Instead, she raised her chin and looked defiantly at him. "I warn you, o-colonel-sama, I will not be in the same room as that man."

"You *warn* me?"

She kept her eyes fixed on his.

His moustache twitched. He raised his sword a fraction.

"You know," he said with a tired sigh, "you really should not wear so many ornaments in your hair." He finished his whisky with a gulp. "People might think you are a prostitute."

Cautiously, she began to remove the ornamental clips. Her

hair fell around her shoulders. She felt the touch of cold metal on her throat. She flinched. Tozawa pushed some strands of hair away with tip of his blade. She could see a quotation written in Japanese text engraved on the haft of the sword.

"I was to be his 'gift', was that it? You were going to repay him for his good work by offering him me."

"Is that what you think?" A sadness marked his face. "You are so very wrong, Teoh-san." There were red cobwebs in the whites of his eyes. She could almost see the disappointment bleed out of him.

"What will he do to me? I made him lose face in there."

"He will do nothing. He has bigger fish to fry than worry about you."

The ends of his black toothbrush moustache glistened with whisky. For several moments he watched her, studied her mouth and eyes.

"Go home," he ordered.

She went.

3

On a high Tibetan hilltop perch, with the wind gusting and the earth brown and hard, Sum Sum watched from a distance as her mother's body was carried in a white cloth and laid in a foetal position on the cold stones. Soaring above, in a rising current of air, a pair of vultures watched, black tip feathers extended, their wings bent forward slightly.

The village *daodeng*, the man overseeing the burial task, set alight a clump of juniper to attract more birds. The fragrant incense rose with the wind. More vultures appeared.

They landed within a few feet of Sum Sum's mother. Bristling their bushy neck plumes like feathery boas, they patrolled the corpse, circling it, hopping from stone to stone. First five or six drew near and then over a dozen arrived, followed by another dozen.

Sum Sum knew what was coming next. She held her breath. The *daodeng* raised his axe to his shoulder and brought it down on her A-Ma's spine, severing her into several parts. The vertebrae snapped like faraway gunshots. Next with a long knife he began tearing the muscles from the bones in long strips and mixing *tsampa* flour into the separated flesh. Finally, with a low whistle, the *daodeng* invited the birds to begin feasting, clapping his hands and encouraging them as he would a flock of sheep.

Throats stretched out, their pale beaks and foreheads suddenly polluted with blood, the vultures began squabbling in their squalling tones. Sum Sum watched her mother slowly disappear.

Entrails were snatched from beak to beak; guts and organs were gorged on.

She decided she wouldn't stay for the crushing of the skull.

The Tibetan sun rose above the horizon line, extending coral shadows from its copper-coin eye. Sum Sum turned away and made her way down the hillside path.

The wings of her earflap hat beat against her cheeks as she rushed to meet her brother, Hesha. A sergeant with the Gurkha Rifles, he was returning that morning from the Burmese front on four days' compassionate leave. She wanted to hug him hard to her chest and feel his heart beat against her ear. It was excitement that made her hop over the stones, not sadness. It was excitement that blurred her eyes with tears.

For the first time in almost seven years, Sum Sum found herself alone with her brother. They were at their family home, a house made from sun-dried bricks and timber posts. She draped a white narrow scarf, a *kata*, across his shoulder and bowed. Hesha accepted the scarf with both hands. "Look at you," she said. "Skinny as a skeleton in a desert."

As they settled down on the floor, on horse fur cushions in front of a short table, sipping hot cups of butter tea from wooden bowls, she began to tell him about their mother's passing. Hesha listened in silence, dipping his head every few moments with reverence, speaking the names of deities in praise of her memory.

Hesha looked relieved when Sum Sum said that many birds came to feast on her flesh. "Let us hope that her soul has migrated." She wanted to tell him more but the words knotted in her throat.

He trailed a finger across his forehead and gazed out of the window, into the sky. He blew on his bowl of butter tea, eyeing the stacks of firewood and the saddle gear on the floor. "We are destined to lose the ones we love otherwise we would never realize how much they meant to us."

Sum Sum touched him on the arm. "Here," she said, handing him a bowl of *tsampa*. "You need to put some extra layers of flesh on your bones."

Hesha accepted the *tsampa*, which he ate with his hands, and together they reminisced about their early childhood before Sum Sum went to work abroad, beyond the plateau. "Do you remember the kites you used to fly in the springtime?" she asked.

Sum Sum watched her brother's face crack into a smile. "Old widow Bayarmaa used to chase after me with a broom each time my line got tangled up with her washing."

"And do you remember the day A-Pha took you to the horse festival and you rode a Mongolian pony?"

"I ended up back to front on the saddle!" They laughed out loud.

After a quarter of an hour Hesha gave a muted yawn. The thought recurred to Sum Sum during this uncharacteristic lull in conversation that perhaps Hesha might wish to talk about his recent exploits. She asked him if being a sergeant meant he was assigned a great deal of responsibility. "Many responsibilities," he replied.

"Like what?"

"I am in charge of a platoon. I must set an example on the battlefield to my men. And when not fighting there is also equipment to maintain which I have to oversee."

"Tell me about Burma. You never write."

His face grew solemn. "I do write. I write many letters, my sister, but not to people I know." She told him she didn't understand. "I write to the families of the dead. Each month five maybe six letters to Nepalese mothers and fathers. I tell them about their sons who have been shot or stabbed or blown into the sky. The words are like black ravens visiting my heart. I am sick of writing." Hesha turned his face away, shielding his hurt from her. Sum Sum recognized the ges-

173

ture. It was the same reflexive manoeuvre he used to make as a boy whenever A-Ma scolded him.

Sum Sum touched his shoulder and offered him more *tsampa*. After which he told her that his battalion had been transferred out of Rangoon and onto a fighter carrier. "Possible recapture of Malaya is the talk."

Sum Sum nodded her head and said no more.

An aircraft flew overhead. The locals called it an iron bird. Sum Sum knew it to be an American C-87 transport on its way from India. Hesha told her that ever since the Japanese blocked the Burma Road, the allies airlifted materials over the Himalayas to supply Chiang Kai-shek's forces in China.

Another two days passed before she pressed an envelope into his hands. "If you find yourself in Penang and the war is over. You will do this for me." He looked at the name on the cover and dipped his chin with reverence.

"It is the one letter I will not mind delivering." He saw the sadness in his sister's eyes. "How long has it been since you last saw her?"

She stiffened. "I ran away from England in 1937. I abandoned my best friend eight years ago." Even now, after all this time, the fact made her equilibrium shift; it was as if she was stepping off a moving carousel.

"And no contact since?"

She shook her head at the question and felt her face go hot. "No contact since."

For a second she tried to smile, to make light of it, but she soon faltered. The guilt fell on her as the rain falls on the grass.

She'd fled England for Malaya, using Uncle Big Jowl's boat ticket and the money left in the red *ang pow* packet. She'd given Lu See no warning. There'd been no mention of returning to Lhasa. Early one morning, she fed her baby, packed her things and left. The ship from Felixstowe took her to Penang. And as soon as she stepped onto dry land she felt like a traitor.

Back on Malay soil, she did not have enough money to journey on to Tibet. So she slept rough. She got a job helping a hawker, crushing sugar cane to make into juice. Not once did she contact anyone from the Teoh clan for help. Eventually, she saved enough to continue on to Chittagong, taking a slow boat from the Straits of Malacca though to the Bay of Bengal. A fortnight later she was in Lhasa.

The guilt had burned inside her ever since, yet she knew in her heart that what she'd done was right. Her sacrifice had been necessary.

Five days following her mother's sky burial, Sum Sum walked to the village of Cloudy Treetops, removed her tribal toe rings and enrolled with the Ani Trangkhung Nunnery. She joined not because she had become truly religious; it was because she did not have anywhere else to go. At 28 she was by far and away the oldest of the initiates.

Urged to memorise the thirty-six novice vows, she set down the square rug which only novices were sanctioned to use and sank slowly to one knee. All around her young women murmured into their singing bowls, rubbing the rims to produce a melodic resonance.

Kneeling, palms joined below the chin, with her eyes locked on a guttering red candle, Sum Sum heard the temple caretaker's voice trail through the incense smoke. "Are you prepared to take refuge under the guidance and protection of Buddha, Dharma and Sangha?" enquired the elderly lady.

"I am," replied Sum Sum softly.

"Are you ready to renounce all worldly relations and possessions?"

In the background the *vajra* tapped the bell lightly and Sum Sum, eyes closed, emptied her mind, visualizing the parasol of white light embracing the compound.

"Yes."

The caretaker of the temple placed her thumb on the top of Sum Sum's skull and applied gentle pressure. Sum Sum heard a *snip*. Then, feeling her head tilt to one side, her thick mane was tugged straight and a masticating noise sounded in Sum Sum's ear as the long bevel blades pared thick handfuls of hair from her scalp.

The hair tickled the skin of her arms as it fell to the floor. Sum Sum wanted to reach up and run her fingers over her head to feel what was happening, but her palms remained joined below her chin.

The metal jaws clipped and pruned, lopping off one clump after another.

"What do you do with all this hair afterwards, lah?" whispered Sum Sum.

"*Sshhh!*"

"In England they buy long hair like mine to make into wigs. You should do that too, no? Sweep up floor and send to wig makers. Maybe can use money to buy sharper scissors."

"Keep still and be silent, please."

She watched the guttering candle for several moments. Her eyes widened a fraction when she saw the cut-throat razor.

"What's that for, lah?"

"What do you think? Stupid question! Like teaching fish about water! Look at how the other girls keeping so quiet as they wait their turn. Do like them, will you please?"

Someone in the shadows cleared her throat, a protest, thought Sum Sum, at the noise they were making perhaps.

The razor rasped against Sum Sum's skin. "Ow!"

"Ow, my foot. Keep still."

The blade ploughed a pale pathway through the fine black stubble.

Eventually, the temple caretaker flicked Sum Sum's ear-lobe with a finger and told her to go over to the next building to meet with the prayer hall manager to collect her robes.

Prayer hall manager Jampa's office was across the courtyard. It had distant views of the snow-mountains and the Potala Palace with its profusion of 'wind horse' flags that resembled multicoloured Kleenex.

Sum Sum lifted the dragon doorknocker and let it drop. *"Yar Pep!* Come!"

The small room was Spartan, equipped with nothing more than a desk, three wooden chairs, a hurricane lamp with an oiled wick and a woven wall hanging depicting White Tara. Sum Sum glanced at the image of the Mother of all Buddhas, noting her seven eyes, searching out the ones in the middle of her forehead and on her hands and feet. A solitary latticework window, sealed with translucent paper, offered a hazy view of the stream and the hills beyond.

Prayer hall manager Jampa, a portly septuagenarian with the face of a little piglet, squeezed her cheeks into a smile and made a click-clack sound with her tongue. "You have had your head shaved. *Yakpo ndug*, good."

Sum Sum ran a hand over her bald pate. *"Ayo Sami!* I must look like a freshly laid egg. Am I allowed to wear an egg cosy when it gets colder?" She felt like giggling but decided against it.

"You will be expected to keep your head smooth. Caretaker of the temple will provide razors. Ay-yi, but what is this? Your garments are loose. Come closer, I want to look at your robes."

Prayer hall manager Jampa adjusted Sum Sum's maroon shawl and lower robe, tightening the cloth at the waist. "These simple clothes may symbolize renunciation but we must still maintain an orderly appearance. Now, please, take a seat."

Sum Sum sat down, placing her hands respectfully on her lap. She eyed the desk. It was lined with paper scrolls, ox horn writing brushes with rabbit hair nibs, an ink stick, a purple-hued ink slab and a stone brushwash.

Prayer hall manager Jampa leaned across her desk and offered Sum Sum natag snuff, which she kept finely ground in a yak horn container. A breeze slithered through the cracks in the latticework window.

"Just a little on your thumbnail will do," said prayer hall manager Jampa.

The scrolls of paper twitched in the light breeze. Sum Sum took a quick snort and then held her head back as if anticipating a sneeze. After a few seconds she gagged.

"Is it too flavoursome for you?" Prayer hall manager Jampa grinned, her eyes flaring theatrically.

Sum Sum let out her breath, which appeared like a smoky dust through her open mouth. "By Dharmakaya heaven! What do you put in this? Chilli powder, no?"

"Ground cloves, cardamom and juniper tree ash." Both women's eyes were watery with tears. "*Ndug're*. Good. Works wonders before 5 a.m. prayers. Wakes me up every time. I offer it to all the novices on their first day here; it helps settle the nerves I think. Better not let the abbess hear about it otherwise she'll have my insides for breakfast."

Both made contented click-clack sounds with their tongues.

When Sum Sum settled down, prayer hall manager Jampa extracted something from her desk folder and handed it to her. "*Ndug're*. Time for administrative business. We have decided that this will be your Dharma name."

Sum Sum received the square bit of paper. It was beige with red Tibetan letters scrawled on it.

"*Sengemo*? Lioness?"

"It is a good name. It is in accordance with your lineage – your father was a great soldier, was he not? Lioness suits you. I also want you to wear these mala beads over your wrist. Each bead is made of bone. Use it to help with your prayers."

Sum Sum thanked her.

"When you enter this nunnery you leave your history behind," the old lady continued. "You leave your memories behind. You must allow those memories to rust. What is past is past. Out in *that* world people create their own sadness. It is not the case here."

The prayer hall manager peered at her folder. *"Ndug're.* Now it is time to discuss what your tasks will be. As you are aware, unlike monks we do not receive payment of any kind for performing ritual services, therefore we cannot afford to feed everyone here the same way the monastery can. Here you will gain knowledge and the teachings of the Buddha but you will be asked to work to help sustain the community. Yes?"

Sum Sum nodded. *"Tuteche."*

"What are you skilled in? What can you do? You know how to use the Tibetan spindle?"

"Sorry, prayer hall manager."

"Humphh. You know how to work the fields?"

Sum Sum flashed her neem-nurtured white teeth. "I spent time in the rice paddies when I was a child."

"But nothing since?"

"Some vegetable growing when the earth is not too hard."

Prayer hall manager Jampa pinched her chin and let out another *hmphh* of amused dismay.

"So what can you do, *Sengemo*?"

Impulsively, Sum Sum went to twist a strand of hair on her head that was no longer there. "Cook. I am a tip-top cook, lah!"

"By the scorching sun, you'll be so lucky. Kitchen duties are for more established members. We can't have you poisoning us with undercooked food, now can we? No, you'll do laundry duty. *Ndug're!* You will start as a washing hand, scrubbing clothes by the riverbank. Is that agreed?"

Sum Sum nodded. *"Tuteche."*

"Now that is settled, let me remind you that chastity is essential and that contact with others outside of the Ani Trangkhung Nunnery is discouraged in your first five years. After that you may attend the annual horse festival on the grasslands. If you wish to send word to people you are advised to seek advice from an elder first. Is there anyone you wish to make contact with before final acceptance?"

Sum Sum felt pleased that she had managed to see her brother Hesha, but now she thought of Lu See. She so wanted to tell her where she was, what she was doing, longed to know if she and the child were safe. Eight years now, eight years without contact. She now left it in the hands of fate. If she was meant to see her friend once more then Hesha would let her know.

"No." She dropped her gaze. "There is no one."

"*Ndug're.*"

Prayer hall manager Jampa reached for her yak-horn container. "Spurn all worldly goods; you have nothing now besides a gown and sandals. Study your scriptures well, work hard and become a learned and kind nun." She made a click-clack sound with her tongue. "Inner peace and strength to you."

Sum Sum rose from her chair, fingered her mala beads and dipped her head. "Inner peace and strength to you."

4

By the middle of August 1945 everyone knew that the Japanese had lost the war. News of the Hiroshima and Nagasaki bombings were greeted with a mixture of wonderment and awe – how, people asked, could an entire city be obliterated in a matter of seconds?

In Po On Village, the change in the air was almost tangible. People on the streets were smiling again. Moreover, old American jazz songs could be heard on gramophones instead of the *Aikoku Koushinkyoku*, and the store owners began to erect English signboards once more, replacing those written in Katakana.

Colonel Tozawa was a changed man too. For a while he pretended all was well but he couldn't keep it up. He grew quiet. He stopped eating.

"Please, o-colonel-sama," urged Lu See, bowing with her hands on her thighs, "you have not touched any food for days. You must eat."

His face looked gaunt. He had not slept for ages. And he kept polishing his sword.

Lu See suspected he was planning to kill himself.

She did not want to see that happen. He had kept her and her family safe from the other Japanese all this time, and she respected him for it. *So you think he is our guardian angel, now?* she heard her mother say. And, as always, she felt a need to defend him. *But why? You care for him? You love him?* No. But she cared what happened to him. At times, especially when he was drunk, he had frightened her, but he had been courteous towards her too. He never treated her like his property. Yet, she also knew she must not mistake his lack of abuse as an act of kindness.

"Would you like me to prepare a shepherd's pie?" she asked him now. "Or your favourite bread-and-butter pudding?

He gazed at the *Katana* sword mounted on the wall and then studied his hands, looking inward like a grieving father. "Soba noodles," he said, through gritted teeth. "I have grown tired of British food. Make me something from home. Soba noodles with tofu and pickles."

Yes, of course, o-colonel-sama." She turned on her heels.

"And Teoh-san . . ." His voice sounded as soft as the rain. Their eyes met. They stood under the slowly revolving fan for several seconds. "Thank you."

Prior to the outbreak of war, Tamarind Hill was a fine sprawling residence that sat on the outskirts of a vast rubber plantation.

It was perched on a rise with views of the Juru River and embraced both Eastern and Western architectural influences. The grand Entrance Hall had floors made from Italian marble, the Chinese-style doors and staircases were constructed with Rain Tree wood and the elaborate cast iron bathtubs were shipped over from Shropshire.

There was an ample verandah at the rear that overlooked a coconut grove, a library stocked with English and Chinese literature, a billiard room, a mahjong studio and a gallery that housed a rare collection of blackwood chairs inlaid with mother-of-pearl. What's more, when the patriarch, Lu See's father, was in residence the major-domo raised the flag of St. George at dawn to alert the Woos of his presence.

But all that was gone now. Now there were nothing but hollow, cobwebbed rooms full of flies dozing on windowsills and mildew curdling in the heat.

On September 13th, the commander of the Japanese 29th

Army, Lt. Gen. Ishiguro, surrendered to Lt. Gen. Ouvry Roberts, Commander of XXXIV Indian Corps at the Victoria Institiution in Kuala Lumpur. Chaos followed.

"All requisitioned homes to be returned to their owners," read Lu See. "By decree of the Imperial War Office." She stood in the village square and turned from the poster to her fellow onlookers. "Finally a sense of order!" they cried. But there was no sense of order to it; vigilante gangs roamed the streets, black marketeers were set upon and villagers clashed over food. Violence erupted with pepper-shaker randomness. The police had lost control; some of them even threw away their uniforms.

Colonel Tozawa left the big house soon after. A civilian car waited for him in the drive, parked under the shade of a tamarind tree. The car flew a white flag and was marked with 'surrender crosses'.

He bowed and offered his hand to Lu See. "It is not safe for you here, Teoh-san. I recommend that you do not return to Tamarind Hill for some time."

As soon as Colonel Tozawa withdrew from the house looters stripped the house clean. The marble floors were dug up and the metal gates torn from the earth, even the giant cast iron bathtubs were taken, leaving only the dust-shadows of their clawed feet.

When the looters left, Lu See paused at the entrance to her old home with her daughter Mabel and Uncle Big Jowl. Despite the hardships of occupation Lu See's uncle appeared only slightly diminished. "Me?" he said when asked about his continued corpulence, pressing a set of podgy fingers to his breast. "I'm turning hollow-chested in my thinness, no?" He would beam: "No, lah, truth is I eat coconut meat. Five coconuts each morning. And I don't have to pay a banana dollah. Comes free from the tree, aahh!' Dressed in long shorts, an open neck shirt and white plimsolls, he resembled a pygmy hippopotamus in tennis attire. He was little changed except that he'd grown prone to offering advice in the middle of conversations that seemed completely out of context.

"How long do you think we will have to wait before the British return in force?" Lu See asked him.

"May take two-tree weeks, lah. There is a small British presence here already to ensure capitulation terms are observed. In the meantime expect more of this sort of thing. There are armed gangs in Kedah and Pahang ransacking, taking what they can." They stepped over the charred remains of a Rising Sun flag. Lu See picked through the splintered glass, with a sick feeling lodged in her throat, as if she'd been forced to swallow a tar ball. Uncle Big Jowl swayed from side to side as he walked. "You think maybe they haven't seen enough bloodshed, hnnn?"

"Are all the big houses ruined?" Mabel said aloud.

"Not all." He made a face. "The Woo house was untouched. The bloody-crafty-buggers hired a team of armed guards to protect it."

Lu See stretched her face toward the sun. The day, with its clear, clean sunshine, seemed to echo her hopeful mood. She recalled Second-aunty Doris's words: *Remember, keep a green tree in your heart and perhaps the trembling leaves will stay away.* "Well, at least now we can make a fresh start."

"Fresh start is like a kite with the cord broken. We are at the mercy of fortune, meh?"

"I'll plant cabbages and leeks and sweet potatoes. Mabel can help."

"Be careful of eating too many sweet things, aahh. Bad for teeth and general health."

Lu See took her daughter's hand, cushioning the girlish fingers in her own and led her inside. She felt Mabel grip her palm tight. She gave it a precious squeeze.

"It's so empty, Mama."

"My friend, aahh, Chan Yee, the man with hair like a porcupine, remember? He died of too much sugar. Heart could not take it. Salt very bad too – look what happened to your Ah-Ba's ankles."

Mottled light shafted through the grey windows.

Uncle Big Jowl fanned himself with a banana leaf, winced and then started complaining about his arthritic knees. There was a smell of damp coming from the walls. "Not much left of it, hnn?"

"They've taken everything, even the door handles," said Lu See. Her voice echoed in the emptiness.

"Not so," Uncle Big Jowl boomed. "I found a crate of your father's old English books."

"All the encyclopaedia books?" When she was a little girl her father used to balance her on his knee and read from the *Encyclopaedia Britannica*. "Is his copy of *The Household Physician* there too?"

"I'm sure so." He nodded. "I also discovered the old ancestral portraits stacked in a room at the back, aahh."

"What do you mean, not the portraits of Grand-aunty Ying?" Lu See contorted her face to look like a witch.

Uncle Big Jowl started sniggering. "The original bride of Frankenstein."

"Must've scared the hell out of the Japs when they first set eyes on her, she's about as good looking as a basket of crabs."

"*Ai-yooo!* Don't be cruel to the crabs."

They laughed, clapping the air with their hands.

"And what about those poor looters? Can you imagine what they must have thought, breaking in here in the dead of night and seeing those beady eyes staring down at them!"

"Must have pee-peed in their sarongs."

"And turned to stone." Uncle Big Jowl's guffaw was rich and rolling.

As they bent double with laughter, the gloom retreated for an instant.

For the last three years Lu See had forced herself to be stoic. She'd closed her mind to the sleepless nights, the stories of Kempeitai arrests, the talk of raided homes and vanishing

185

friends. Instead, she'd tried to make her home life as normal as possible; she made sure nobody missed a birthday, a dumpling ceremony or a Chinese New Year dinner, even if the shortage of sugar and eggs made the cakes less sweet and the dumplings less rich.

"Your birthday's not far away," she said tousling her daughter's hair. "Maybe we can clean up the house in time."

"When is it *your* birthday, Mama? You never say and we never celebrate."

"That's because I don't like being reminded of it."

"Why?"

"Because I don't!" Lu See cringed at the harshness of her own voice. She immediately smuggled the image of Adrian grappling up King's Chapel roof to the back of her mind. "I'm sorry, I didn't mean to shout."

"That's okay, Mama." Lu See smiled into Mabel's eyes. When Mabel smiled back she really lit up. Lu See called her 'my brave little *pendekar* warrior' and she'd done everything possible to protect her from the horrors inflicted by the Japanese.

"Children aren't scared of a thorn bush until they get one snagged on their leg," she said to Uncle Big Jowl at the height of the terror. "As long as I keep her out of sight, she'll be fine."

"But she has eyes; you can't hide the ugliness from her. When two buffaloes fight it is the grass that gets trampled, aahh."

Her daughter was almost nine years old and throughout the entire war Lu See had seen her cry only once and it wasn't even the day her grandfather died. It was the day they'd been forced from their home; the day Mabel's childhood innocence ended.

Uncle Big Jowl used to say that what he loved most about Tamarind Hill was that it was so calming. But in 1942 the Japanese shattered that peace. They swarmed in from the north, from near the Thai border. They came overland, but rather than slink through the jungle they pushed down the north-south road on lorries and bicycles. And as they swept through villages and towns they frisked whomever they came across and relieved them of their cash and wrist-watches. When they reached Tamarind Hill the soldiers told everyone to form a line and pulled the youngest female servants to one side and bundled them into the back of a truck. Lu See came dashing out to protest and immediately saw that it was a hopeless cause; the Japanese had fixed their bayonets in anticipation of trouble; there were already 18 to 20 village girls huddled together in the rear of the truck, all frozen stiff with fear. Some had bloodied noses and mouths. They would have seized Lu See too if Colonel Tozawa had not appeared on the scene soon after.

The Colonel stood on the seat of his open top scout car and to the ululating cries of the victims declared that only three girls per village would be acquired. "Staff sergeants, I want to make this clear. Keep a rein on your men. Any breach of this order and the culprits will answer to me personally. Three per village, no more, no less. We must maintain discipline!"

"Mama, they're taking Ah Ling away!" bawled Mabel.

"I know," Lu See replied, trying to block out the wailing. White-faced, she wrapped her hands round Mabel's shoulders and shielded her with her own body. "Look at the ground Mabel, look at the ground, don't look up," she said, struggling to keep the hysteria from her own voice.

From that day on, through to the end of the war, both Mabel and Lu See flinched each time they heard a truck pull up, their hearts skipping a beat or two.

Ah Ling was the kitchen maid; a young cheerful provincial girl. She was 23 years old. Lu See never saw her again.

With Tamarind Hill back in her possession Lu See worked from dawn til dusk; she ploughed the land, dug up the spent stalks of lemongrass and the last of the onions and sewed fresh seeds into the soil – easy crops like tapioca and sweet potato. Bit by bit she put the house back together. She aired the rooms, swept the floors of shattered glass, fixed up the bedrooms, put fresh sheets on the beds, set out rat traps and boarded up the broken windows. She also began bringing back items from the village tip which had been abandoned by looters, things like a dressmaker's mannequin, old umbrellas and walking sticks, even a badly damaged sewing machine. They were things she hoped she could barter one day; trade for food perhaps? If anything, the Japanese occupation had taught her to be frugal.

Meanwhile, Peter and James used their carpentry skills to replace the damaged floorboards and door handles and erected a swing in the garden out of an old bicycle wheel. Mother made clothes from old curtains and cut slippers from ruined rubber tyres; the dresses Mother sewed for Mabel often even had pleats on them, like a window blind.

They were long, exhausting days and at night, streaked with dust, with the sun setting, Lu See would slip Adrian's old wristwatch off her wrist and slump on a chair. The wristwatch had stopped ticking long ago but Lu See could not bear to dispose of it – not just yet. It was as if Adrian were still with her as long as she kept the watch close to her pulse.

For these brief moments, with the wristwatch loosened, Mabel rubbed palm oil into her mother's rough hands to soothe the calluses and moisten the cracked skin. After which Lu See ran a comb through Mabel's hair, teasing the knots out, before arranging it into a long plait.

Several weeks had passed since the Japanese surrender. Behind the big house, in the old vegetable garden, Mabel found Peter and James picking through the weeds as they pulled lemon grass shoots from the earth. Both wore over-size civil service shorts. As usual they were squabbling.

"Certainly not. No, I won't do it," said James, eyes protruding like marbles. He started to perform jumping jacks and recite the book of Ruth.

Peter folded his arms across his chest and threw him a dark glance. "Well, I'm telling you the meeting is at nine tomorrow morning and you're expected to explain what happened."

"Are you deaf? I said I'm not doing it."

"Well somebody has to account for why five hundred sheets were issued with the wrong overprint."

"They'll just have to classify it as printer's waste."

"Even so, somebody has to take responsibility."

"I'm not doing it!" With a violent yank James jerked a handful of lemongrass over his head. Bits of soil and earth dribbled down his collar and the back of his neck.

"Watch it! Clumsy!"

"Oh quiet!"

Lu See appeared at Mabel's shoulder. "What on earth are the two of you bickering about now?"

Peter rolled his bulging eyes, shaking the dirt from his shirt. "Your genius brother here allowed the 'Rebirth' stamp series to be overprinted with *Burmese Occupation* all across the face. The Inspector General is furious."

Lu See tried to suppress a smile. "James, you nitwit, didn't you check the proofs?"

"Look, I can't be expected to work the new system."

"And what system is that," said Peter, shouldering his brother aside. "The one that sends letters across the world with postage stamps saying we've suddenly been overrun by the Burmese?"

"You're the one in charge of quality control."

"But you're meant to check for imperfections."

"And it's your job to sign it off."

"As Jehovah is my witness you are the most incompetent person I have ever worked with."

"To be precise: so are you."

189

"Well at least we agree on something."

"Precisely."

"But you're still in the wrong."

James shook his head. "You are such a *fan-tung*. No wonder Irene Ting refused to marry you."

Lu See, stooping to tend some wild mint, waved her arms in the air. "Truce. Truce."

"Only if James admits he's wrong," said Peter.

"You always have to have the last word, don't you?" shot James.

"I don't."

"See?"

"See what?"

After a while they threatened to glue each other's mouths shut.

Giggling, Mabel glanced at Lu See and winked. "You know, Mama," she said. "Sometimes I'm maximum glad I'm an only child."

"Well, my maximum-glad only child, I have a job for you," said Lu See. "The Japanese used the village church as a stable for their horses. Let's grab some brooms and buckets and clean it up. And when we're finished we're going to go into the jungle and dig up some treasure."

"What treasure?"

"It's something that belongs to the church. You'll see."

Several hours later, the church was looking and smelling like its old self. Lu See and Mabel had scraped and scoured and scrubbed away the stink of the horses. They also managed to restore the pipe organ console and pedal board to something like its former glory. Some of the stop knobs had gone missing and there were some hoof dents in the organ case but Lu See couldn't complain.

"There's not too much damage," she said, running a damp towel over the top panel.

Mabel stepped in and ran her fingers up and down the keyboard. "Why is there no sound?"

"For that we'll have to go into the jungle and dig up the treasure."

With a cock of the head, Uncle Big Jowl grinned, toying with an earlobe. He was at the entrance to the church looking in. "Aahh! You have done wonders."

"Well, somebody had to do it."

"When will we collect the pipes? Maybe after the British regain full control?"

"Yes, let's wait until law and order is fully restored. There are still looters about."

"Your father would be proud of how you've restored not just the church but the house too," he said, puffing on his cheroot.

"If he hadn't taken to the bottle and shot himself he could have seen the end product himself." She detected only a hint of regret in her own voice.

"Drinking hair tonic. Stupid-stupid, aahh."

"Ah-Ba was ill by then. He wasn't right in the head. But what do you expect? The Japanese forced him to sell the rubber estate at $50 an acre to the Mitsui Group. Before the war it was worth what, $300 an acre?"

"More like 400 dollah. Aahh, you know my friend, Perak Suan, aahh, he died last week of lung disease. Don't ever smoke, very bad for you, tell your daughter too."

"Why are you smoking then?"

"This not smoking, this keeps mosquitoes away. My grandfather smoked Sumatran cigars until he was 94."

"And then he died."

"No. He switched to using a pipe. Anyway, I never inhale."

Bemused, Lu See loosened the broken wristwatch on her wrist and gave the skin beneath a rub. She shook her head. "What were we talking about?"

"Japanese buying rubber estate from your father, aahh," he said, cocking his head.

"Yes, and then they seized his Bentley."

"Which they had the gall-galls to call a gift to the Imperial Nippon Government." The big man snorted, rubbed the tip of his head with cigar ash and shook out his shirt. "Gave him a certificate and called it a gift. Bloody robbers, aahh."

She remembered her father withdrawing deep into himself. By then they were living in the Chinese-style dwelling by the river. He barricaded himself in the wet kitchen with a revolver and drank. When he finished the whisky he went on to the last of the brandy, and then he turned to the hair tonic and aftershave, and finally to the gun. *Huffed and puffed and blew his brains out.*

When she was at her lowest ebb she'd think about this. She'd think about the day she found him with the top of his head blown off.

Lu See puffed her cheeks out. "You know, near the end, his hands shook so much he couldn't hold his razor steady. I had to shave him myself."

Uncle Big Jowl placed his thumb and index finger to his throat. "Damn-fierce tragedy. Life is like this, without head or tail."

At the mention of her Ah-Ba a curious cold had flooded Lu See's veins. Now she went outside and sat on the church steps. She shut her eyes and pressed her palms to them.

5

The following day, with the sun filtering through the tamarinds, Lu See and Mabel strolled down the windy road that led to the village. Mabel jumped and skipped behind her mother. "What are we going to buy from Mr Ko's shop, Mama?"

"We'll have to see what they have, my little warrior. There's still very little we *can* buy. Everyone's short of food supplies, so I thought I would barter these turnips. With school term starting tomorrow, you'll need a new pair of shoes. I don't know if those rubber-tyre slippers will last much longer."

"Princess shoes? With bows on them?"

"Yes, your majesty," Lu See said, walking backwards, bowing and whirling her hand showily as if greeting royalty. "Bows as big as wings."

Mabel spread her arms out wide and pretended to fly like a bird. "Mama, look at me. I'm a crow. *Caw-caw!*"

They could see the toddy shop in the distance and the palms above swaying; a breeze running through the village had brought children out to fly their kites. Lu See shielded her eyes from the sun, blinking as she plunged from light to shade, and peered over her shoulder at Mabel who now hopped to grab at the vines that trailed from the eucalypti, which stood in silent ranks. Then she broke into a run. She came tearing down the road and skidded to a stop. That was when Lu See saw them through the trees, snaking through the leaf litter.

The guerrillas emerged from out of the jungle like ghosts; it was the first time she had ever seen them in broad day-light; they called themselves the Malayan People's Anti-Japanese Army. Otherwise known as the MPAJA. Their uniforms were a mottled khaki and those that wore caps showed three stars on the rim. Leading them was a man in his late sixties with a face like cracked porcelain and lips as thick as sausages. Lu See noticed a young boy by his side with a Japanese service pistol stuffed in his belt; he couldn't have been more than ten.

Someone from the pith wood shop began to clap and cheer, acclaiming them liberators; others, in quieter voices, branded them vigilantes. A dog tied to a coconut tree barked as they approached. The chickens scattered and the village goose honked. Grasping the handle of her turnip basket, Lu See watched the group strut down the main street, heads held high and shoulders thrown back. There were one or two Malays amongst them but the majority of the bedraggled-looking fighters were undoubtedly Chinese.

They barged into the toddy shop. After a short while they reappeared, dragging a man by the heels. His face was already swelling from numerous blows. The villagers gath-ered in the square. Almost immediately, Lu See recognized the white suit.

"Japanese informer!" a woman shrieked, baring her teeth. "He's the one that accused my husband of keeping a wireless radio, saying he listened to Allied broadcasts."

"He's a Woo!" someone yelled.

"So what if he is! He knows what's coming to him!"

Kneeling, the man lifted his hands towards the gathering crowd, sobbing like a child, pleading for their help. The onlookers stood paralyzed.

One of the MPAJA soldiers shoved him with his foot.

Lu See stood on her toes, straining to see if it was who she thought it was. The MPAJA soldier struck him in the face. His head twisted. There was a mole on his cheek.

Mabel looked at her mother in alarm. Quick as a shot, with the man's screams ringing in his ears, Lu See took her daughter's hand but Mabel's leg muscles had locked with fright. "We must go," hissed Lu See. *"Now."*

The little girl's feet suddenly came alive. "Yes, Mama."

"Don't look back, Mabel. Whatever you do don't look back."

There was a thud of wood on bone as they drove their rifle butts into the man's chest. The snap of ribs reverberated around the village square. Lu See quickened her stride, almost pulling at Mabel to keep pace.

The dog continued to bark.

"What about her!" someone yelled. "The one that worked for the Colonel!" Other voices joined in, surrounding her like a blanket, but the pulsing in Lu See's ears drowned out all sound, all thought. Her instinct was to get away, as fast as possible. Turning past the toddy shop, she dropped the basket of turnips. She and Mabel hurried up the windy road towards the big house, close to sprinting now, feeling as though at any second someone was going to grab them from behind and pull them down.

The sun beat down. But despite the heat from the day Lu See's blood ran cold.

That night Mabel fell asleep in her mother's arms. Having kissed her eyes shut, Lu See caressed her daughter's head and then carefully removed Mabel from her bosom. She went to the verandah and stood in the shadow of the moon. Her mother appeared at her shoulder. "Are you all right? Hungry?"

Curtly: "I'm fine."

"You cannot tell lies to me. Your face the same as when you eat bitter marrow."

"I said I'm fine." She folded her arms. "I'm always fine. I've been fine all my life. Forthright, resilient and fine, that's me." She turned her mouth down.

"Don't make that face, Lu See. Your father hates it when you make that face."

"Ah-Ba's dead, Mother."

"I know he's dead. What makes you think I don't know he's dead?" She shook her head.

"You still sleep with his slippers at the foot of your bed."

Mother ignored that. "Mabel told me what happened today in town."

"It was nothing, just a settling of old scores. They got hold of one of the informers." Lu See pictured the man the MPAJA soldiers were attacking. It was him, she was certain of it; it was the Black-headed Sheep.

"Nothing?" Mother shot her a look. "What do you mean nothing? They killed the man. They strapped his body to the angsana tree by the church and placed a sign over his head. There's talk that he was a Woo as well."

Lu See covered her mouth. "So he's finally dead." She closed her eyes, wishing she could share the news with Sum Sum.

"I heard you were chased," said Mother.

"We weren't chased." She rubbed the skin of her forehead. "I wish Mabel wouldn't make things up."

"This would not happen if you had husband. Your father, he felt the same every time we discussed you, he got worried sick, saying, 'She must find a husband before she turn old like dried prune.'"

Lu See didn't want to get into this – the last time they talked about her widowhood her mother made out she was responsible for her father's depression. All that worrying, she claimed, made his mind bloat up, like a balloon full of heavy water.

"And then you ran away to England and came back with a baby!"

Uncle Big Jowl appeared at the door. "Baby? Someone pregnant? Not you, Lu See?"

Lu See pinched finger and thumb to the bridge of her nose, dramatically. "No, I'm not pregnant."

"So, who?" Nonplussed, he looked to his sister then to his niece; when neither replied he left the room.

Mother shook her head. She looked at her hands for several moments. "Shameful, meh, that your father should kill himself like he did." She sighed. "Now I have to wear my grief like an open wound."

Lu See squeezed the skin between her eyes again. They'd found him barricaded in the wet kitchen with the gun by his side and an arterial spray of red garlanding the wall. His body lay at a grotesque angle and at first Lu See couldn't work out why the top of her father's skull was missing, why his tongue hung on his chin, why there was a sliding mass of blackness over his forehead. That was when she registered the flies. Swarming like a black bubbling crust over the angry raw flesh.

They placed a towel over his face and together she and Mother scrubbed the blood and brain scrapings off the wall, unable to say a word. They looked at one another as if to ask *are you okay?* But they weren't okay. They wouldn't be okay for a long, long time. They rolled a blanket out and helped set him down, stretched out as if asleep. They covered all the mirrors in the house and left him in the main room smelling of camphor and oil-smoke; just sat and watched over him until the city policeman arrived. There was no wake, no fancy funeral. They couldn't even afford chrysanthemums.

"Call me old fashioned, nah, but you should have a man to support and protect you. At this rate only man who will come for you is undertaker when you old. Tell me, who will take care of you, Lu See, when I die?"

"Mother, please."

"And you are already so lonely to boots."

"I'm not lonely."

"You should have married Cheam Chow when you had the chance."

"Shouldn't you be telling me to take my time, to wait for love to come to me, to be careful and not get hurt?"

"No." Mother stared at her, motionless. "You should find a man. You want me to speak to matchmaker?"

"*No*, I do not." Lu See folded her arms across her chest and turned away.

"Mabel, your daughter, she needs a father figure, but no, you too stubborn to marry."

Lu See snapped. "I *was* married once. And he died! Or have you forgotten?"

"Not forgotten." She tilted her head this way and that. "Nobody has forgotten. Especially not the Woos. When you returned from England without Adrian, many of them reproached you! They still reproach you." Mother saw the look in Lu See's eyes and extended a consoling arm. "All I'm saying is you should have married *aaa-gain*, find someone to take care of you, take care of Mabel. Now look what happens, people chase you down the street."

"Oh for God's sake!" Lu See couldn't hide the annoyed twang in her voice.

"Not God's sake, young lady, it is our sake I'm worried about. I told you time and time again, don't work for the Japanese. I said if they lose the war there will be all hells to pay."

"How else was I to bring food to the table? How else was I going to keep the family from harm?" Mother pretended not to hear. She seemed to be able to suck the insides of her ears shut. She scratched her palms. "Whatever you think, Tozawa protected us."

"And who will protect us now, meh?"

A pointed silence.

Remorse etched across Lu See's face, peeking out like the tips of an adulterer's shoes from behind a curtain.

"They will come for you eventually," said Mother. She

sipped from a cup of tea, which she placed on the verandah ledge by the trails of bougainvillea. "They will call you lousy traitor and shave your head and tear your clothes from your shoulders like call girl."

"Trust you to say such a thing."

"What? You want me to put sugar in my mouth and tell you sweet lies? I'm simply warning you. They will tie a can to your tail and run you out of town. Best maybe if we all go to Kuala Lumpur where nobody know you."

"I've done nothing wrong. I'm not going run away like a criminal."

"*Cha!* You putting us all at risk."

"I'm staying. It will all get better when the British return, just wait and see."

"Stubborn. Pig-headed. Proud." Mother prodded her finger at Lu See with each adjective. "You say you spend the whole war protecting Mabel and now with new danger loomings you choose to do nothing."

Lu See gave an exhausted sigh. Her mother always fiddled with her head like this, like a dentist picking at a painful tooth. "I am not choosing to do nothing. I am standing my ground. I haven't done anything wrong."

"You sided with the Japanese."

"I never sided with them."

"What do you mean never?" she hissed at her.

Lu See wanted to throttle her mother senseless. She wanted to grab her by the throat and shake her. Not because she was asking for it. Not because she deserved it. Simply because it would shut her up.

"I worked for Tozawa because I knew he would shield us – you, me and Mabel – from other Japanese. It was self-preservation."

"There is no law-order here. One stray accusation, one lazy-bits of finger-pointing and they will come with fire torches and burn this house down. Their rice is boiling over."

"Mother, you're being silly. We just have to be patient; it will soon die down."

"Patience was never your strong point."

"The villagers know us. We've always been good to them."

"Damn-short memories. They forget all we did for them before the war. What they remember now is that you worked for Colonel Tozawa, in his household."

"And that's all it was, work, simple, honest hard work. I didn't betray anyone. I didn't exploit anyone." Lu See swung at a trailing bougainvillea vine with her hand, but it was her voice that was thorned with anger. "I didn't sleep with the bloody man. I wasn't his bloody mistress!"

"Foolish and stubborn, that's what you are." Mother snatched her cup of tea from the verandah ledge and retreated indoors. As she disappeared she called out of the gloom: "Come, nah, if you are hungry. I will cook you something to eat, no more talk."

A light rain began to fall. Every plap, plop and sploosh seemed to be trying to tell Lu See something. *Is Mother right?* she wondered. *Should I pack up and run? Would they really cut off my hair?*

Lu See felt her breath pull tight. She trembled. The night was beginning to cool but she wasn't cold. A tremulous sense of playing with fire seized her. There was something she had to do.

She stared in the direction of the village, but her gaze went beyond the tiny swell of yellow lights in the distance. She needed to see the body.

Somewhere in the distance Lu See heard the sounds of firecrackers exploding. *Or is it gunshots?* She couldn't be sure.

As she made her way down the drive she could see the silhouette of the church up ahead, lit by the light of the three-quarter moon. She rubbed her hand over her face and then hid her trembling hands under her armpits.

She crossed the field.

The angsana tree waited for her. Stalks of tall grass on either side of it were trampled down. There were footprints in the mud left by the men who had strung him up.

Her heart beat like a hammer against cloth. She approached the tree and noticed a stool had been kicked away from under him. She forced herself to look up.

The men had left him for the crows and monitor lizards to feed on.

The body swayed gently from the hanging rope. The noose was tight to the trachea; it made his face contort like a gargoyle from a cathedral perch. Mouth pulled taut in a grimace, chin on his chest, eyes open.

She searched his face in the dim light. *Yes,* she said, *there's the mole. It's him pumpkin-head. He's really dead.*

Satisfied, she started back across the field, before pulling up. A shiver went through her. *Wait! There's something not right.* She turned slowly, then ran back to the tree and looked again at the leering skull. The grimacing face seemed to mock her. She reached for the stool and stood on tiptoes. With a sense of revulsion she pushed her hand into the tangle of hair and lifted the head to the moonlight. *There's the mole . . . but . . . there's been a mistake. Something's wrong here. Something's muddled.* And suddenly she realized. *It's on the wrong cheek. The mole is supposed to be on his left cheek not his right. It's not him. It's not the Black-headed Sheep.*

She felt powerless. It was like waking from a nightmare and wanting to scream only to find not a muscle in her throat could move.

For the first time she wished she still had Colonel Tozawa to protect her.

6

As the Tibetan grasslands turned green, the festival of the mountain gods drew a crowd of villagers, all bestowing offerings of food to the deities. They gathered by the *ndekheng*, the village shrine, women on the left, men to the right, to burn conifer branches in the *sangkong* furnace. Dancers beat rectangular goatskin drums and swayed in circles, entreating the heavens to grant a bountiful harvest. And in the centre of it all the *lhawa*, the trance medium, spoke in garbled tongues, exorcising the soil of evil, as his male disciples pierced their cheeks with long metal needles.

Not far away, assembled under the shade of a tree, Sum Sum and her fellow novices sat at Jampa's feet. Wild flowers grew everywhere, pale green shoots pushing up through the dry earth. They were in the middle of a lesson on the sacred Ayurvedic texts.

"Caterpillar Fungus," Jampa expatiated. "We use its flesh to strengthen the body's immunity and to regulate blood pressure." She removed something from the lining of her robes and made a click-clack noise with her tongue. "*Ndug're*, here we have a piece of Indian Snakeroot. You identify it by its lush green leafage and black berries but the part we use is the root. The story goes that a man from Burma watched a mahout feeding this root to his uptight elephants to pacify them. Now it is used as a hypertension drug in the West."

Sum Sum had heard much of this all before. Her mother had been a 'tip-top medicine woman'. Listening to prayer hall manager Jampa drone on about indigenous herbs and their role in medical science was like listening to the ticking of an old clock with the pendulum oscillating lazily from side to side. It was lulling her to sleep. She felt her eyelids droop and her jaw muscles tweak.

Her boredom must have registered on her face because Jampa called out her name, "Sengemo!" she commanded with a smile that could eat through steel wool. "Will you kindly summarise what I just said."

Taken aback, Sum Sum blinked. She hadn't been expecting a question. Unnerved and a little embarrassed, she recovered by mumbling something about an elephant.

Without giving her a chance to expand, Jampa thrust her right hand under Sum Sum's nose. "Smell that?"

Drawing everyone's attention to the bit of dried tuber in her hand she began to bay. "Snakeroot," Jampa bellowed in the manner of a lunatic reciting her mathematics tables. "Known in Sanskrit as *chandrika*. Treats hypertension. High-blood pressure. Lowers fevers. Harmful to women during pregnancy. Also used as antidote to the bites of venomous snakes." She glared at Sum Sum. "Sadly, it does not help to concentrate the mind. And don't sulk, Sengemo, it ruins your face."

It was turning out to be a bad day. Only that morning Sum Sum had been scolded by the caretaker of the temple for startling the reclusive abbess. The abbess had been seated at a bench that overlooked the valley, enjoying a sense of calm. She was singing a quiet, rambling mantra to herself, a hundred-syllable hymn. Nobody was to disturb her. The dawn air was fresh and cooling; there were birds twittering in the trees. She was halfway through the Vajrasattva *yik gya* when Sum Sum, without waiting for permission, promptly sat down by her side.

"Ai-yoo, beautiful sunrise, no? They call me Sengemo. What's your name?"

Sum Sum had barely perched herself on the bench when the *tsampa* really hit the fan. The caretaker of the temple rushed out from the shadows with her finger wagging and her robes flapping. "What in the name of Moggul and Trazil do you think you are doing?" she hissed like a wounded adder. "Leave Her Reverence alone! This is her quiet time! Away! Away!"

The abbess glared at Sum Sum, eyes fixed like twin cannonballs. "Give her fifty lines of the *Tengyur* to copy out."

How was I to know she was the abbess? Sum Sum complained to herself over breakfast. *It's not as if she wears a brass nameplate on her chest.* She peered at the shaven-headed septuagenarians slouching over their bowls at high table. *Everyone here over the age of fifty looks alike, lah!*

"Country Mallow, Giloy, Bitter Oleander, Night Jasmine, Khas-khas," Jampa's voice broke into her thoughts. Sum Sum was back under the shade of the tree once more. "Indian Pennywort, Senna, Wild Indigo." Jampa rattled the names off with a crash, thud, bang, like a frenzied woodchopper. "Even the petals of the Hibiscus flower are used in our medicines. Can anyone tell me how we use the Hibiscus?"

A fat little novice raised her hand. She had a round face and the traces of a moustache. Sum Sum thought she could have easily played Oliver Hardy onstage.

"I know all about Hibiscus," she said in a shrill voice. "My grandmother used them for treating her carbuncles."

"*Ndug're!* Very good. Yes, beat the flowers into a paste and use as a poultice over the swelling."

"What about you, Tormam, what do you know of Hibiscus?"

Everyone looked over at the shy person sitting near the back. Sum Sum immediately recognized her as the young woman who slept beside her in the dormitory. On hearing her name, Tormam blushed and stuttered. "I . . . it . . . it can be used to heal . . . the leaves can be crushed and mixed with water . . . to help problems with the passage of urine."

"*Ndug're!*" beamed Jampa.

Just then they all heard the sound of an aircraft overhead.

"Iron bird!" someone shouted. A small black speck moved slowly across the bright, white clouds.

"Come," said Jampa. "Let us go now in search of Yarchagumba."

Yarchagumba was a fungus that grew on the heads of caterpillars. The ancient Tibetans knew it as the 'herb of life' and believed it had the power to cure headaches, respiratory ailments and impotency. Once a week, during the summer months, the novices were instructed to enter the Sera Valley and fill five baskets with it.

The women traipsed off into the meadows in search of the larvae. Flies followed them and buzzed about their faces. They descended the steep valley and came to a pasture with moist ground. Here they crouched and began sifting through the dirt with their hands. All around them were the mountains. The wind blew sheets of white powder from the top of the peaks.

"Found one!" cried Sum Sum. She held aloft a dead caterpillar. The fungus visibly sprouted from the top of the creature's head like a set of horns. Tormam came over with a basket. Together they raked the ground for over an hour, pushing their fingers into the soil, occasionally pulling out a scaly-skinned insect.

At noon the sound of another passing aircraft distracted them. Sum Sum squinted and looked up. She saw the iron bird falling from the sky, half-rolling and then diving.

Moments later they all heard a crash. There was a clatter of steel against steel and the thud shook the ground. Jampa paled visibly; Sum Sum jumped. It felt as if someone had thrown a large sack of rice at her feet. Before anyone else could react, Sum Sum and Tormam were racing across the valley floor towards the downed plane.

It was a C-87 and it had crash-landed in an area of countryside devoid of trees and people. Sum Sum saw a long black trail gouged in the fresh grass and the metal fuselage shining in the sun two hundred metres away. The starboard wing was missing and there was damage to the tail; the closer she got the more she feared the plane would catch fire.

Sum Sum felt Tormam's hand on her arm. "The men in the plane. Will they be dead?" asked Tormam. "I'm scared to see the blood."

"We must try to help them. If you see blood just imagine it's strawberry jam."

Tormam looked nonplussed. "What is this strawberry jam?"

Parts of the engine were hissing. It sounded like gas escaping from a radiator. Sum Sum climbed up onto the main body of the aircraft. She tried to slide back the cockpit hood but it was jammed. She rubbed frost off the surface of the window and peered through the glass.

The crew sat upright in their seats. Their faces were hidden by their goggles and breathing masks. Not one of them moved. They looked asleep.

By now, the others had arrived. Most of the initiates, together with prayer hall manager Jampa, simply stood there, clutching the skirts of their robes, unsure how to proceed.

"Fetch me a large stone," ordered Sum Sum.

Someone reached over and handed her a tapered rock the size of a bitter melon. Shielding her eyes, Sum Sum smashed the glass of the cockpit and removed the splintered debris. The three-man crew remained in their seats, strapped in tight. The pilot was in his flying suit. His gloved hands still grasped fast upon the stick.

Sum Sum crawled into the cockpit. One by one, she placed her fingertips on each man's neck. She took a deep breath. It confirmed what she'd already suspected – the crewmen were all dead.

There was no blood. No arms or legs were twisted into knotted shapes. They'd either died from the impact or from oxygen deprivation.

One of the other novices climbed into the compartment before Sum Sum could stop her. Entranced, she began to fiddle with the pilot's buckles, trying to undo the straps. When that failed she placed a hand on the throttle, then started to twiddle with a reflector light. She played with a trigger and flicked a red button from *safe* to *fire*.

"Stop that!" Sum Sum commanded.

Other novices peered through the cockpit entrance now. Rather than look at the dead crewmen, they reached in and fingered the displays by the instrument panel. Hands tapped against the oil pressure gauge. Thumbs pressed the rev counter, the altimeter, the oxygen and petrol dials.

"Stop it!" cried Sum Sum.

"Who made you the abbess?" protested the Oliver Hardy lookalike in a shrill voice.

"There may be bombs aboard. What you want to do, blow us all up?"

When all the novices scurried away, Jampa's face appeared at the cockpit roof. "Are they Americans?" she asked, panting.

Sum Sum nodded. "Yes, look, here are the eagle wings on his chest. And see, lah? It says USAAF on the flight suits."

"But the war with Japan is over. The Dalai Lama announced it Himself. The Japanese surrendered. Why are these planes still flying? Why do they keep airlifting weapons over the Himalayas?"

Sum Sum spotted a paper dossier by the pilot's hip with the words *Top Secret* stamped on its face. She undid the fastener. Inside there were charts and hand-drawn maps. The words were written in English.

Sum Sum finished reading and looked at Jampa who had been studying her every expression. "According to this, the Americans are preparing for a new war in China. A war between the Chinese Nationalists and the Chinese Communists. This time, I think the battle is going to be waged closer to home."

Jampa and Sum Sum stared at one another. They heard the door of the hold being forced open. It was the villagers. They'd arrived on their horses. Already they were stripping the plane clean.

Seconds later they made out a groan. One of the airmen was still alive.

They lifted the injured airman into a yak-hide blanket and carried him back to the nunnery.

They laid him flat on the courtyard floor, under the shadows of an overhanging eave. One of the novices knelt by his side and placed a cooling jasmine cloth to his forehead. Sum Sum lifted a bowl to his mouth. The taste of the warm butter tea appeared to soothe him. Carefully, they removed his flying jacket and undid the front of his shirt to ease his breathing.

Everyone gathered round to get a look.

The whispering ceased as soon as the abbess emerged from her rooms. Like sparrows stilled by the shadow of a hawk, everyone grew quiet.

Looking harassed, Jampa bowed her head and spoke first. "He came through the clouds on an iron bird, over the great mountains."

The abbess stood back and examined the airman critically from a distance as she would a yak whose milk had grown sour. "We have very strict rules. Men are not allowed."

"We understand that, your reverence," said Jampa between tightened lips. "However, the stranger's wounds seem grave."

"You must take him to the monastery. The High Abbott will decide how to treat him. Only he has the ripeness and wisdom for such things."

"But if we move him he will die," Sum Sum challenged. "We can save him if he stays here. The monastery is several miles away."

Jampa click-clacked her tongue, anxious to diffuse the tension in the air.

Radiating disapproval, the abbess locked eyes with Sum Sum. "We know nothing of his kind. Look at him; he has ink pictures on his chest. These white men are men of war, they are as hard as their far-flung accents. We must leave this to the High Abbott. And you, Sengemo, must learn to hold your tongue. You are in a nunnery now. You cannot say something simply because you want to. Continue showing dissent and you will find yourself struggling to remain here."

Sum Sum nodded gravely back at her but did not lower her eyes submissively. She felt no regret about speaking out. Affronted, the abbess shook out her robes and retreated to her rooms, vanishing through a little doorway.

Sum Sum fixed her thoughts on the abbess's words. The phrase 'struggling to remain here' took on new meaning. She gave a puff of exhaustion and felt a flutter of emotions – defiance, pride, anger and dread. It was the dread of being alone once more. But right now she didn't care what the abbess thought. She'd done a good thing. She'd helped save a man's life. And if they didn't appreciate her then she would leave.

Sum Sum marched off towards her dormitory. The whispering began again as soon as she was out of sight.

7

It was late afternoon of the Mid-Autumn Festival and a fortnight into the Malayan liberation.

The day had been stifling – to Uncle Big Jowl it was like being smothered by a steaming-hot towel in a barbershop. Slouched in the coolest nook of the big house, he fanned his sweaty cheeks with a banana leaf, wearing the expression of a man who had just realized he'd boarded the wrong bus.

From the garden he heard the violent thud of hammer on nail; from the kitchen he smelt the warm red-bean perfume of freshly baked moon cakes.

Mabel, in flannel pyjamas, padded across the floor in bare feet and sat on his lap. "Your mother traded some old umbrellas for a packet of red bean paste, I see," he said. "Aahh, if you become as resilient as her, I will be proud."

"Guess what?" said Mabel. "Uncles Peter and James are squabbling again."

"*Ai-yoo*, such bloody nincompoops. In the old days we were lucky, aahh! Nobody really ever argued apart from your grandfather and Second-aunty Doris, God rest their souls." Uncle Big Jowl removed a monogrammed hankie from his pocket and wiped his brow. "In those days, living in such a big home with so many others, if you didn't like someone, aahh, it didn't matter. You had an argument with your brother? So what! You go sit at dinner with your uncle or your sister or your nephew, or your sister-in-law or one of your five nieces. Every meal was twenty, maybe thirty people, sometimes more. And after we eat we play mah-jong."

Mabel stared up at the huge, glistening face. "More than thirty people?" She rested her face on his tummy as if it were an overstuffed pillow.

Uncle Big Jowl rocked her on his lap then winced. "*Ai-yooo!* Bloody arthritic knees! This fifty-eight-year-old body's no good, lah!" He wiped his brow again and shook out his shirt. "Family and friends all mixing together like jigsaw puzzle in a box. After a while you forget you ever had an argument with your brother in the first place."

Just as he said this, two raised voices interrupted the nail-hammering.

They went to see what the squabbling was about this time, Uncle Big Jowl swaying from side to side as he walked. "*Ai-yoooo!* What on earth are you pair of maddos doing now?"

"What does it look like we're doing?" answered Peter, hitching up his oversize shorts. He had a mallet in his hand. His gaze was bright yet glassy like a radical priest with an opium habit. "We are preparing for the second coming! I'm building James' coffin."

"And I'm building Peter's. His is going to be a Toe Pincher."

"Next, we're going to design the lettering for our head-stones."

"But why, aahh, aahh?" exclaimed Uncle Big Jowl, performing a double-cock of the head.

"It's cheaper," said James with a nonchalant shrug, "and it reminds us of our own mortality." He stooped to plane the side of a plywood panel.

"Cheaper?" Peter protested. "This has nothing to do with money."

"I remember you saying it would be a good investment."

"Yes, a *spiritual* investment."

"Nonsense, you were thinking about the money."

"Are you calling me a Cheap-Charlie?"

"I cannot believe you're my brother, we have nothing in common," James sighed.

"Not true, we both like satays. And cabbage and – "

"You are such a child!"

"Oh and you're not!"

Fidgeting in his oversize shorts, James pinched his knee-caps together. "Listen, can we continue this later? I need a pee-pee break."

Uncle Big Jowl looked at Mabel and rolled his eyes. "Pair of top-class nincompoops," he muttered.

Just then Mother and Lu See appeared at the bottom of the drive, waving Union Jack banners to get their attention. "They're coming, they're coming!" Lu See cried. "Hurry! Or you'll miss them! Drop the mallets and grab the mooncakes!"

With several trays of mooncakes in hand, Lu See led the charge as they raced down the windy path into the village. The kampong was lined with cheering people brandishing flags, giving the thumbs up, hopping up and down in excitement. Bunting and messages of welcome hung from the upturned eaves of the village temple. A ribbon of children, arms linked, yelled like mad in front of a home-made *Arc de Triomphe.*

"Here they come!" The crowd pressed forward. A convoy of heavy vehicles kicked up dust in the near distance. The rumble of engines and the rattle, clank and squeak of metal gears and steel springs grew closer. Vickers Light tanks, Bren-gun carriers and armoured cars thundered up, bouncing over ruts, arriving with the hubbub and anticipation of the carnival coming to town. As they slowed to a snail's pace the villagers ran alongside. An officer in a jeep, with his beret folded into his shoulder lapel, made V for Victory signs with both hands. All about him people clapped with glee.

A dozen more Bedfords crawled past as teenage girls teased out their hair, beckoning flirtatiously. Everyone rang their bicycle bells and squeezed their *toot-toot* hand horns. The armoured vehicles slowed and wheezed to a stop to take in the celebratory atmosphere. Bringing up the rear was the infantry – The Royal Lincolnshire Regiment in berets and the Gurkhas in terai hats; row upon row of dark tropical green, chanting and whistling as their boots thrummed the ground.

Lu See stared at the lines of solid Himalayan faces and briefly thought of Sum Sum. Somewhere behind her Uncle Big Jowl waved his Union Jack frantically.

Peter and James began singing 'God Save the King' as others flung rice and coconut shavings into the air. Mr Ko, the shopkeeper, held aloft the village goose which gave an *onk-onk* of complaint. Two little boys, legs lubricated by adrenaline, ran alongside with a handful of wild flowers showering the troops sat along the turrets with yellows and pinks; one of them mounted a tank to shake their hands.

"Where are you heading?" someone yelled.

"Kuala Lumpur!" came the reply.

And then they were gone, like a child's balloon seized by the wind. The last of the armoured trucks sped by, heading south towards the capital, trailing cast-iron drifts of dust to the sound of grinding machinery and lead shot grumbling in a drum. A few of the barefoot boys ran after them.

A firecracker went off in the distance. "*Gung hei! Gung hei!*" cried Lu See, passing out mooncakes to the hungry boys and girls. "Compliments of the Teohs. Enjoy them while they are warm!" Nearby, women from the Woo household removed round cakes from woven baskets, distributing the circular pasteboard packages to the elderly. Lu See exchanged polite nods with them.

The children danced about the village square, banging gongs and watching the sun slide beyond the horizon and oohing as the bright full moon materialized in the sky. Red paper lanterns appeared on the end of long bamboo poles – butterflies, carp and rabbits lit from within by trembling candles.

"Can I play too?" asked Mabel, hopping from foot to foot.

"Of course you can," replied her mother.

Lu See watched the children skip along arm in arm. She

smiled with pride, but jerked her head round on sensing others staring at her. And there they were: the men from the jungle, the MPAJA soldiers. Watching her like buzzards over carrion.

Each of them had similar hard-boned faces – square cheekbones, sharp jaw lines and dull-black hair. The tallest and oldest, thought Lu See, the one barking orders, with the bare chest and fat rubbery lips, he must be the leader.

Strutting with thumbs in belts, they swept around the village square, circling like buzzards. Lu See could smell the sweet scent of their clove cigarettes. She counted their weapons: two of them held *parangs*; the others all carried rifles slung across their shoulders. And then there was the boy too, the one she'd spotted only days earlier, the ten-year-old with the Japanese service pistol stuffed in his belt.

A drunken river fisherman stumbled towards Le See. His dishevelled face resembled a shipwreck with eyelids lowered at half mast. She happened to be right in his line of vision.

"You!" he yelled, spraying spittle and lurching like a boxer on the ropes. Lu See's features pulled tight. "I know you!" She took a step backwards, but he followed. The alcohol made him daring and he was spoiling for a fight. "You are the treacherous woman who sided with Tozawa." Faces pivoted in their direction. The children stopped dancing and banging gongs. Laughter ceased.

The celebratory mood vanished.

"You think just because you are a Teoh you are immune? We dealt with a Woo the other day. Don't think we won't do the same to you." The drunken fisherman, wagging his finger, was joined by the woman from the pith wood store and a barefoot goat herder.

"When we had nothing to eat, she would go and buy him black market sugar!" the woman accused. "I saw with my own eyes!"

"And when she finished her work, his car would drive her to her home, like she was big city concubine!" cited the fisherman.

The goat man began to whip up the crowd, chanting, "Japanese friend, we will find you in the end!" His matted, stringy chin-beard swayed as he strode up to Lu See. She could smell him now, rank and stale like a wet towel in a bag. "What should we do with her?" he bellowed. "Thought you could get away with it, eh?"

Lu See held his gaze, calmly. "Get away with what, exactly?"

"Leave my daughter alone!" cried Mother, clutching Mabel close.

The drunk hiccupped: "Tear off her clothes! Shame her!"

The goatherd pulled a pair of shearing scissors from his knapsack. "We cut the wool from goats and whores," he said.

Uncle Big Jowl, sucking in his stomach, tried to muscle his way in but was seized and held back by several of the villagers as others, a large boisterous group, formed a ring with Lu See at its centre. Lu See felt a woman's nailed hand reach forward to grab at her top. The cloth ripped, exposing her bare shoulder.

"Let's teach her a lesson!" yelled the drunken fisherman.

Just then James stepped forward. He pointed a hand to the moon like an Old Testament prophet. "The upright are the ones that will reside on this earth. The wicked will be cut off from the very world, and as for the treacherous, they will be torn away from it.' Proverbs 2:21. This woman is innocent, leave her be."

The goat herder arched his eyebrows with surprise and glared at James' clean-shaven face, taking in his pop-eyed gaze. "Who the hell are you?"

"I am a lamb of Jehovah."

"Lamb?"

"Yes, lamb. Baa-baa, lamb." James smiled a beatific smile.

Temporarily nonplussed, the goatherd fluttered his hand to shoo James away.

"Happy are the mild-tempered ones, for they shall inherit the earth." James beamed with eye-bursting gusto. "I strongly advise you to leave my sister alone," he said. "She has committed no crimes. And you really ought to shave off that beard. Beards sprout from the forelock of Satan."

"Precisely!" howled Peter from within the melee, finding his voice.

The goatherd shoved James to one side. Lunging, he snatched at a length of Lu See's hair and pushed her to the ground amongst the chicken droppings. She fought back, but the years of grappling with livestock had made the man strong. A strip of teeth and upper gum flashed as he snared another handful of her mane.

"Renounce!" he insisted. "Renounce what you did."

She saw a glint of metal by her left eye. The jaws of his shearing scissors bit into her hair. She let out a short sharp gasp. Black clumps of hair fell to the ground like scorched wheat.

She grasped his wrist, holding him at bay. People, their expressions grim and fortress-like, made clicking sounds of encouragement. They jostled forward, eager to witness the Teoh woman being punished. She waited for someone to cry out that she was innocent, that all this was a huge mistake, but nobody did.

"I've done nothing wrong." Her voice was small and did not sound like her own. "Get Mabel away from here," she heard herself say. The very thought of her daughter watching this made her chest jump and rear. She'd once read about a village in Borneo that apprehended offenders by doping a parrot, taking it to the identity parade and urging it to fly onto the shoulder of the guilty party. Usually the parrot landed on an innocent who, wrongly accused and powerless to do anything about it, was hanged or beaten with bamboo canes. Lu See's predicament felt exactly the same.

Lu See clenched her teeth. Whatever happened she was going to maintain her dignity.

Women tugged their earlobes in consternation. Men watched with the serpent stares of moneylenders. Somewhere in the background she heard Mother objecting vociferously and her brothers pleading.

A momentary stillness settled. And then a gunshot cracked the air.

Lu See looked to see the MPAJA leader with the rubbery lips by her side. Bare-chested, the tall old man aimed his firearm between the goatherd's eyes.

Lu See focused on the leader's smooth, sinewy forearm. She saw the tendons contract as he thumb-cocked the hammer of his revolver; muscles like walnuts pushed under the dark skin. She watched as he adeptly pressed the muzzle a fraction above the goatherd's eyebrows.

His sweat-shined knuckles twitched.

The goatherd's mouth opened and closed like a dying goldfish. The crowd watched transfixed. The goatherd dropped his shearing blades.

Nobody moved; it was as though the entire village had stumbled into the centre of a minefield and didn't know where to place their feet.

All of a sudden Lu See heard herself speak, surprising herself as words tumbled out of her mouth. "Please don't hurt him," she said. "I can see why he is angry, but please don't shoot him."

The tall old man ran a tongue across his rubbery lips. The goatherd's eyes darted about as if for a place to run. But his legs had set with cement.

The old man's finger kissed the trigger, caressing it lightly

"*Hum gaa chaan!* Open your eyes, you miserable lot of satay suckers. You see how this woman is? You accuse her of treachery yet forget how she gives out mooncakes to your children. You threaten her yet when the tables are turned she begs for mercy on your behalf."

The MPAJA leader lowered his revolver and gave the goatherd a kick in the arse to help him on his way. Watching him scuttle off, he threw out a calloused hand, which Lu See clutched. The sky came rushing at her too quickly as he pulled her to her feet; she put a hand on his shoulder to steady herself. "This woman is neither a traitor nor a colluder; she is an asset to this village," he added. "I expect you to treat her as so. *Sai yun tau!* Dead man's head!"

Gasping and almost rigid with shock, Lu See glared at the sea of faces. Her voice trembled. "We have all been through a terrible war," she said. "Some of us have suffered more than others, but let's not kid ourselves - everyone suffered at the hands of the Japanese." Her insides shook like a reed. "Everyone lost someone or something dear to them. We have all swum in the same water, but we are all different; we each have our own personal moral code. Mine was to do whatever I could to protect my family. I worked for Tozawa; it's true; I cooked in his kitchen. But every day felt like I was sacrificing a piece of my soul. In return he paid me a small amount of money. I never gave myself to him. I never revealed any secrets. I never passed him any of your personal information. If you think that is a crime then so be it, but I know I have done nothing wrong. I can hold my head high."

Lu See snapped her mouth shut; she wanted to wail angrily at the crowd, wanted to wave a fist at them. But she just glared at them. The woman from the pith wood shop backed away. The drunken fisherman scratched his throat and beat a retreat to the toddy shop. Ko, the shopkeeper, stared at his feet. Gradually, with embarrassed coughs and guilty collar-tugs, the rest of the squirming throng dispersed.

Mabel rushed up and leapt into her arms. The force of her body sent Lu See back a step.

Lu See buried her face in her daughter's neck. She looked at the tall man and thanked him.

"My name is Foo. My friends call me Fishlips. And this here," – he ran a hand through a boy's straggly hair – "this here is my grandson, Bong. His parents were taken by *Kempeitai*. They never returned."

Lu See smiled at the boy with the Japanese service pistol stuffed in his belt; a boy with thirty-year-old eyes in the face of a ten-year-old. "Hello, Bong. This is my daughter Mabel."

"Hello," he replied, looking Mabel up and down. "You ever held a gun before?"

"Come now, grandson, enough excitement for one day. Time we made camp." He spun on his heels and marched off.

As he turned into the jungle foliage Foo smiled at Lu See as if to say, *You owe me one.* And then he vanished.

Only later, having returned to the big house, when reality set in, did Lu See retreat to the back garden to throw up long pink strands of half-digested mooncake. With a violent shaking she leaned her weight on the wall to recover and realized that her mother had been right all along.

8

That night Lu See found Mother lying flat on her back on the billiard room floor. She had her arm flung above her head. She did not appear to be breathing.

"Mother! Have you fallen? Mother!"

Her mother stirred. There was half a walnut shell over her left eye and a crudely rolled lit cigar smouldering in her ear.

"What the hell–?"

"All okay!" blurted Mother, sounding anything but okay. "This is old-village acupuncture therapy. No need to panic!" she said sounding panicky.

"Why do you have a walnut on your eye?"

"I soaked it in herbal tea. For treating eye disorders. And burning dried moxa leaves in ear helps circulation."

"I didn't know you had an eye disorder?"

"I don't." She lifted a pyjamaed leg and bent it at the knee. "It's my nerves. Seeing what happened to you make them shake all over."

Lu See wanted to tell her not to worry, but what good would that do? All her mother did these days was worry and complain.

"I told you about the reprisals, but you always too stubborn. The shame of seeing you kneeling in the dirt today." Her hand went to her heart. "How can I hold my head up in this community now?"

"It won't be for much longer. I discussed it with Uncle Big Jowl and we've decided to make the move to Kuala Lumpur." Lu See peeked out the window for any sign of villagers. "He will put the house and the remaining acreage up for sale. We will start a new life in the city. Maybe I can open a small restaurant or something."

"Restaurant," Mother said with disdain.

"But there's something Uncle Big Jowl and I have to do before we leave. We have to reclaim the pipes we buried years ago and restore the church organ to its former glory. I owe it to Second-aunty Doris and Tak Ming."

"Restaurant," Mother repeated. "One of the most powerful families in Penang state before the war . . . and now? Running a chop suey house," she spat. "What am I going to do, wash dishes?" Lu See pretended not to listen. "I'm sorry but I still cannot forgive your father selling our land to the Japanese. And for so cheap too! We used to have status . . ." The smoke billowed from her ear. "In one foul-bowel swoop he turned us into paupers! Paupers!"

"Calm down, Mother. I thought your generation was meant to be good at hiding your feelings?"

"How can I hide when your father acted like fishmonger on a hot day? Everything sell, sell, sell."

"His actions kept us alive."

"Alive? Who cares about alive? What about our social standing?"

Exasperated, Lu See made for the kitchen. She brewed herself a cup of Boh tea and leafed through the newspaper. "What's this?" she said, reading a headline. "Mother, Uncle Big Jowl!" she cried, racing into the living room. "Listen to this! It says here that the chairman of Hip Sing Rubber Processing Co. confessed on his deathbed that he was responsible for the 1935 dynamiting of the Juru River dam. He claimed he did it in an attempt to ruin the nearby plantations and buy up land on the cheap."

Her uncle winced. "Bloody no-good scoundrel, aahh! That fellow like a spider creeping behind a stone."

"Wait, there's more. It says that he conspired with the late Woo Hak-yeung, an unashamed Japanese collaborator, who had been cast out of the Woo clan years before. Woo Hak-yeung's body was discovered hanging from a tree in Juru last week in what was believed to be a retaliation killing."

"Woo Hak-yeung was known as the Black-headed Sheep," said Uncle Big Jowl.

"The man with the mole. So it was him. He really is dead. I must have been wrong; the MPAJA did kill him. Don't you see what this means? It means an end to our feud with the Woos."

"Nonsense," said Mother, walnut still attached to her eye like a pirate's patch, "this feud started years before that bloody dam-bursting."

"But we can start afresh now. Forgive and forget."

"The Woos never forget. Never!" said Mother, removing the smoking cheroot from her ear.

Lu See puffed out her cheeks. "Well, I have never had an issue with them."

"They will always see us as their enemies," Uncle Big Jowl said. "Look how they treat Mabel, their own granddaughter. They refuse to acknowledge her."

"Well, in order to know your enemy you must befriend him, or at least pretend to be his friend, no?"

Uncle Big Jowl fanned himself with a banana leaf. "What are you suggesting, Lu See?"

"We ask them over."

Uncle Big Jowl's chin dropped comically like an accordion jaw. "Ask them over? What, aahh, to a tea party?" He laughed, pretending to hold a teacup with his pinkie in the air. "Cucumber sandwiches on the lawn, snooty British-style?"

"I was thinking more a shot of coconut toddy."

"*Hnn*, this country in middle of a food crisis and you want to host a party, is it?" smirked Mother.

"I'm trying to mend bridges. I want to talk with Matriarch Woo."

"That stubborn old sow? *Cha!*"

"You will only provoke them, aahh. Speaking of provoke," he said to Mother, starting one of his tangents. "Eye injury can provoke cataracts. You should remove the walnut."

"When was the last time a Teoh asked a Woo to anything?" said Lu See, feeling a flicker of impatience.

The big man scratched his forehead. "Apart from to knock heads together like coconuts? Never. At least not in my lifetime."

"Well, there you have it. Time to put that right."

Uncle Big jowl shrugged. "Better to have Indian pissing out of wigwam than have him pissing in."

The next day Lu See ground her ink stick onto some water and, using a brush, composed an invitation on a Chinese scroll, carefully writing the important family names in black lettering. When she finished and dabbed dry the ink she sent a barefoot village boy round to Swettenham Lodge, the Woo compound, to deliver it.

"What, lah?" the townspeople asked. "It must be a trick."

Within hours Lu See received a reply – a short one-word response accepting her offer of drinks.

From a cabinet in the billiard room Lu See brought out the only glasses she had in the house, a set of mismatched goblets, and set them out on the dining table. She wiped her hand on her skirt and realized her hands were sweating.

"*Chee-chee!* This is how trouble starts," said Mother. "When you invite a cobra into your house, expect nothing but trouble." She eyed the mismatched goblets. "You better prepare some small chow. People come expecting food. You better pick up your socks if you want to do everything on time."

"I think the expression is 'pull your socks up', Mother."

"You look nervous. Do you feel nervous?"

Irritated, Lu See snapped, "Yes, Mother, I am nervous. Aren't you?"

"Why should I be nervous? You are the one who invite them." She removed her spectacles and polished the lenses against her sleeve. "All this your idea."

"Yes, I'm well aware of that."

Mother tilted her head this way and that. "And a bad idea to boots. How many of them do you expect will come?"

Lu See took a cloth and wiped the goblets of dust. "I think we'll see the head of the family and perhaps one of his sons."

"One of Adrian's brothers, meh?"

Lu See swallowed and felt her throat catch. "I expect so."

Her mother shook her head and scratched her palms. "You know they'll come here and start blaming you for his accident."

Lu See gritted her teeth. "Well, I can't change that. I'll just have to swallow it."

"If you didn't run off to England he would still be alive, I bet that is what they say."

"Mother!" She threw the cloth onto the table in protest. "Have you any idea how hurtful your comments can be sometimes?"

"Hurtful? How? No, why hurtful, hurtful to who-ah?"

"To me, to all of us. What is it with you?" she challenged.

"I speak my mind, that's all. And if you don't like . . ." She washed her hands in the air. ". . . not my problem. I say what I think." She eyed her daughter. "Aya, don't look at me like that. Why don't you sit down? Now you are even making me anxious, pacing back and forth, back and forth like a betel nut worm."

"Please, just let me get on with this, will you? I want this to work out."

"*Cha!* Waste of time."

Lu See shrugged. "We'll see."

Mother couldn't resist not getting in the last word. "See, my foot."

The following day the cookboy from the Woo house came with a box of pineapples. He bowed reverently and announced that owing to a family illness Woo-sang senior would not be coming after all and to please accept the gift of fruit as an expression of regret.

224

"Damn-powerful outrageous!" bellowed Uncle Big Jowl. He drew on his cheroot and smoke hung blue in the air. "We've been jilted, aahh."

Mother tilted her head this way and that. "See? I told you, waste of time, liao. Don't look like that, Lu See, you know it's true."

The cookboy placed the box of pineapples on a table and turned to leave.

"Wait!" cried Lu See as he drifted out the door. "Who is ill?"

"Grandson number one," he replied.

"Hold on," she said. "I am coming with you."

When Lu See arrived at Swettenham Lodge armed with her father's copy of *The Household Physician* the cookboy told her to wait in the poorly lit drawing room. She'd been in the house but once before, on her return from England, to inform the family of Adrian's death. The patriarch turned her out and told her he wanted nothing to do with Mabel, his granddaughter. It had been a traumatic experience, one she preferred to forget. For several minutes she glanced about the Woo drawing room, getting her bearings, wondering how many of the objects had been here in Adrian's time, how many he had touched with his own hands.

Moments later a parade of Woo women appeared in neatly ironed dresses and stiff smiles. The matriarch of the family stepped forward and greeted her with folded hands. "How is the child?" asked Lu See.

"His condition has worsened," replied Matriarch Woo solemnly.

"May I see him?"

"Why?" asked the child's mother, a young woman of about twenty-five, her voice crackly and breathless.

"I want to help."

"Unless you are a doctor I doubt you can help. And what is the point of calling a doctor if there is no medicine to be bought?" said one of the older aunties.

"Besides," offered another with an intense look, "all the doctors have run off to Kuala Lumpur where the money is better."

Lu See squared her shoulders. "I may not be a doctor but I have a book of medicine with me."

A pointed silence filled the room. The aunties exchanged reluctant noises. "Let me at least see him."

"Very well," said Matriarch Woo.

They led Lu See up the stairs to a dim outpost of the sprawling house. In the child's room Lu See pulled up a chair so that it was next to the bed. She placed the back of her hand on his forehead. He had a high spiking fever and no longer recognized his own family.

"Where is the pain?" she asked the boy. "Is the pain sharp like a cut or dull like a bruise?"

When he didn't reply his mother responded on his behalf. "In his stomach and he has been wetting his bed every hour. We gave him rancid brinjal and vinegar but his fever will not break."

Lu See knelt at the child's bedside and ran a cool, damp towel over his face. She placed her palm on the boy's abdomen and ironed it gently with the flat of her hand. Then she touched the lower right side of his tummy and pressed down. The boy barely moved. Frowning, she could feel the abdomen was distended. "Not appendicitis, otherwise he would have jerked with pain."

"His lips have turned white."

"He's dehydrated. Get him to drink more water."

They applied a wet cloth to his mouth and dribbled water onto his tongue.

With a quiet strength, Lu See stayed by his side for several minutes unsure what she could do. She studied the young boy's pale face and the blades of his narrow shoulders and thought of Adrian. *He would have looked like, as an eight year old. He would have looked just like this.*

Tenderly, she stroked his hair. She tried to recall what it was like to see Adrian's face, what it was like to hold Adrian in her arms; when he was warm, when he was whole. But she couldn't remember; the weight of grief had seen to that. She pinched her eyes shut and tried to squeeze the memories out. Her hands went to a piece of loose thread attached to her sleeve. And like a reflex her mind unspooled, taking her back to the hospital at Addenbrooke's and its institution-green walls.

A nurse wheeling a trolley of kidney dishes immediately abandoned what she was doing to help Lu See to a bench in a big empty corridor. "I want to see my husband," she said, but the nurse gave her a sympathetic look that said, *Now's not the time; he's lying on a marble slab.*

She sat on the plain wooden bench, shaking in her overcoat, the sleeves of her cardigan pulled down over the backs of her hands. Every so often she stared at the wall clock, but dark spots bobbed before her like black watermelon seeds. Only when the same nurse offered her a cup of tea did she notice that over an hour had gone by. She placed her hands on her tummy, her eight-week pregnant tummy. For the first time that day she realized the child would be fatherless.

Only last night Adrian had pressed his face against her tummy. She vaguely remembered him kissing her belly button through her dress, tickling, making her laugh. And the more she giggled the more he tickled. Had that been yesterday or some other evening?

Lu See felt a panic grow within her. She looked about and hoped the nurse with the white cape and red cross embroidered on her bosom would come and sit with her. But she didn't.

She waited; she thought about the future of her unborn child, and waited.

Finally, the coroner appeared. He wanted her to come

with him. He and a houseman led her into an old iron elevator that took her down to the windowless basement.

The houseman flicked a basement switch. Overhead lights sparked on. She saw a raised table at the centre of the room with the contours of a body shrouded by a white sheet. The houseman stood by her side in case she collapsed.

"All right," the coroner said in a steady, composed tone. "When you're ready."

She nodded.

He pulled the white sheet from Adrian's motionless frame, exposing his wan chest and small pink nipples, his arms arranged by his sides. The first thing she noticed was the bones protruding through his upper chest. His clavicle and ribs had splintered and pushed through the skin.

Lu See started gasping for air.

Adrian's eyes were closed and the overhead lights turned his cheeks the blued white of an iceberg. He was as pale as a wax model. The back of his head looked warped, caved in almost; it was where he must have struck the ground, she thought.

"Is this Adrian Woo?" asked the coroner.

She looked at him. His lips were dry and cracked, flecked with blood. The hair he was always so proud of looked sleep-tangled. She nodded.

Tremulously, Lu See touched him. She wanted to feel his warmth. There was none. He was a piece of marble, nothing but a cold shell. She leaned closer. His smell still floated on his skin. "Come back, Adrian," she whispered inaudibly, lovingly smoothing his hair. She pressed her open mouth onto his flesh. "Please come back to me."

The coroner pulled the sheet over Adrian.

"Please don't cover him up."

She crumpled over her husband, her arms around him, embracing him. She wanted to cry out again and again but her throat was closed.

Her eyes remained riveted to the white sheet covering him

as she was led away. It was as though her feet had been snatched from under her.

She was falling.

Some time later, Lu See found herself back in the big empty hospital corridor, on the same wooden bench. She cocooned herself in her arms and waited.

Her hands began to tremble. She felt stripped bare, like a tree ripped of its leaves. An hour passed, followed by another. Then the administrative nurse appeared with a bespectacled man from the hospital's accounts department. He carried a clipboard. Handing her Adrian's wristwatch, wedding ring and house keys, he wanted to know if she wanted them to make arrangements and pick out a casket. In hushed tones he asked her what was to be done with the remains.

The remains. The word burned like a flame in her chest – a moment of sickly realization.

She stared at the wristwatch and the gold band in her hand. The wristwatch had stopped ticking. Lu See retched once; then twice. Whirling round she was sick on the floor, her insides gushing out like bilge water squeezed from a sponge.

Lu See flipped through the pages of her father's old leather bound tome. Adrian had mentioned something years ago about Arrowroot.

"I think he may have a urinary infection," she said to Matriarch Woo.

"What can we do?" the mother despaired.

Lu See searched through the index, flicked from one silverfished page to another, found the section headed *Maranta arundinacea*. "It says here that Arrowroot plant is abundant in certain parts of Asia and produces soft, oval-shaped leaves up to ten inches long. Look, here's a picture. The Malay word for it is *Koova. Fun koat* in Cantonese. White flowers. Currant-like berries. Apparently it grows inland, in

229

well-drained soil." Moments later the entire household staff went into the forest armed with lamps and candles in search of the tree.

At long last they returned with a basketful of rhizomes. Lu See instructed them to grind the rootstalks into a powder and mix it with boiled water to make a thin gruel. Propping his head up, Lu See dribbled spoonfuls from a bowl into the boy's mouth.

An hour went by. Fresh candles replaced the guttered ones. Lu See kept vigil over the boy.

"His fever is breaking," announced the child's mother.

Lu See approached him and felt for the radial artery on his wrist. "His pulse is stronger." She saw the sweat gleaming like copper off his forehead. "Perspiring will help cool him down. Just make sure he drinks plenty of water."

"He is sleeping soundly now," observed Matriarch Woo. "I think the medication has worked."

"Then I shall leave you," said Lu See, folding her hands in farewell.

As she left the room Matriarch Woo called after her. The old lady took Lu See's arms in hers. "For years I have hated you for returning without my son. For years I blamed you for his death. For years I have ignored my own granddaughter . . . and for that I feel regret."

Lu See studied her face, which still carried the haunted struggles of a mother who'd lost her son.

"Thank you, Lu See," she said. They looked deep into one another's eyes – Adrian's mother smiled a sad smile. "I wish," she said in a soft voice. "I wish there was some way, some key into the past to change things, but there isn't."

"All my memories of him are sealed in one place . . ." her voice trailed off. "Like a shrine."

"Thank you for healing the child. I can see now why my Adrian married you."

Lu See dipped her head and kissed the old lady's hand. When she reached the bottom of the stairs she slipped off

Adrian's old wristwatch and left it on the hall table before retreating into the shadows of the night.

With the help of a military chaplain, Uncle Big Jowl obtained the use of an army lorry and three shovel-wielding coolies.

He drove the lorry to the periphery of the jungle and instructed the coolies to start digging at a spot marked with a gravestone.

Lu See and Mabel knelt close by in the undergrowth, shaded from the sun. "Is this where the treasure is?" Mabel asked, trying not to sound excited.

"Yes, just be patient," replied Lu See. Her face was scarlet with anticipated triumph.

One of the coolies held back the encroaching elephant grass as the other two stuck their shovels into the earth. Ten minutes later they stopped working.

"Have they found it?" cried Mabel, running up to peer into the excavated ditch.

Among the coarse earth and broken weed stalks, wedged into the soil, was a large wooden box.

"What's this?" Lu See demanded. "This wasn't here before. We put down canvas." She looked at Uncle Big Jowl, trying to make sense of it. "I don't understand. We didn't bury this, we buried pipes," she told the coolies. "Copper pipes. I wrapped them myself in oiled canvases."

"No pipes here," proclaimed the head coolie. "You want us to bring it up?"

The coolies lifted the box out of the hole and placed it on solid ground. The box was about three-feet long by two-feet wide. It was coated in a green moss.

Everyone stared at it.

Uncle Big Jowl crouched down and placed his hand on the lid.

"Careful!" warned a coolie. "The Japanese might be responsible for this. It may be booby-trapped!" But Uncle Big Jowl didn't withdraw his hand. Rather, he positioned his other hand on the far end of the lid and dug his fingers into the grooves, easing it off its hinges.

"What do you see?" asked Mabel, almost hopping now with excitement. "What's inside?"

Uncle Big Jowl removed the canvas covering.

Lu See stared in horror. She shrieked and shielded her daughter's face with her arm.

Coffin flies flew up from the putrefying skull.

Worms had eaten away the animal's eyes. Its face was pulled back in a grimace. Only bone and tufts of black curly wool remained.

It was the severed head of a sheep.

9

It was the ninth week of Sum Sum's apprenticeship. At precisely 5 a.m. she woke for the daily morning prayers. The cold bit into her toes and feet as she shuffled into the hall and joined the murmuring mouths. It was her job to light the endless rows of yak-butter candles in the prayer hall. With a long taper she bent forward time and again, reciting the Kyema Kyhud, stumbling over the words which were punctuated with ringing bells and cymbals and deep horn blasts. One after the other the tiny flames illuminated the massive gold statue of Shakyamuni Buddha, draped in saffron and yellow cloths.

The lamps gradually brought the image to life – Buddha seated on a lotus pedestal constructed from inlaid gold leaf panels with the upper section of the throne reinforced with vertical *vajra* sceptres

When the final lamp was lit, Sum Sum knelt on her novice carpet and quietly, unhurriedly looked about for Tormam.

Tormam still slept beside her in the dormitory. She had the somewhat easier duty of replenishing the Seven Bowls of Water on all of the altars. Sum Sum gave the young, shy-faced girl a wink as she took her position beside her on the novice rug as all around her the shaven heads bobbed in prayer, up and down, up and down, like windup toys.

Later, the new companions sat next to each other, in the breakfast hall. Bowls of *tsampa* lined the long wooden tables. Everybody ate with their fingers.

"Listen, we have been here for weeks, lah, and still nobody had told us where we can have baths. Do you know where we can go to wash?" asked Sum Sum, worrying the mala beads on her wrist.

"Tormam paused from chewing her barley balls. "Wash?"

"Shush!" someone warned and all the initiates, some of whom were no more than fifteen years old, dipped their heads.

After breakfast as they lit incense and spun the prayer wheel, Sum Sum asked again. Tormam gave her the same blank look and reply. "Wash?"

"*Rey.*" Sum Sum made gestures with her hands as if rinsing her armpits and back.

"I do not understand?"

"In your village don't you have a stream or an outhouse?"

"I'm from a family of nomads. We did our business in the open. To clean ourselves we rinsed our faces in yak milk. I was never allowed to wash my hair. My mother said it would freeze on my head."

Sum Sum raised her eyebrows theatrically. "You mean to tell me you have never had a bath, lah?"

Tormam looked at her blankly.

They grew silent, contemplating their barley balls.

"What are we going to do about this?"

"About what?" said Tormam, nonplussed.

"This . . . this no-bathing scenario," Sum Sum replied, not sure what to call it.

"I have no idea what you are talking about. Look, Senge-mo, finish up your breakfast. It is almost lessons time."

The following morning at precisely 5 a.m. Sum Sum nudged Tormam awake with her elbow. She'd spent half the night staring out of the dormitory window, gazing at the fingernail sliver of moon, dreaming up an idea; all around her the other novices slept, open-mouthed, filling the dormitory with the sounds of snoring. *Aiyo! Like sleeping with a band of piglets.*

"I've got it," she said, watching Tormam wipe the sleep from her eyes.

"Well don't give it to me, whatever it is. I am too tired."

"No, listen. I have a plan, lah." She peeped over her shoulder to assure nobody else was listening.

"A plan?" Tormam said, her tone nonchalant – until she saw the expression on Sum Sum's face.

They dressed and made their way to the prayer hall, thirty women in a crocodile line, bare feet padding across the floor. Scarves of incense perfumed the air. "This plan of yours, what – "

"SSHHH!" quietened prayer hall manager Jampa.

Several pairs of buttocks clenched tightly together.

In a hushed voice: "What is this plan?" asked Tormam self-consciously. When she spoke she always looked as though she had made a mistake and hadn't really meant to say anything at all.

Leaning towards her, Sum Sum whispered fiercely, "The plan is for you to experience heaven."

"You are going to kill me and send me to Nirvana?"

"Not that sort of heaven."

"The scriptures say there is only one type."

"*Aiyoo!* Did your mother drop you on your head as a baby? No, I am going to collect water from the river and heat it up and you are going to sit in it."

Tormam's eyes blinked at this. "You are going to boil me alive."

Sum Sum gave a sigh. "Yes, in hot water."

In the prayer hall Tormam arranged herself on a novice rug. "And this is a good thing."

Sum Sum lit a row of yak-butter candles with a long taper. "Keep your voice down. Yes, it is a good thing."

"You have either become enlightened overnight, Senge-mo, or you have been chewing Chinese opiates."

"Trust me."

The village of Cloudy Treetops was named after the trees that sat in near constant cloud at the top of the hill. In spring, with the snows melted, goat herders gathered here for the new succulent grass, while the novice nuns pounded laundry on the washing stones along the banks of the nearby stream. Beyond this, dwarfed by the landscape around it, was the Sera Valley, where the American plane had crash-landed.

Sum Sum squinted into the distance, searching for any signs of the abandoned aircraft; the fuselage of the crashed C-87 was no longer visible. It had been dismantled, stripped clean piece by piece, by villagers and nomads alike; the cargo of guns and military equipment pilfered to be sold across the border. There was nothing to show that it had ever been there bar some broken glass and the tatty scuff of earth where the tyres had skidded on landing. It was as if a hole had opened in the ground and swallowed it up.

Sum Sum thought about the poor airman.

Word had arrived from the monastery that he'd failed to recover from his wounds. Sum Sum remained convinced they could have saved him if he hadn't been moved. She blamed the abbess. However, she knew she had to grow beyond that now, especially as her relationship with the abbess seemed to have healed. Of course, she continued to make the odd blunder; she was still getting used to monastic etiquette, but gradually she was gaining the sense that she belonged.

"Come, let's see how long it takes to reach the water," Sum Sum said to Tormam.

Swathed in a yak-hide blanket, it took ten minutes for Sum Sum to walk from the nunnery to the banks of the stream. The terrain beneath her feet was gravelly and dry, the grass as tough as coir. On her return, under a persimmon sky, gazing at the winged roofs of the Ani Trangkhung Nunnery, she said to Tormam, "This is my plan." She set down her basket of damp, freshly washed robes and rubbed the needle-sharp chill from her hands. "We do this, lah. We take a hand sled with two empty rice barrels on its back and pull it to the river's edge. Once there we fill up with river water or ice chips and cart it back to the drying room, you know which one I mean, the room used for drying yak dung for fuel." Tormam nodded, rather wishing the nunnery had running water. "We may have to do this several times."

"And if someone asks what we are doing we say . . .?"

"What do you mean?"

"Why are we transporting barrels? Is it drinking water for the table?"

"No, lah, the kitchen do that."

"What then?"

"We are making soup."

Tormam blinked at this. "Soup, well, yes, of course. Why wouldn't we be?"

"No, listen, lah, I am serious. You see all these scrubby plants growing wild here. It is traditional Tibetan medicine, what English call wormwood, can be treatment for malaria. We say we are boiling up an herbal soup for the abbess."

"The abbess?" cried Tormam, who panicked at the mere thought of the elderly priestess.

"Yes, for the abbess, and the herbal soup requires plenty of clean river water."

"You have already been in trouble with the abbess. Can't we get water from the kitchen, from their round vats?"

"No. They will get suspicious. We fetch it ourselves from the river." A supressed smile of anticipation washed across Sum Sum's face as she spoke. "You excited?"

"I honestly cannot wait."

Sum Sum ignored her friend's sarcasm and watched a pair of grey wolves trot along the distant hills in search of sheep. "*Hnnn.* You just see, no? I will draw you out like nail to a magnet."

Behind the red gate-doors of the drying room, the charcoal stove roared under several round vessels of boiling water.

The ceiling, made dark by years of smoke, was low. The room was ill lit and in the dimness the spare robes that hung from wall hooks resembled crumpled ghouls. Sum Sum and Tormam huffed and puffed as they shuffled across the room hefting ice-chip-laden tin buckets. They tipped one bucket of frigid water into an empty rice barrel and went back out to retrieve another. "Hard work, no?" said Sum Sum jovially. "You excited yet?"

"Uncontainably so. It is like coming face to face with the Yeti." Tormam frowned with sarcasm. "Nail to magnet, my foot."

"*Ndug're.* It will be worth it. Trust me," said Sum Sum. Her eyes shone with a mischievous light.

Tormam made a face over her frost-numbed fingers, stretching them out as if checking to see if they were all still there.

After twenty minutes, with the room smelling of charcoal smoke, the two rice barrels were three-quarters filled with ice chips and river water. "Now for part two." Sum Sum wrapped a length of cloth over her hands and approached the charcoal stove. "Come help me." They removed a cooking vessel from the heat and eased it over the lip of the barrel, tilting it with care. The scalding liquid ran over the ice and immediately hissed. Great gouts of steam hit them in the face. "Again," said Sum Sum breathing quick, panicky breaths. They went to get the other round vessel. More mist filled the room.

"Is this supposed to happen?" asked Tormam, eyeing the steam with suspicion and laughing.

"I'm not sure. Are the ice-chips melting?"

They could hardly see each other through the vapour. "I think so, slowly."

"What should we do?"

"Boil more water!"

Tormam went to stoke the charcoal. "I cannot see a thing! Too much steam!"

"Shhh!" hushed Sum Sum, hoping nobody could hear their whispered giggles. "We mustn't get caught."

They started giggling even more.

At long last Sum Sum and Tormam were in their make-shift tubs. Their robes and mala beads lay on the floor in a heap. Following some oohing and aahhing, the girls squeezed into the barrels and sat with knees curled to their chests, their heads resting on the rims, both arms hanging loose, water up to their collarbones. The flesh on their shoulders shone pink and the ends of their fingers wrinkled like prunes. Their eyes were shut.

Sum Sum forgot where she was, forgot all she'd done and all she should have done, forgot about everything but the feel of the water on her skin; as welcome and warm as springtime rain.

After a short while Sum Sum stretched her arms like a cat in the sun and looked over at Tormam. "What's the matter? It sounds like you're crying."

"No, no, it is because I am so happy. This feels so wonderful and you are the first person in a long time who has done something so nice for me."

Sum Sum inclined her face and reached out to touch her friend's hand.

Just then the red gate-doors crashed open.

Prayer hall manager Jampa stood at the threshold, hands on hips. Her face swam with anger. "By the mother of all Buddhas, what do you think you are doing?" she cried, sounding like a startled goose. "Get out of those barrels this minute!"

The girls scrambled for their clothes. As soon as they put on their robes, they stood side by side, sodden and shivering like a pair of shaven-headed kittens. Steam rose from their scalps.

Glaring with her piglet nostrils aflare, prayer hall manager Jampa ordered them to withdraw to their dormitory. "Go and think about what you have done. Go and pray for forgiveness from the eternal Gods of the mountain. You'll be lucky if the abbess doesn't throw you out for this!"

"Please don't tell the abbess!" mewed Tormam. "It won't happen again."

"It was all my idea," said Sum Sum staring defiantly at prayer hall manager Jampa whose face was now so red Sum Sum thought she might be having a heart attack. "Leave Tormam out of this."

"*Humph!* Who are you to tell me what I should or should not do?"

"All I am saying is if anyone should be punished let it be me." The words slipped out before she could stop herself.

Tormam yelped. Squirming, she folded and unfolded her hands, marvelling at Sum Sum's outspokenness.

"Such insolence!" The words swished like a horsewhip. "I will send for you both later, once I have decided what to do with you." Jampa eyed the steaming water in the barrels and shook her head at them. "I am so very disappointed in you." She clapped her hands violently. "Now go!"

Back in their dormitory, melodic chanting resonated through the walls together with the music of *damaru* drums and *rolmo* cymbals. Secluded from the other novices who were all at evening prayers, Sum Sum stared at her hands, as if searching her lifeline for an answer. "I'm sorry, Tormam. Are you angry with me?" Head down, it looked like she was trying to see into the future. "I don't want you to be angry, lah."

Tormam smiled. The truth was written in her eyes. "Of course I am not angry." She covered her mouth as she giggled. "Actually it was good fun." Her face coloured as if embarrassed to admit it.

Almost as an afterthought Sum Sum said, "You know some tip-top Englishman writer once said, 'The greatest pleasure in life is doing what others say you cannot do'. I think he makes sense, lah."

"How do you know about English-Minglish writer?"

"I have been to England."

"You have not!"

"Have, lah. In summertime it gets dark at eleven at night. And I've travelled in a motorcar with no roof and seen Cluck Gable in moving pictures. Seems like long-long time ago." Sum Sum went quiet and searched the palms of her hands again.

"Tell me about your past." Tormam sat forward.

"My past? My past is all mist now." Thumbing back through the years, she thought of Lu See and Cambridge and all that she'd left behind. There was so much she wanted to tell her shy-faced friend but she remained tight-lipped. The previous day Tormam had asked her about her earlier life, about marriage and children, if she'd ever considered it. Sum Sum looked at her for a prolonged moment, and replied – *Yes and no*. The same expression of regret was in her eyes now.

She decided to change the subject. "Jampa was cuckoo-clocks crazy annoyed, no?" She clicked her tongue.

"I thought she was going to burst open with fierceness." Tormam stopped herself from giggling again. "I suppose we ought to pray for forgiveness."

Suddenly Sum Sum touched her wrist and immediately grew concerned. Her eyes started wandering over her robes and across the plain plank bed.

"You lost something?" asked Tormam.

Sum Sum scanned the floor and felt her cheeks glow hot. "My mala beads." She touched her wrist again.

They searched all over. "You must have left them by the tubs. You will have to go back."

"By Dharmakaya heaven, we are supposed to be confined to our dormitory. I'm scared to go back alone in case Jampa is there. She will skin me alive. Will you come with me?"

They flitted down the corridor and through a hall strung with guttering candles and crinkles of shadow and incense burning from stoneware pots

Soon they were at the red gate-doors of the drying room. Sum Sum stretched out her hand to grasp the door handle but then stopped herself.

"What?" asked Tormam.

"You hear that?"

"Hear what?"

They cocked their heads to the noise. "Sounds like a quarrelling seagull," said Sum Sum.

They pressed their ears to the thick gate-doors. "By Dharmakaya heaven, it's Jampa."

"She is singing!" Tormam's eyes widened. "She is sitting in the bath water, in *our* bath water, and singing!"

An ejaculatory cry of joy thrummed through the walls. Sum Sum stamped her foot. "What nerve!"

"It is not fair. What should we do?"

"Let's come back in an hour. She'll be gone by then. Of all the nerve, *ai-yoo*!"

An hour later, the two girls returned to similar cries of joy. "What, lah, still?" They sat on their haunches, limp with disappointment, hands cradling their chins. "You'd think she'd had enough by now, no?" Another impassioned whoop pierced the air. Followed by another. "It seems the piglet queen cannot relinquish her throne."

Tormam shook her head. "But wait. Does that sound like singing to you?" The whoop turned into an enraged howl. The girls approached the door and peeked through a tiny slat. Sum Sum turned to Tormam. "Something's happened to her. She has a cuckoo-clocks crazy look on her face, her eyes are wild and rolling about like marbles."

They pushed though the gate-doors. Jampa glared at them; her eyelids, eyebrows and lips were twitching uncontrollably. "I'm stuck!" she screamed, teeth chattering. "Stuck, stuck, stuck!" The words lashed the air. "By the scorching sun, I have been sat here shivering and alone for an age!"

"We thought you were singing."

"Singing?" She squawked like an angry hen. "I was calling for help!" Every muscle on her face was in spasm. "Well, don't just stand there gawping. Help me out of this wretched tub! I'm freezing! And bolt the door behind you!"

Tormam and Sum Sum snuck their hands under prayer hall manager Jampa's armpits, but she wouldn't budge.

"*Ayo Sami!* She is wedged in like a Mongolian tick. Lift!" cried Sum Sum. Cold water sloshed on to their robes on its way to the floor.

"It's my hips," cried Jampa in a hoarse voice, her lips blue. "They're jammed to the sides of the barrel. Here," she threw one of her saggy breasts aside. "Can't you see?"

Sum Sum peered at the folds of bunched skin and the waves of goosepimpled flesh. "Let's tilt the rice drum on to its side." It was half-full of water now and easier to shift. "Gravity will help us, no?" With Jampa's arms resting on their shoulders they eased the barrel sideways and began to heave and grunt and pull. Stiff-necked, faces pinched, nostrils flaring, everybody strained their limbs and tendons.

The girls began to giggle.

"Don't you dare laugh!" scolded Jampa, the skin of her face pulling tight. "And not a word of this to anyone!"

Sum Sum bit her tongue. There was a subversive twinkle in her eye.

They clamped and clawed and kneed. Little by little they worked Jampa's body free. Purple patches appeared all over her skin where it had scraped along the barrel walls. Eventually with a final tug and a sharp exclamatory yowl her puckered buttocks popped free like a cork.

Jampa flopped across the floor like an injured flounder. Euphoric and trembling all over, she gave a cry of delight and immediately the girls began to rub her legs back to life. Sum Sum, thinking Jampa resembled a desiccated plum, all pink and raw and wrinkly, grinned from ear to ear. "It feels like someone has taken a ruler to my bottom cheeks," the old lady mused. They moved her close to the heat of the smouldering charcoal stove and covered her in spare robes. Head drooping, body slumped, Jampa peered at the girls and hoisted a warning finger, but then seeing the impish expression in Sum Sum's eyes a smile spread over her face. Seconds later all three burst into soggy laughter.

After lights out Tormam leaned from her bed, over the lip of plank wood, and angled her head in Sum Sum's direction. The sheen from her shaven scalp reflected light from the Tibetan moon. "Hey," she hissed across the gulf. "I've been thinking about you making that journey to England. Why do you never speak about it, never speak about your history?"

"Because I don't want to." Sum Sum stared at the ceiling, eyes roving the blackness.

"Why, did something bad happen?"

Sum Sum's heart skipped in her chest. "Yes, something bad happened and I don't want to talk about it, you stupid or something, is it?"

"I was only asking," said Tormam, sounding hurt.

"Don't look like that. Go to sleep," Sum Sum said with a suppressed querulousness, refusing to allow her memories a foothold. But it was too late – already her past had begun to snatch at her, with all the accompanying should haves, would haves, how and whys.

Sum Sum felt a tiny urge to confide in Tormam – to tell her about Lu See and Adrian, Pietro and Cambridge, Aziz even, but she couldn't. She had a secret she dare not tell anyone – not her brother, not the abbess, not Tormam. All she could do was put the urge out of her mind.

She'd made a sacrifice back then, in her eyes the ultimate sacrifice; something that cut so deep it left a wound that still wept. Even now, the heat of guilt filled her chest.

Tomorrow will be a new day, she said to herself . . . *as new as an infant's fingernails. Right now I just want to forget.*

The thing was, no matter how she distracted herself, it always came back to her. In the small, dark hours of the night, lying on her back, the memories flooded in. Despite herself she proceeded, cautiously, step by step, through the events of her twentieth year, pausing at each landmark, unfurling the episodes one by one until she settled on the day her child was born.

She'd gone into labour late.

Push! Ayo . . . bloody . . . Sami! Push! PUSH!

Outside, beyond the shaded window, grey pre-dawn clouds darkened the cobbles of Bridge Street as rain began to fall, pocking the glass, making *plink-plink* noises. Mrs Slackford propped a pillow under Sum Sum's head. "Yew want me to fetch Lu See from Jesus Lane?" *No*, thought Sum Sum. Adrian had not been dead long. *She is still grieving, curled up in bed, legs clutched to her chest. Leave her in peace.* "And are yew having the baby here?"

"What, you want me to go behind bushes like hillside women in Tibet?"

"I'm talking about hospital."

Sum Sum shook her head. "No, I have baby here."

There were clean towels, scissors and a pail filled with scalding water at the ready. Mrs Slackford applied a cold, damp cloth to Sum Sum's face and told her to take in several deep breaths before pushing once again.

"Wooden spoon!" Sum Sum caterwauled.

Mrs Slackford returned from the kitchen seconds later. Sum Sum clamped the wooden mixing spoon between her teeth. *Okay, push. PUSH! And don't go screaming like you cuckoo-crazy.*

The rain hit the glass.

Teeth clenched; Sum Sum squeezed her eyes tight. Mrs Slackford puffed out her cheeks to mimic the breathing mechanism. "Big shove now, dear."

Another half an hour passed. Sum Sum threw off the damp cloth on her forehead and sucked air in, feeling her face glow hot and her toes grow colder. With her whole body trembling, her stomach bulged before her eyes like an angry, pink-veined Humpty Dumpty head.

"It's coming, dear, never yew worry." Mrs Slackford, a pair of horn-rimmed spectacles balanced on the end of her nose, adjusted her pinny and positioned her elbows between Sum Sum's legs, mouthing encouragement. Spoon clamped between teeth, Sum Sum bit down and arched her back as another overwhelming contraction wrung her insides.

"Big shove, dear," ordered Mrs Slackford.

Push! Aiyo Sami! Push! And don't cry out otherwise you'll attract evil spirits. She shrieked with pain.

"That's it, dear, let it all out. Think of yer husband and how proud he'll be. Mr Aziz, isn't it?"

She thought of the man responsible for her condition and let out another shriek. *I'm going to kill you, for doing this to me. Kill you.*

With the mad staring eyes of an out-of-control downhill skier Sum Sum pushed. After a while some instinct led her to attempt labour in a squat, gripping the bedpost for support and allow gravity to do its job.

The muscles in her face knotted.

If I ever get my hands on you! Sum Sum clenched her teeth and strained.

Sum Sum felt the baby shift inside of her, tunnelling its way through the birth canal. The room began to swirl with colours. She bit hard on the spoon and squeezed again. A tearing agony ripped through her.

"Oh, look!" exclaimed Mrs Slackford. "Oi think it's on its way."

Sum Sum, feeling as though her insides were being shredded to make confetti, gripped the bedpost and pushed even harder.

The head crowned.

"Am I too late? How is she?" It was Lu See, entering the room and removing her overcoat. "I sensed something. I had to come over."

"Oi see it," cried Mrs Slackford as she eased her hands over Sum Sum's stomach and pressed. "Oi see the shoulders now! Here it comes." A wrinkled creature with gummed bluey-pink skin slipped out. Seconds later the placenta and fetal membranes followed in a warm gush. Mrs Slackford held the newborn by the legs and slapped its little bottom. Shocked by the light, it gave off a spluttering, bilious cry as its tiny hands tried to snatch away the glare.

Lu See gave a yelp of delight and helped with the towels.

"A darling little girl," Mrs Slackford said, tying the umbilical cord before severing it. "Have yew a name for her?"

"Yes," Sum Sum replied. "Her name will be Mabel."

PART THREE

August 1957

1

The jungle at night was menacing. It was dense and hulking and smelled of rotting vegetation. Mabel kept her gaze transfixed on the swaying blackness of the thicketed interior; purposeful; alert; right eye peering down the barrel, the other clamped shut; finger feathering the trigger. There had been activity up ahead, she'd been sure of it. Straining, she stared beyond the tangle of vines dangling from the tall mass of trees.

There was sound all around her. Somebody had once told her that the jungle was quiet at night. They were dead wrong. The tree frogs were like a brass band; the cicadas the percussions.

She made a low whistle by fizzing air through her front teeth and Bong, five yards to her left, whistled back. His spectacles caught a glint of moonlight. Once more her finger feathered the rifle trigger. Scribbles of movement seemed to bend against the forest floor. Mabel waited, feeling the perspiration trail down her forehead. The salt stung her eyes. The topsoil felt damp on her elbows. All about her snarls of tubers and rootstock chafed the flesh of her body.

Somewhere out there leaves skittered along the scrub and trees creaked. The sounds of tree frogs piped louder. Little explosions of noise amplified a hundredfold in the dark. Then, in the near distance, a branch snapped. Craning her neck, immediately Mabel's gaze snagged on a small hunched figure – a ball of grey against the black backdrop, like the contours of a man moving on all fours across the ground. She wanted to shout Bong's name aloud; instead she forced another stream of air through her teeth. Breath control, she said to herself. She was peering through the rifle sight aligning her target. Her finger curled itself tighter around the trigger. She mouthed a whispered prayer. Muscles began to twitch along her cheek. She inhaled lightly and held her breath.

The night drew in closer. Time folded in on itself.

Suddenly, out of the mouth of the dark clearing, a bearded pig came shuffling and snorting into the open. Snout to the ground, it was scavenging for discarded fruit; bits of rambutan and mangosteen tossed out by the monkeys.

Thankful, Mabel exhaled and lowered the gun. Her neck muscles felt like sprung coils. Although she carried a weapon, Mabel was in fact the company medic; she had never fired her gun in anger. The thought of maiming or killing somebody appalled her. Rolling on to her back, her eyes drifted towards Bong. She made out the metal rims of his round glasses. The glint of ivory betrayed his beleaguered smile.

She'd been asleep in the wet, dark place, in a *basha*, a temporary shelter made of *attap*, where toadstools grew and gibbon excrement peppered the overhanging leaves, when Bong had roused her, shaking her shoulder. She'd slept for no longer than an hour but already her clothes were damp with mist. He'd heard a rustling in the trees, he said. Earlier they'd been tipped off by local tribesmen that the Security Forces were near. The entire camp had been put on high alert. Along the perimeter they'd set up man-traps and spring snares out of vine, wire and supple willow trees.

It was another three hours until dawn.

All around her was raw nature – leaping, crawling, slithering, flapping. None of which Mabel could see. Spiders scuttled across her hands. Mosquitoes buzzed her ears. Each time she nodded off a fly or stinging bug would land on her and creep across her mouth, waking her with a jolt. The jungle, where everything was food for something else, had nibbled at her for months; now it threatened to eat her alive. She began to dream of mutton rendang washed down with iced lemonade, soft pillows made of Indochine cotton, the easy feel of toilet paper on her skin, the simple delights of clean, cool water in her hair. It was at moments like these that she wanted to return home.

With daybreak came the mass choir of voices. A troop of gibbons sang high up in the trees, repelling their infringing rivals. This was quickly followed by an orangutan's rich baritone.

Mabel washed in the yellow river, her bathing sarong wound under her armpits. She was a bag of bones and had lost her natural stockiness yet she still went about her business with a muscular air. Sharp collarbones protruding, there were insect bites all over her arms and legs. She cupped her hands and scooped water on to her throat. The water clawed at the inflamed parts of her unsoaped skin. Looking up, she saw a sprawling chalky sky, dawn light shimmering at the jungle's edge, the world still thick with shadow. Two kingfishers were flying overhead. A hundred yards upriver, crab-eating macaques were splashing in the shallows, noisily celebrating the capture of her hand mirror from her bag some time in the night.

Pinching her nose, Mabel submerged her head under the cool, muddy water. Her dark hair flowed about her like a cloud of ink; she ran her fingers through to work out the tangles and pick out bits of leaves and earth.

The day had started with roll call at 6.45 a.m. Earlier, Bong, their unit commander, had gone around poking the sleeping with a stick to wake them; prodding them as he would an injured, weary horse to see if it might flinch. Next, together with her band of communist insurgents, Mabel breakfasted on fresh water prawns and *arak*. Dressed in rubber boots, khaki uniform and peaked cap with a red star, the guerrillas then conducted an hour of weapons training and drill. Afterwards, some of the men kicked a small rattan ball about in an impromptu game of *sepak raga*. Others lounged on string beds, hidden behind palls of woodsmoke. A few sat under trees, dozing, hands propped on cheeks.

Being a mobile unit, they had erected a temporary shelter. Shacks were crafted from bamboo, planks and beams held together with coir and coconut-husk fibre, palm fronds were spread across everything to hide them from enemy planes. When they decamped, drinking water was strapped to shoulder blades in stoneware jars. Ceramic bowls and metal cooking pots were held in rice-straw bales to prevent them knocking against each other during transport through the jungle.

As soon as everyone was ready to move out, Bong called them to form a large circle. They were a ragged crew of underfed, filthy irregulars, pocked with scabs and scars and gunshot lacerations. As the medical officer, Mabel could almost hear the scuttling of lice in the seams of their clothing. She stood at the front, amongst the elongated shadows, doing up her hair with wooden pins. A hunter's green medic's bag was hitched across her back, a Chinese-made rifle hung from her shoulder. She wiped the perspiration from her brow with her sleeve. Her hair was damp with sweat. The heat was already cutting into her skin.

Bespectacled and well-spoken, Bong started off by handing out the monthly allowance per man of M$26, raised by extorting villagers, then proceeded with a pep talk.

"Great social change," he began, putting his Sten gun down and adjusting his round glasses, "such as the abolishment of slavery, the end of colonial rule, the overthrowing of capitalism, the striving towards a higher social order, all start with public awareness. It was us, the MNLA, who first advocated the end of British rule. It was us who formed the trade unions in Selangor. The people out there in the kampongs" – he pointed beyond the jungle, puffing out his chest – "are all behind us. Soon they will all rise up against the white running dogs. Remember we are freedom fighters, not rebels! Bolshevik Warriors, fulfill your duties to the last. Long live Mao Zedong! Long live the Malay Communist Party!"

He touched his spectacles once again, leaving rifle grease on the lenses. He removed them and wiped them with the end of his sleeve.

Behind him, birds cawed and something in the distance screeched. Suddenly, a huge palm tree frond dropped from the sky and came crashing down on to the ground. "Also remember," he added, raising a hand and drawing a finger across his throat. "More people die of falling trees than snake bites, crocodile attacks and drowning in mud. So keep vigilant! And if the water in your bowl wriggles don't drink it."

2

Throughout Kuala Lumpur and the Klang Valley people gathered in tea shops to listen to the 3 p.m. radio broadcast. The transferral of power from Britain would take place at midnight the following day, thirty-six hours from now, declared the newsreader. Members of the Malay, Indian and Chinese parties would stand in darkness for two minutes to mark the official handover. Shouts of '*Merdeka*' would ring across the land.

On Macao Street an enormous, brass pig's head towered over passersby as they paused to listen to snippets of news coming from the crackling radio. Some of the Chinese reached up and touched its snout for luck; others, mainly the Muslims, shuffled away without making eye contact. The brass pig belonged to Il Porco. And Il Porco belonged to Lu See, who was preparing a fresh batch of her popular rosemary shortbreads. Using Sum Sum's recipe, she'd been making rosemary shortcakes every day now for the last twelve years; ever since they sold the big house in Juru and moved to the capital.

Lu See lived in the rooms above the restaurant. Next door there was a compound where a group of five Muslim families lived. In the summer, during the school holidays, it was like a small village, a miniature kampong, with mothers in headscarves calling out "Ismail!' and "Yasmine!" and "Younis!' at all times of the day, and where hens and roosters scratched about in the dirt and children sang and laughed as they played badminton. Separating Lu See's shophouse with the compound was a ten-foot wall and a wide monsoon drain scrawled with scribbles of barbed wire to keep the sewer rats from climbing over.

Once in a while, the family headman, Abdul bin Kassim, would leave a basket of fresh mangoes on her doorstep. When she thanked him profusely, he'd stroke his tightly rolled beard, as curly-ended as a Persian slipper, and then touch his *songkok* shyly.

Lu See opened a tin of Eagle Brand condensed milk and almost straight away flies started to buzz all around her. A new song by P. Ramlee was playing on the gramophone. She had just whisked an egg into her mixture of flour, sugar and butter when Dungeonboy slid a crooked finger into the blending bowl.

Lu See immediately slapped his hand away with her long wooden spoon. "Don't eat anything that contains raw eggs. How many times must I tell you!"

"Yes, yes, I know, lah. Udderwhy I catch Sam and Ella."

"Nincompoop!"

"Cannot help, lah. It sweet like ice cream." He sucked the sugar from the frighteningly long nail on his fifth finger – usually reserved for ear scraping and nose drilling.

"Do that again and I'll chop your pinkie off, understand?"

"Okay, lah." Dungeonboy chuckled. He was a short, quick-witted Malayan Chinese of about twenty with a chubby, shiny face eternally folded in smiles.

Lu See poured the mixture into a baking pan and shoved it into the Florence oven. Afterwards, spanking flour from her batik apron, she emerged from the tiny kitchen into the restaurant proper. Set in a two-storey building, with bright orange shutter windows and narrow verandahs called five-foot ways that shielded pedestrians from the sun, Il Porco was a small eatery set on the corner of Macao Street and Hokkien Street, close to the Old Market Square. From Market Street to Il Porco you passed mainly Muslim-owned establishments and certainly no other restaurant that served pig meat.

The first time Lu See told anyone she was opening an eatery that specialized in roast and stewed pork they thought she was mad. "Pig restaurant?" Uncle Big Jowl cried, cocking his head. "What about the Muslims next door, aahh?"

"I admit, it's a bit provocative," she replied matter-of-factly. "But I spoke to the neighbourhood Imam and he gave me his blessing. I'm not doing anything illegal. The building was going cheap."

Once he'd sampled her rosemary roast pork, Uncle Big Jowl almost collapsed. "Crackling so crunchy it fills your head with noise!" He patted his tummy with delight and agreed to be her silent partner, taking a 10 percent stake.

Six months later, despite the occasional sour looks thrown her way by her Islamic neighbours, business was thriving. KL's culinary hotchpotch of diners had never experienced cuisine quite like it. The Chinese and Indians came in droves and on Saturday lunch, the busiest time of the week, Lu See often had to squeeze twelve people together at a table designed for eight.

Where its exterior was colonial, the compact interior of Il Porco was classical *Nyonya*: blackwood chairs, round marble-topped tables, wooden screens, washed-out portraits of Lu See's Grand-aunty Ying scattered along the walls and a huge lacquer panel in Chinese that read *Tung Jao Gung Jai* meaning 'We are all in the same boat'.

After shelving away a few plates, Lu See paused and slowly twisted her lower back first this way, then that. Her movements were stiff. She was going to be forty-one years old, her legs remained willowy and her body was still angular, but today her stomach was killing her. She stood motionless for a long moment with her arms crossed over her tummy and her head turned heavenward.

"Is that a new yoga position? You look like an Egyptian mummy," said Stan Farrell. Since their initial meeting on the MS *Jutlandia*, his hair, like Lu See's, had grown a little salt-

and-pepper grey over the years. It hadn't taken him long to find her on his return from the war. He took a quick sip of *teh tarik* and then replaced the cup on the table between his truncheon and peaked cap. Dressed in khaki shorts and shirt, knee-high socks, Webley revolver and Federation of Malaya Police badge, Stan looked every inch the policeman. Apart from the hockey boots, that is.

Lu See bent forwards a fraction, keeping her arms folded. "It's the only position which doesn't hurt. Why the ridiculous shoes?"

"For protection." He grinned, parting his lips to reveal his infamous gravestone teeth, which could signal ships off the coast. "They extend past the ankle, you see?" He lifted a leg. "You ever see a leech?"

"Only in *The African Queen*."

"Keeps the leeches off when I'm out in the swamps chasing guerrillas."

Guerrillas like Mabel, she wanted to say. Instead, frowning and with a sudden craving to break wind, she said, "All set for the handover?"

"Duke of Gloucester's flying in tomorrow for Abdul Rahman's swearing in ceremony." He popped a gumdrop into his mouth, opened the *Straits Times* and turned to the funnies page.

Several Chinese patrons were slurping thick rosemary-infused *baan meen* pork noodles; several bottles of Tiger beer sweated by their elbows: transistor radios screeched. A tangy smell of pork belly stewed with shallots flavoured the air. Fans whirred overhead.

"And you're definitely staying on?" she asked, reaching for a swig of milk of magnesia and returning to her mummy pose.

"Hell yes, I'm staying on. In fact, I think I'm the only *gweilo* copper who's not leaving. Everyone else is being sent home. Besides, I've got Mum to look after. She likes living in this country," he said, watching her sip from the cobalt-blue bottle. "Anyway, why would I leave? I was born here. I'm entitled to stay, unlike the rest of 'em." He took another suck of tea as he read the comics. "What happened? To your tummy, I mean. Something you ate?"

"I'm not sure. It might be muscular. It started when I threw a heavy bucket of water over Dungeonboy."

"Sounds interesting. Was he drunk?"

Lu See straightened up and rubbed her abdomen rhythmically. "No. During last night's blackout, he set his hair on fire lighting the candles."

On hearing this, Stan swallowed the wrong way and choked, forcing a jet of warm tea to shoot up his nose. Both she and Stan burst out laughing as he wiped his face with a handkerchief. "Poor chap. He's only been here a week. Why on earth d'you call him Dungeonboy?"

Still laughing, she said, "Because he lives in the basement under the stairs. There are no windows down there. He calls it his dungeon. His real name's Ah Fung."

"Any references? Know much about him?"

"Not much except that he thinks he's Doris Day. He worked as a dishwasher at the Coliseum Club for three years."

Stan stood up. "I'll have to check him out. D'you mind if I look at his IC?"

Lu See shrugged and called him over.

Stan studied Dungeonboy's identity card as he stood beaming and chuckling in his starched white house coat. There was a small patch of burned hair to the left of his fringe. "Wah! You thing me Communist, boss? Of course not, lah! Hey, you likey Doris Day?"

"That's a mighty dangerous looking fingernail you've got there."

"Good for picking locks. Me number one expert lock-picker, boss!" He laughed, winking theatrically at Lu See. "Only joking-joking!"

Stan returned the identity card and looked at Lu See. "Bit

of a fruit cake if you ask me." They smiled at each other and allowed their eyes to linger. Not for the first time, she subconsciously wanted to go to bed with him. She wondered if that was a semi-erection in his trousers.

"Well, best be off." He left his tea money on the table and held his baton in his hand as if it was a flower. "Oh, I almost forgot," he said, reaching into his back pocket to pull out a folded piece of thick, white cold-pressed paper. "What d'you think? It's the front of the restaurant. I did it over the weekend."

Lu See's eyes gleamed as she smoothed out the creases of the watercolour. It was a work unique to Stan – a creamy violet shopfront, light pink skies and dark ochre-green shadows. There were two hawkers in the foreground, their faces were salmon red, and bang in the centre of the composition, made with rapid strokes, was 'Il Porco' in cool ultramarine.

Lu See gave a contented sigh. "It's lovely."

"How're your own pictures coming along?" he asked.

"Haven't done much. I used to do a portrait of Mabel once a year, or at least I did until, well, you know."

"Still no news?"

"No." She stretched again, wincing at the pain in her stomach.

"Well, you know what I always say – no news is good news, unless you're a journalist."

"All I know is that she's somewhere deep in the jungles of Johor." As she stretched, her back made popping noises that sounded like an old man cracking his knees.

"How can it be," said Stan, "that Mabel spends two years training to be a nurse then leaves three months before her final exams to live like a monkey in the jungle?"

Mother, eavesdropping from the other side of the restaurant, tapped her cup with a spoon in protest. "*Cha!* As soon as she started her monthly and hair sprouted between her legs she was with that Bong fellow."

Stan raised an eyebrow. "The Malayan Communist Party member?"

Lu See nodded. She was about to tell him that she'd known Bong since he was a child but something stopped her. There was a part of her that admired Bong; something about him – his recklessness and passion – reminded her of Adrian.

Adrian and Bong. The scholar and the soldier. Apart from their shared devotion to radical socialism there was little to link the two men. One dreamed about a communist state, the other fought for it. Whereas Adrian's intellectual approach was all youthful enthusiasm and theory, Bong relied on discipline, stealth and sabotage.

"You were such a good mother. It's not fair," said Stan.

"Fair?" Lu See sighed deeply and shook her head at Stan because it sounded like such a ridiculous thing to say – this implication that life had to be *fair*.

Turning her gaze towards the cash register she scooped up the coins on the table. Eventually she said, "Mabel was always iron willed."

"Stubborn girl . . ." said Stan. "Did you . . . did you ever meet any of her friends? Ever come across someone nick-named 'the mule'?

"Mabel rarely introduced me to her friends," she sighed. "She kept them all close to her chest." Thinking she had to look strong in front of Stan, she lifted her head with purpose and added, "Can't go on moping about it. And I don't need any finger-wagging I-told-you-sos either, Mother."

Mother gave a *harrumph* from the other side of the room and turned her face away as if to imply she was bored with it all.

"You must miss her," said Stan.

"Every minute. And every minute of not knowing where she is makes it worse." The ache in her stomach intensified.

Stan nodded. There wasn't much more he could say. "Well, as I said, best be off. See you next Friday." He cocked his head to one side. "Started, farted, stumbled fell . . .?"

"Yes, see you Friday, Stan Farrell. Good luck tomorrow night." They shook hands a little awkwardly and moments later he vanished through the battered swing doors into the bright tangerine sunshine.

Kaching! Lu See dropped the coins into the tray of the cash register. She checked that nobody was looking before pulling a red $10 bill from the note stash. Hurriedly she snuck it into an envelope labeled 'Juru'.

Then she turned to watch Stan go. Often, when she saw Stan walk away like this, she thought of the final scene in *Casablanca*, where Rick stands in the fog watching the plane carrying Ingrid Bergman fly off to neutral Lisbon. Stan often reminded Lu See of Humphrey Bogart – more Rick Blaine than Sam Spade. There was something so calm and appealing about Stan; a quietness, like the reassuring comfort of a mid-afternoon nap.

"He give you picture-drawing," said Dungeonboy, taking up his broom. "Maybe you make good *rabak rabak* boyfenn-girlfenn?"

Lu See did not react to this. It was true, she mused, they would make 'good boyfenn-girlfenn' and it was not the first time the idea had been suggested.

Once in a while she caught herself standing motionless over a pork knuckle stew, staring straight ahead, thinking of the way Stan laughed by tossing his head back, and how his infectious laughter made her feel. She had realised that over the last few months she'd been wondering about him more and more, but having an affair with Stan was not an option. Of course the idea had crossed her mind many times, but she knew she would never be able to go through with it. He was a friend first and foremost. *Yes, he's single, yes, he's kind, but why would he want to get involved with a forty-year-old widow?*

It didn't stop her from fantasizing, however. And whenever she thought of him she felt happy rather than forlorn, so where was the harm in that? What was wrong with a little romantic escapism? Nothing, she decided. Was he off home to feed his cat this minute, she asked herself? Did he hover by the stove with a frying pan in hand on Sunday mornings to cook himself and his mum eggs on toast? Did he go out dancing at the Roxy after dark, or did he spend all his social hours drinking with his police pals at the Spotted Dog? She didn't know for sure, but she did know that she was growing increasingly curious about Stan's private life and in her secret daydreams she wished she could be a part of it.

Sometimes she would join Stan for dinner and a game of rummy at the Colony Club. And now and then he would share a coffee alone with her at a *kopitiam* and look deep into her eyes. But each time she reached into her emotional self she was frightened of finding a black void; scared that her passion had long been extinguished; snuffed out within the pale green walls of a Cambridge hospital.

3

Before the planned ambush the entire company waded into the Tengi River up to their chins to rid themselves of the reek of sweat and cigarettes. Stripped to the waist the men scrubbed themselves hastily, quietly, conscious of the hovering ever-hungry mosquitoes.

Unlike them, the British patrols were noisy, stumbling through the wilderness like buffaloes. The sound of a branch snapping could be heard over a hundred yards away and Bong claimed he could smell a Welsh Borderer's hair oil and mint-flavoured chewing gum a mile off.

Mabel washed the jungle grit from her eyes and ears.

"Quick-quick-quick," Bong encouraged. "Pythons may be in the water. One minute you're swimming, next minute they grab you and pull you away." Of course, everyone knew he was exaggerating, but they also knew that pythons could stay submerged for almost half an hour.

Coincidentally, as he was saying this, a snake emerged from the opposite bank and skimmed along the top of the river towards Mabel. She watched it moving; a thick, black snake that seemed as comfortable on water as it did on dry land. It was a large cobra and it was not the least bit afraid of people. When it got within ten feet of her it stopped and locked eyes with Mabel. She caught her breath. Anyone who knew her could read the fear on her face by the way her nostrils flared.

Bong told her to move back slowly, away from the water, to not turn around. The cobra swished away, unfurling like a whip.

Shortly afterwards, as everyone dried off and two or three soldiers were sent in search of slugs to eat in the prickly grass, Bong went through the strategy one more time. Under his direction they were going to surprise a convoy of British soldiers with what he liked to call 'the Venus flytrap'.

Malay independence might have been only days away, but the Malayan Emergency was far from being lifted. The continual conflict between Commonwealth troops and the Malayan National Liberation Army (MNLA) had lasted since 1948, nine long years. There had been thousands of casualties, including the high-profile murder of the British High Commissioner, Sir Henry Gurney. The MNLA not only wanted the British out, they wanted Communist rule.

From the way Bong's shoulders were held, stiffly squared, and the charged atmosphere around him, Mabel could tell that he meant business. Standing at the back of the group, she listened to his instructions as they rehearsed their plan.

She was exhausted from the endless months spent in the jungle. Emaciated, her arms and legs punctured with ulcers and insect bites, her uniform torn to shreds. The pallor on her face had turned grey.

She loathed these barbaric surprise sorties – she didn't mind derailing mail trains or slashing rubber crops and it was all very well defending a communist camp from British patrols but watching men being gunned down left a dry sickness in her stomach. Nevertheless Bong was adamant that they had to make a preemptive attack. *Dyaks*, headhunting trackers from Borneo, were assisting the Security Forces. Each day a unit of South Wales Borderers, led by tattooed tribesmen with four-foot blow-pipes, was gaining ground on them. Earlier a local villager informed Bong that he'd seen these *Dyaks*, clad in only loincloths and with tigers' teeth in their ears, about six miles to the east. He said they resembled savages and carried dried human heads on the ends of poles, the eye sockets stuffed with seashells.

Bong said they needed to make a show of strength. Mabel was going to stick her hand up and ask if this was going to be like what the Americans called a turkey shoot, but controlled herself at the last second. She had once grilled him on whether he ever felt for the men that he killed. He considered the question. "Of course I do. But any empathy I might feel is neutralized by my love for the Party."

They burrowed into the heart of the jungle. Hundreds of photographs of smiling, well-fed, surrendered Communists lay strewn across the forest floor and in the treetops. Mabel picked up one of the thousands of propaganda leaflets air dropped from the sky into the jungle each day. She read the words: *We understand what you have done is for the Revolution. But you are a human being and we all make mistakes. Surrender and all will be forgiven. Surrender and you will be treated well.*

The undergrowth swam with oily mud.

The soles of Mabel's shoes often got sucked by the clay. The effort of lifting each leg burned the muscles in her legs. Eventually her feet became saturated and she felt the wet earth ooze between her toes. "Out of the lion's den, into the lion," she whispered to herself, letting her gaze wander over the rainbow of tropical greens. "It's like an endless road through hell." All the while the team kept their heads down, focused, mud in nostrils, aware of the snakes and other hazards all around. Mabel repeatedly snagged her shoulder bag on thorny vines. Sweat stung her eyes. Trailing thorns pulled on her clothes, tearing them further, and the deeper they crept through the belly of the *ulu* the more her hair got snagged on ropes of dangling vines.

Finally, dropping her head, exhausted, she had to stop. She made a noise to attract Bong. *"Psst!"*

He turned.

"What is it?"

She gestured for him to approach her. "I need to pee."

He shook his head no.

"Serious! I need to pee!"

Behind his round glasses, Bong blinked his eyes. Mabel hopped from foot to foot like a gecko on hot cement.

"If I piss my pants, the whole jungle will smell it and come running!"

He made a sign to the others with his hands and they all dropped into a crouch. "Follow me," he growled.

He led her away from the men into a space where elephants, feasting on palm trees, had torn open a clearing. As they walked she took his hand. Brown dirt and gun grease under his fingernails. She realized that, at the prospect of being alone with Bong, she was getting aroused. Finding a nook where she could relieve herself she asked, "Are you going to watch me?"

"Of course." He was grinning like a schoolboy.

"So you're a maximum crazy pervert too."

Bong stuck his tongue out and crossed his eyes.

"Stop it!" she shushed, trying to suppress her giggles. To her delight Bong kept pulling silly faces. In one fluid movement Mabel yanked down her overalls and squatted, laughing and peeing in little squirts.

Sat on her haunches she could see nothing of the sky when she looked up. The roof of the world was a thatch of vegetation. The foliage was so green and thick that it left a malachite scorch mark on the back of her eyelids whenever she blinked. There were no signs that anyone had ever been here before. Only rarely did light stream in through a hole; a thin ray of sunburst through dagger-shaped leaves. She picked a leaf off a tree and curled it to make a whistle. Then, remembering the need for silence, she unfurled it and dabbed the spot between her legs.

An hour later, the whole party emerged out of the swollen mass of vegetation. Pushing through, they crept out of the belly of the forest, out of the skyless canopy. In the clearing they could see the main road about a half-mile away; but first they had to navigate a gorge. The drop was steep, at least thirty feet. Mabel, using the aerial roots of a strangler fig tree to gain purchase and grip, slid down on her bottom, spilling into the muddy chasm below.

Bunched into groups of four, spread twenty metres apart, watching the road through binoculars, the predatory wait began. In the clearing wet leaves glistened in the sunlight. Bong, hunched behind an uprooted tree, glared into the low horizon with one eye closed, like a sharpshooter on a shooting range. Mabel wondered if she would die today, if Bong might. Her face muscles and her limbs hardened; even the air seemed to blur and stiffen, making things sway around her. The waiting made her breathless, flared her nostrils.

An hour went by. Mabel was daydreaming, staring at a rhinoceros hornbill feasting high up in a tropical rambutan tree, admiring its beauty, when the first crackle rang out.

"Let fly! Right flank! Right flank!"

The scatter of gunfire threw foliage to the forest floor, showering the air with splintered leaves.

Mabel ducked her head and covered her ears with her hands. The ground pinged and zipped with ricocheting bullets. Boots thumped the earth all about her. "Grenades!" Bong cried, firing his rifle from the hip, recoiling with each shot. "Get the grenades off! Come on! Pour it on them!"

Amid the shrieking monkeys, a Sten gun opened up, ripping through the vegetation. One of the men to Mabel's left spun round like a top. A wound on his neck appeared as brilliant and red as a bird's-eye chilli. Without hesitating Mabel fetched a long strip of bandage from her bag and applied direct pressure to the hole, feeling the fountain welling through her fingers. "Leave it to me!" she shouted. "Let go!" Mouth gurgling, tongue sticking out, his hands clawed at his throat; she had to fight him off and pin one of his arms down with her knee. A deep growl came from the depths of his stomach as a dark stain of urine soaked through from in the man's groin.

One after another grenades discharged, clapping the breath out of her. In the corner of her eyes, the armoured car erupted with a *cha-whump*. A tree burst overhead and a branch came swishing down. Grapeshot debris fell from the sky.

"How is he?" Bong asked, shielding her with his body, firing his gun intermittently.

"Bleeding severely. I cannot tell yet if the airway is obstructed." She bent down and listened to his chest, felt his ribs rise and fall with shallow breathing "Quick, help me get him upright. Take off his cartridge belt."

"Medic! *Mediiiiiiiiic!*" A frantic voice screamed in the distance.

"His airway is clear. Bong, keep your hand over this bandage. Press hard. When it's soaked through don't remove it. Just apply these new bandages over the old ones, understand? Just squeeze tight, then bind it. Use this bootstring if you have to. He's going to be all right."

"Where are you going?"

"Over there."

"Over there?" he repeated. A large vein on his head grew pronounced. "No, stay back!"

"Look, let me do my job!"

She ran as quickly as she could in a crouch. A bullet zinged past her ear like a needle of dark light, thudding into the tree behind. She'd never felt so exposed and unprotected, so full of purpose. A fire was burning in front, plumes of sooty smoke billowing from an armoured car. Five, six, seven men had been belched forth from the twisted husk of metal, their faces blackened, elbows twisted and snapped. Burned as black as soy sauce.

She heard the cry for help again.

A blond British soldier was slumped on the road behind the blazing vehicle, his ruined clothes splashed with black blood.

"Where are you hurt?" She spoke quietly and assuredly, crouching down beside him.

"Leg and stomach I think." He began to shiver violently.

A puncture had opened up in his belly like a mouth, as round and dark as an antique coin. There was also a fist-sized hole in his hip – red on the outside and white sinew and exposed bone within, making Mabel think of a ruptured apple.

She immediately searched for an exit wound. "Stay with me," she said. "What's your name?"

"Evans, Corporal Johnny Evans." His face contorted.

"Keep your eyes focused on me, all right, Johnny Evans? Stay with me! Keep focused!" She grasped at the two torn ends of material by his hip and ripped them further. Saturated with blood, the wound felt like wet, warm bread. "Are you still with me, Johnny?"

"I'm afraid." The muscles on his neck stood out like blades.

"You needn't be afraid, Johnny," she replied, removing scissors from her bag. She cut through his clothes. His guts were opened up like a tin of tomato soup. She pressed her hands flat against his stomach, which kept his insides from spilling out.

"What the hell do you think you're doing?"

She looked up and saw Bong looming over her.

"Saving his life." She jabbed a shot of morphine into him.

"You can fucking stop that right now. We don't have enough bandages and morphine as it is."

She dragged her eyes across his face as a farmer drags his hoe across the soil. "And you can fucking start acting like a human being for once in your life!"

He tried to wrench her hand from the soldier's abdomen, but Mabel was fired up now. "Don't you dare!" she cried and kept her fingers splayed, pressed over the crater with the flat of her hand.

"He's the enemy."

"For God's sake, shut up and help me! The bullet's lodged deep inside him. His spleen is punctured. I've got to stop the bleeding."

Bong looked at Evans. His body was shaking but his face looked calm now. "Do you have a smoke?"

"A what?" said Bong.

Evans inhaled and exhaled loudly. "Cigarette."

"In my pocket," Bong said, reaching for his packet. He lit one and placed it between the Welshman's lips.

The ground about them looked as though it had been saturated with wine; Mabel's uniform grew spattered with burgundy. She worked on Evans for several minutes, digging her fingers into him. "There it is." She'd found the slug and tried to gain purchase on it. The wound made a sucking sound as she pulled the bullet from his flesh. "Keep your eyes focused on me, Johnny Evans!"

When his eyes glazed over, half-closed and unblinking at the twilight, Mabel stiffened, curled her fingers into balls and thumped him hard across the chest.

She worked on him for several minutes, straining to get his heart to work.

Eventually, Bong draped an arm around her shoulders and eased her to her feet.

The steel carcass of the armoured car continued to smoke in the background. All the British soldiers were dead. Flocks of crows charcoaled the sky, heading for the coast, fleeing the sounds of guns.

She rubbed the filthy mess of tarry blood off her arms with a clutch of leaves. Already Corporal Evans' blown-apart stomach was crawling with ants.

That night Mabel built a platform from bamboo and settled down on her makeshift cot. Having tied several tourniquets and set a broken wrist, she scrubbed the dried blood from her fingernails and tried to forget what she'd seen earlier on.

In the near distance men from her platoon were busy either cleaning captured machine guns or sorting ammunition belts.

She fell into an abbreviated sleep. Mosquitoes stirred her awake every few minutes. She tossed and turned, still hearing the ricochet of screams, eventually having to cover her face with a jacket before falling into a deep slumber. She was lying on her front when her right arm slipped from the platform bed and dangled towards the rainforest floor.

A few hours before dawn she woke up having dreamed she was in a hospital with a fractured elbow. Half-asleep and woolly-headed, Mabel tried to take off the cast on her broken humerus but quickly worked out she wasn't wearing a cast and was busy tugging on the huge fold of leathery skin which had enveloped her arm like a sleeve. It was then that she woke with a start. The night was still and coal black. There was a high, musty smell all about her and her shoulders ached. When she moved a fraction, she found that her right forearm had gone numb and heavy. Groggily, she jerked her hand from the elbow but found it had become a dead weight. "Damn it," she hissed. "Bloody pins and needles." Still on her front, she pulled her jacket from her eyes with her left hand and tried to roll onto her back. It was then that she came face to face with it: the Pontianak – the vampire of Malay folklore with its elongated tongue and terrifying fingernails that ripped out a person's sex organs. She stared at it, lips agape. The lean, flat head was the size of a king coconut. Its eyes were bright yellow like shiny stones with narrow, slit pupils. The rotten fangs gaped at her.

As she reared back, she suddenly realized with equal horror that it wasn't the dreaded Pontianak at all but a serpent. A massive reticulated python was inches from Mabel's nose. Its snout was butting her chin. She could smell its breath as it inched its hinged jaws over its prey. It took Mabel several seconds to realize that the prey was her own right arm, that the snake had deadened it with its coils. The python had taken it in, up to her shoulder. She was being eaten alive.

Opening her mouth wide, Mabel began to scream.

4

"Paupers!" Mother bleated to no one in particular, folding her legs under an Il Porco table. "The bloody old fool turned us into paupers." She was looking at her bank book.

"What happened?" Dungeonboy asked Uncle Big Jowl who was tucking into a plate of *char siu faan*.

"Nothing, aahh! Missie-Mummy's still damn-powerful bitter that before he died her husband signed over the banking and rubber concessions to the Japanese in return for his safety. Once a year or so, she has volcano-tantrums."

Mother clacked her tongue. "Worse still, it drove my sons deeper into the clutches of those Jehovah's. You think that having one Jehovah's Witness in the family was bad enough, but both brothers claiming to be 'enlightened ones'? The nincompoops truly believe that blood transfusions are against God's will. What will happen if either of them has accident? *Chee-chee-chee!* I tell you, I'm at wit's end!"

"Accuse me, you likey coffee dis morning, is it, Missie-Mummy?" asked Dungeonboy.

"Coffee? Your coffee tastes like durian dust. Bring me toast-bread with condensed milk."

Lu See appeared from the kitchen. "Morning, Mother. You look a bit frayed at the edges."

"Frayed? I'm not frayed," she said, sounding frayed.

"Are you feeling all right?

"*All right?* I'm better than all right. How about you? Stomach better?"

"Not really. Might be an ulcer."

"I wonder if it is from filthy germs. How many one-eyed

dogs have you taken in today?" she said derisively, looking hard at Pebbles who was busy nibbling a front paw. "Why *must* you bring in from the street? *Cha!* Such dirty animals! Licking their . . . their . . . things all the time!"

"I'm giving them a better life. They get a nice roof over their heads and a proper bath once a month. Who knows how long they'd live with all those crazy drivers out there. Isn't that right, Pebbles?"

Pebbles flattened her ears and wagged her tail.

"Soon, nah, everywhere will have ticks and fleas. Look how it scratches itself all day long! You should throw them all back, liao!"

Lu See's mouth soured.

"Later you go back inside kitchen and think about what I say for ten minutes then decide I'm right. Your mother is always right."

"Why is it that every time I speak to you I feel as if I'm being forced to drink vinegar?"

"*Cha!*" She spoke across Lu See. "You see how she make me feel welcome here?"

"Please don't take offence, Mother, but sometimes you're as welcome here as a doctor with a rubber enema hose."

"I come all this way to see you."

"Mother, you live two streets away."

Mother raised her eyebrows, and slipping on her batwing reading glasses, started on last week's crossword puzzle. Smiling faintly, she said, "Bring me hot milk tea, nah. One of your special cups of *teh tarik*."

Lu See adjusted her apron and clucked her tongue. Reluctantly, she made her way to the kitchen to boil some water. Inside, the tubes of the radio began to glow – Dungeonboy stared at the black dial of the Zenith console radio.

"She's such a bloody interfering . . . So *kaypoh!*" Lu See blurted to Dungeonboy as she spooned tea leaves into a pot. "I bet she comes here just to check up on me."

The radio played a Peggy Lee song. Dungeonboy clicked his fingers out of rhythm to the music.

"If she ever asks you about me, don't tell her anything!"

Dungeonboy sucked his teeth and nodded like a metronome. His eyes remained glued to the powdery black grille. Before working at Il Porco he'd never come across a radio.

"Do you understand? Are you following me?"

"Of coss, I follow you like my own shadow."

Seconds later Peggy Lee's voice faded.

'. . . and now it's time for Malay Woman's Hour,' said the radio presenter, 'where our own Dr Chow and Mrs Gangooly will be discussing the health benefits of star anise . . .'

"Were you listening to what I just said?"

"Yes, lah! No tell Missie-Mummy anyfing."

"And why not?"

"Because Missie-Mummy just like fart bubbo in bath tub. Gets up everyone noses."

Lu See rubbed the skin between her eyes. Something bubbled painfully within her bowels. "Well, that's not quite what I meant, but I think you got the gist of it."

She emerged from the kitchen with a cup of *teh tarik*. Mother raised her eyebrows at her and brushed imaginary dust off the table top. Under her batik apron, Lu See's summer dress had a small hole near the right shoulder. As she placed the cup down, Mother glowered as if she'd just witnessed Lu See pawn off another family heirloom, just as her husband had done during the war. She raised her index finger and prodded Lu See on the arm. "*Chee!* What happen to you? Your dress is torn?"

"I'll mend it later."

"I'm glad," she said, sounding not the least bit glad.

"This is a restaurant not a clothing boutique. That'll be sixty cents for the tea and toast."

"What happen if you hit by a bus? What will the ambulance men say if they saw you in such rags?"

"I think if I was hit by a bus my first concern would be staying alive, not how my clothes look."

"You really are giving us Teohs a bad name."

Uncle Big Jowl winked at her. "This coming, aahh, from someone with enough make-up on to make an Ipoh prostitute blush."

"See what I have to put up with?" she addressed an imaginary audience. "No respect for Ah-Ma!"

"Joking-joking, lah." The big man said placatingly.

"I mean," Mother said, gesturing at Lu See with a square of toast slathered with condensed milk. "Your mother's not a snob-snob or anything, but I believe that appearing well groomed and dressing elegantly helps social standing, no?"

Of course, Lu See knew that Mother was right. As the owner of Il Porco it was imperative that she looked her best. She just didn't want to give her the satisfaction.

"No wonder you cannot find a man, lah," her mother continued, scratching her palms. "You should really take notes."

"I'm perfectly happy being by myself, thanks very much," Lu See said.

"Yes, I'm sure you are."

Lu See gave a resigned shake of the head. She pulled up a chair and sat down beside her mother, more to relieve the pain in her tummy than anything else. They looked at each other. "I'm almost 41."

"And I'm 64. No springtime chicken. Past my prime."

"You were past your prime when Churchill was born."

Mother looked out into the middle distance, back at her imaginary audience. "Cha! See how she talks to me?"

"The truth is I'm too old to find a man. Lord knows I'd love to have someone take care of me, someone to help with the restaurant, with the dogs." *Someone to have wild sex with.* "But what are my chances. At my age, what's left for me?"

"Great-uncle Loo got a woman pregnant when he was 84, aahh!" Uncle Big Jowl snorted.

Lu See smiled, as did Mother. They broke into giggles. "Maybe there's hope for me yet. More toast?"

"No, I rest." Mother extracted a Malayan dollar from her pocketbook and handed it to Lu See.

"True, at your age you have to watch your weight." *Kaching!* went the cash register.

At thirty seconds to midnight the music stopped. Elvis Presley was half way through *Teddy Bear* on Radio Malaya when the sound snapped off.

There followed twenty seconds of dead air before a clipped Empire accent solemnly described the lowering of the Union Jack at the Selangor Club and in its place the new Federation of Malaya flag was hoisted at exactly 12.01 a.m. "After 83 years of British control, Malaya is now a sovereign independent nation." He went on to say that it would remain in the Commonwealth, adding that the Commonwealth Far East Strategic Reserve would add support to Malaya's external and internal defences and that the country's Emergency Regulations were still in force. He also noted that an unspecified number of senior British police officers and judiciary staff would stay on to oversee the successful transition.

It was a humid and sticky night. Stan's shirt was stuck to his back. He plucked at the parts where his shirt stuck to his skin. All about him families were out in force and revellers were setting off fire crackers, drinking Coca Cola and Green Spot through paper straws, and shouting 'Merdeka! Merdeka! Freedom! Freedom!' Most of the people, he was sure, didn't even know what the term meant.

He made his way through the chaos of hawkers where earlier, at a stall, he ate a portion of *otak-otak*, the delicious fish paste custard wrapped in banana leaf. Multi-coloured banners fluttered from streetlamps. Windows were strung with fairy lights. Tall palm trees dripped with lustrous bunting. A Malay man in a *songkok* was dancing down the street, blowing a trumpet. Next to him, a fat Chinese fellow was hitting the back of his wok with a pair of chopsticks. Everywhere people were singing and shouting. 'Malaya is for all Malayans!' they cried, watery-eyed. Despite it being Ramadan month the Malays were out in full, waving their country's new flag aloft; having fasted between *Fajr* (dusk) and *Maghrib* (sunset) they were finally letting off some steam. Car horns blared; radios sang. From dilapidated rooftops residents clapped and whooped as young children, clutching on to their parents' necks, waved at the crowds. It was way past their bedtimes but they'd been caught up in the adults' excitement and were wide-awake, not knowing why everybody seemed quite so happy.

Along Petaling Street roadblocks, sand bags and barbed wire clogged up traffic. Nearby, Stan stood with his truncheon ready, overseeing a cordon of over a hundred other policemen as they linked arms outside Independence Stadium. They formed a line separating the UMNO delegates from the masses. UMNO was the country's largest political party. "For the love of Rita! Keep the bloody line tight, sergeant!" he cried.

"Yes, saar!"

Stan didn't like this district; Old Pudu Road, a few streets down, was a hotbed of spies, informers and double agents. *Spies.* The word made him think of Mabel. He remembered the day she ran off.

He was lunching at Il Porco the afternoon Mabel telephoned to say she wasn't coming home.

"What do you mean you're not coming home?" Lu See asked, talking quickly into the receiver.

"It's Bong. He wants me to be with him." Her voice was calm.

"You can be with him here. You don't have to leave. Why must you leave?"

"Because I want to."

"I don't understand."

Stan recalled looking at Lu See and seeing the panic mist her eyes. What's happened? he wanted to ask.

When she replaced the handset on the cradle slowly, defensively, she told him Mabel had gone to join the Communists. She spent the rest of the day with her head in her hands.

Stan wiped his brow with his sleeve and scanned the area. A small group of St John Ambulance girls waited by the post office, smoking by the colonnades amidst the scribbles of barbed wire. With a surge of invigoration, Stan climbed up on to the bonnet of an armed personnel carrier to get a better look at the crowds streaming in from Sultan Street. In the far distance he saw the giant billboards for the Rex Cinema. He reached into a pocket and pulled out a sweet. Popping a Caramel Bullet into his mouth, standing with arms akimbo, he could make out Robert Mitchum's droopy face promoting *The Night of the Hunter*.

He looked back into the throng that had gathered on the boundaries of the *padang*. A group of women with paper fans were sipping bottles of Green Spot out of straws, faces alight with pleasure. Moments later he heard a rallying shout. Two Sikh officers had fallen onto their backsides as they chased after a Chinese man on a bicycle. He had a long mane of hair gathered into a ponytail. Bursting though the junction, he rode the bicycle at speed, all the way up to the police line. Stan watched as he skidded to a stop, balanced a sandalled foot on the road, withdrew a pistol from his belt and aimed it at Stan's face. Before Stan could move, the man squeezed the trigger.

5

By ten the next morning, the corner of Macao and Hokkien was spilling over with gossip. "You heard about the attempted murder of the police inspector, is it? Yes, the one with the tombstone teeth! Cannot believe-lah! Him one damn-fierce lucky bugger! You heard that the gun got jam-jammed and misfired, otherwise he sure to be dead as doornail and pushing up daisies, no? What happened to the gunman? The shooter got away, lah. Ran off zigzag-aloo into the crowd and disappeared vanish!"

Lu See listened to the jawing and chitchat with a thankful heart. She mouthed a silent prayer that following their failure the perpetrators wouldn't make a second attempt at Stan's life.

Into the glare, she glanced down Macao Street, at the clock tower. She still felt a pang at no longer having Adrian's watch, but giving it away had cemented the reconciliation with the Woos.

The stretch of road was overflowing with cobblers, street-barbers and tin tinkerers using antiquated tools. Hawkers pushed trolleys, pinching squeeze horns as they passed. Small Indian boys went from door to door, skipping over the monsoon drains, peddling Hindu movie magazines and song posters, and with Hari Raya approaching the *serunding* stall owners were busy cooking vast quantities of meat floss, stirring the pasty mixture over low fires for hours on end.

Shielded from the sun, women gathered in the shade of the five-foot-way exclaiming over the price of pineapples and soap and the shortage of sugar as they returned from morning market. Despite the Malay economy emerging from the post Korean war slump, luxuries remained dear and fears lurked of currency depreciation.

Nearby, alongside the lake by the red mosque, a kite festival was taking place. Lu See could hear the squeals and laughter of excited children. Swigging from a bottle of milk of magnesia, she emerged from the restaurant's threshold into the steamy heat that swamped the city. A *zakat* collector had set up a counter by the roadside to raise alms for the poor. Several people were already lining up to pay the tithe before Hari Raya. Next to him, beside a 'Drink Milo' advertising sign, a bill was being plastered onto the wall. It read:

"Rewards for Information. Substantial rewards will be paid to all who cooperate with the authorities in providing information about Communist Guerrillas and Gangsters. Useful Information EARNS CASH."

Suppressing a scowl, Lu See noticed a discarded rattan basket at the corner of the street. She went across and swept it up. Might come in use one day, she said to herself.

Shortly afterwards, an armoured police van rumbled by with a Magnavox public address system; a recorded message blared out that citizens were required to name known Communists and their supporters.

Inside, the phone rang. Lu See ignored it; she had long since stopped hoping that it might be Mabel calling and she did not accept reservations so she couldn't fathom why anybody would want to call her.

"*Wai-eeee!*" hollered an old man from within Il Porco. Old Fishlips Foo, the former MPAJA fighter, the resistance movement that fought against the Japanese, was eighty now and each day he planted himself in the same chair from ten in the morning to six in the evening. If he wasn't slurping his soup or shouting tyrannical orders, Fishlips was busy scratching his legs and burping whilst complaining about his long-dead wife. Almost as annoying was his constant staring at other people's food – and it wasn't a casual passing glance either, but a proper visual inspection. Only when his daughter came to fetch him at six o'clock did the restaurant get any respite. He did serve one useful purpose, however. Whenever the phone rang, Old Fishlips, perched near the telephone counter, would pick up the receiver with a resounding '*Wai-eeeee*!' and rail loudly at the befuddled caller about the terrible state of the world.

Lu See felt a wave of nausea coming on. She reached into her *samfoo* pocket and removed a small cut-glass atomizer of rose water, which she sprayed on her face. When that didn't work she applied a judicious smear of mentholated Tiger Balm to the points of her forehead and settled down in a corner of the restaurant where she self-medicated with milk of magnesia and fluffy white bread dipped in cabbage juice.

As she sat in one corner, she watched Old Fishlips in his cotton singlet scratch his legs in the opposite corner.

"How's the soup today, Mr Foo?" Lu See asked, smiling at the liver-spotted face.

"Too hot! Always you try to burn me."

Lu See touched her wrist to her forehead with exasperation. "Give it a blow and it will soon cool down. Who was on the phone, by the way?"

"Dead man's head! Another crossed line, would you believe! These bloody rubber-estate gossipers! All they do is talktalk and badmouth us Chinese! What gives them the right to think they're better than us? Bumiputra they call themselves! Princes of the earth! Bloody joke! *Hum gaa chaan!*"

"Mr Foo, language please."

"*Sai yun tau*," he muttered under his breath. "My grandson, Bong, he understands me. He knows what I mean."

Colouring, Lu See sidled up beside him with coffee cup in hand, looking as if she'd dabbed spits of rouge on her face. "Mr Foo, please. We've talked about this before. We don't mention Bong in public, remember?"

"You've known him since he was a boy." He blinked, arranging his thoughts. "The British gave our resistance fighters medals for what they did against the Japanese, awarded Chin Peng, the leader of the Malay Communist Party, an OBE – "

"Yes, yes I know. But the world was a different place then."

Old Fishlips Foo grunted. "Yes, now only thing young people can think about is American imperialist cinema."

Half way through her cabbage juice, a Ford Anglia police car puttered to a stop on the kerb, avoiding the monsoon drain. Seconds later, dressed in donkey-brown khaki with shiny silver buttons, Stan strolled in. Removing his cap he dropped into the chair beside her.

"You look very dapper today," she said.

"Do I? Thanks." He ran his fingers over his chin. "After my little brush with death I thought I'd treat myself to a proper haircut and shave at Cutthroat Chan's. You're not looking so bad yourself, by the way. In fact I'd say you look rather stunning this morning. Is that a new dress?"

Lu See's face reddened like a slapped bottom. "Sorry, I'm not good with compliments." She paused. "Fancy a cup of tea?"

Stan refused politely. "Actually, this isn't a social call." He cleared his throat. "52 Squadron air dropped millions of propaganda leaflets into the jungle last week telling everyone the war's over. There're rumours that the Reds might be planning a truce with the new Malay government. Of course there's no way in hell that'll happen."

"I heard the same on the wireless."

"Special Branch now has a detailed list of nearly all known Communist guerrillas across the whole peninsula, with photographic records of every bandit. Those that don't give up the fight within the next ten days won't stand a chance of survival."

"Why are you telling me this?"

"Special Branch is aware," he cleared his throat again, "has been aware for quite some time actually, that Mabel's with the Reds and that she's the mistress of one of its hardcore elite, Bong Foo. They also know you're her mother and that you serve tea every day to Bong's grandfather." He aimed his chin at the old man.

"What are you saying? That I'm under suspicion now?" Stan stared at her. His silence turned her blood cold. "Am I going to be pulled in and interrogated?"

"I hope not."

Lu See watched her mother shuffle across the room. Mother didn't speak, but Lu See could tell she was listening. "Is that why you keep coming here? To keep an eye on me? To see if I'm passing secrets to the MCP?"

Stan put his hand on his heart. "No." He shook his head. "I come because I like the food here and I like you."

"So, you're saying I'm not a target."

Stan patted her hand gently and smiled his toothy smile. "I'm an ex-RAF rear gunner. We never lie about our targets." He reached into a pocket and extracted a gumdrop. "All I want to do is bring Mabel home in one piece."

Lu See looked at him with suspicion. "Does this have anything to do with the attempt on your life?"

The phone rang.

"*Wai-eeeeee!*" hollered Old Fishlips.

"So, what do you suggest I do?" she asked, making a helpless gesture.

"Dead man's head! *Sai yun tau!* Crossed line again!"

"I want you to find Mabel before it's too late," he whispered as though revealing a state secret. "The Reds that surrender will be treated well, some may be sent to a rehabilitation camp, but the majority'll be allowed to get back to their daily lives. Those that don't surrender face a mandatory death sentence. They'll be executed without trial."

"Oh, that's wonderful news," she said sarcastically, all of a sudden hearing a tone in her own voice she didn't recognize: irrational bitterness. "And how do you expect me to go and find her? Do you think I should wade through the *ulu* shouting her name?"

With a blister of curses rattling off her tongue, Lu See stormed out to the back of the restaurant to the small courtyard. Drying tablecloths hung on lines of rope attached to trees. Scrub boards leaned against the walls. Everywhere you looked there were pots and pots of rosemary bushes. This was her private garden. It was the garden where Mabel as a young teen learned to do headstands; where Mabel first announced she wanted to become a nurse; where she used to sit in the shade and revise for her Senior Cambridge Examinations, where she blew out the cake candles on her nineteenth birthday – the last birthday they'd spent together.

It was a place that held many memories. It was also a good place to think.

Twenty minutes later Lu See returned feeling as deflated as a tattered windsock. She sat down besides Stan and hung her head in despair. "Sorry about that. My stomach's been killing me. The truth is," she paused, "I feel so helpless."

"Don't worry, I have a plan," he said, keeping his voice low. "I want you to keep this to yourself. Can you do that for me?" He threw a suspicious glance over his shoulder and then stared hard into Lu See's eyes. "I can find Mabel. I can bring her home. But it won't be easy and it's a little risky." Lu See encouraged him to go on. "I can't talk now." He slipped her a card with an address scribbled across it. "Meet me at this location tomorrow morning at ten. And make sure you're not followed."

The address on the card led Lu See to an obscure building near the railway station. She made her way down Victory Avenue on foot, passing the Moorish domes and minarets, and turned discreetly into a narrow alleyway.

There was a door at the far end. Lu See knocked three

times and was met by Stan. "Sorry for all the cloak and dagger stuff," he said, shutting the door behind them. Once inside she saw five women seated at a row of typewriters and a gigantic map of Malaya pinned to the back wall. The place smelled of rubbing oil and typewriter ink. "Is this your office?"

"It's one of several we use." Noticing her wince, he asked. "How's your tummy?"

"The same."

"Could be an ulcer."

He led her through a gloomy corridor and into a communications room where a man in shirt-sleeves manned a bank of telephones. She saw two post-office clocks, one showing Malay time, one London time. Several other rooms branched off from here to the left and right, some with red lights lit over the closed doors.

Crouched by a filing cabinet, a Malay woman in tortoise-shell spectacles looked at her.

"This is May," said Stan. "May, make sure I'm not disturbed."

He grabbed a door handle and yanked it.

The interview room was windowless and bare apart from a small table and a pair of wooden chairs. They sat. Stan removed a gum drop from his pocket and popped it in his mouth.

"Right, let's get straight to it, shall we?" he said, flashing his teeth. "As I mentioned yesterday, I think I can find Mabel and bring her home."

"How?"

"Our dandruffy boffins have devised a battery-operated radio receiver, the same type as the ones used by the guerrillas. The only difference is that when switched on our model transmits a silent signal, a type of homing device that can be picked up by our spotter airplanes flying overhead. Once we get a 'fix' on their positions, we'll drop in a load of non-lethal bromide gas and surround them, forcing them to surrender. There'll be minimal force applied."

She looked at Stan. "Why are you telling me this? Surely this is all classified information."

"We need your help. This fellow Bong, Mabel's troop leader, is a very slippery customer, he moves around the jungle like a ghost. To get the radio receiver to him we have to ensure that in his eyes it comes from a reliable source: who better than Mabel's mother?"

"You want me to betray my daughter?"

"No," he grunted, "I want you to save her life. So long as she's with Bong she won't turn herself in. This way we can nab them and ensure her safety."

He watched her, analysing her reaction.

Lu See shook her head slowly, saying, "You throw the stone, but hide your hand."

"I'm sorry?"

"And if the stone misses, I get the blame, is that it?"

"No, that's not it."

Lu See looked at the ceiling, unsure. "I don't know—"

"She'll be executed as a terrorist if you don't do this."

"How can you be certain your plan will work?"

"I can't guarantee it'll work, Lu See, but it's the best chance we'll get."

"What if something goes wrong? I mean . . ." she hesitated, at a loss for words.

"You're going to have to trust me." He glanced over his shoulder as a reflex. He pushed an envelope into her hands. "Here's three hundred Malayan dollars. This is what I want you to do."

Lu See listened and nodded, listened and nodded. When Stan finished explaining, she rose from her chair and followed him out into the communications room.

There was a man standing under the post-office clocks. He was dressed in an immaculate white suit. He had his back to her. One of his shoulders was lower than the other.

And she was suddenly overcome with fear.

Stan took her by the elbow. "No," she whispered.

"For the love of Rita! What is it?" Stan demanded impatiently.

"Him?" she hissed.

The man in the white suit did not turn around.

Stan pulled Lu See by the elbow and soon she found herself in the gloomy corridor, well out of earshot. "Do you know who that is?" she spat, staring Stan hard in the eyes. "That's the Black-headed Sheep."

Stan drew her aside and kept his voice low. "And now he's one of our most important agents." Lu See felt as if her head was about to burst.

"He's supposed to be dead!"

Stan shushed her.

"The papers reported he'd been killed by the MPAJA. And I saw a man, hanging dead from a tree in Po On Village. I thought at the time I'd been mistaken, that it wasn't him, but the newspapers . . ." Her voice trailed off.

Stan shook his head. "Somebody else, made to look like him."

"I don't understand."

"The man you saw was a doppelganger, probably a drunkard or a beggar from the south, hired to look like Woo Hak-yeung. They dressed him in a white suit and paid him to stroll into the village toddy shop and start mouthing off that he was the Black-headed Sheep. Poor sod never saw it coming. The villagers were hungry for blood."

"But Woo Hak-yeung is a murdering war criminal, a traitor to the Crown."

"Yes, we know all about his past. But the thing is, during the war that piece of garbage in there was one of Japan's top informers. He knew everything about the anti-Japanese guerrilla movement. How they used the jungle, how they communicated, how their finances worked. Those same people who were in the MPAJA are now Communist terrorists. Look, I don't know what happened between you and him and frankly I don't want to know. The thing is, we need his help, Lu See. If we're going to win this war, we need him. And that's really all I can tell you."

Lu See watched Stan's eyes, scarcely able to breathe. A pressure in her throat was building. His words had a nightmare quality; all of a sudden she felt as though she was in the middle of a dream, locked in a room with a monster.

"You'll still do this for us, won't you?" he said, eventually. "You'll still go through with the plan?"

The pressure in her throat increased. She hardly heard what he was saying. Slowly, she nodded.

I should have known, thought Lu See, *I should have known he'd come back and haunt my dreams.*

She remembered the feeling of helplessness when she'd discovered the organ pipes were gone; dug up and replaced with a rotting sheep's head. When had he done it? When had he switched them? It must have been some time in 1943, soon after he'd befriended Tozawa. Had he been watching her all the time? She pictured him laughing at her, at her stupidity. The copper would have been invaluable to the Japanese war effort – smelted down, it would be used for wiring electrical equipment and radio components. The Kempeitai would have rewarded him handsomely for it.

The bastard, the bloody bastard. Of all her ghosts the Black-headed Sheep was the one that had never been laid to rest.

Her blood ran cool again as his face, his mole, the ugly slant of his shoulders all came to mind. And she knew, that despite the dangers, she was going to have to expose him.

Rain clouds marked the KL skyline, spilling moisture. Lu See looked at the clock. A sudden spasm streaked through her gut. Ignoring the pain, she concentrated on the time. It was almost 4 p.m. and the city seemed to hold its breath as the usual daily downpour approached. The wet rooftops, warped from the monsoon rains, rang out with the call of the muezzin.

Allaaaahu Akhbar! Allaaaahu Akhbar! Subhaan-Allaah wa'l-hamdu Lillaah wa laa ilaaha ill-Allaah wa Allaahu akbar wa laa hawla wa la quwwata illa Billaah.

The late afternoon heat, combined with the effects of Ramadan fasting, were making people heavy-lidded. Along Macao Street some of the Muslim eateries had drawn curtains across their windows so that the hungry could snack without guilt or recrimination.

An Indian woman in a sari floated by, a section of her stomach showing; the skin paler than her face and arms. It was Mrs Viswanath from the spice shop. As she passed the restaurant, she waved a languid hand at Lu See. "*Selamat Siang,*" she sang.

Lu See nodded at her and checked her watch again, waiting for the top of the hour.

Wobbling her head, Mrs Viswanath's scarlet bindi shone between her eyebrows as she smiled.

To distract herself, Lu See turned to the porcelain ewer and basin at Il Porco's entrance where diners washed their hands before and after meals. Presently, the ewer was a quarter full and Lu See topped it up with fresh water, adding half a lime to give it a squeeze of scent.

A minute or so later she poured herself a whisky and threw it back in one gulp, wiping her mouth with the back of a hand like John Wayne in a Wild West saloon. Then she snatched the large brown parcel from behind the counter and headed down Macao Street, pushing past the lottery ticket vendors. Dressed in lightweight *samfoo* and her favourite *kasut manek* beaded slippers, she looked like any other middle-class Chinese woman in the city.

By the Tung Wah Association assembly hall on Klyne Street an elderly gentleman practising tai-chi arched his eyebrows at her. She dropped a white handkerchief and stepped on it with her right foot. He twisted his chin towards an alleyway.

Here she found a small room dug from a hole in a wall. Through the narrow door, just wide enough to allow one person through at a time, she saw a dim naked bulb drooping from the ceiling. Inside, seated on a wooden stool, a bald man in a string vest with a toothpick between his lips shot her a what-do-you-want glare. There was a mirror on the wall and several pairs of scissors and combs thrown together on a brass tray. The place smelt of Brylcreem.

"Yes?" he challenged. She regarded him. His spectacles magnified the size of his squinting eyes, making them appear far too big for him.

"I'm Teoh Lu See. I am here to see the mule."

His gaze travelled down her face. "There is nobody here by that name."

She persisted. "Do you know why I have come?" The man feigned ignorance, examining a hairbrush for hairs. "I think you do," she said. "My daughter Mabel, you know who she is. I want you to give her this money and I want her to have these things." She opened the brown parcel and pulled out Carlisle bandages, linen gauze pads, water purification tablets, a bottle of aspirin and packets of sulfanilamide and $300.

"I don't know what you are talking about," the man said unconvincingly.

"Look, these things could help keep her alive."

"Who sent you here?"

"I've been trying to contact my daughter for over a year!" Lu See exclaimed, almost pleading.

His face softened a fraction. "How do you know about the mule?"

Lu See swallowed. The heat in the airless room was making her perspire; she brushed a strand of sticky hair from her face. "Fishlips Foo told me," she said. "I have known Bong and his grandfather for years." The man held her gaze. "Use the money on anything you think she and her unit needs, medicines, swabs, food. Can you do this for me?" The man eyed her; his face a map of suspicion. "I can also get my hands on battery-operated radio receivers."

The man said nothing.

"Please don't make this more difficult for me. I should have done this earlier, I should have supported the cause earlier, but I was afraid. I am still afraid."

"I run a barber shop," the man said. "I really cannot help you."

"I have a dozen battery-operated radio receivers in my home. Please allow me to donate them to the barber shop."

The man looked at her. A spark of shrewdness hid behind his eyes.

She made to leave. As she turned he said, almost inaudibly, "I will see what I can do. You are aware we will take the radios apart to check for explosives?"

"As is your right."

"There's one more thing." She extracted Stan's calling card from her sleeve and placed it on a tub of Brylcreem. "On this card is an address. It is a secret place. There's a man who goes there from time to time. He wears a white suit and has a mole on his left cheek. Woo Hak-yeung. You'll remember him as the Black-headed Sheep. During the war he killed many of our friends, many of your colleagues. Perhaps you thought he was dead. Well, he's not. He's alive and he's still killing your colleagues. Do with him as you feel fit."

The man pinched the skin between his eyes. "Someone will contact you about the radio receivers. Do not come back here again."

6

Later, it was business as usual at Il Porco.

"More *teh tarik*!" roared Old Fishlips from the far corner with despotic ferocity.

"Your pulled tea is on its way, Mr Foo. Just be patient," Lu See said. She was in her kitchen, slicing carrot discs. In annoyance the old man flapped the pages of his newspaper and belched.

After fetching his tea, Lu See kneaded her lower abdomen with her thumbs, massaging a spot to the left of her navel. Her stomach cramped more often now and there was blood in her stool. She was sure, too, that she was nursing a fever.

She went to the cashier's desk, removed a piece of writing paper and sat down. Pebbles nudged her with his cold moist nose and because Dungeonboy was sweeping the floor with a broom Lu See was forced to pick up her slippers as he swept up under her.

"*Tsk!* Impossbo, impossbo," he complained, with a grin.

"What is impossible?"

"*Alla mak*, keeping *nee gor* floor clean-ah, of coss! Impossbo! *Ayaahh*, everywhere dog hair! Like when toothless Grandma Fung tries to eat hard, raw carrot. Impossbo!" He laughed.

Mother, seated by the door, adjusted her batwing spectacles. "Lu See, did I tell you that your brothers will be paying you a visit soon? They want to give you earbashing for allowing Mabel to run off the way she did."

"Why on earth would they do that now? Mabel's been gone for ages!" Lu See bristled.

"At first they relied on prayer, hoping Jehovah would bring her home."

"And when prayer fails, they come to badger me. What's it got to do with them, anyway?"

"That's what I say, but you know what James and Peter are like, all holy-than-thou. They always such busybodies."

"I wonder who they take after, aahh!" Uncle Big Jowl strolled in swaying from side to side like a top-heavy bus. "A plate of *char siu faan*, please." He threw a letter on the cashier's desk. "Post just arrived. Looks like you have a fancy letter from the Italian Embassy. See?" He gestured with a salami-like finger. "Says so on the back."

The telephone rang. "*Wai-eeee!*"

Lu See wiped the palms of her hands on her apron and ripped open the envelope and saw a gold-embossed card with an invitation to drinks with the new ambassador. "Strange," she said aloud. "I wonder why they asked me?"

"Maybe they need a new chef, aahh!"

"That'll be the day." Lu See smirked and turned towards Dungeonboy. "Have you done the washroom yet?"

"*Tung yet jun!* Soon-soon, lah. Finish dog hair sweeping first, lah."

"*Hum gaa chaan!*" Fishlips slammed the phone down.

Uncle Big Jowl eyed the invitation. "Friday 13th. Bad joss, bad joss, aahh." He cocked his head. "Never sit at table when thirteen people are seated. Never so long as there is still teeth in my mouth." He knocked three times on his wooden chair. "Are you going to go?"

"To the Italian Embassy?" She shook her head. "Not my cup of congee."

Mother's ears perked up. "I'm not surprised, just look at your appearance – moth-hole in dress, no eye shadow. You think she was *hut-yee*. Sometimes I think you steal clothes from the dustman."

"You know, Mother, I've been thinking. When you're old and senile I'm going to send you out to work at the chicken farm in Pagoh and force you to pluck feathers for ten hours with all the other old, mad, stinky people."

"*Cha!* No respect. You see how my own daughter speaks to me?" she said to her imaginary audience.

"And at the end of every day I'm going to bring my dresses with holes in them for you to mend."

Mother started to grin. "Terrible things she says, meh?"

"And if you refuse to comply I'll jab you with a stick. Mother, stop laughing!"

Mother covered her mouth but continued to giggle. Lu See turned to Dungeonboy, who had taken up his mop. "Scrub the footprints off the toilet seat while you're at it."

When he'd gone Lu See at last found a moment to herself. She remained at the cashier's desk and played with a pen cap, deep in thought. Eventually, she began to write.

When will I get to see you again, Mabel? I find it horrible imagining you in the jungle surrounded by leeches and spiders. Are you in constant danger? Is there anything to eat? Are you hurt? You wanted to be a nurse at school. What happened? Why did you go and do this? Was it to punish me? To reject me for not telling you sooner about Sum Sum?

When, just after the war, Hesha came with that letter saying she was safe and well I wanted to tell you there and then but you were so young. I suppose I was selfish – I was frightened of disappointing you, losing you. I depend on you for love.

I worry so much I cannot sleep at night. I wait and watch from the window. What did you think of me, of your family, when you went off to fight for the Communists? The house is so quiet without you. The dogs miss you. I imagine you think you know what you are doing, know what you are fighting for, that you are proud that you have a cause, but remember those you have left behind. I am your mother, not your birth mother it's true, but your mother all the same. Like it or not, I am. I raised you. I kept you safe for so many years

Lu See stopped writing in mid-sentence. She realized her

lips were moving, muttering Mabel's name under her breath; she crumpled the paper in her hands and threw it angrily to one side.

I kept you safe for so many years. Lu See closed her eyes and clung tightly to the words.

She took a breath and recalled the day Mabel's eyes found hers and blazed with such shock and distress Lu See had been reluctant to meet them.

Mabel had just returned from nursing school and she was frantic. "The administration department is questioning if I am Chinese?"

"What? Why?"

"They have initiated race-based quotas. Malays get first choice of courses available, followed next by the Chinese and finally the Indians. They say from the colour of my skin I might be an Indian. They want clarification."

"Your complexion isn't dark."

"No, but it isn't as fair as most Chinese. And I'm too pale to be Indian."

"It's simply that milky-chocolate shade because you used to spend hours in the sun when you were a child."

"Please don't lie. I know when you're lying. I'm nineteen years old. I've had to live without a father all my life. Tell me, was my father really Adrian Woo? Or was he an Indian?"

"Mabel, really, you mustn't – "

"It was something I never wanted to ask. I never even suspected anything until a few years ago, when I realised that I didn't look like the other Chinese girls at school. But I never dared ask. Well, I want to know the truth now."

Lu See absorbed her daughter's words and shut her eyes briefly.

"Is there something you want to tell me?"

"Mabel," said Lu See. "Please take a seat."

She sat down at the kitchen table. Lu See sat next to her and took her hand. "A long time ago I promised myself you would learn the truth about your life, that I would confess everything . . . I promised I'd tell you one day."

"The truth about my life?" repeated Mabel. "What are you talking about?"

Lu See stroked her daughter's hair. "Please, just listen." Searching for a tissue in her pocket, she began in a wavering voice. "There is a woman in Tibet, a woman called Sum Sum, who is a great friend of mine, almost a sister, perhaps even more than a sister . . . A long time ago she accompanied me to Cambridge, to England, to the place where you were born." She paused, frustrated that her words weren't coming out right. "What I'm about to tell you has no bearing on how I feel about you. I love you, Mabel. None of this was ever meant to hurt you. Sometimes we keep secrets to protect the ones we love. You are my daughter." Her eyes began to fill up. The fingers on both her hands knitted together in prayer. "You will always be my little girl."

Mabel rose and took a small backward step, putting both hands to her mouth. "What are you talking about?"

"The thing is, Mabel, my darling, Sum Sum left you to me when you were only a few weeks old. Not long after Adrian died." Her voice trembled. "Not long after my husband died, I miscarried. I was in a terrible state, broken apart. I'd lost my husband and my baby. I was broken apart. Only Sum Sum understood how to heal me. She realized you would heal me."

When she lost her child in the weeks following Adrian's death, Lu See's anguish had known no limits. In her darkest moments she feared her psyche had fractured. She often wondered what would have happened if she hadn't been forced to look after Mabel. If she'd been left with only grief to fill her soul. Would she have done something drastic? Would she have lost her mind? Might she have taken her own life? The answer more often than not was yes. And Sum Sum had known it.

Lu See had hidden the secret for so long, shielded it, the way a beautiful girl would protect an ugly scar on her arm with long sleeves. Now, seated in front of Mabel, shoulders slumped, she felt as if she was about to be sent to the gallows. She looked into Mabel's eyes and wished there was something she could say to comfort her.

"You're saying that everything's a lie. Everything about me is made up."

"No, of course not."

"First I had to grow up without a father and now this! Do you have any idea what it was like not having a papa when I was at school? All the girls used to ask what does your papa do, what does your papa do? You know what I told them? I said he was a ship's captain, sailing the seven seas, that's why he was never at home. And now you tell me this!" Stricken, she looked at her hands intently, inspecting her skin tone, her short fingers, as if seeing herself for the very first time. "So my mother, my biological mother, is living in Tibet?"

Lu See blinked a quiet yes.

Mabel's expression grew serrated, like the edges of a bread knife. "Why?" The anger filled her up. "Why did she abandon me? How could she – I was her child." She was pacing backwards and forwards in her beaded *Nyonya* slippers. "And why didn't you tell me before – and don't say you were meaning to, you wanted to, but it was better I didn't know!"

"Do you think I haven't thought about telling you? I've thought about it every day for the last nineteen years."

Mabel's arm whipped through the air. "Who else knows about this?"

"Only Uncle Big Jowl and your grandmother."

Mabel took out a fork and carefully stabbed the back of her hand.

"What are you doing? You'll hurt yourself!"

"I'm making sure I'm not in some horrible dream." She dropped the fork.

"I was there the second you were born. I fed you, cradled

300

you, bathed you, put you through school. Made sure you wanted for nothing. Who do you think put coins under your pillow when you lost your first tooth? Who taught you to ride a bicycle, to tie your shoelaces, to count to one hundred? I taught you what's right and wrong. I left Cambridge, never sat my entrance examination, so that I could return with you in my arms. I've taken care of you since—"

"This isn't about you." Mabel interrupted. "It's my life that's been turned upside down."

"Who protected you from the Japanese soldiers during the war? When there was no food to eat, who pawned her rings and necklaces so you could have an orange or a packet of biscuits to eat?"

Mabel looked away. She gnawed her bottom lip.

"I'm sorry," said Lu See, whispering, threadbare. "I should have told you about Sum Sum, but . . ."

"But what?"

"I was scared of losing you. When I left Malaya, when I eloped, I left duty and family obligation behind. But then you were born and I had to embrace them all over again." She clasped her hands together. "In so many ways, you were a blessing."

"Did she know me?" challenged Mabel. "Did she . . . did she breastfeed me, coo over me? Did she put pink ribbons in my hair? Or was I always unwanted?"

"You were never unwanted."

"Oh, really. I suppose she abandoned me because she loved me so much."

"No, because she loved *me* so much."

Lu See rose from her chair and went across to the Florence stove. She filled the kettle with water and put it on the boil and spooned tea leaves into a pot. Reaching under the sink, she pulled out the bottle of Dewar's, unscrewed the cap and took two long swigs.

Mabel's eyes were red and moist. "I want to see her."

"You can't . . . Tibet is shut off from the world." Lu See's voice went dead on her as Mabel turned her back and stomped upstairs. Lu See heard the slam of a door, the sound of a bolt being dragged shut, followed by a wail like an angered bird-cry. Alone in the kitchen, Lu See listened to her daughter stamp about her room, hearing the darkness close in on her. "What have I done?" she mouthed.

Eventually all went quiet and in the silence she felt something inside her strain and break in two, like a guitar string, strung too tight for nineteen years, finally snap.

"More *teh tarik!*"

Lu See jolted free from her daydream. She found herself sat with pen cap in hand at the cashier's desk. She told Dungeonboy to see to Fishlips Foo and wondered if, at this very moment, Mabel was being shot at, or worse, floundering in a shallow ditch bleeding to death. *God's sake Mabel! Why are you doing this to me?* Why, when I always taught you not to venture outside after dark, not to visit the Tung Wah Association assembly hall on Klyne Street and certainly not to speak to the watermelon sellers who everyone suspected to be communist spies. *Maybe I pushed her away, into the arms of the bandits. If you tell a child never to smoke cigarettes, one day it'll lead to an exploratory puff behind the garden pagoda.* Lu See let out a protracted sigh. *Boiling water will both soften a carrot and harden an egg.*

Mabel longed to be independent, to be forward-thinking, but the moment Lu See told her about Sum Sum, she grew rebellious and rash too – *didn't she realize how dangerous it was for her to have joined the Malay Communists?* She'd be tried as a traitor, and where did that put us, her family; will I, thought Lu See, be branded a sympathizer for raising a daughter this way?

A few years ago, before Mabel disappeared, Lu See would bump into Mrs Kuok in church or Mrs Viswanath at the Indian spice store and one of them would say, "I saw your Mabel with that MCP boy. You must be so ashamed." But Mabel had never caused her mother to feel shame; rather the women's words led to a kind of fear to rise in her, together with a swelling of sorrow in her chest.

Lu See rubbed her eyes with her palms and glanced at the crumpled sheet of paper on the floor. She picked it up and set fire to it with a match. Mabel had been gone for over a year and in that time Lu See had never been able to write a letter through to the end. What was the point, she asked herself. There was no place to send it in any case.

7

The giant snake had come across Mabel's dangling arm probably thinking it was a type of rodent. Having wrapped its coils around it, slowly numbing the flesh, the python began to feast. By the time Bong heard Mabel's screams, the python had realized its mistake and was desperately trying to disgorge its dinner. "Kill it!" she shrieked. Without hesitating, Bong hacked into the snake's dense body, running a *parang* across its thick olive skin, severing its spine; already half of Mabel's arm had been expelled by its strong cheek muscles. When they pulled the snake free from her she found that her saliva-soaked fingertips had already started to wither and break down from the python's digestive juices. All along her arm and forearm, its long, backward-curved teeth had dug into the tissue, locking onto flesh as it swallowed. The shock put her to sleep for most of the day.

"Let her sleep," Bong told his men. "Make sure she doesn't develop a fever from infection. A snake's mouth is full of bacteria."

They observed her throughout the morning, as the stickiness of the night was cooked and burned off by the sun. While they prepared the python for the pot, removing its head and cutting a deep incision along its belly to remove the innards, they watched her as she slept in the shade. Before long, her clothes had turned black with sweat.

They took her perspiration to be a good sign.

As soon as she woke at noon Mabel fretted over the wounds on her arm. She prodded the bandage with the tips of her finger, hoping that the mercurochrome and antiseptic powder were strong enough to fight off potential sickness from the python's bite. Flexing her right hand, she noted how the skin of her fingertips was fluffy and had turned a curiously pale shade of purple. Fortunately, there didn't seem to be any infection.

The stress of the last forty-eight hours had exhausted her. She was ravenous. She was always ravenous now. Her late-afternoon meal had been a bowl of grilled grasshoppers, shredded green bananas and a thumb-size dollop of rice. She couldn't stomach eating the thing that had come so close to eating her. Apart from the fruit that fell from the trees, there was so little food that they usually had to rely on villagers smuggling rice to them in bicycle tyre tubes and hollowed-out pineapples, but with the unexpected arrival of a hundred and fifty pounds of python meat, the camp was buoyant.

"You must rest," insisted Bong.

"No," she said with sinewy brusqueness, "I want to keep maximum active. What can I do?"

"We're not moving base until tomorrow. You can help secure the perimeter if you like." He searched her face. "Are you sure you feel up to it?"

"I'm sure."

The men helped create several covered pits that when trod on impaled its victim on bamboo stakes. Mabel used Bong's *parang* to whet the tips of the bamboo. She'd been working for almost an hour and had just completed constructing a nightingale floor around the camp – a floor specially con-structed out of dry *attap* fronds that popped and crackled if trodden on – when she felt a chill up her spine. She pivoted to see who was creeping up behind her but saw no one. The bright yellow eyes of the snake flashed though her head like serrated hooks and immediately she thought of the Pontia-nak again and tried to dismiss it as silly primitive super-stition. But with darkness fast approaching Mabel couldn't help but think of stories regarding the haunted forest and remember what she'd been told about the underworld – that dusk was the time of day in Malaya when the bad spirits came out to cause harm, searching for isolated souls to inhabit.

As she returned to camp a wind was blowing. The trees creaked and groaned. They were huge trees, taller than the houses she grew up in; so tall that when fruit fell they hit the earth with a splat. In the sparse light Mabel checked the bandaging on her aching right arm as well as the small cut on her left elbow, caused by tree thorns. The damp weather caused skin to swell, making it soft and easier to cut: septicaemia and inflammation were a constant threat. Thankfully, the wound looked fine. She peered up into the darkening sky; soon it would be as black as a witch's cauldron. All about her men sat about nursing bandaged arms and legs; they hovered around the open fire, waiting for the water to boil in the earthenware cooking pot.

Arranging herself for the evening on a stubble of fallen sunwarmed leaves, under a pyramid of palm flags, Mabel removed her medic's bag from her back and emptied its contents. Lit by the light of a dammar torch, she laid out a sheathed knife, needle and thread, a bottle of antibiotic pills, two tinkling bottles of mercurochrome, a flask of fresh water, three grimy sachets of antiseptic powder, a dozen tubes of morphia, cotton rags for bandages, syringes, a roll of sticking plaster, a tin of sulphanilamide tablets and a sepia photograph of Teoh Lu See standing at the entrance to her restaurant in the city, smiling, waving at the camera; her pale hand long-fingered and elegant. Mabel looked at her own stubby short-fingered hands. Her nails were shot – split to the cuticles and caked black with mud. As a child she'd wondered aloud why she looked nothing like Lu See, asking Uncle Big Jowl: *why is Mama so tall and fair and I'm short and dark?* Of course nobody had revealed anything. Your father wasn't very tall, was usually the stock answer.

Mabel removed the wooden pins – ones she'd made herself out of bamboo – from her hair and shook it free.

There was another photograph of Lu See crammed into her back pocket, but the daily diet of rain and heat had all but rotted it to shreds. She tugged it loose and gazed at the mottled face of her 'mother', her mind fertile with accusations.

If only she'd told me earlier, thought Mabel. Why had she tried to hide the fact that my real mother abandoned me? Why wait until I was nineteen before telling me? The fact that she'd maintained the lie for so long hurt. It made my whole life a fiction; it made me a fraud. Had she been protecting me from the truth? That I was a bastard child? Mabel gritted her teeth; she didn't need protecting.

Mabel often wondered what might have happened if she'd found out herself, accidentally. Would that have been worse? Perhaps if she had found out earlier, her life would have taken a different course. Maybe she wouldn't have run off with Bong; perhaps she'd have continued her studies; she might have even made plans to go in search of her birth mother. She certainly wouldn't be here now, getting even with the world.

But whom am I really punishing – Lu See or myself? Talk about cutting off your nose to spite your face!

Mabel inhaled a deep lungful of air. She didn't feel bitter about it any more, didn't feel as if the sky was pressing down on her like a black hammer, but she did feel that familiar chest twinge whenever Lu See popped up inside her head.

And then there was the letter. The letter from her real mother to Lu See written on the day they parted – *the day I was abandoned, discarded like a toy in a sandbox*. This she housed in her waterproof map pouch, free of mildew and mud and insects. Lu See said that Sum Sum had left it on the kitchen table for her.

She read it through for what must have been the hundredth time:

Lu See, my sister, my friend,

I write this letter in middle of night while you still sleeping. When you wake up I will be gone. Please understand that this is the most difficult decision I ever make. I am leaving, Lu See. The Gods have summoned me and such is my destiny – to return to my ancestral home. Something happened to me when I first came to Cambridge which make me realize I must return to my homeland, return to my mother and return to my religion. I only wish I could speak to you but I know you will stop me.

When the baby is exactly a month old, Lu See, you must paint the tip of her nose with soot from the underside of a pan to keep away envious ghosts. Even though at first this baby's scent is not what you crave and the smile is not your own baby's smile, I know you will grow to love her. Be good to each other. Right now, I think you need her, and she needs you.

I found Uncle Big Jowl's red *ang pow* envelope and will take just enough to pay for train journey to Felixstowe. I will use one of the boat tickets to reach Penang. From there I will find my way to Tibet. Please do not follow me or try to stop me for this is the direction my life must take.

One thing you must do for me is register baby's birth. I learned that this must be done within first 42 days. Give her the Teoh family name. She will wear it with pride.

I have bought enough KLIM powder milk to last 3 months. I also give you my blue note book full with Pietro's recipes and many rosemary pots. I am sorry I did not tell you I was going to leave. If I did I know you try to stop me.

I will always treasure you.

Sum Sum.

Mabel folded the letter and replaced it in the waterproof pouch.

Not far away, Bong was settling himself down for the evening. She watched him rub his tired face, his eyes too laden with sleep to focus on the map spread across his knees.

In the past few weeks whenever they went on scouting trips within the forest, not an hour went by without Mabel and Bong exchanging clandestine touches. She'd known him since that first day he'd appeared out of the forest in 1945, with a Japanese service pistol stuffed in his belt.

They'd met again after his grandfather had swapped the jungle for the city and bought a bicycle repair shop in KL. And as a teenager Mabel was forever wheeling her rusty vintage Hawthorne in for repairs – a retreading here, a bolt tightening there. Although she did not realise it at the time, she'd been in love with Bong since her final year at Convent Bukit Nanas. He'd gone around the campus stealthily trying to recruit young women, although most girls were intimidated by his easy confidence and bold stare. Not Mabel though. She just grew jealous when she saw him chatting to her classmates. His passion for the cause was irresistible, and even though she didn't truly believe in the communist doctrine herself, she joined the movement: her physical need to be by his side was stronger than her political doubts.

There were occasions of course when she found living in the jungle almost intolerable, but each time she threatened to leave he would say it wasn't for much longer – just one more month, one more week – and then he would make love to her and she'd fall under his spell all over again.

But they rarely made love nowadays; an officer could not be seen philandering with his medic, the only woman in his platoon. Curiously, Mabel found that the longer he restrained himself, the more excited she grew. These pauses in passion added a new dimension to their relationship.

His status didn't stop them from playing silly pranks on one another.

Earlier, as she was building the nightingale floor, Mabel had caught a tiny tree frog and imprisoned it in her pocket. She crept over to where Bong was resting and, whilst his back was turned, inserted it into his water canteen before crawling back to her bed of leaves. Watching from the corner of her eye she sat cross-legged, waiting for Bong to put the canteen to his lips.

Five minutes later Bong gagged and Mabel immediately fell about, hand over her mouth, choking on her laughter. Sliding over to her on his hands and knees, he gave her bottom a sharp slap. "What am I going to do with you?" he admonished.

Mabel drew him close, cuddling him from behind, burying her face between his shoulder blades. "I know what you can do with me . . ." Her left hand brushed the front of his trousers, pulling at the drawstring belt.

"Aren't you supposed to be injured?"

"I am. I need tender and devoted care."

"I thought you'd had enough of snakes for one day."

Her fingers wandered on, searching and finding the growing bulge in his pants. "Perhaps we can have a jungle wedding," she whispered playfully.

She waited for him to turn around and give her one of his withering glances. When instead he simply smiled, her heart lifted. "Maybe I'll wear a tiara of jasmine flowers in my hair or have a garland of white frangipani looped on my wrist." He grunted, taking her hand and placing it to his lips. "And you, my handsome groom, will wear a crown made from dangling crocodile teeth. What do you say?"

"Maybe," he said with a chuckle, wrinkling the sides of his mouth.

"Really?" She stared into his eyes. "You'll consider it?"

He turned over and held her close. The evening sky was being lit by the light of fireflies. "Yes, I'll consider it."

A week later, with rain drenching the makeshift camp, Mabel huddled under a banana tree canopy. "Bong, how much longer can we go on like this? Living like animals, being hunted?"

He was fiddling on the dial of a radio receiver. "Quiet, I'm trying to get the right frequency." The radio emitted a strange high-pitched sound.

"We're like a bunch of bank robbers on the run from the

law." She threw a pebble at him. "You've dedicated your life to the Party. Your father did the same before he was killed by the Japanese. All for what?"

"It won't be long now. The MCP leaders are trying to negotiate a truce."

"I've heard that one before."

"No, really."

"Do you promise me?"

He kept tuning the radio. "I promise you. Not much longer. Then we'll have all the time in the world to be together."

She manoeuvred through the rain and hugged him. "Tell me again, why you do this, what you believe in."

"I've told you this before many times."

She snuggled up against him. "Tell me again."

"Before this all started, before the fighting began, the Chinese in Malaya had nothing. They were denied the equal right to vote in elections. Apart from the very wealthy, very few had any land rights to speak of. We have changed all that."

"I'm so proud of you."

"Proud of me?" His spectacles slid down to the tip of his nose. "How can you possibly be proud of me? Have you seen this ragtag army I lead?"

"I'm proud because you believe in something. You care about your cause. I love you for that."

"Do you?"

"Of course I do, you silly fool!"

"Well, you're only human."

She eyed the radio receiver. "Where did that come from?"

"It came from our man in Bilang village, together with some cash and several boxes of ammunition." He banged the receiver set. "Just wish I could get the thing to work."

Cocooned in this blanket of intimacy, Mabel pressed her cheek into his chest. She breathed in his scent and sweat. Her mother once told her that life was not made up of days or weeks or even years, but of moments. Feeling Bong's arm around her shoulders with a *son et lumière* supplied by skylarks and fireflies, watching the phosphorescent jade insects dance a tango to the beat of the rising moon, this was one of those moments.

She closed her eyes, contented.

They held one another until somewhere in the distance they heard a crackle, scarcely audible, a faraway sound like King Kong cracking a finger knuckle.

Suddenly, the men spotted a shadow in the sky; the shadow of a vulture spreading its wings. Alarmed by the whirr of an engine, they got to their feet just as the RAF Hornet swung down from the clouds and aimed its machine guns at the forest floor. For the briefest of moments Mabel's breath seemed to suspend, hanging high in the trees. A small tremble of fear passed over her face, flaring her nostrils.

"Put out the torches and the fire!" someone hollered.

The aircraft sound swelled.

Instantly, Bong was scrambling, shouting orders, reaching for his rifle. "It's the radio," he cried. "They must have rigged the radio."

Bullets peppered the overhanging foliage, punching fist-size holes into the ground. Moonlight came streaming through, etching shadows, throwing glints of silver on the forest floor. Birds scattered. Gibbons leapt in panic from tree to tree, swinging from branches a hundred feet tall, searching for cover.

Instinctively, Mabel fell to the ground and wedged herself against a tree root. There was another sharp pop of gunfire as the plane tore through the nimbus. "Run!" someone yelled. She picked up her feet and sprinted, zigzagging with her arms shielding her face, losing sight of the world around her. After several seconds she slid to a halt and lay breathless as her elbows sank into the mud. She wanted to get up and flee but she didn't recognize this part of the jungle; she might run out of cover and running might expose her and get herself shot. She clamped her eyes shut and prayed.

A low inhaled whistling came from the skies. She felt the air pressure drop. The explosion that followed seemed to blow a hole in the atmosphere. Mabel's chest and stomach emptied as earth and rock erupted, pitching gouts of earth into her face. The harrowing WHUMP split the air, jolting the bones loose in Mabel's vertebrae. She was thrown headlong across the oily sludge like a human javelin.

Soil splinters rained down on her. A red mist filled her eyes. She tried to move, but parts of her body had gone numb. Eventually she rose to her knees and found the world had fallen silent except for a buzz of silver noise shrilling in her head. She shouted but couldn't hear her own voice. Splattered with her comrades' blood and gristle, she screamed out their names but heard no reply. The loud metallic tocsin ringing in her head just grew louder and louder.

All about her hot fragments of bomb matter lay sharp and hissing in the ground. Everything was caked with dust and debris. She realized that at any given moment another shell might explode. But she didn't care. All she wanted was for the red mist to disperse and for her head to stop ringing. All she wanted was for the blood to stop oozing from her ears. And then gradually the smoke began to clear. A dead man's face peered into hers, his jawbone white, teeth exposed. She held up her arms to protect herself and saw others shrieking all about her open-mouthed but silent. Flesh hung from branches like threads; charred trees tilted and collapsed; mutilated birds lay burning, cooking in their feathers. A panic gripped her heart and her teeth began to chatter uncontrollably.

Wiping the gristle from her eyes, she began to grope through the mud. Her hand happened upon a severed foot. A few yards away sprawled a man. His chest had been blown open. Part of his spinal column jutted out. There was nothing left of him from the knees down. Only then did she see the round glasses.

Seconds later another low inhaled whistling dropped out of the skies. She ran for cover. The shockwave snapped her head forward; a white heat stung her shoulder. And then the forest turned black. Too black to see.

8

A full ten days had passed since Lu See donated the dozen battery-operated radio receivers to the Communists. She hadn't heard anything new from Stan. There had been no further communication from 'the mule'. She was a bag of nerves. Rather than partake in conversation, she sat by Il Porco's cash register and listened to her mother and Uncle Big Jowl prattling on about how Malaya was changing for the worse.

"I mean, it's the way they look at me sometimes," Mother told Uncle Big Jowl as they sipped *teh tarik*. She was complaining about the Malays. "It's just like the way they looked at Lon Chaney Jr., you know, when they realize he is about to change into the Wolf Man. As if there was some sort of monster inside of me."

"What you expect from a bunch of inbred satay-eaters!" cried Fishlips from across the room.

"Do you mind, Mr Foo! This is private conversation," Mother retorted.

"Hum gaa chaan!"

"This sort of problem will only get worse," said Uncle Big Jowl. "Plenty of tension growing, aahh, between Chinese and Malays. Chinese are only just seeing the effects of Article 153 of the constitution recognizing the Malays as 'special class of citizen'. Singapore is making one stink of a fuss."

"Well, I'm pleased you agree with me," said Mother, sounding not the least pleased. She scratched her palms.

Later, having shut the restaurant for the night at 11 p.m., pulling down the iron grille at the front with a pole, Lu See went to the cash register and extracted a red $10 bill from the note stash and shoved it into the envelope marked 'Juru'. She then climbed the stairs and stepped through her dog gate. As soon as she clicked on the ceiling fan and removed her apron, hanging it on the back of the door, she was greeted by six wagging tails and yelps of delight.

The dogs were all waiting to be fed. She filled the six bowls in her high-ceilinged kitchen with biscuits and scraps, and then lit mosquito coils and stationed them by the window. Shortly after, following a quick bucket shower, she pushed her way past all her accumulated possessions. Amongst the mountains of old books and newspapers was her frayed eel-skin trunk, Mabel's rusting Hawthorne bicycle, several brass pots and pans, a dressmaker's mannequin, bamboo stepladders, cushions, walking sticks and umbrellas lashed together with string, sewing machines, a massive Radio Flyer wagon and a huge collection of paints and canvases.

It was all junk, but Lu See didn't have the heart to throw any of it away. Since the war, ever since she lost everything to the Japanese, she'd been a compulsive hoarder. Nothing, however beaten up or old was thrown away; everything she kept carried an emotional resonance, but after years accumulating things she now had no place to put them. Still, she was convinced that one day all of these bits and pieces would have bartering value.

She looked at the clasps of her old eel-skin trunk. Many years ago she had hidden something in there: a letter from Sum Sum written as she sailed from Felixstowe, fleeing England and leaving Mabel and Lu See behind. She had promised never to show anyone that letter, never to tell. It was a secret between Sum Sum and Lu See. The trunk had not been opened in years.

She picked up the dressmaker's mannequin, ignoring the ache in her stomach, and tried to stuff it into a cupboard but the doors had warped from the humidity and the dummy's arms kept creeping out.

At that very moment the electricity cut off. Not just in her apartment but across the neighbourhood; streetlamps, building lights, lanterns extinguished. Plunged into blackness, Lu See groped her way along the wall, bumping into all manner of things, feeling her way through the darkness like a catfish using its whiskers against the river floor. "Dungeonboy!" she called down the stairs, into the abyss.

"*Haak mung mung, haak mung mung!*" he yelled back, before breaking into yet another Doris Day song.

"See if you can find the candles, will you?"

He sang a gobbledygook of mixed-up lyrics.

"They should be somewhere in the kitchen, maybe in the chopstick drawer."

Dungeonboy soon put his head around the door with a flashlight; he had found the candles and lit three of them. Lu See fed some batteries into her radio. The station was playing Bill Haley and the Comets.

"Okay, lah," he said, chuckling, admiring the flames. "No burn hair today!"

"No, thank goodness. Goodnight, Ah Fung."

"Goo-nye, Missie."

Lu See retired to her bedroom and lay on her bed for several minutes. "Knackered," she said aloud, burying her face in the plump white pillows. Running the restaurant drained her. She hadn't been prepared for how much work it was – the daily grind of cooking, cleaning, going to the wet market. Back in her student days she'd have the stamina to study for ten hours without a break, but this sort of toil was back-breaking. It exhausted her and her tiredness often made her impatient, quicker to argue with people. Sometimes she grew frustrated that she wasn't pursuing an academic career. All those good grades wasted, she thought. Still, she had to push on and make ends meet.

Recently, there had been mornings when she didn't feel up to going to pig alley to buy fresh cuts of pork. She couldn't stomach seeing the hogs hung in the open air, some with their testicles still attached so that the shoppers knew what they were getting. But then the sight of her batik apron hanging on the back of her door would give her the strength to ignore the pain in her intestines and before she knew it she'd be stirring a stew pot and sprinkling rosemary into the stock, keen to see the first customer come through the door.

She closed her eyes. Her stomach still ached and she was sure, again, that she had a mild fever. She tried to lift her knees into a standard yoga position but failed because one of the dogs came barrelling through the door and attempted to climb aboard, balancing on its hind legs and pawing the mosquito curtain. "Not now, Pebbles. Mummy needs her rest. You stay on the floor." Obediently, Pebbles wagged her tail and busied herself by sniffing the bed legs, which were stuck into Campbell's soup tins filled with water to stop invading ants.

Moments later, feeling restless, Lu See got up to clear away the tower of magazines on her desk and return to a letter she had started three days before. It was a letter to Sum Sum. After returning from Cambridge in late 1937 she had heard nothing from her friend for eight years, not until the end of the war, when Sum Sum's brother, Hesha, had delivered a letter. That was when Lu See learned that Sum Sum had taken vows at the Ani Trangkhung nunnery in Lhasa. But however hard she tried Lu See could not obtain official permission to enter Tibet to visit Sum Sum. The Tibetan Foreign Office consistently refused to grant her the necessary travel permit.

Pen hovering, her eyes scanned the page:

My dearest Sum Sum,

Still no news of Mabel. I know I wounded her by telling her about her parentage, but I cannot understand why she must rebel like this and risk her life for a cause she hardly understands. Was I too protective of her? Is she now redressing the balance by rebelling? Now that the tables have been turned I know how my poor mother must have felt when I ran off to England all those years ago.

Things are quieter in KL now, but there is still tension in the streets, especially now with the new constitution. I fear there is bad blood growing between the Chinese and Malays.

Things are quieter for me too. At night, I often feel like a little seed left to germinate all alone. When I cannot sleep I listen to the house creaking. It's almost as if it's talking to me. Often I wonder if there is a ghost here. Thank God for my dogs! Have I ever told you about my dogs? There's Pebbles the dominant, assertive mother of three, her tiny pups Lightning, Thunder and Rain; there's Boris with the curly tail and happy eyes, and finally Goose, a black-haired spaniel who likes to howl at passing fire trucks.

Guess what? I found the painting I did of you on the MS Jutlandia. It was in an old trunk. It's faded terribly but I can still make out the old pumpkin-head!

I want to send you photographs of Mabel but I'm told that letters going in and out of Chinese Tibet are heavily censored, that photographs of any kind are destroyed.

I asked Stan Farrell about Aziz. I know you once said you didn't care what happened to him, but I feel you ought to know. Stan wrote to the War Records Office and finally received a reply a few weeks ago. Aziz was killed in action in Burma fighting with the 50th Indian Tank Brigade in 1943.

Lu See stopped writing. She pictured Aziz and his waggling head, laughing and joking with Sum Sum on the deck of the *Jutlandia*. The candlelight flickered and distorted her face. She looked about the room without seeing anything. Shaking off the memory she opened a packet of shrimp crackers and then took up her pen again.

The newspapers still print the names of captured guerrillas; sometimes they even name those that have been killed. Mabel may be hurt, hurt badly, but there is no way of knowing. I wish I'd spent more time with Mabel, more time hugging her. I'm sorry to sound the way I do. Perhaps I'm a sentimental fool. We've had yet another blackout and I think it's affected my mood.

Do you remember the three-legged crocodile those men caught on the tongkang all those years ago? I think about what those men said – that it was a curse, that the missing leg would reappear in your dreams and snatch away your firstborn.

This must be the hundredth letter I have sent you, yet still there's been no reply. Perhaps you never receive them. I wait for news. I yearn for news. But answers never come.

Lu See set her pen down and lit a fresh mosquito coil.

The weight of worry made her heart heavy. She hung her head and closed her eyes. The room was silent apart from the distant sounds of chorus frogs clicking from the house drains.

A shout from outside made her jump. When she opened the window she saw a black Fiat 600 with red diplomatic licence plates and twin Italian flags attached to the bonnet. Its headlights illuminated the unlit street.

A man in a white suit and fedora paced about below, huffing and tut-tutting like an agitated hen.

"Who is it? Who's there?" she cried, but the man did not look up or respond. The red licence plates made her recall the invitation to the Italian Ambassador's residence on the 13th. Today was the 13th. She hadn't gone, hadn't even bothered to reply. Was the man here to reprimand her for not turning up? Had she caused a diplomatic ruckus? Surely not.

She peered down at the man in the fedora and debated whether she ought to find out what he wanted.

She glanced in a mirror. *Look at the state of me. I've got no make-up on. And my hair!* She tried not to imagine how she would look to a visitor: a rather lonely, flat-chested, eccentric Chinese single mother who lived with her stinky dogs in an armpit of a small shophouse full of pre-war junk . . .

She heard a hyena laugh emerge from below.

. . . who'll die one of those big city old lady deaths, all alone in her room, probably trapped under something heavy, where nobody will find her for weeks until the smell gets so bad that it drifts down the street . . .

Lu See smiled at her own moroseness.

She descended the stairs and jerked the iron grille skyward.

The man in the fedora turned at the sound. His hat was tilted at an angle, obscuring his face. On seeing her, he planted his feet wide apart like Gary Cooper in High Noon, and held his hands at his sides, fluttering his fingers as though about to draw.

She noted a papal amount of rings on his hands. A bright pink handkerchief cascaded from his breast pocket, rustling in the night breeze. Then he reached up and snatched his fedora away to reveal an enormous forehead. "Brah-haaa!"

His teeth shone like silver lira coins.

"Pietro!" howled Lu See. She rushed up to him and held him tight. "Is it really you?"

"Oh, my dear loo seat. It's so wonderful to see you." He laughed, head thrown back, with a broad smile on his face.

"What on earth are you doing here in Malaya?"

"Doing here? I'm the new Italian Ambassador, you silly moo, and the new Italian Ambassador simply hates being stood up. The last person to stand me up was that pretty second year Botanist from Caius." He swept a hand to his brow ostentatiously. "When you didn't show – *quelle horreur!* So after the party ended, I nipped into my little Feee-yat and abracadabra my boyfriend's an actor, here I am."

"I cannot believe it," she said, hopping on her toes in delight. "I just cannot believe you're in KL."

"I know! They sent me to some treacherously ghastly places before, full of fat-witted fop-doodles. Places where the so-called elite hold their knives like pencils and drink tea out of saucers. But you know what they say." He smoothed the lashes of his eyes with a bejewelled finger. "Travel broadens the behind."

Lu See hugged him again. "Will you come inside?"

"Actually, dear loo seat, I was thinking of a late supper at Fatty Crab's. I'm ravenous. You know what it's like; I never eat at my own parties."

"I can cook you something here. Do you like curry noodles?"

Pietro looked aghast. "Make me fart like a Roman emperor. No, it's Fatty's or bust. Besides, I fancy a glass of their Chateau de Coques Roche."

"But I'm not dressed, look at my hair – "

"You are a raddled old mess, aren't you? Not to worry, just give your cheeks a pinch for colour and . . ." He removed the satin trim from his fedora, made a bow for her hair and smiled at her. "Tah-dah! Cinderella's all tubbed and scrubbed for the ball. Simply wonderful being a girl, isn't it?"

Fatty Crab's was by the racecourse, a ten-minute drive away. Wedged in the front of the Fiat in between a hornbill and Pietro, Lu See felt a bit like a sausage roll.

Pietro's teeth emerged from his mouth. "He's called Hartley. He's a gift from the Sultan of Selangor."

"He doesn't bite, does he?" She studied the bird's red eyes and its capacious beak and casque.

"No, but he has a scorching wit. Just keep your nose away from him; he might think it's a palm nut or a cocktail sausage. Speaking of sausages: what news of my favourite Tibetan, Sum Sum? I gather you resuscitated her old blue recipe book."

Lu See squeezed her eyes shut in despair. She'd spent most of the previous day making phone calls to the Chinese Embassy; once again she'd been denied an entry permit into Tibet. "Her brother Hesha occasionally sends me word. He's in a Gurkha regiment. He writes to tell me that she's in good health, living in a Tibetan nunnery."

"Get thee to a nunnery!" bayed Pietro, which set Hartley's wings flapping. "Oh, I do love my *Hamlet*!"

"I'd do anything to see her again."

They passed the Sikh temple on Bandar Road where devout Punjabis slept in the gardens on rainless nights. Further along a farmer was blocking the way as he led his water buffalo across the street with a net of pineapples strapped to its back.

Pietro tooted his horn and drew a sideways look from Lu See. "I heard about Mabel joining the Communists," he said.

"How?" She felt her cheeks go warm.

"Oh, the usual diplomatic chatter. With a little finesse one can find out almost anything." He kept his eyes on the road. "Funny isn't it, how Adrian turned to the Communists, and now Mabel. I do miss Adie so much. He was a wonderful man. Look, you'd better get Mabel out of the jungle soon, dahling. The British boffins have devised a new gadget; a radio with a tracker." He paused, but Lu See said nothing. "When the guerrillas turn the radio set on it sends a secret signal, a type of homing device that can be detected by spotter aircrafts. Once they make a fix on the camp they bomb it to kingdom come. They're taking no prisoners."

Lu See's blood turned cold.

The following evening Lu See shut the restaurant for the night as usual at 11 p.m., pulling down the iron grille at the front with a pole. She'd been nursing a hangover for most of the day, courtesy of the five whisky *stengahs* she'd downed with Pietro at Fatty Crab's.

Lu See pinched the skin between her eyes and went over her conversation with Pietro. She'd told him about Stan and his deception.

"How could he? How could he do this to me?" she bawled.

"Perhaps he didn't know." Pietro shrugged.

"Didn't know? Of course, he knew! He's deceived me all these years, pretended to be my friend."

They had talked deep into the early hours, until the popadums and cigarettes grew damp in the night air. Nothing Pietro could say could console her.

Earlier in the day she'd rushed over to see 'the mule' on Klyne Street, but found the barber shop's narrow door boarded up. Neighbours said the police had hauled the owner away. And when she telephoned Stan she got no reply from his home and was told he was 'out station' when she called his work number.

When Pietro came over to console her she was frantic. "What can I do?" she cried.

He held her in his arms. "There is nothing you can do. The best thing is to ensure that you don't get into a state over this. You're looking a bit peaky. You need to rest."

"I've signed her death warrant, Pietro. I've killed my own daughter."

"Go upstairs and rest. Will you promise me, you get some sleep?"

She nodded.

"Do you want me to stay?" he asked.

"No. I'll be all right."

She watched Pietro climb into his Fiat and drive off.

At the top of the stairs the dogs were all waiting to be fed and once she clicked on the overhead fan, hung up her apron and filled the doggy bowls with scraps, she went to her bathroom cupboard in search of a tin of Tiger Balm for her forehead and a bottle of milk of magnesia.

She passed her bedroom and saw her plump white pillows piled high behind the mosquito curtain. The news about Mabel, the shock of it all, had made her incredibly tired. She looked longingly at the pillows. *Like a set of warm cream buns nestled together*, she thought. Right at that moment she wanted her bed more than anything else in the world, but as soon as she applied the mentholated salve to the twin points of her temple, she heard a faint banging on the iron grille below.

"Oh God! Not again. Don't these people have homes to go to?"

Expecting to find the black Fiat parked once again in the street below, she peered out of the window and was about to shout: "Go home, Pietro. I'll be fine." Yet when she looked from the window, there were no cars at all in the deserted roadway.

When she heard the indistinct banging once more against the iron grille, she cursed like a Malaccan sailor.

Dungeonboy came running to tell her, all panting and excited, "Somebody at door, Missie – somebody small and like black shadow at door."

She went down the stairs to lift up the metal shutters. "It's probably Mr Pietro." She told Dungeonboy to fetch a stick in case it was a burglar.

"What do you want?" she yelled. Then, filled with a sudden sense of foreboding, she placed her palms on the grillwork and jerked it skyward.

The metal clattered.

A young, painfully thin woman stood with her head bowed. The smell of the jungle was on her, in her skin and clothes. There was grit and dirt on her face and crushed earth matting the ends of her hair. One arm, her right arm, was supported in a crude sling.

Lu See caught her breath. Her mouth fell open. She threw a hand against the wall to steady herself. "Oh my God," she gasped, "Mabel."

9

Eight years had passed since the Chinese crossed the Jinsha River to invade Tibet and for seven of those years the monasteries remained untouched. There was no sacking of temples, no offences aimed at the monks, no quarrels with Tibetan religion. But then one afternoon in the spring of 1958, that all changed.

It was the day of the horse festival. Many hundreds of people, including nuns and monks, flocked to the grasslands to enjoy the entertainment. Setting off at dawn, it took Sum Sum and Tormam three hours to reach the venue; as they trekked along the hillside trails a pure crystalline sunshine washed the plateau gold, gilding the nomadic sheep that gnawed at the fresh green felt. When they reached the grasslands they found a hive of activity.

Yellow and blue tents set up days before dotted the plain. Over the snowy passes, caravans of pack-horses and donkeys appeared laden with bricks of tea and great blocks of salt. Pilgrims passed through – devotees from Nepal and Sikkim – offering sutra streamers and aromatic smoke to the Mountain Gods, whilst merchants and nomads and pedlars came from far and wide to do business. Leather traders arrived from Mongolia. Chinese vendors of gold, turquoise, borax and musk set up wooden stalls in the temporary market. A Manchurian silk dealer laid out several colourful bolts of fabric as Bhutan rice suppliers haggled with farmers, behind him a Muslim spice runner exchanged salaams with an Indian indigo broker whose white teeth flashed bright against his burnished skin. Everywhere people wheeled and dealed.

There were archery contests, feats of balance, rope-walking, tumbling and wrestling. Local women, wearing their hair in plaits, mounted their yaks to get a better look. Many had their babies strung to their backs. Sum Sum and Tormam joined them to watch the horsemen show off their skills. One of the disciplines was to fire their arrows at a coloured pole while riding at full gallop. With the springtime sun warming her scalp, Sum Sum oohed and ahhed as the riders thundered past, enjoying their graceful athleticism, applauding as the arrowheads found their mark. Amid this constant activity, pilgrims burned green cypress branches for incense and spun their prayer wheels.

Later, she and Tormam collected alms from the horsemen in fox-skin caps as they fed barley straw to their stallions. Not far from them she saw clusters of red-robed monks, young and old, gathered for ritualized debate. The young monks sat on the hard ground as an older monk faced them. Every few seconds an elder would rush at his fledglings, arms flailing and clapping, to launch obscure questions of Buddhist orthodoxy. The older monks lunged and the younger ones parried, soon a sharp rat-tat-tat of voices filled the dry air as these thrusting debates grew fiercer and more boisterous.

In the background several open fires burned. Warmed by the flames, people ate on small blue Tibetan rugs, offering their neighbours yak dumplings and deep-fried flat bread. Sum Sum sniffed more delicious smells of cooking. She saw the glistening flesh of spit-roasted mutton, the saddles of venison, the hind-quarters of deer and goats and beef turning on long metal rods, dripping meat juices into the flames. The trailing scent-scarves of food reminded Sum Sum of Cambridge, of May Week, when whole oxen sat roasting on the lawns of Trinity and St John's, ribs showing like the staves of a boat. Try as she might, she couldn't help salivating.

Crows hopped about cackling as they edged closer to the fire. Their cries crescendoed when a group of boys threw stones at them.

At midday, with the sun as sharp as the edges of a knife, Sum Sum's mouth, throat and nostrils grew parched. A windblown silk trader offered them butter tea, which they drank from wooden bowls. Sipping her tea, Sum Sum looked up from her bowl to see pinheads on the horizon moving along the Tea Horse Road, a cloud of dust trail on the stony ridges. Shimmering charcoal spots against the pale grasslands, they grew larger with each passing second. They spread like dark stains.

Within minutes, several dozen thick-legged Chinese soldiers arrived on horseback; carnivorous men with leathery, thunderous expressions, casting blue shadows. "Faces so sharp and ugly, they scratch the wind," observed Sum Sum.

They pulled a woman from her long-haired yak; her scream was as shrill as a false note on a violin.

A skillet-faced officer, full of false bravado, spoke in his guttural northern tongue, jabbing the air with aggression. He slapped a hand against his rifle; his eyes were like a pig slaughterer's.

When he spat a bullet of phlegm by his feet, leaving a dull green smear, Sum Sum knew the festivities were over.

As soon as they returned to the nunnery Sum Sum and Tormam were confronted by prayer hall manager Jampa. "Ay-yi! They have stolen our country," the old lady said as soon as she heard their news. "Do you know how they stole it? Under threats of death. A Tibetan delegation to Peking was forced to sign a 17-point plan handing control to China. When ministers in Lhasa complained to Peking claiming the treaty was not legal because it was signed under duress and because there were no official Lhasa seals to certify it, the Chinese said they don't care."

"But it is wrong," said Sum Sum, as prickly as a Himalayan porcupine. Tormam could not speak: she was stunned. They walked through a narrow corridor into a candle-lit room adorned with frescoes of bodhisattva Tara. Several nuns sat in meditation; in the dim light their heads, brown and pitted and hairless, looked like overgrown potatoes.

Jampa, lowering her voice, continued, "Then Lhasa says that under some rule called Vienna Convention, treaty is null and void. So what do Chinese do? They send in military." She reached into a leather satchel concealed in her sleeve, pinched off a thumb of snuff. "All this happened a few years ago. But now there is unrest in Kham and Amdo so Chinese shut the door to the Land of Snow. They clamping down on all festivals and on monks."

"What will happen to us?" asked Tormam.

The yak butter candles guttered. Juniper and written prayers burned in censers. Jampa took another hit of snuff and rubbed the skin between her eyes. "Things will get worse for all of us. The abbess says the Communist invaders will suppress and mutilate our culture."

"Do you really believe that?" questioned Sum Sum. She couldn't believe this was the same communism that Adrian had advocated in Cambridge.

"When you have lived as long as I have, you believe everything about the Chinese. Their arrogance has no limits."

Sum Sum stamped her foot. "I wish I had a chestnut pan to hit all Communist invaders' heads!"

"There is open fighting on streets in eastern parts of the country." Jampa leaned in close, collusively. "Some people even gossip-talk that the Chinese invaders want to kidnap our young God-king."

The girls sucked in their breath, shocked to hear such words spoken aloud. Their fingers stiffened with imaginary cold. *"Ndug're.* Come," said Jampa. "Let us engage in meditation." Jampa closed her eyes and made her face appear calm and at peace. When Sum Sum shut her eyes too all she saw were the red posters plastered on the walls of the town – posters showing the face of the one they called the devil-man, Mao Tse-tung.

10

Folding into each other, they held on as tight as they could. Just to feel her daughter's touch made Lu See want to cry. They pressed foreheads together.

She could not believe how skinny Mabel was, how gaunt her face had become. She touched her all over as if checking she was still intact. With her matted hair full of bugs and muddied skin she could have been a vagabond. Eventually Lu See heard a high voice from the basement. "Missie, is you? Is ok to come upstair?"

"Yes, yes, Ah Fung. It's my daughter, Mabel," she said wiping away her tears. "Look at me, bawling like a watering-can."

Dungeonboy climbed up to the top of the basement steps. His look was full of bewilderment.

"Please heat up this evening's pork stew and boil some fresh rice," she instructed. Like any mother, Lu See's first instinct was to feed her daughter; perhaps if she could succeed in nourishing her child, all was not lost. "Also fetch some clean bath towels and soap. Hurry, hurry! Then I want you to make the bed for her. My daughter is home to stay."

He flipped his thumbs skywards. "Of coss, no problem, Missie."

Mabel was home. Yet as the days went by Lu See began to panic. What about the authorities? Should Mabel go into hiding? Was she on a 'wanted' list?

Taking the initiative, Lu See went to the nearest police station and told them that her daughter had returned voluntarily from the jungle weeks before but had been ill with dengue fever. *"Ai-yahhh!"* exclaimed the duty sergeant. "Dengue terrible thing to catch, meh? My brother had it last year. They call it bone-breaking disease. Your daughter better now?"

"Yes, she is."

"Here, I fill out this report and send to Special Branch for you. When did you say she come back?"

"Five weeks ago." She lied, naming a day. He filled in the date with a pencil.

"And she returned home voluntarily?"

"Yes. Will she have to go to a rehabilitation camp?"

The duty sergeant made a face. "I don't think so. Only senior officers of the guerrillas are forced to. But she will have to come in for interview and remain on probation. Give me your telephone number. I will call you."

"Will she be all right?"

"Ai-yahh! Don't worry, lah. Emergency is over. This country has other things to worry about now."

Mabel went for the interview a week later and was given the red 'all clear' chop on her papers. She didn't tell them she was close to Bong Foo. And even if they knew, there was no way she was going to voluntarily incriminate herself. Rather, she said she didn't really understand the Communist cause, that she was cajoled into it through peer pressure, that she felt shame for disgracing her family. She also claimed that she had wanted to surrender months before, but her superiors had threatened to have her shot. "I was the medic, you see. Without me, they would have succumbed to all sorts of infections. I helped injured enemy soldiers too, so I suppose I was saving lives on both sides. I never raised a gun against a Commonwealth soldier."

She also told them she was terrified of her mother. "I knew she would raise maximum bloody hell when I came home, so I kept delaying my return." The interviewers, all men, said they understood that Chinese mothers could be very strict. They laughed when she told them how often she was smacked on the bottom with a wooden ruler. When they stopped laughing their faces turned serious.

"You have shown suitable remorse," the chief-interrogator said. "However, it is our recommendation that you return to this station every week for the next twelve months and check in with our duty officer. Just to ensure that you do not relapse."

With the ordeal over, Mabel returned home.

She tried to fit back in. But having been away for so long, she found it hard adjusting to life in the city. For one thing, her civilian clothes, left behind in her previous existence, felt awkward. And when she looked at herself naked in the full-length mirror, she saw a stranger – her ribs jutted out and her arms were like reeds. There were damp blisters on her feet. She touched the scars on her shoulder, red weals like wrinkling red chillis. Her arm was fully healed from the python bite, but as she stroked her thighs and her pubis she wondered if her periods would recommence once more; the weeks of eating jungle food had put a stop to her monthlies.

Everywhere she went she walked silently, the way she'd been trained; it felt strange walking on dry land and not pulling her feet out of sticky mud. She found it odd, too, not having to lug a pack around all day. And she felt defenceless without her gun. I'm not the same person I was, she told herself.

She still couldn't understand how she had survived when everyone else had been killed. Why am I standing here scarred but alive, when all those others are lying dead in the forest?

She felt disconnected from the people around her, and the more she tried the harder it was to regain her sense of self. It took a while, but then one afternoon she stood at the entrance to the restaurant and saw her mother at the cashier's till, her grandmother scratching her palms and Old

Fishlips complaining about his soup. It was a scene she'd witnessed a thousand times and yet she suddenly saw it in all its splendour and complexity. She saw her family, and this family was a symbol of all that was valuable in the universe.

That same afternoon she told her mother and Old Fishlips about the explosion; how, to her despair and confusion, her entire platoon had been killed, how it took her weeks to find a way out of the jungle.

"So, Bong is dead," prompted Fishlips.

Mabel gave a tiny nod. She sat with her hands in her lap, heavy as an infant. She could still feel his thick hair under her fingers.

Lu See went to make everybody a cup of tea. On her return she said, "I am so sorry, Mr Foo."

"I suspected as much but waited for you to tell me. I raised him up. He was a good boy."

Mabel stared at her hands nestled in her lap and nodded again.

"How did he die?" asked the old man, his eyes now honeycombed with blood vessels.

When Mabel mentioned the radio and the strange noise it emitted, Lu See demanded to be told more: where had the radio come from, what sort of noise had it made? Mabel looked at her, blinking; she searched her memory; it was like looking for needles in the hay, but eventually she came across a splinter of shining metal. She went quiet for a moment and then said, "The radio. Now that I think about it, it must have been a trap. They wanted us all to die." Those twenty words turned Lu See's blood cold.

The following afternoon Stan Farrell paid Mabel a visit at the restaurant and asked her to identify certain faces in a selection of mugshots.

Lu See strode up to him and slapped him hard across the face. Stan cupped his hands in front of him and repeated over and over that 'it wasn't meant to happen like that.'

Mabel heard the words 'radio set' and 'betrayal' and 'the Black-headed sheep' but didn't understand. She didn't want to understand. What's done is done, she said to herself. Nothing now can bring Bong back. Instead, she went to her room to get away from Lu See's screaming and flopped face down on her bed.

Later, Lu See told her never to speak to Stan Farrell again.

Mabel didn't ask why; rather she concentrated on getting her life back on track. But it was hard. Losing Bong was hard.

The night sounds were different. She missed the thrumming drone of insects that drowned out all thought. The air smelled thinner. Gone was the close scent of wet earth and heavy rain, the smell of wood rot and decay. She noticed too that the people in the neighbourhood behaved differently; they kept their distance, rarely offering a hello when she strolled up and down Macao Street, never once volunteering a smile. In fact they regarded her with suspicion. *Is it because I used to be a rebel?* She couldn't tell. Mabel was reminded of the crocodiles in the Tengi River; cruising the yellow waters with only their thick globular eyes visible. She felt as though she was being watched all the time.

After all that had happened to the country, it just wasn't possible to say *selamat pagi* or exchange *jo-suns* any more if people suspected you had a Communist past. They may have supported her secretly, but now with the Emergency lifted she was shunned.

"You must eat." Lu See said over the pork stew, "Look at you, all gristle and bone. We have to fatten you up."

When she said this, Mabel felt like a pig being plumped for slaughter. But this was a Chinese mother's way of expressing affection; feeding the ones you loved. Earlier, whilst listening to *Malay Woman's Hour* on the Zenith radio, Mabel heard Dr Chow and Mrs Gangooly discuss the differences in parenting cultures. *'Because we Chinese find it hard to convey tenderness in a Western, physical way, through hugs and kisses, we spoil our children instead. And punish the hell out of them if they do something wrong!'* That was when Mabel thought of the old Cantonese saying: *Da see tung, ma see ngoi – Hitting is caring. Scolding is love.*

"Please eat more." Lu See poked one of Mabel's ribs for emphasis. "Look how thin you are."

But Mabel's stomach wasn't accustomed to so much food; it had shrivelled and needed time to adjust. "I'm used to eating only tiny morsels . . . off plates made of leaves," she told Lu See. "It's been a while . . ." She flinched. A thin *pop* sounded in her head.

"And why are you so jumpy?"

Mabel kept quiet. *Pop-pop-pop!* The vague noise resembled distant gun shots. *Like machinegun fire. Crackling inside my head.* It immediately brought back memories: Corporal Johnny Evans with black ants swarming over his stomach; Bong with his chest blown apart; corpses with hideous staring eyes. She had to guard against thinking of their faces.

One night Lu See awoke to Mabel's nightmares. She stood outside her daughter's room with the hall lamp on and listened to the whimpering, the yelps of panic, the kicking and squirming, waiting for the inevitable scream to come. The feeling of helplessness engulfed her.

Later, sitting by her side, with Mabel bent double as if with stomach cramps, Lu See helped her dry her eyes on the edge of a pajama sleeve. "I'm sorry," sobbed Mabel.

Lu See told her daughter there was no need to apologize. In the dim light of the hall lamp, she took her hand and stroked the skin toughened by a thousand mosquito bites, inspecting the scars made by rattan vines, the red weals on her shoulder caused by Stan Farrell's bomb. "All you need is time to heal," she said, calming her fears. If she was broken, Lu See would help pick up the pieces. She watched her daughter fall back into sleep, careful not to disturb her, watching her face, listening to the creaks of the bed as she dreamed of men roasting in their own skin.

Lu See banged the receiver down. She'd spent the last hour making phone calls to the Chinese Embassy, speaking to their visa staff. Once again she'd hit a wall. "Why must they make it so difficult? It's like climbing Mount Everest." The previous day Pietro had called his Chinese counterpart on her behalf, only to be informed that all entry permits into Tibet were 'temporarily' denied. It seemed to her that each time they unravelled one layer of bureaucracy, another layer materialized.

Irked, Lu See set down her cup of tea and watched how Mabel used her fingers to press each mouthful of rice into a ball and transfer it to her mouth. "Don't you use a fork and spoon any more?" she asked.

Reaching for some cutlery, Lu See caught the shadow of a man hovering by the five-foot way outside.

Mabel chewed slowly. "It's been a while," she said, "since I used a fork." Her voice was brittle.

Lu See eyed the stranger at the entrance. She'd seen him before. He was the elderly man she'd spotted practising tai-chi by the Tung Wah Association assembly hall; he was one of the mule's accomplices.

Lu See pretended to read from the *Malay Mail* front page. From the corner of her eye she watched the man drop a white handkerchief. He trod on it with his right foot.

Lu See folded her newspaper and stepped out into the open. As he moved off she followed him at a distance. The streets were quiet. The sun was setting and worshippers were preparing themselves for Maghrib prayer. Near the railway station, passing the Moorish domes and minarets, they entered a narrow dark alleyway. That was when she saw the Black-headed Sheep. He was dressed in his characteristic white linen suit. He looked as if he was on his way to work. As they approached he paused and glanced over his shoulder. The failing sun threw an orange halo on his face.

Lu See stopped. In the amber-hued half-light several slim-waisted figures emerged from the shadowed alcoves, surrounding him. They carried meat choppers.

A far off muezzin announced that there was no God but Allah.

Lu See watched the attackers close in. Her fingers tightened into a strangling clench.

The choppers made brief patterns in the air. As if in slow motion Lu See's hands travelled to cover her eyes. She heard metal tear into flesh and bone, and a howl – a startling baying sound, like a calf taken from its mother.

Retreating, Lu See kept shielding her eyes, but caught flashes and glimpses. Crawling around in a circle, he gripped the base of a wall for support. His hands smeared the stone with red streaky marks. Blood oozed from his sloping shoulders. His jacket stuck to his skin like crimson cellophane; he looked as though he wore a bright red saddle on his back. Beneath it, his torso trembled. The spittle at the corners of his mouth thickened into a milky foam. A sound escaped from his throat, hissing like a three-legged crocodile.

She'd wanted him dead. But not like this. Not like this.

One of the assailants edged forward. He held a long-bladed sword.

The moment the Black-headed Sheep lowered his head, exposing the nape of his neck, the man gripped the sword with both hands and swung.

Across the street people emerged from the mosque. Maghrib had ended.

The decapitated corpse of notorious gangster and Japanese war sympathizer, Woo Hak-yeung, aka the Black-headed Sheep, was found in an alley near Victory Avenue yesterday evening. A Samurai sword, believed to be the murder weapon, was found beside the body. Police suspect the act was a revenge killing for crimes committed by Woo during the Japanese occupation. A CID spokesman said they were not ruling out underworld involvement. Previously, rumours abounded that the Black-headed Sheep was killed in 1945 by the MPAJA. It turns out these rumours were unsubstantiated. The Malay Mail

For a while, Lu See was unable to move. But then, all of a sudden, she dropped the newspaper, moved over to her typewriter and inserted a single sheet of paper. She felt her fingers rest on the keys, then tapped:

Dear Pumpkin-head,

We finally got the bastard. He is dead.

Lu See

She wound the paper out of the typewriter, folded it in two and sealed it in an envelope. It was over, definitely over. A part of her wanted to shout and scream and hurl things against the wall. Bitterness exuded from every pore. However, after several minutes, she felt her spirits lift as the echoes of her past died down. She took several deep breaths and sensed that, once and for all, a chapter of her life had come to an end, and a new one was about to begin.

When she returned to the breakfast table, Mabel was still eating with her hands. "My goodness, look at your fingernails. Weeks later and still black underneath."

Mabel made a face. "No matter how hard I scrub the dirt won't go away."

"We'd better clean them up if you're going to come and work in the restaurant."

A *chi chak* scurried across the wall. "Who says I'm going to work in the restaurant?"

"What, you mean you don't want to spend the rest of your life submerged in cooking smoke and scrubbing pots and pans?"

"I'm a nurse. I'm going back to nursing."

Lu See arched her eyebrows a millimetre; her lips twitched with pride. *Brave girl. She's seen men with their limbs torn out, their souls too, yet she still wants to return to medicine.*

"Well, if you want to go back to nursing I'll put you in touch with Dr So. He'll get you back on the course and you can work part-time in his clinic."

Men with their limbs torn out . . . Were those the images she saw in her sleep? Were those the ghosts lurking on the backs of her eyelids, waking Mabel at night?

There was so much more she wanted to ask her daughter – have you forgiven me, will you run way again, do you still love me the way you used to – but now was not the time for such questions. Lu See gazed into Mabel's eyes. "So many months I thought you'd been swallowed up by the ground. But you're home now."

Mabel smiled a weak smile, which gradually grew broader and broader. But then her smile froze. "Mama, what is it? What's the matter?"

Lu See clutched her middle. A violent spasm tore through her stomach.

Mabel's reached forward, hands hung in mid-air, suspended like prayer flags.

Her mother was vomiting blood.

11

Losar, the Tibetan New Year Festival, was supposed to be one of the happiest occasions for the nuns, but because of the Chinese religious clampdowns the celebrations were muted.

The day started with the high-pitched ting of bronze cymbals. The altar table gradually grew thick with offerings of water and lotus flowers and rice. The abbess addressed everyone and spoke of the lotus flower being the symbol of purity. "It grows in the muddiest of waters," she said, "with its beauty undefiled. This is how you must be to the world."

Afterwards, all the nuns went to the giant prayer wheel in Barkhor Street and wished for peace in their broken land.

Everyone was excited, ringing bells and brandishing *dorjes*.

In the town some of the monks wore pointed yellow hats called *Gelugpas*, others wore red scholar's hoods. They waved banners of cloth and soon, as if on cue, a masquerade started. Devil-dancers in black hats adorned with feathers and men in grotesque masks acted out scenes from religious stories where demons captured lay people and called for the monks to save them. The monks charged forward theatrically and frightened the devil away.

There were lamas blowing six-foot long copper horns. Others blew on conch shell trumpets; a deep, rich blast of sound. But before anyone could light any of the butter lamps, Chinese soldiers appeared, spitting phlegm. They ordered the monks to stop what they were doing and pack up their things. Kicking over a wall of prayer stones, they said all religion was poison and then they forced an elderly lama to strip naked in the town square.

"I wish I had a chestnut pan to hit all Communist invaders' heads. They spit and jeer at us," Sum Sum said. She could feel her heart thumping like a temple drum. On the streets of Shigatse and on the outskirts of Lhasa anyone wearing the sacred red robes was at the mercy of Chinese soldiers.

Tormam's voice was unsteady. She said, "I hear of big fighting in Amdo and Kham." She gnawed at her fingers, which Sum Sum knew meant she was trying not to cry. "Some people are saying that Americans are helping the uprising with guns, saying American planes dropping rifles somewhere south-side of Lhasa for resistance movement."

"Terrible things are happening to the roof of the world." Sum Sum felt a dull ache stretch her insides, as though her stomach had been drained. The kitchen still had some grains and plenty of yak butter, but the nuns now ate only once a day, usually *tsampa*; every fifth day they were given rice with nettle spinach and wild onions.

With the spring of 1959 came quail's eggs and seasonal turnips.

The prayer wheels spun.

As the soldiers approached, forming a line like a row of privet hedges, the nuns gathered.

A monk from a neighbouring monastery came tearing down the beaten earth road, arms stretched wide like a bird to bar the soldiers' progress. They cuffed him across the face and pebble-sized droplets of blood fell from his split lip. As he rushed at them again, arms flapping this time, they grabbed him high up by the shoulder and beat him. Tormam, watching, doubled over as though someone had kicked her too.

Outside in the main courtyard, with the rain coming

down, the abbess stood on helplessly, fists clenched, with a grimace-smile painted on: an imprisoned elderly bird.

The nuns filed out and formed a link-line across the entrance to their home; Jampa took Sum Sum's hand and Tormam held the other. The officer in front unclipped his holster and brandished a pistol.

All the nuns backed away, apart from Sum Sum.

A slow fuse burned within her. Eventually, for all her boldness, she took a step back too.

Tormam, whose face was arranged into an expression of wild-eyed confusion, darted a concerned look at Jampa and hugged herself against the cold. Sum Sum leaned over to console her and whispered a heated message into her ear.

The soldiers stomped to a halt. Jampa shouted for the men to leave with a determination she usually reserved for prayer. Tormam placed a comforting hand on her arm as the rain spat into their eyes.

Sum Sum stared hard at the men and then whirled round and tore down a hallway that led to the kitchens. A minute later she was back with a basket of quail eggs. Her heart thudded in her chest so hard it blurred the edges of her vision, but despite this, her aim was true. The first egg landed with a splat on the officer's shoulder, spilling yellow yolk over his epaulettes. The next smashed against a soldier's cap, dislodging it from his head.

It was all a distraction. Tormam, ribcage swelling and falling over her lungs, took her cue and with a rumple of robes vanished unnoticed into the prayer hall.

The abbess's mouth thinned to form a smile, closing like a narrowed fan. Sum Sum threw three more eggs, but before she could let off another the officer's hand was over her chin, cupping her jawbone forcefully. Her jaw hinge gave a tiny crack under the pressure. He leaned in close, tracing her cheekbone with a knuckle. She was convinced he could hear her heart pounding. When she struggled, he loosened his grip and she wrenched free.

The smell of raw garlic crackled in her nostrils. The odour oozed from his pores and breath.

She tilted the basket and the remaining eggs fell and broke across his boots. "We will have to bottle that breath of yours, lah. Must not let it go to waste."

He showed his teeth, looking as if he intended to bite her breasts.

"You could curl hair with it." Hearing this, the officer tipped his head back and laughed uproariously. Sum Sum thought he laughed like crazy-crackpot Captain Bligh or Pirate Blackbeard. She waited to see if he would swing his arm round and break her nose with one sharp flick. She stared at him, defiant.

When he stepped clear of her she gave an audible sigh and clutched at her solar plexus in relief.

He hitched his thumbs into his belt and spoke with his chin in the air. "Our great leader and modernizer chairman Mao Tse-tung has declared that religion is poison. And as a result our mineralogist." – he stepped to one side to allow a smaller man through, jabbing a finger in the direction of the prayer hall – "Comrade Compatriot Suen will be liberating all the stones from the Buddha icons. After which our metal people will come to make itemizations of all brass, copper, silver and gold artifacts. Every ritual object here is to be confiscated and taken to be melted in the foundry. When these metal people come I urge you to make them welcome and offer them tea and *tsampa*."

Yes, thought Sum Sum. I'll make them *tsampa*. *Tsampa* made with mule dung. May the wrathful deities of the *Bardo Thodol* drink their blood.

The officer and the mineralogist found Tormam stuffing a bronze of Buddha Akshobhya into a basket of freshly laundered spiritual robes.

They slapped her several times and turned the rooms over, one by one, starting with the prayer hall. They tore up floorboards, kicked over ritual bells and *vajras* and ripped open novice rugs. They hauled down sections of shelving, which collapsed with a crunch, like the sound of rice paper crumpling in your fist. When they reached the kitchen, they shook the turnips from their sacks and rifled through the chests of tea. The officer in charge eyed the hot cauldrons of soup. They found another bronze statue in a vat of yak butter. The officer, appeased now, grabbed a wooden spoon and sunk it into the cauldron of hot soup. "Ugh! Taste is terrible." He grimaced. "Right, I want everything itemized for the metal people. Give me the list and I will hand it to them. If anything goes missing there will be hell to pay."

As soon as they left prayer hall manager Jampa took Tormam aside. There was a cut on her top lip. "How is your face?"

Tormam did not reply. Instead she nodded and led Jampa and the abbess to the kitchen and the cauldron of hot soup. With a wooden paddle she fished out two large pouches made from goat hide and deposited them on a work table. She undid the straps with a cloth wrapped round her fingers and removed the priceless statues – a massive golden image of Shakyamuni Buddha and a 15th century figure of Harit Tara, cast in solid gold and inlaid with rubies. They were the nunnery's most sacred possessions.

The abbess smiled at Tormam. "Inner peace and strength to you."

The following day fighting broke out in Lhasa. A battalion of dob-dobs – monk soldiers – wearing red armbands and with their faces soot-blackened attacked a Chinese foot patrol using spears and cobblers' knives as weapons. Hundreds of protestors backed them up throwing rocks in support of the Dalai Lama. A wave of Chinese troops arrived and when the protestors threw stones at them they drew their weapons and fired on the people. Like flower buds after a frost they fell to the ground.

The military commission imposed a dusk-to-dawn curfew. When this stirred up even greater hatred the Chinese shelled the Dalai Lama's Summer Palace and set it ablaze. The resulting fires spread to the nearby buildings. Many hundreds died in the inferno.

Sum Sum could smell the burning flesh. The Chinese troops burned corpses in Barkhor Street throughout the day, tossing limp charred bodies into the giant pyre.

Prayer hall manager Jampa and the abbess were deep in conversation as they padded barefoot across the courtyard.

"What were they talking about?" asked Sum Sum a little later. She fingered her mala beads.

"I don't know," Tormam replied. "They went into Jampa's office and closed the door. But they mentioned your name."

"My name?"

"Have you done anything wrong?" asked Tormam. Sum Sum shook her head. "Well, I think they are going to want to see you."

The abbess's mouth curled and quivered. "The Dalai Lama has fled. The gates of heaven have closed."

Sum Sum and Tormam were in prayer manager Jampa's room, heads bowed reverently. The abbess was close to tears. Her words shocked everyone into silence.

Jampa's mouth grew thin. Eventually: "The abbess and I have decided," she said with deliberate calm. She was peering down at her desk now, laying her hands on its surface, fists clenched. "We have decided that the situation in Tibet will only grow worse. Knowing this, we must save our sacred statues. The Chinese will keep returning. One day they will find them. They will find them and destroy them." She unfurled a scroll, an ancient hand-drawn map of Tibet and Bhutan. "We believe this is the route taken by the Dalai Lama. It is treacherous and strength-sapping and . . ."

"And . . .?" Sum Sum urged her along.

"It is our hope that you and Tormam will follow in their footsteps. Deliver our sacred golden image of Shakyamuni Buddha and our beloved Harit Tara into the hands of His Holiness."

Sum Sum registered the words and information but was unsure what to say.

"Will you do this for the sake of our nunnery?" pleaded the abbess.

"Why us?" asked Sum Sum.

"You are both young and loyal and exceedingly resourceful," replied the abbess.

"If a little mutinous," added Jampa.

"It has taken us time to appreciate you, Sengemo, but appreciate you we do. You have a wilful character and a genuine heart. We trust you," continued the abbess.

"Will you do this?" said Jampa.

Sum Sum and Tormam exchanged looks. "Yes," they replied. "Of course, we will do it."

"*Ndug're.*"

"But how do we do this?" said Tormam.

"You walk," replied the abbess.

"Walk?"

"Yes," she said triumphantly. "To India."

The skin on the back of Sum Sum's neck stiffened.

"Yes, to India," Jampa repeated decisively. Forgetting for a moment that the abbess was there she took a pinch of snuff from her yak-horn container and snorted noisily. "This map will guide you. I have outlined your course with landmarks. You will cross the Indian border at the Khenzimana Pass. Give them these papers." She handed them two scrolls. "Tell them who you are and that you seek political asylum. If they do not understand you keep repeating the Dalai Lama's name over and over. Whatever happens they must not send you back."

"And take this firebag." The abbess gave them a leather

pouch. "Inside are flints, tinder and boxes of matches. Keep it dry. This bag more than anything will keep you alive."

The abbess spoke in a strangled tone; the words crackled like dry leaves. But it was what she'd left unsaid that made the blood leave Sum Sum's face. She read the warning in the old woman's expression: *Lose this bag and you will freeze to death in the middle of nowhere.*

For the first time there were dark circles of worry under Jampa's eyes.

The abbess found them boots for the long journey; the soles were made from thick yak skin and the upper made from buff. Jampa insisted the girls wrap cloth over their feet within the boots to stave off the cold and told them if the cloth should wear through they were to stuff their boots with yak hair.

"*Ndug're!* Also, this is for you," the abbess said to Sum Sum. She handed over a brick of paper, held together with twine. "Letters from your friend in Malaya. We have held them in safe-keeping for you. Usually we do not allow contact from outside for the first twenty years, but we feel you are deserving of this."

Sum Sum bowed her head and tucked the letters under her arm. For several moments she did not say anything: she was dumbstruck. All this time, Lu See had been writing to her and she never knew. At length: "May I ask something? I want to send word to a friend that I am leaving. If I write a short message will you ensure it is sent?" Jampa assured her that she would take care of it. Sum Sum hesitated before continuing. "There is more. I have broken a rule. In the last few months I have used a postal-runner, a *dakpa*, to carry several messages out of Tibet. I wanted this person to know what is happening in Tibet, hoping somehow they could help. Now, I just want them to know I am alive."

The abbess simply nodded.

*

Both Sum Sum and Tormam were given earflap hats, sheep-skin jackets with the wool turned inside out, thick gloves and several layers of insulating underclothes. They each tied eight taels of silver in a cloth over their waists and secured prayer box amulets round their necks. They filled small leather pouches with tea, butter and barley-flour. Then Jampa escorted them to the prayer hall where the abbess blessed them with a sacred Tantra.

"Look at you, as calm as Namtso Lake on a summer day, lah," said Sum Sum to Tormam. Her friend returned a nervous smile.

They set off at dawn with two shoulder bags apiece. Tormam was given the golden image of Shakyamuni Buddha; Sum Sum was to look after the figure of Harit Tara.

The nuns erected windhorse prayer flags in their honour. When Jampa hugged her, Sum Sum tried but could not speak. It was as if she had stones in her mouth.

Heading south-west, aiming for a scattering of dwellings made almost entirely from goat and oxen horn, and onwards towards the 16,000-foot Chela Pass, they walked at a steady pace. A quick scan of the field behind assured her that they were not being followed.

They walked until the moon was high in the sky. That first night they settled down by a rock cave. In the far distance, an outline of watery orange lights pooled: flickering fires lit by nomads that necklaced the hills.

The following morning they looked back on their progress and caught a last distant sight of Lhasa.

Two days later they descended to the valley of the Brahmaputra River. They crossed the broad stretch of water via a rope-and-barge ferry. Using a thick black rope which stretched from bank to bank, several men pulled the barge across the current. By now Sum Sum's feet were beginning to ache.

When they reached the town of Chidisho and came across a horse and yak caravan that was heading south-east for the hamlets of the Himalayan foothills, they almost collapsed with exhaustion. They refreshed themselves with *tsampa* and butter tea and were told by one of the traders that the salt caravan, made up of thirty yaks carrying heavy saddlebags, was heading off at daybreak. He said for a tael of silver he would let them ride with them, sharing a horse.

For the next two weeks the thud of hooves and the swishing of whips was a constant sound in their heads. Tormam had ridden as a young girl, so she took the reins with Sum Sum tucked up behind and their bags lashed to the saddlebow. They navigated narrow mountain passes and crossed semi-frozen streams. The yak herders clicked their tongues to calm and guide their beasts, always keeping a keen eye on the lead yak which had red tassels tied to its ear and a prayer flag strung on its back. It also had a string of bells secured to its tail. If the lead yak lost its footing and tumbled to its death down a crevice, the bells would alert the entire caravan. Fortunately this happened only once. After which, each time their horse neighed, Sum Sum's heart leapt to her throat.

At nightfall they set up camp and huddled in yurt-like canvas tents. Saddle sore, Sum Sum lay down gingerly by Tormam's side on sheepskins spread out on the floor. A fire was lit to keep the jackals and wolves away. They ate *tsampa* and stale flat bread, starting each meal by dipping a hand into the *tsampa* and throwing droplets in every direction for luck.

At dawn the traders flicked salt on the morning fire to seek assurance from the mountain gods. If the fire crackled as the salt fell upon it, it meant a storm was far away. If the fire stayed silent, it meant a storm was near.

Tiny villages made up of ten to twelve houses came and went: places the herdsmen called Shopanup, Lhuntse Dzong and Jhor. The names meant nothing to Sum Sum.

The caravan route ended at a small settlement made up of stone huts. The girls found that they had descended into a valley full of greenery and buzzing insects. Dismounting, Sum Sum stroked the horse's muzzle. She laced her hands behind her head and stretched. The long ride had driven hard nails into her buttocks and thighs.

They rested here for a day, regaining their strength. They ate a lavish supper of barley soup, turnip dumplings and flat bread stuffed with peppers. Sum Sum restored her food supplies, refilling her leather satchels of tea, butter and barley-flour; she also gathered several fistfuls of yak hair for insulation and tinder and bark resin for making fire.

In the morning, Sum Sum unfurled Jampa's scroll and peered at the ancient map; there was a landmark up ahead; she looked to the rising sun and worked out her directions. The traders gave them dried meat and a fresh store of safety matches, waved farewell and pointed to the distant mountains. "From now on we go on foot. That is the direction we are heading," Sum Sum said to Tormam. "One of the men said we must look out for a huge cavern shaped like the mouth of a bull; after that we head south for a set of twin peaks."

They entered the grasslands. Sum Sum noted the terrain beneath her feet was soft and waterlogged, very different from the hard brittle ground surrounding the nunnery.

Gradually, they began to ascend. The greenery turned to stubble, then rock and then to snow. The air grew thinner as the temperature fell. Eyes downcast, heads bowed as though inspecting the boots on their feet, they climbed the mountain trail. Once in a while they glanced up in search of the sun to use it as a compass. Sometimes Sum Sum jammed a stick upright in the ground, waited several minutes and traced the movement of the shadow.

"Are we lost?" asked Tormam.

"Not yet," Sum Sum reassured her.

They came to a rope bridge. Sum Sum stared at the overpass. All she saw were three pieces of cordage, one for the feet and one each for the hands. "I hope you are a good rope-walker, lah," she said to Tormam, who peered over the sheer drop. There was nothing but eternity below.

At the lip of the bridge she shunted Tormam in the back. "Come, lah, we have to hurry. Cannot do this after dark."

"I'm scared of heights," Tormam admitted.

"You want me to go first, is it?" Tormam nodded. Sum Sum adjusted the bag on her shoulders and reached for the hand cables. As soon as she secured a firm grip she stepped on to the foot rope. Her boots sent down a rain of little stones. Almost at once she experienced a terrifying swaying. When the swaying subsided, she took a few tentative steps forward, concentrating hard to keep her head steady and upright.

"Don't let go!" cried Tormam.

"You and your stupid advice!"

Sum Sum's first instinct was to not look down, but then she realized that she had to in order to place her feet firmly on the cable. When she was half way across she felt the ropes begin to swing and shake again. She pulled too much to the left and overbalanced. Her right foot rose and kicked at fresh air. Tormam screamed. She caught herself and pulled herself straight and once more waited for the swaying to subside.

"The trick is to take your time," she called out to Tormam.

"I thought you were dead!"

She peered over the chasm, which was several hundred feet deep. "It's easy once you get used to it." Ten minutes later they were both safely across. Tormam was ashen-faced and her hands were trembling.

"Let's go back and do again, lah," said Sum Sum. "Fantastic exciting, no?" Tormam punched her in the arm.

12

The Zenith radio blared, rattling the windows. Lu See and Mabel were in the back courtyard. An electric fan spun behind a thick block of ice, driving cool air into their faces. As usual, tablecloths hung on lines of string, drying in the heat. Scrub boards leaned against walls and the dogs lay out in the shade, hidden from the afternoon sun. Cries of 'Younis!' and 'Yasmine!' flew across from the neighbour's compound.

"To recap the international headlines for November 20, 1960: President Dwight D. Eisenhower to authorize the use of US$1m to resettle Cuban refugees arriving in Florida. South Vietnamese President Diem survives another coup attempt. The funeral of actor Clark Gable takes place in Hollywood . . ."

Lu See allowed the news of Clark Gable's interment to brew for a while before taking up the scissors again. She thought of Sum Sum and how she had once adored the King of Hollywood. "For goodness' sake, keep still, Mabel, stop twitching like an anxious bride."

"I never asked to have my hair cut."

"Your head looks like a chrysanthemum. Hospital regulations state that all scrub nurses must keep their hair short, above the shoulder line."

". . . and the International Red Cross estimate that 90,000 Tibetans lost their lives in the recent uprising against Chinese occupying forces."

Lu See darted into the kitchen "What was that about Tibet?" She felt a panic strike her gut like a hot stone.

Mother appeared with a dog by her feet. She shooed it into

the back garden. "There's been fighting in Tibet. Many dead," she said matter-of-factly.

"But what about Sum Sum? I have to do something."

"Do what?" Mother said, scratching her palms. "Go rescue her?" She snorted. "Like a blind monkey, swinging from tree to tree?"

Lu See pursed her lips.

Dungeonboy said, "Maybe you ask boss-Stan to help. Pow-lice always good at finding people."

Lu See didn't reply, but Dungeonboy could guess by her expression what she thought of his suggestion.

"*And now it's time for Malay Woman's Hour,*" said the radio presenter in a tinny voice, "*where our own Dr Chow and Mrs Gangooly will be discussing whether bananas cause constipation . . .*"

Mabel shouted from the courtyard: "Please hurry up. I have to clock in at the hospital before five for the evening shift." Her head gave an involuntary twitch.

"Surely you can be a few minutes late, Mabel?" said Lu See.

"Of course I cannot. You know how things are since the British left. A Chinese person has to work three times as hard to get recognition."

Lu See nodded. Under the new constitution the Malays got the best jobs.

"*But first we give you a musical interlude with . . .*"

Lu See returned to her barbering duties. "Keep your head straight, please." Mabel, balanced on a tall stool amongst the pots of rosemary bushes, adjusted her bib for the hundredth time.

"It's causing maximum anger amongst the Chinese and Indian staff."

". . . *Elvis Presley's new hit song 'It's Now or Never'.*"

"Dungeonboy! Please turn it down in there!"

From the depths of the kitchen, Dungeonboy tweaked the

volume control but remained glued to the Zenith's black dial.

"Knock, knock! Aahh!"

The voice was unmistakable. Lu See, Mabel and all the dogs swung their heads round in unison. Uncle Big Jowl leaned against the outer door frame. "Any chance of a plate of *char siu faan*?"

"I'm just finishing off here, take a seat inside."

He slapped his tummy with delight. Moving with hippopotamus stateliness, he turned heavily, swaying from side to side as he walked.

Mabel shook the bib free and swept hair from her clothes. She caught up with Uncle Big Jowl and helped him into a blackwood chair beside Pietro. Pietro pinched the brim of his fedora and raised it. "*Buona sera*," he said, sipping a glass of lime juice with his little finger held in the air. He was eyeing the nearby table which bore a smoky glass case of rosemary shortcakes.

Yanking at the creases of his trousers the big man slumped down heavily.

"The freight train has landed," observed Pietro.

"Bloody troublesome knees. *Ai-yoo!*" He winced. "So," he growled, squinting at Pietro with suspicion. "Lu See says you a tip-top diplomat, aahh. Tell me, what makes a good diplomat?"

Pietro, looking pristine as ever with a knotted silk cravat at his throat, fluttered his eyelids. "A good diplomat is someone who always remembers a woman's birthday, but never her age."

Uncle Big Jowl puffed out his cheeks, made them as round as dumplings. "Oh, by the way, Lu See, aahh, your brothers, have come to see you."

"Peter and James are here?" exclaimed Lu See. "Where?"

"Up in your rooms. James is wearing his maddo homespun clothes."

"Bra-haa! Is that who it is?" cried Pietro. "I thought Gandhi had made an appearance."

"Apparently they have come from Butterworth for a Jehovah's conference."

"Dishy fellow nonetheless – he'd look fabulous in polka dots." With an imperious tilt of his chin, Pietro watched Lu See race up the stairs. He stretched a flaccid wrist in the direction of the smoky glass case of rosemary shortcakes but Mother slapped his hand away.

Through the open door Lu See could hear a deep-throated mantra. She found her brother James meditating between a stack of old books and the dressmaker's mannequin. Attired in a white toga-like shawl and silk-lined slippers with socks held up with garters, he sat cross-legged, chanting, with a palm branch in his fist. *"Om, om, Rama . . . Om, om, Hare om."*

She knocked on the doorframe and his eyes sprang open. There was the look of the zealot about him; his gaze bright yet glassy like a radical priest with a drug addiction. "I thought you were a Jehovah's Witness." She smiled. "What's with all this Buddhist chanting?"

"That's what I said," exclaimed Peter. He was dressed in his usual baggy shorts and shirt, examining an old walking stick.

"In these troubling times, I'm hedging my bets, God Shiva allowing."

"I don't know what the elders will say about this." Peter waved the cane at James.

"Please get that stick out of my face."

"It's not in your face, it is in my hand."

"Precisely."

Lu See interrupted them. "Why on *earth* are you dressed like a sadhu from the Batu Caves?"

"I'm in shirt and tie all week at the Postal Department, trussed up like a chicken. This is my way of letting off steam."

"And who's this?" said Lu See, suddenly noticing a stranger hovering by the shower room.

James got to his feet. "May I introduce Dr Rafit Patel."

She studied the little man, her eyes guarded. He wore a navy blue suit and had a pointy chin. He removed his silver pince-nez as he stepped forward to take her hand.

"Birth certificate says Rafit Patel, but please call me Ralph," the doctor said in a voice as clear and shiny as a diamond dipped in ghee.

"Whose idea is this?" Lu See asked, her face beginning to purple slightly.

"Mine." Mother was standing at the door, fists on hips.

"I've already seen several doctors."

"All useless," barked Mother. "Last time you vomited blood, you spent three days in hospital and still they scratch their heads. Dr Rafit is – "

"Please call me Ralph," he insisted.

Mother shot him a withering look. "Dr *Ralph* is an expert in his field."

The doctor approached cautiously, hands folded like a priest. "I would like you to come in for some tests."

"I've had all the tests and they were inconclusive. They said it was probably ulcers."

"What harm then to come in for a few more?" His tone was gentle and coaxing.

"I've been poked and prodded and clucked over quite enough."

Everybody looked solemn. Lu See walked up to the window and pressed her forehead to the glass.

James shut his eyes. "*Om, om, Bhadaraya . . . Om, om, Rama . . .*"

"Quiet, James!" scolded Mother.

"Just a couple of blood and urine tests," the doctor said, cajoling now. "To put your mother's mind at ease."

Lu See felt the colour drain from her face. She hated having her blood taken. "Will it be just the one blood test?"

"Two at most," he conceded.

Mother came to stand by her side. "What are you thinking, Lu See?"

Lu See dug her nails into her palms. She didn't say anything for a long time. "I'm thinking I don't want to know. Whatever's the matter with me, I'd rather not know."

"Often it is the not knowing that makes people worse," said Dr Ralph. "The anxiety builds and builds. I can give you peace of mind."

Breathing rapidly, Lu See said, "And what if it is bad news? How does that offer me peace of mind?" She stared at her mother but she was talking to the doctor.

"Well, that is where medical science comes in." His voice soothed her. "Please," he said. "Come with me now to my clinic."

He held his hands out to the sides, palms upwards.

"Come, dear madam," he said, shifting his weight forward.

Lu See followed the doctor down the stairs and into the glare of Macao Street.

It was late afternoon and the muezzin called the faithful to *Asr* prayer. Lu See muttered a quiet incantation to herself, as children, stripped to the waist, played with a rattan ball, running around in circles chasing the sunlight on their backs. For the first time in many years she felt scared of what the future might bring.

Lu See climbed into Dr Ralph's car. Twenty minutes later, he motioned for her to sit in a chair in front of his desk. She sat very still and tense.

He spread out a number of diagrams on his desk, anatomical drawings of the human body, showing the digestive tract, the stomach, the large and small intestines, the rectum and anus. The major organs such as the heart and lungs and liver were coloured red. The intestines were shaded green.

Lu See pointed her eyes at the ceiling, as though there was something exceptionally interesting up there. She was so nervous she hid her gaze from the doctor's.

"Once I examine you, I will have a finer idea. First, we will analyse your blood and urine for anaemia and inflammation. After that we can talk."

He led her to a small surgery where a female assistant waited by an examination bed. There were instruments laid out in metal trays.

After about an hour Dr Ralph said, "Let's talk in my office." His voice was calm. Lu See settled into the same chair as before. "What I am about to tell you is not easy to hear." He took a breath and adjusted his pince-nez. "Our tests confirm that you are suffering from anaemia, which indicates to me that you may be bleeding within the intestines. I will wait for the urine samples to confirm this. I will need to proceed with further tests but your symptoms are compatible with a most uncommon illness."

Lu See's mouth went dry. "Is it cancer?"

Dr Ralph frowned. She waited for his response, scared his words might snap her in half.

"At this stage, I would say no, but I cannot rule it out." He set his lips in a grim line. "However, the abdominal cramps, the fevers, the weight loss and nausea are all consistent with deep ulcers in the intestines. These ulcers puncture holes in your bowels resulting in fistulae and abscesses." He pulled a file towards him and looked at her over the top of his silver pince-nez. "Medical reports from your hospital stay last year have you diagnosed with Sprue, a digestive disturbance caused by an allergy to gluten." He clasped his hands together tightly. "But I believe you have an advanced form of Crohn's disease."

Lu See stared at him. She had never heard of such a thing. "And what does that mean?"

The doctor took a handkerchief from his pocket and dabbed his pointy chin. "It means you have a disease with no known cure."

Lu See swallowed. "Is it serious?"

"Ordinarily, it is not regarded as life-threatening." The doctor removed his eye-glasses and rubbed the skin where the clip made a mark. "But in your case, you've vomited blood on two occasions. So I would have to say that it is serious."

"Are there pills I can take? Can you remove the ulcers?"

"The disease is difficult to diagnose because the symptoms appear only gradually. To be absolutely certain I will ask you to come to the hospital for a barium sulphate X-ray. No, please, dear madam, do not look so alarmed. It is not as frightening as it sounds. Do not worry your brain over it. You simply drink a mixture of barium sulphate, tannic acid and gelatin, after which we X-ray you. The solution acts as a contrast medium in X-ray photography, meaning it will show up white in the images."

Lu See did not say anything.

The doctor asked, "Have you endured a lot of stress in your life?"

"Well, let's see. My husband died a few months into our marriage. I miscarried. My home was taken over by the Japanese. My father shot himself in the head. My daughter ran away for months to fight in the jungle." She paused. "I'm sure there's more."

He nodded with a solemn look in his eyes.

"Doctor, tell me the truth, please. How long do I have?"

He took a breath. This time it was his turn to look at the ceiling. "It would be unprofessional of me to speculate."

"I'm asking you, for my daughter's sake. How long?"

"If you are lucky, ten, twenty, perhaps even thirty years."

"And if I'm unlucky?"

"You mean if the vomiting of blood persists?"

"Yes."

"Twelve to fifteen months."

Only when she was out on the pavement, crossing to catch a cycle rickshaw home, did she allow her body to release its anxiety. Her legs went weak. She only just made it into the seat of the waiting pedicab.

13

Sum Sum trudged ahead, head down, pushing against the wind. The wind felt like something solid and raw as it bounced off her face. 'Not long to go,' she muttered every now and again to keep her spirits up.

She pressed on, resisting the knifing wind. Eyes fixed on the next resting-place – a belt of trees or a cluster of craggy rocks in the far distance. *Keep going. Keep going.* With each step Sum Sum repeated the message, willing her legs forward.

She held an unshakable will to survive.

They walked for hours in silence; mostly because they would not be heard above the wind-rush. They tied thin cloths over their eyes to fend off the glaring sun and snow blindness. Occasionally they smiled through the cold and fed off their partner's determination.

They carried on through a snow-flurry until Tormam sank to her knees. "I'm too tired!"

Earlier, Sum Sum thought she'd heard voices behind her. She wondered now if the Chinese were after them. She pictured the officer with the laugh like Pirate Blackbeard, unbuckling his holster and shooting them dead.

"Get back up!" cried Sum Sum. "Remember the yak that was left behind? I'll do the same to you. I'll relieve you of your bags and leave you here!" She helped her friend to her feet. To work out how many hours of daylight they had left, Sum Sum raised her hand parallel to the ground, with the sun just above the hand. Every finger down to the horizon meant 15 minutes. She counted eight fingers. "We have another two hours of daylight," she said.

Muscles aching, they marched on, staring blankly at the carpet of snow ahead, keeping their centres of gravity low. They passed the skeleton of a bird. It made them think there must be trees up ahead.

"Not long to go! We rest when we find shelter."

An hour later, out of desperation, with no shelter in sight, they chose a slope with a natural wind block and started scooping out a hole in the snow with their gloved hands and a trowel made of tree bark. They dug and dug until their arms and shoulders ached. They tunnelled at an upward angle. After forty minutes they crawled inside their burrow, just wide enough for them both to fit through, entering feet first. Once settled, they stopped up the gap with packed snow and punched a small ventilation hole through the top. "All that digging . . . I'm perspiring so much," said Tormam.

"Me too. Quick, lah, we must stay dry," said Sum Sum. "Reach into the bags for change of undershirt. We have to get out of these or we will freeze to death."

Elbows and knees banging, they wrestled into fresh clothes. They jammed yak hair under their garments for added insulation and held on to one another for warmth, legs entwined, hands pressed into armpits. "Tormam, if I died up here, would you eat me?"

"I would think about it . . . not for long . . . but I would pause for thought."

"I bet your hind loin is damn tasty, lah."

"And I bet your shoulder joint would be delicious roasted over a fire."

They giggled over this for some time. Short of breath and shivering from head to toe, terrified that the walls might collapse and trap them underneath the weight of ice, they dared not close their eyes. They listened to the wind and the shifting snow make eerie screeching noises overhead, until eventually, exhaustion claimed them.

The following morning, with the Himalayan sun breaking through the clouds, Sum Sum and Tormam dug free of their shelter. Their throats were parched with thirst and their lips crackled with dryness. Sum Sum, squatting, flattened the ground with her hands and lit a small fire to melt some snow. The snow water tasted good. They ate the last of their dried meat and butter. Yawning and grumbling they shouldered their packs and continued south. Sum Sum set her eyes on the horizon; Tormam screwed up her gale-filled face and muttered long curses under her breath. Ahead of them was only endless whiteness and empty land; miles below and miles in front.

Hours and hours later, flayed by the wind and sun, they descended to a safer elevation below the treeline. As they walked down the uneven slope, the snow began to spoil. The slope grew so steep it hurt their knees and jammed their feet into the toes of their boots. Coming from the exposed upper reaches of the mountains, it took them some time to adjust to the brooding oppressiveness of the forest.

They foraged for food, pulling aside lichen and rotten tree branches. They searched hidden animal holes. But all they found were earthworms and grubs.

Extracting leaf mould and dirt from their supper they settled down to eat. Tormam held up a grub. "You swallow first."

Sum Sum, eyes wide with mischief, chewed with her mouth open, ready to spit it out. "Tastes like stale English Stilton." She grinned at her. "Try, nah." They ate, moving their jaws mechanically, squatting with arms wrapped round shins.

They gathered dry sticks, twigs, moss and pine pitch from the ground and built a ring of rocks. Using the abbess's firebag, they lit the tinder with a match and added kindling and bark resin, carefully blowing on the fire to build it up. Gradually, they added firewood to the flames, building a teepee of sticks around it.

Sum Sum warmed her pink, stiff fingers by the flames, wondering aloud if she'd ever be able to feel her fingertips again. She looked into Tormam's eyes. Both refused to admit how lost and hopeless they felt.

14

In the OR Mabel switched on the monitoring equipment at the head of the operating table and laid out the various surgical knives, scoops, scalpels and specula on a sterilization tray. She tested the hand-operated blood pressure sphygmomanometer. She fiddled with a knob on the ventilator and checked the infusion pump. Next she prepared the necessary blood bags, volume expanders and intravenous drips. Finally, she grouped metal clamps and clips in a line and positioned Sklar forceps with angled heads next to a severe-looking set of flat-handled curved scissors.

Having prepared the patient's skin, Mabel set down the dish of iodine swabs and looked at the surgeon. His expression was unreadable through his surgical mask but she guessed he was contemplating the best angle of entry. He reached out his hand, flat and expectant, to receive the scalpel from her. She pressed it into his palm as he stood over the patient and watched him make a long careful incision in the upper right part of the stomach, just below the ribs. The scalpel tip sank into the skin, slitting it with a clean, silky sound.

The blood oozed out, black and tarry. Immediately Mabel wiped it with an absorbent swab so he could proceed. An hour later, after cutting the bile duct and blood vessels leading to the gall bladder, the surgeon clamped the skin and with needle holders stitched it tight with suture thread.

"How are you holding up?" he asked her, running a curved needle through the skin.

"I am fine," she replied a moment later, applying a primary gauze dressing.

His eyes did not stray from her hands. "You mother is coming in for treatment today, or did I hear wrong?"

She secured the secondary dressing. She felt her head twitch. "No, you heard right. She will be having several X-rays in thirty minutes or so."

"Join her as soon as you finish up here. Take the afternoon off. You've earned it."

Mabel pressed the last bit of tape firmly down and gave him a long sideways glance. "Thank you. I will."

After sponging her hands and forearms in the scrub sink, Mabel changed out of her surgical gown and took the stairs to the ground floor. She bought herself a bag of Gandour hard-boiled candies from the hospital canteen and watched the catering staff wipe the table surfaces with damp cloths and set out a roll of paper napkins with the cutlery sets.

In the kitchens *mee hoon* noodles, tinctured yellow with turmeric, sizzled in a hot flat wok.

She was hungry but the only thing she could think of was her mother. A few minutes later she was in Radiology.

Through the hospital windows the broad sweep of the distant Genting Hills shadowed the horizon.

Lu See and Mabel sat side by side in the waiting room.

"I saw that surgeon you work with," said Lu See. "Is he single?"

Mabel did not reply.

"He's very handsome."

"Please don't start with the matchmaking."

"I'd better get the red engagement cards printed," Lu See teased.

"Stop it!"

"Look at your nostrils. Whenever you get angry they grow the size of the Batu Caves."

"I mean it, it's not funny."

In the ensuing silence, Mabel studied her mother's face;

she watched a muscle twitch on her neck, urgent and swollen as the throbbing throat of a tree frog.

"Are you laughing?" challenged Mabel, feeling the corners of her own mouth lift. Both women broke out in giggles and Lu See squeezed her daughter's hand affectionately.

"Has Dr Ralph given you the barium sulphate to drink?" Mabel asked.

Lu See nodded, mouth wilting at the sides. "Tasted like liquid chalk."

It was Mabel's turn to squeeze her mother's hand.

Lu See's name was called by the X-ray technician. She entered a small windowless room and lay down on a bed. She was told to hold still first on her left side and then on her right. The room was filled with a loud humming noise. She had several X-rays taken.

Some time later Dr Ralph invited Lu See and Mabel to his consulting-room. His smooth voice dropped an octave. "It is as I suspected," he said. "Only more advanced."

His words were like small explosions in her chest.

He took a long breath through his nose, took a handkerchief from his pocket and dabbed his chin.

"So how do we go about treating me?" Lu See asked.

Dr Ralph tried to sound confident and reassuring. "First thing is to prescribe a course of antibiotics to stop any infection. Next we will look into anti-inflammatory drugs. Failing that, we will explore the surgery route to remove fistulae and other obstructions."

Mabel grasped Lu See's sleeve in a supportive gesture.

Lu See set her jaw. She leaned forward, both elbows on her knees. "And this thing I have, this . . . this . . ."

"Crohn's disease."

"Has no cure."

"We can treat it." He pulled a file towards him. "We can minimise its spread, try to contain it. But the symptoms will keep returning. It will continue to flare up in different parts of the digestive tract. Often more aggressively with time."

He gave a tiny apologetic shrug of the shoulders. "I wish there was more medical science could do."

Lu See's whole body became very still. She was silent for several moments.

"Would a change in her diet help?" asked Mabel.

"Fish oils and eggs can benefit."

"What about alternative medicine?" said Lu See. "What about acupuncture or herbal remedies?"

The doctor made a face and bowed his head. "Please do not worry your brain with such things. The best treatment for you will be antibiotics – "

Lu See did not let him finish. "There must be another way."

Dr Ralph's forehead became a field of wrinkles.

"In the Himalayas there are healers." Lu See straightened in her seat. "The Tibetans have been developing holistic cures for over 2,000 years."

"Please forgive me, dear madam, but holistic medicines can often do more harm than good. Western medicine is the only way to approach this."

"I want to go to Tibet," she insisted, letting her frustrations get the better of her.

"And what is it you hope to find?"

"An answer!"

Dr Ralph looked at her with a sad expression. His eyes were soft and compassionate. They said: *My heart goes out to you but please don't do this. Don't go clutching at straws.*

Lu See rose slowly from her chair; she thanked him and left the room, dry-mouthed, closing the door quietly behind her.

From Dr Ralph's consulting-room Lu See took a taxi straight to the Chinese Embassy. She pushed through a set of revolving doors and emerged into the reception hall, noting to her surprise, that the place was deserted. The cavernous white foyer resembled a mausoleum. Set along the walls were solid rectangular benches, each the shape of a child's coffin. A giant portrait of Mao Tse-tung stared down like a benevolent god with a wart on his chin

Lu See saw a single counter window positioned at the far side of the foyer. She crossed the wide expanse of floor.

The Chinese girl behind the counter had a greasy fringe. She was filing her nails and did not look up even when Lu See cleared her throat.

"What? Can I heppjoo?"

"I want to apply for a visitor permit to Tibet," said Lu See.

Smiling, the girl inspected the fingernails on her left hand. "No can."

"But you haven't even seen my documents."

The girl spoke over her shoulder. She said something in a Chinese dialect that Lu See did not recognize. A man's laughter emanated from somewhere behind the partition.

"I'd like to see your supervisor."

"No can."

"And why is that?"

The girl ignored the question. She set down her emery board and proceeded to explore the outer rim of a nostril with her thumb.

"Excuse me! I want to see your superior."

"No can."

"Why?"

"You wan talk abow Tibet entry permit?"

"Yes. I've written countless letters and telephoned your visa department God knows how many times."

"You telephone again tomorrow."

"But I don't want to telephone tomorrow. I'm here now. Where is your supervisor, please?"

The girl looked at her for the very first time. She stretched forward and tugged on a cord with her fingers. Suddenly a bamboo chick dropped down. The counter window was now closed.

Lu See banged her fist against the glass.

No response.

She turned and was immediately confronted by a consular official in white shirtsleeves and black trousers. He seemed to appear out of nowhere like a jack-in-the-box. It startled her.

"What is your interest in Tibet?" he asked. "Why do you wish to visit?" He had short thick legs and bad teeth.

"I have a friend in Lhasa, a very dear friend."

He stood with his thick legs wide apart like a man about to swing an axe. When he spoke only his upper lip moved. "At this point in time all avenues to Tibet are temporarily closed. The country is undergoing a peaceful liberation. We must give it time to rebuild without outside interference."

"And what about the poor souls left there?"

"These *poor souls*, as you call them, are gaining from China's generosity. New schools are being built, new roads. It is like renovating a house. Such things take time. In years to come people will see how we have helped and modernized Tibet. We have improved the lot of the Tibetan people."

"Is that what you call it?" Lu See pushed past him, talking as she walked. "I call it ruling with an iron fist." She reached the revolving doors and looked into the man's expressionless eyes. "I call it governing with brute force, imposing your beloved Chairman's totalitarian hell on a deeply religious people."

Seconds later she was being escorted to the main gates by a uniformed guard. "You know I'm right," she shouted. A curious feeling of elation filled her. It felt wonderful berating them this way. She took a deep breath and yelled at the top of her voice. "You know I'm absolutely bloody right!"

15

Sum Sum ploughed on, head down, thrusting against the wind. This was the final push; she could see the end of the mountain range ahead. The Punjab Himachal border was a mere thirty miles beyond the ridge. In the far, far distance she believed she could see a black outline of trees and smoke billowing from a forge as blacksmiths pounded metal on anvils.

"We are down to the last hour of sunlight." She urged herself on; counting out her steps: seven, eight, nine, left-right, left-right, fifteen, sixteen, seventeen, right-left, right-left, until her mind began to drift from exhaustion. She found herself thinking about a train ride. A train ride she'd taken years ago. The train chugged through a jungle tapestry, then through kampong villages, and a little later she got the sensation of nearing a town. The scenery changed – dirt roads were replaced with tarmac; shanty huts with shop-houses; the sounds of cock crows and fragmented car horns; buildings sprouting up like bamboo shoots. Juru. Was it Juru? And then someone was calling to her. The sound brought her back to earth. She told her legs to keep moving, left-right, left-right, seventy-nine, eighty, left-right, left.

New memories now: a city in England; King's Parade; the Backs; trees in leaf along Jesus Lane; Fitzbillies cake chop; college oars mounted on the walls of a pub; croci sprouting on Parker's Piece; the kitchens at Christ's; Pietro's laugh; the first time she held her baby girl.

Hours. Hours came. Hours went.

Her legs were stiff and heavy.

Her lips and cheeks felt frozen solid. A couple of jaw flexes got her face muscles working again. She looked behind to check on Tormam.

She saw the drag left behind by her own footsteps and was gripped by a paroxysm of fear.

Tormam wasn't there.

16

Coolies employed by the H.M.O. pushed handcarts carrying anti-malaria-oil; they entered the bus hubs and recreation areas and pumped the air with spray-clouds. The mosquito-men squeezed into storm drains, into hard-to-reach places, and directed their squirt-gun nozzles into nooks and crannies.

Not far away from the *ktts-ktts-ktts* of the spray cannons, Lu See clambered up a wooden step-ladder with an armload of Eagle Brand condensed milk. She shunted the tins indiscriminately on to the top shelf and looked down. Three pairs of eyes pored over the front page of the *Malay Advocate*. Mother, Dungeonboy and Pietro grappled with the lead article, almost falling over one another to digest the news.

For weeks now, since Singapore's merger with the Federation of Malaya in September 1963 the talk had been of the rising tide of ethnic disharmony and the deep mistrust amongst the races; fear and frustration threatened to boil over.

"And who exactly are the LPM nowadays?" Mother inquired with casual disdain.

"Look, I insist you stand on my left," said Pietro. "I've gone a bit quiet on this side."

Mother shuffled around. "I know they call themselves the Labour Party of Malaya, but surely they're communists through and through. All they do is promote Chinese heritage and education and spread anti-Malay sentiment."

"They're all as bad as the other, fuelling racial and religious hatred to win votes," Pietro said, dreamily.

Mother tilted forward on her elbows. "I read in the papers that one of the LPM members was shot by the police a few days ago resisting arrest."

"Only after a rival politician was hacked to death in Penang by Chinese radicals," Pietro conceded with a fainting sound.

"Is true?" asked Dungeonboy.

"Cross my heart and hope to see your Jap's eye."

The phone rang. Fishlips Foo picked up the receiver. "*Wai-eeeee!*"

He slammed it back down and scratched his ankles, muttering, "Sons of the soil these Malays call themselves! *Hum gaa chaan*! More like sons of night soil." He eyed the next table. Uncle Big Jowl, necklaced with perspiration, was launching into a bowl of vegetable soup.

Lu See climbed from the stepladder and stretched her arms over her head to ease the ache in her stomach. The phone rang once more.

"*Hum gaa chaan!*"

Lu See snatched the receiver out of the old man's hand. She heard a hissing on the line like the sizzle of palm oil on a hot wok, followed by voices and the click-clack of type-writers. "Yes? Who is this?" she said.

"This is P.K. Au from the *Malay Advocate*."

"Yes?" Lu See fumbled with the telephone cord as she spoke. From across the room Pietro stuck his tongue out and flicked a piece of bread at her. She turned her back on him. "And how might I assist you, Mr Au?"

A tiny square of bread struck her back.

"I'd like to write a piece on your restaurant, Il Porco. Perhaps we can discuss the details face to face. I would like to interview you, come and see the restaurant, perhaps take some photographs."

"And sample the food of course," she added.

"Huh?"

"I assume you will want to review the food for your article."

". . . yes . . . er, yes . . ."

Lu See exhaled down the phone. "Mr Au, what exactly do you intend to write about?"

She heard him hesitate. "We are running a story on racial provocation leading up to the election. Can you confirm you deliberately try to bait your Muslim neighbours by serving pork? Is it true that you–?"

She banged the receiver down hard.

"Who was that?" asked Mother, scratching her palms.

"A reporter. Those bloody vultures love stirring up trouble." She marched into the kitchen and returned with a bowl of vegetable broth for Fishlips Foo.

Fishlips tipped his liver-spotted tortoise head towards his soup and took a sip. He grunted in disgust. "This soup is lousy." His spoon clinked against the bowl. "All watered down. No taste!"

"Uncle Big Jowl likes the soup," said Lu See.

"Look how fat he is. He eats anything."

"You've been ordering the same soup every day for the last ten years, Mr Foo."

"And every time, no flavour. Also how come my portion so much less than his portion? Always you try to cheat me."

"I'll fetch you another bowl if you want more," Lu See said.

"Why you think I want more? Soup has no taste."

Uncle Big Jowl mopped up the cracker crumbs on the table with his middle finger.

"What word from within the walls of Troy?" asked Pietro.

Lu See had no idea what he was on about.

"Oh, you are a howling monkey," he roared with a gleam of teeth. "Tibet? Sum Sum?"

Lu See shrugged. She'd tried. She'd really tried. But no one was prepared to tell her anything. The radio and press reported conflicting news. Only last week a regular customer sat down for a plate of pork and announced that China was at war with Tibet. Lu See spread her hands in a plea. "I call the Chinese Embassy continually and keep getting brushed aside. I called them three times yesterday but they were deliberately vague, denying all knowledge of a 'crackdown' in Tibet." Her mother grunted. Lu See recognized Mother's look. It meant she thought Lu See was wasting her time trying to track down Sum Sum. "So I went to the Chinese Embassy in person, again," she continued. "An awful woman with flat feet made me wait, then I was herded into a small room with nothing but a bare desk, three chairs and a couple of men in Mao suits. They asked me more questions than I asked them. And what did I get out of them? Nothing."

Pietro paused in the middle of sucking on his long cigarette holder. "Typical diplomats."

"I even spoke to someone in the Red Cross and telephoned the Indian High Commission – nobody was willing to say anything about the Dalai Lama or the situation in Lhasa."

"Oh, Archimedes' screw! Poor old sausage. She's a survivor, is our precious Sum Sum. Let's hope she follows the Dalai Lama's lead and fiddles a ride over the border to Dharamsala." Pietro, sipping tea, opened his diplomatic pouch, as was his habit, and sifted through the low-priority mail. He opened a seemingly incongruous-looking letter with a nail file and then, without warning, sprang to his feet, pressed his fedora to his head and bolted out the door.

"What happened to him?" asked Mother. "He late for a hair appointment, is it?" Just then she spotted Lu See lifting a red $10 note from the till and sticking it into an envelope. Mother inhaled audibly. "What you doing?"

"What does it look like I'm doing?"

"Are you stealing?" She emphasized the last word.

"It's none of your business, Mother."

"Are you gambling, is that it?"

"I don't gamble."

"Drinking! You take the money and hide it, then use it for your drinking!"

"Look, it's my restaurant, I can do what I want with the proceeds."

Mother glared at her, more curious than stunned. "Your uncle and I are silent partners. We own 10 per cent. Maybe you conveniently forgotten." Lu See felt her cheeks grow warm and hid her embarrassment by showing Dungeonboy a chipped teacup.

The telephone rang once more. This time Lu See was quickest off the mark. After a moment she replaced it on its cradle. "That was James. He says there are several thousand people taking part in a march. He told us to close up the restaurant."

"Close up? Why?" asked Uncle Big Jowl.

Lu See wasn't sure. "All he said was that they were chanting Maoist slogans and provoking the Malays with slit-throat gestures."

Everyone, including Fishlips Foo, scratched their heads. Unfazed, Lu See stacked a clean plate in Dungeonboy's outstretched arms, then another. As soon as he had shelved them, he slammed the shutters and returned to wash more dishes. A minute later they heard something. Dungeonboy, at the basin, up to his elbows in soap suds, urged everyone to be quiet. He strained his neck to one side, wiping the soap residue from his arms with a dishcloth.

A noise approached, throbbing and subterranean, thrumming through from the ground itself like the rumbling sound of heavy rain pulsing in the distance.

Lu See, Mother, Uncle Big Jowl, Dungeonboy and Fishlips Foo crept toward the restaurant's bright orange shutter windows and peeped out, spellbound.

One by one the legion materialized like ants spilling from a blazing anthill.

Howls of voices whipped the air, echoing back and forth between the shophouses. Throngs chanted *'Malai Sai! Kill the Malays! Malai Sai! Kill the Malays!'*

Swarm after swarm of Chinese demonstrators filled the

maze of streets, jamming the five-foot ways, tumbling in like a downward rush of water from a broken dam. *The East is Red! The Communist Party is like the sun! Wherever it shines our doctrine will spread!*

It was like the roar of approaching rapids.

Lu See clapped a hand to her mouth. She recognized the scene; she'd seen it before: 1936, London. The mob behaved like an out-of-control funeral procession baying for the blood of the dead. *"Malai Sai! Malai Sai!"*

Mother's hand went to her throat. "You hear what they're saying about the Malays? They say they're going to kill them. Shall we call the police?"

"I can't believe this is happening," said Lu See.

Huge posters of Chairman Mao waved high in the air, peering down from the heavens, levitating over the multitude like a godhead.

Chairman Mao is the red sun in our souls!

Arm in arm, they marched, many in flip-flops and wearing only shorts and singlets, brandishing little red books, each one carrying either a picket, a *parang*, a cudgel or a flaming torch. They yelled at the Malays to crawl back to the jungle and tore down the tin tinkerer's sign, stomping on it as if it was a mangrove snake.

"Where are they heading?" Lu See wondered, clutching the fabric of her *kebaya*.

"Why must they come through here, don't they realize this is a Muslim area?" cried Mother.

"That's precisely why they've taken this route, to provoke the Malays." Lu See poked her head out into the sea of migrating bodies, raising herself onto her toes. She paused there. The clingy smell of sweaty bodies filled her nostrils, and then, much more worryingly, the oily stink of rag torches being lit.

Already dimples of destruction were visible: carts overturned here; lamplights and window glass shattered there. Most bystanders had fled in fear, but a few stood transfixed.

Some of the local street vendors huddled into a traffic podium at the end of the road like a frightened flock of sheep, staring with bewildered gelatinous eyes. As the crowd thickened they packed themselves ever tighter.

That was when Lu See saw Pietro. The throng pulled him from his car and jostled him to and fro. She also spotted her Muslim neighbour, Abdul bin Kassim, being manhandled. With the wall of noise still ringing in her ears, Lu See lifted the iron grille and dashed outside. She snatched a burning torch from somebody's hand and waved it to thin the rabble in her path. "Don't you dare touch him!" she screamed.

A Chinese man had his fist around Abdul bin Kassim's tightly rolled beard; another was tearing his *songkok* in two.

"What do you think you are doing?" she spat.

The scrum hesitated. "We are teaching these Malays a lesson."

"This man is my friend and neighbour. He lives next door to my shophouse restaurant."

"Shophouse restaurant?" One of the men flicked his eyes about. He was thirtyish with stick-thin legs. She indicated Il Porco with an arm. "That is your restaurant?" He teetered with surprise.

"Please. Look at all the damage you've done."

"But they were asking for it," replied a man with a pimple on his nose.

"The only people asking for it are the politicians. They are the ones responsible for drafting these concessions." She pressed herself forward. "If you have a problem with my friend Abdul bin Kassim, you better think twice. All the years I have been here, not once has he complained about my pork restaurant, not once has he petitioned me to move away." The heat of the torch coloured her face. "What the hell are you people trying to do? Cause a race riot?"

"We want the government to hear our plight. The Malays are getting all these privileges – "

"So you decide to burn their businesses down. That's just

stupid," she cried. "Put your *parangs* away. If you want to be heard, demonstrate outside the parliament buildings. Leave us alone. On this street we are all Malayans. We are all equal."

The man with the pimple lowered his eyes and frowned at his bony feet.

Lu See's eyes blazed. "Who is in charge of this lamebrain rabble? This is just wanton destruction. You're acting like animals. Soon you'll be tearing into people with your bare teeth. You," she addressed the man with the stick-thin legs, "What do you do?"

"I'm an electrician."

"Is this a reflection of how you live?"

"How I live? I live a very civilized life, I'll have you know," he said, taking offence.

"Who do you live with? Your ma, your wife, children?"

"My wife and I have two daughters."

"What would they say if they could see you now? Attacking poor, innocent people." The man frowned at his feet too. "I'm sure they would be very sad. A nice, intelligent man like you . . ." Lu See glared at him for several moments.

"Sorry," he told his feet. A number of men stared at him unsure what to do next.

A minute later, Stan Farrell's Ford Anglia came into view with winking lights and the bee-boo-bee-boo of sirens.

Abdul bin Kassim dusted himself down and retreated to his house, just as Lu See saw Pietro push his way towards her. "Let me through, you horny-thumbed brutes," he yelled.

Gradually, the group moved off. They made almost no noise as they went their separate ways.

Wanting to avoid Stan at all costs, Lu See took Pietro by the arm and led him back to the restaurant, through the tidemarks of vandalism.

As soon as she sat down, Dungeonboy pressed a cup of *teh tarik* into her hands.

Reversing buttocks-first on to a sturdy wooden stool, Uncle Big Jowl sank down with a thump like a wobbly sack of spuds. "You lucky, aahh. Mob like that can go damn-powerful crazy, lah. They act without head or tail."

"Ten years ago I would have come out there with you," said Fishlips. "*Hum gaa chaan!*"

Mother, too, fussed over her. "*Chee!* When did you get so bossy, ordering grown men around, hnn? Who did you learn from?"

"I wonder," she replied, squeezing Mother's arm. Lu See turned to Pietro. "You left here very hurriedly earlier."

"Yes, I received a letter. A rather disturbing letter, actually."

"I could tell. From?"

"The abbess from Sum Sum's nunnery."

Lu See straightened up quickly, as if jabbed by an electric cattle prod. "The abbess? From Sum Sum's nunnery? I don't understand. How? Why has she been writing to you? Oh God, has something happened to Sum Sum?"

"She's all right." He looked sheepish now. "Sum Sum's been writing to me for some time now. The clever moo tracked me down by getting in touch with my old Cambridge college; urged them to forward all post to me."

Lu See felt a tinge of jealousy. "What does she write about?"

He looked at her levelly. "Up until recently, not much. Bits and pieces about wanting to smack Chinese communists over the head with chestnut pans and whatnot. But the last two letters have been most disturbing. Pleas for help, no less. I think she might have been worried about Chinese censors so it was a bit cryptic and cloak and daggerish. A bit like unravelling Rapunzel's tangled *tuchis*, but I've managed to piece it all together: she's going to follow the Dalai Lama to India."

"What? Alone? Across the Himalayas?"

"According to the abbess's letter, it would seem so, yes, and across to Dharamsala."

Lu See felt a low panic in her gut. "But I read in LIFE that the Dalai Lama went with horses and . . . and Sherpas. Going alone would be suicide."

"What's wrong?" asked Mabel. She was preparing for her night shift at the hospital when she spotted her mother from the corridor.

"Nothing," Lu See replied, tossing woollen socks and thick winter clothes she hadn't worn in years into her eel skin trunk.

They were in Lu See's bedroom above the restaurant. Mabel pushed aside some cushions and sat at the end of her mother's bed. "It's something awful, isn't it? You're going away to die. You've decided to end it all in some secluded place, like a wasteland or an underground grotto. Old elephants do the same thing when they think they're about to die. They go to an elephants' graveyard – some dark cave in the wilderness."

Lu See folded a scarf and placed it neatly on a woollen cardigan.

"That's it, isn't it?"

"No," Lu See said. "I'm not going in search of some cave in the wilderness."

"What then? Tell me! It's bad news. I can tell it is bad news."

"I wouldn't call it bad news. Actually it's all quite exhilarating."

"Exhilarating?"

"Yes." Lu See reached across her suitcase and pulled out a folding map.

"What's this?" asked Mabel.

"It's a map of India."

"For heaven's sake, I can see it's a map of India. But what's that got to do with you? Is that where you're planning on going?"

"Not just me. You are too." Lu See turned to Mabel. She was beaming.

"Oh God! I've seen that look on your face before. It's your crazy look. What is it?"

"I'll tell you later. Go pack your bags. Bring a thick jacket and winter clothes."

Mabel did not budge from the end of her mother's bed. Instead she kept eyeing her nervously. "What the hell is going on?"

"If the doctors here can't help me, then I'm going to go and find it myself."

"Find what? What on earth are you talking about?"

"I'm talking about a cure, Mabel. I'm going to go find a bloody cure."

That evening the restaurant was quiet.

Lu See and Pietro were chatting over a pot of tea when they heard a rap on the iron grille. Stan Farrell stepped gingerly across the threshold with his police cap tucked between arm and ribcage. "Sorry to interrupt. Just wanted to say all is calm again. Most of the demonstrators have gone home."

Lu See blew the froth from her tea. "I thought I told you never to step foot in here again."

"Yes, quite right. I'll be off then."

"No, sit down," ordered Lu See.

Stan did as he was told. Hunched over, he pressed his hands tightly between his knees.

She glared at him. "I haven't forgiven you."

"I know you haven't."

"And I never will. You're a weasel."

Pietro smoothed his eyebrows with a thumb. "Careful, dahling, little boys love being insulted by little girls; it makes them feel loved."

"You're a weasel and a snake."

"Fair enough," said Stan. "But I need you to understand that I was set up, just as you were. I never knew about the bomb. I never set out to hurt you or Mabel."

She raised a warning finger. Her eyes raked his face. "Whatever you say isn't going to change things between us. You realize that, don't you?"

Stan drew his lips uneasily over his sticking-out teeth.

"And you, Pietro, I saved you from a beating earlier on. That mob would have really roughed you up."

Pietro set his delicate jaw. "Oh, dahling, you can be such a melodramatic Mary."

"Shut up!"

Both men jumped in their seats.

Lu See kept her finger raised like a weapon. "And because you both owe me, you're both going to do something for me."

"I am?" whinnied Pietro.

"We are?" said Stan.

"You are."

"What?" they asked, swallowing.

"Pietro and I are going on an adventure."

"An adventure?" cried Pietro. "Where on earth to?"

"You are going to accompany me to Dharamsala, India."

Pietro blanched. "Bronte's withering tights! India? What, with all those beggars you can smell at twenty paces?"

"Yes, Pietro, I'll need all your diplomatic weight behind me. And, Stan, you spent a year in Bombay, you have your contacts. You can find out for me how we get from Madras to Himachal Pradesh."

"When're you going?" asked Stan.

"Next week," said Lu See.

"Oh, Edesia's enema! How am I going to cope with all that curry?" yelped Pietro. "What about my wind?"

"Put a cork in it," said Stan.

"Oh, *brah-haaa*, very droll, slippery Stanley, very droll indeed."

"But what do you hope to achieve, Lu See?" demanded Stan.

"What I've been trying to achieve for the last twenty bloody years: find Sum Sum."

"How do you know she's at Dharamsala?"

"It's the home of the Dalai Lama's exiled government. If she's anywhere that's where she'll be, at the Geden Choezom sanctuary for exiled nuns." Lu See went to the telephone and picked up the receiver. "But there's one last thing I must do before we leave. I have to take Mabel back to Juru. There's something I need her to see."

Mother, who had been eavesdropping, suddenly piped up. "Juru? Why on earth are you going back there? Cha! That place now attracts a lower class of people if you ask me."

"Let's just say I have some unfinished business to look after." Lu See dialled the number for the hospital and asked to speak with Mabel's superior, the handsome surgeon. She informed him that her daughter was taking the following day off. And he wasn't to protest.

17

On arrival at Juru train station, Lu See and Mabel rented a pair of bicycles and took the road to Po On Village.

With the sunshine breaking through the clouds, they rolled straight through the country lanes, skirting long-legged chickens and kampong women wearing sarongs tied above the chest. They trickled by little streams, pootled through a mango grove where the air was sweetened by fallen fruit and the early-morning rain. Pumping their legs, they climbed up a broad hill, passing a troop of monkeys and an austere-looking water buffalo with an equally austere white bird on its back. Grasping their handlebars tight, they juddered into a field of sugar cane wilting in the heat, before stopping to admire six barefoot boys playing *sepak manggis* in the shade.

Potholes slipped beneath Mabel's wheels. She hit a puddle and with a shout of glee sent a blanket of spray up over her ankles.

When they reached Po On Village they were amazed that the place looked exactly as it had done in the 1940s. Up ahead they saw the village square, empty now except for some dogs and the odd chicken. Beyond the Chinese Temple was the old toddy shop, the pith wood store and the mosquito-net maker. It was as though they'd been transported back in time.

"Are you going to tell me why we've come back?" asked Mabel.

"You'll see," replied her mother. They cycled in the direction of the big house.

"Are you taking me to see our old home?"

"No."

Mabel's curiosity was fully aroused now. Just as she was wondering where Lu See would lead her, they stopped by a 10-foot high wooden gate. An Englishman in a bush hat came striding out of a lodge office to greet them.

Under his hat, Mabel noticed his complexion was as glossily enamelled as a glazed roast duck – a planter's face, baked stiff by the tropical sun. He carried a bamboo switch tucked under his arm like a swagger stick. Both women smoothed their hair into place.

"Mabel, meet Mr Charlie Fosler." Mabel alighted and shook hands. "Charlie runs one of the large rubber estates here."

"Ayup, ladies," he said in his gruff Yorkshire accent.

With the formalities over Charlie led them over some worn stone steps towards a curve of field and a plantation house by a copse of angsana trees.

Under the angsanas, streaks of moss glinted emerald in the sunlight. Charlie led them through his house and into the drawing room. An Anglican priest rose from a chair as soon as they entered. He was in his late fifties with grey hair and florid cheeks.

"Well, hello, Lu See," exclaimed the priest.

"Father Louis. How nice to see you again." Lu See placed an arm on Mabel's shoulder. "May I introduce my daughter, Mabel."

"An exciting day, what?" said Father Louis. His long fingers folded over Mabel's outstretched hand.

"Delighted to meet you, but I really don't know what this is all about."

"Nor should you. Your mother's been planning this for years, coming down to see us in secret."

Mabel's face was a question.

"No idea? Well, then, we'd better show you," said the priest, giving her a wink. "Let's go for a walk, shall we?"

A few minutes later they emerged from the copse of angsana trees and came to the Anglican Church, perched on the river's edge.

"The Japanese used it as a rice storage facility. Left it in horrid disrepair. And of course, as you know, the pipe organs were stolen. Your mother tidied it up but the Juru Diocesan Trustees Association simply had no funds to replace the damaged floors and pews."

"We approached the Chinese Synod but they could not help either," added Lu See.

"It was a desperate time." The priest placed his arm on the heavy teak doors and pushed them open. They entered the fresh, white-walled interior. "But thanks to your mother and her negotiation skills, we prevailed."

Shafts of sunlight streamed in through the coloured-glass windows. Fans on the ceilings whirred silently.

Lu See led Mabel by the hand. "I worked out a plan, and we came to a formal arrangement with the surrounding estates."

"The tin miners refused point blank, but the plantation companies agreed to contribute."

"Grudgingly, mind you," said Charlie Fosler with a grin.

"They agreed to donate cent of revenue per planted acre."

"And your mother put in the rest."

"You did?" said Mabel.

"Every week I took $10 from my share of the restaurant takings and donated it to the fund." There was a hint of quiet pride in her voice. "It took me fifteen years until we had enough."

"Enough for what?"

"The new pipe organ, of course."

"Ah, that's where I coom in," said Charlie Fosler.

"Charlie's uncle sold us the original copper pipes."

"It dint tek much for me to persuade the old bloke to cast a new set at a knock-down price. You being a return customer and all."

"And here it is," beamed Father Louis.

Lu See came forward and stroked the solid console base. The case work was in oak, shiny and highly-polished. The organ employed both mechanical key and stop action. "It's beautiful," she said. She examined the pedals and then, finally, gazed up at the pipes. The copper glinted in the sun as if coated with grease. "Absolutely beautiful."

"Thought you'd like it," said Charlie Fosler. "We put up the memorial tablet for you too."

A brass plaque hung to the left of the organ. It read:
This pipe organ was donated in memory of
Teoh Tak Ming 1915-1935
AND
Adrian W.S. WOO 1912-1936

Lu See looked at it and smiled.

Lu See and Mabel chose a pew and sat side by side.

Father Louis folded his long fingers across the keyboard.

Just as Lu See shut her eyes a blast of sound shuddered the air – the opening bursts of Bach's Prelude in C Major. The notes swirled in circles, around and around her head. They rose and fell. The eddying swell of noise permeated the walls, shook the ground and trembled the leaves on the trees outside. It drowned out all thought and knocked the breath out of Lu See. This was what she'd waited so long to hear; this was the music she'd sung to as a child, in the choir.

When Father Louis brought his hands to a stop and the air grew still, it felt as though the church had been washed clean. Lu See dropped her chin to her chest. She felt a solitary tear slip down her face, drying on her cheek. It made her skin itch.

Outside the church, Lu See and Mabel stood on the stone steps.

Mabel leaned forward and whispered in Lu See's ear. "I'm proud of you."

"I've had to keep this from your grandmother," she admitted, looking up at the sky. "Otherwise she'd be down here every weekend, sticking her oar in."

"Grandma thought you were stealing from the till. She kept dropping hints that you might be gambling or getting secretly drunk." From her voice, Lu See could tell Mabel was smiling. She glanced at her daughter, half amused.

There was another long silence.

"Fifteen years. I'm amazed you didn't give up."

"I needed to finish this. For my sake, for Second-aunty Doris and cousin Tak Ming's sake."

"You make it sound like an obsession."

"This church is a very important to me. It holds wonderful memories. It is part of our heritage. This is where I hope you will get married."

Mabel smiled; she thought about her surgeon friend. "Did you ever think about throwing in the towel?"

"No. After the war, even though we'd left Juru, I was determined to get the pipes replaced."

"Because you lost them."

"Because of a promise I made to Second-aunty Doris. But also because they were stolen by a man I hated." Her voice grew flat with disgust.

"The man with the mole, yes, Uncle Big Jowl mentioned him once when I was much younger. He was the one that put the sheep's head in the ground."

"You remember that."

"Of course I remember. I was eight years old. It's not something an 8-year-old easily forgets."

"I'm sorry."

"What did he do to you? Why did you hate him so much?"

"He–" Lu See held her tongue. She was about to elaborate but quickly stopped herself. She shuddered inside at her carelessness.

"He what?"

Lu See saw the impatience and hunger in Mabel's eyes; she wanted to hear the full story.

"He what?" Mabel jabbed her with the same question. The colour seeped out of Lu See's face. She tried to think of what to say, dusting her words with a sprinkling of lies. But it was like walking on thin ice. The truth would stab a hole in the frozen water and pull them under. And beneath the ice lurked something dark and wrong and jagged. Long dead. Never to be brought to light.

The night before she left for India, Lu See removed a letter she'd kept hidden in an inner pocket of her eel-skin trunk for almost a quarter-century. It was a letter from Sum Sum. Lu See wasn't sure why she'd kept it for so long without destroying it. Perhaps, she thought, it was because the letter had been written in Sum Sum's hand, and anything belonging to Sum Sum was sacred to her.

Lu See set an ashtray by her elbow together with a box of matches. Tentatively, she unfurled the page and smoothed it flat with the palm of her hand. The blue ink was faded, the paper a little yellowed.

My dear Lu See, my sister, my friend,

I write this from a ship I have boarded from Felixstowe and my heart is crying.

I have left you with my child, I have left you with many unanswered questions. Now is the time for you to know the truth. Soon after we both arrived in Cambridge something bad happened. Remember the day I lost the camera? I told you I had accident and it dropped into the river? Well, I lied. I not drop the camera. I gave it to a man. The same man I saw coming out of the jungle when the dam broke. The same man you saw on the Jutlandia. The man with the mole on his cheek.

He was in Cambridge. He followed us. On day you had college interview that is when he come for me. When he found me, he chased me to a place with no people around.

He catch me. And then he say if I ever tell anyone about the dam he will kill you. Not kill me, but kill *you*. I promised him I will keep quiet and I told him I would do anything if he went away, do anything so that he won't hurt you.

So, I give him camera, I give him all the photographs . . . and I give him me.

He tear my clothes and hit my face.

For a long time, Lu See, I have nightmares. I think I see him everywhere I go. I think I can smell him. But I never see him again after that day.

Some time later, I started feeling sick with baby.

Promise me you NEVER tell Mabel about this. Never tell anyone about the man with mole. You must keep this our secret forever to protect Mabel.

As I wrote in earlier letter, perhaps Mabel's smile is not the same as your own baby's smile, the baby God took away, but I know you will grow to love Mabel. Be good to each other. Right now, you need her and she need you.

I thank the Goddess Tara for all the love and kindness you have given me.

I will always treasure you.

Sum Sum

Lu see lifted her eyes and stared at the ceiling, stared at the slowly revolving fan. And then, without hesitating, she struck a match and applied it to a corner of the page. She watched it burn like an offering to the gods.

18

The journey to Dharamsala involved taking two ferry boats, three commuter trains and sitting in a Leyland bus built in the 1930s for fifteen hours.

Lu See's spirits were light, full of girlish energy. She couldn't wait to see Sum Sum; the anticipation electrified her. Yet she tried not to get ahead of herself – there was no way of knowing if Sum Sum was in Dharamsala, or in Tibet, whether she was even alive at all. But somehow, in her bones, Lu See knew with an unshakeable certainty that she would find Sum Sum. She felt the pull of their friendship and an overpowering sense that fate was drawing close.

Dharamsala. She toyed with the word, rolling it around on her tongue like a salted plum. In Hindi it meant 'sanctuary', a place for injured souls. She wondered if the city in the upper reaches of the Kangra Valley would bring her soul the peace it craved.

Earlier, in Penang, with the thick smell of the sea in her hair, she watched loinclothed Lascars with arms and shoulders blackened from the sun unload a shiny red fire engine with a heavy lift derrick. A shout went up. The fire truck swung in the air like a toy. Children playing street badminton nearby dropped their racquets and gathered about, unable to contain their excitement, whooping with delight as the engine landed on the quay. Their excitement was infectious. It reminded her of the laughter she once shared with Sum Sum.

Then, as Lu See's ship left Penang harbour, skirting the coastline, she stared out at the hills of George Town, at the fields of palm parched by the sun, at the fish farms, tin mines and coconut groves. A farmer reclined in the shade, on a makeshift bed made from coconut fibre rope and the image made her smile; it summed up everything she loved about Malay rural life; everything sleepy and calm.

Despite herself, she was touched by a sense of nostalgia.

Do you remember? Lu See lowered her eyelids. *Do you remember, years before, standing on the deck of the Jutlandia? Watching the port recede from view, embarking on that adventure of a lifetime? You were the girl who'd never travelled beyond the Straits of Malacca. The girl who believed she controlled her own destiny.*

"How little I knew," she murmured to herself. "How little I knew."

She turned and walked, walked all the way around to the bow of the ship, until the barrier at the end stopped her. She gripped the handrail tight and, feeling the breeze in her face, laughed at the sun.

Her lips tasted salt. Her eyes tasted happy tears.

She was on a new adventure.

And she was going to look forward not back.

When they arrived in Madras, Pietro took charge, flashing his diplomatic documents. But getting from Dr. Ambedkar Dock to the dilapidated Royapuram Rail Station proved to be a trial; the traffic jam of trishaws and rickshaws and the seething mass of people made Pietro swoon. "It's like everyone's rushing for the khazi but nobody's got the key," he moaned. Their Ambassador cab swerved past buses bloated with passengers. Each time they hit a pothole Mabel and Pietro yelped.

Their train for New Delhi left at 13.30. They made it with twenty minutes to spare. They were told they had to change at Hyderabad.

The station master wore a pair of open-toe sandals with yellow nylon socks which looked as if they hadn't been laundered in a while. The fat folds on his neck were so deep they'd turned pink and crusty. Swollen like some gargantuan sweaty bean, he brandished their tickets and barked out their platform number.

"This fella makes Uncle Big Jowl look like Fred Astaire," whispered Mabel.

Thirty-six hours later, they alighted at Delhi Junction, pushed through the wall of warped-limbed beggars, and headed straight for the Maidens Hotel.

The following morning at 5 a.m., a bus took them north from New Delhi. Lu See peered out the window, rubbing the mist from the glass with her hand. She stared at the pre-dawn sky, cut and scarred with strips of colour – low clouds lit with orange and pink.

Meanwhile, Pietro pored over the *Hindustan Times*; there was no mention of Malaya in the 'World News' section. "All quiet at home," he said, sounding relieved.

Lu See knew what he meant. There hadn't been any trouble in KL since the incident outside her restaurant; but the fault lines had been drawn; a large portion of the community had been made to feel like aliens in their own country. It was, she conceived, only a matter of time before new racial tremors would shake the city. But she couldn't worry about that now.

She tucked her chin into the crook of her arm and slept.

Five hours later they stopped to stretch their legs and relieve themselves behind the trees.

Three hours after that, they stopped for lunch.

Lu See emerged from the bus to the smells of woodsmoke mingled with the scent of sautéing pine needles and cow-liver mushrooms, and feeling the dry scrape of the wind against her cheeks. The rarified atmosphere made her momentarily dizzy; she took in a deep breath and steadied herself. In the small eatery the band of tourists found themselves seated around an oval table. They were served little round dumplings floating in a dark soup with large mushrooms.

"What's this?" asked Lu See, sniffing the steam.

Pietro glanced about conspiratorially and mopped his brow with a handkerchief. He gave Lu See a 'Ye Gods' look. "It's like something a swamp-dweller might eat."

Mabel offered a corner-of-the-mouth grimace.

Lu See examined the contents of the bowl, smelling it, weighing it first in one hand and then the other, before dipping her spoon in. She wondered whether this was how Sum Sum felt the first time she tried Stilton cheese.

Back on the bus Lu See settled into her seat and stared out of the window. She saw nomads living in tents made of animal hair. She saw windowless houses with shingle-covered roofs and walls made from loam; women in long kurtas, ghaghri, salwars and cholis; farmers working fields clad in kurtas and caps.

Along the road joining Haryana to Mandi she saw snowy mountain peaks, rock monasteries, donkey-drawn caravans. *This is Sum Sum land*, she said to herself, *everywhere I look I see her face.*

Up ahead she saw the rugged, muscled landscape and the outline of mountains stabbed by ice-caps. Itinerant herds of goats dotted the terrain like seedpods.

The bus stopped again in the late afternoon. The rest house had lotus blossom carvings adorning its doors with painted *gyung-drung* swastikas gracing its walls.

"I think it must be market day," said Mabel.

Basket makers, salt traders, silversmiths and weavers lined up to greet them. Their language spilled from their throats as snatched, angular sounds.

Twenty yards along, men hunkering down to shear sheep, white wool scattered like snow about their knees, looked up momentarily and smiled at Lu See's camera. The thinness of the air made everything appear brighter and sharper. The rays of the sun seemed to travel farther.

After a while, they boarded the bus once again.

Lu See had read something – probably in LIFE magazine – about Dharamsala. "It's one of the main towns of the Kangra Valley," she told Pietro as he filed his nails. "And the mountain range encompasses three sides of it which give on to the valley stretching to the south. It's something like 6000 feet. above sea level with very rocky ground."

He stuck a finger to his chin. "Good thing I didn't pack my stilettos."

As they drew closer to Dharamsala, Lu See grew increasingly anxious. *Will we recognize one another, will we still be friends?* What would she see in Sum Sum's face? Perhaps she'd see her own reflection.

As soon as they settled into their boarding house, Pietro decided to hang back and explore Dharamsala proper. "I'll do some souvenir shopping. No point all of us barging in on the nuns and making a scene," he said. Lu See agreed with him.

Lu See grasped the handle of her art portfolio case, touched Mabel's elbow and led her through the bustling pavement life. Mabel had a Tupperware box tucked under her arm. Up ahead they could see the nunnery forecourt through the gates. Snow-splashed mountain peaks surrounded them. They passed letter-writers, *paan* sellers and women hawking rice. A woman with almond-shaped Nepali eyes, who seconds before was caressing her sandalled feet, held out a fistful of rice from a gunny sack. When Lu See shook her head no, she went back to massaging her big toe. A bit further on, under the shade of peepul trees, the letter-writers sat cross-legged on boxes, thrashing at the keys to their typewriters; every now and then they paused to listen to their clients' dictation. Further on still, a *paan* salesman combined betel leaves with lime and tobacco.

Lu See and Mabel passed through the modest set of gates

and into the temple complex. No one told them where to go or where they were allowed to go.

The air was crisp and clean and alive. Due to the steep altitude, their breath sat high up in their chests.

With the autumn chill gnawing at her, Lu See hopped about from foot to foot like a child eager for the loo.

"Well, this is it," said Mabel. "Geden Choezom Nunnery."

They looked up and saw butter lamps burning and nuns sitting cross-legged reciting Buddhist texts.

Overhead, prayer flags shook in flames of blue and white and yellow.

They approached the Dharma enclosure and each gave the *mani* wheels a spin.

"Which way do we go?" asked Lu See.

"Pietro said to head for the private huts next to the Dharma enclosure. I think this might be it."

"God, I hope Sum Sum recognizes me."

"We don't know she's even here. Don't get your hopes up."

"She's here. I know she's here."

They entered a small courtyard.

A few days earlier, Pietro, through his diplomatic connections, had made a telephone call to the local member of parliament; he in turn arranged for Lu See to meet with the chanting master.

Mabel went up to a young nun who was busy tending some flowers and asked for directions to the main office.

Lu See's mouth felt as dry as crust crumbs. She just needed to see Sum Sum's face. Hold her, touch her; she was dying to hear her laugh. Only then would she feel a sense of release.

Blindly, she followed her daughter down a corridor, the way a child usually followed her mother.

The chanting master, or *Umze*, was a sprightly thing called Ven Sengdroma. She wore wire spectacles and kept her hands folded in front in prayer pose.

"*Namas-te.*" Ven Sengdroma greeted Lu See and Mabel with a warm smile and draped white scarves over their shoulders. Balmy jasmine incense and pale candlelight filled the room. Somewhere in the distance Lu See could hear the incantations of gods' names being chanted. "The local member of parliament mentioned you are looking for someone specifically."

"Yes," Lu See said. "Her name is Sum Sum."

Ven Sengdroma's brow crinkled. "But there is nobody who goes by that name here."

"But there must be."

"Is that her Dharma name?"

Lu See had no idea what Ven Sengdroma was talking about.

"We have someone called Sonam who is only thirteen, a child really."

"No, Sum Sum is her name and she is forty five years old."

"Might you tell me anything more about her?"

"About your height. She was with the Ani Trangkhung Nunnery in Lhasa. Please," Lu See heard her voice crumble, "she must be here."

Ven Sengdroma looked blankly at her. "I'm so sorry. It would seem that your long journey has been for nothing. There is nobody by that description that resides here."

"Are you absolutely certain?" pleaded Lu See, desperately trying to hold her poise.

Ven Sengdroma's expression turned inwards; hands reached for a set of mala beads. "You must understand that many of our sisters did not survive the journey. Some were forced to turn back."

Lu See's eyes began to burn with disappointment. *Please, God, don't do this to me. Please tell me she's safe.* She tried one last time. "Aged forty five with a mischievous sense of humour."

Ven Sengdroma's thumb flicked one bead to the next.

"Mischievous sense of humour, you say . . . perhaps you're thinking of Sengemo . . ."

Mabel stopped when she reached what appeared to be a communal reception room. "It's just up ahead. Go out through that back door. It's the first hut to your right apparently."

Lu See paused, conscious of how anxious she'd become – her breath sounded too loud, and the curious frictionless thud sliding about in her head, she realized, was, in fact, her heartbeat. *I haven't felt like this since my Girton interview.* Just relax, she told herself.

She rose up on her toes and bounced on her feet.

"I'll wait here. I think it's best if you see her alone first," said Mabel.

"Are you sure?"

Mabel nodded. "Maximum sure." Yak butter candles burned all about her. "Leave the portfolio case. Come fetch me when you're both ready."

The afternoon sunshine streamed through the slats in the shutters like sparkle-dust. A finger of sunlight illuminated Mabel's face as she perched on a sheesham wood chair and toyed with the new engagement ring on her finger. Her eyes darted to the small but lustrous diamond that lit up her hand.

Her surgeon friend had proposed only days before. Did she love him? Yes. Did she still love Bong? Of course. She would never forget him. But five years had passed since his death and, post-Emergency, she'd had to move on with her life. She'd put herself back together and rediscovered her family. She still felt a penchant for the socialist movement, but instead of fighting she'd found a better way to help the poor – she healed them. Yes, her life was good again. It too was lustrous. It had the gleam of something perfect and intense and new.

Lu See gave Mabel's arm a squeeze of support and made

her way to unit 23-B. Once outside, Lu See looked up at the plate number, marked in red paint with the Tibetan words ??????. This is it, she said to herself. Her heart thumped against her breastbone. Taking a deep breath she rapped her knuckles on the doorframe and waited.

Nothing. No reply. She did it again and gingerly poked her head round the half-open door with an enquiring look.

At the far end of the room a woman sat in shadow. She was hunched and withered in the ailing light. The windows were open and a cool breeze ruffled the pages of a prayer book, yet a sour smell like stale milk lingered.

"Sum Sum?" Lu See called out, tentatively. She glared into the dark, searching the black shape of a face.

It took a long time for the crooked figure to stand up straight from her sitting position. Gradually, she moved out of the shadow, emerging like a withered bat from her shrivelled-up throne. She walked with laboured gasps, shuffling across a rug that had worn down to the weft, taking tiny steps as if weighed down by cement shoes. One pace forward, pause, another pace forward, pause.

The first thing Lu See saw were her chicken-feet hands and the raised green veins which were as milky green as drain water. They looked ice-bitten.

And then a finger of sunlight splashed across her face.

Lu See tried not to gasp. She saw an avalanche of age; the features of a ruined castle, weathered by a myriad of deep spidery lines; eyes blinded by cataracts. When their gazes met, there was no recognition in the woman's expression whatsoever.

"Sum Sum, it's me. Lu See."

The woman tipped her shorn head in confusion. A gurgled emission of air escaped from her throat. That's when Lu See saw the telltale droop and realized she'd suffered a stroke.

Lu See's heart unravelled like a worn pair of rope-soled shoes.

"I've come to see you. After all these years I finally made

it." She tried to sound cheerful. "Mabel's waiting for you too."

The woman blinked. Her face resembled a deflated beach ball. Perturbed, she turned away.

Lu See persisted. "Pumpkin-head. It's me, Lu See."

But to no avail. Slowly and deliberately, the woman turned and, walking with heavy steps, retreated from Lu See across the worn rug. When she reached her chair she sank back down, flecks of froth gathering on her lips.

Lu See watched the woman close her eyes, bowed by the weight of her illness.

A knuckle of despair lodged in Lu See's throat. A dull ache bloomed in her chest. She rubbed a hand down her face and had a sudden mental picture of having to explain this to Mabel. Perhaps if she went to fetch one of the younger nuns, she might be able to help?

Then all of a sudden a chastising voice from behind boomed in her ears. "You cuckoo-clocks crazy if you think that me! She 68-years-old, lah!"

Lu See spun round.

At first the shaven head took her by surprise. But then she registered the face, which was flat and furrowed with a crimp of anxiety between the eyes. It was undoubtedly her. It was Sum Sum.

Lu See stretched out her hands, taking Sum Sum by the forearms; Sum Sum's fingers reached out to hold hers in return. Touching her skin, thought Lu See, was like touching her own flesh. It was the best feeling in the world.

They held onto one another for a long time. They hugged so hard their bones made clicking noises. Hinges creaking, hearts pounding, their lips parted into wide smiles.

Then, laughing, they looked into each others' eyes as though they were nineteen again.

"You look tip-top well," said Sum Sum.

"You've always been a terrible liar. Look at the skin of my neck, resembles somebody's crumpled bedsheets."

"*Aiyo!* What about me? My face so lined it looks like it made from jungle vines."

"Nonsense, your skin's still as smooth as mutton fat. Not too sure about the hairstyle though."

Sum Sum ran the palm of her hand over her bare scalp. "Why must you talk such crazy-crackpot things after all these years?'

Lu See's soul overflowed with elation.

This was Sum Sum, her Sum Sum.

They'd both dreamed of this moment for over a quarter-century. Spilling over with happiness, Lu See squeezed Sum Sum's arm again as if to make sure it was real, that she was real.

And then, quite unexpectedly, the two women burst into tears.

A little later they sat with Mabel in the communal living room. For a long while Mabel and Sum Sum stared openly at each other in fascination, like baffled, spellbound aliens from separate worlds meeting for the very first time.

"I brought you something," said Lu See eventually, breaking the silence.

Draping her blue prayer beads round her wrist, Sum Sum accepted the Tupperware box. She was dressed like all the other nuns, in a maroon wrap-around shirt called a *dhonka* and matching skirt, together with dark socks and sandals.

"What's this, lah?" She prised open the lid. "*Aiyooo!* I recognize these, they're rosemary shortcakes!"

"You invented the recipe. I remember you used to eat two or three in one sitting."

"*Aiyo!* They smell wonderful. Can I try?"

"Of course, they're for you."

Sum Sum took a tiny bite, nibbling at it like a squirrel. She cupped a hand under her chin as the crumbs fell from her mouth, making '*Mmmmmmm*' sounds like a child licking ice cream from a spoon.

"And this is a photograph of my future husband," said Mabel.

"I bet he is magazine-cover handsome, no?" Sum Sum rubbed her eyes and focused hard on the image. "Looks strong like a yak. How long have you been engaged?"

"Only a few days," Mabel conceded with a smile. "He proposed on the morning I left."

"Mabel is going to marry a surgeon," said Lu See, unable to keep the pride from her voice.

"Wah," Sum Sum declared with approval, her eyes radiant.

Then Lu See kept quiet for a while. She watched how attentive and polite Mabel and Sum Sum were with one another, both desperate to make a good first impression. She noted how they tried to make a connection, tentatively holding hands, touching fingers, leaving impressions on the skin shaped like expectant joy. Between them though still nestled a pile of unuttered questions that neither was yet bold enough to ask.

A younger nun came up to them and handed out cups of yak butter tea.

Sum Sum introduced her. "This is my friend Tormam." Tormam bowed her head. "She saved my life many times when walking from Tibet."

"Actually, it was Sengemo who saved my life. I was lost and she tracked my footsteps and found me."

Sum Sum took a slurp of tea. "You like our national drink?" She said to Mabel with a mischievous smile.

Mabel nodded with laughing eyes. "Like drinking a thick cup of oily mud."

Sum Sum launched into a story about eating stinky cheese in England. It made Mabel laugh. And for the first time Lu See realized how much they looked alike, how their smiles were the same, sloping gradually from left to right.

"Hey, you still painting-painting?" Sum Sum asked Lu See.

"Oh, yes, I almost forgot." She reached across and unzipped her art portfolio case. One by one she removed the individual portraits of Mabel – acrylics, watercolours, even the odd oil. "You know, many years ago we had to abandon the big house, Tamarind Hill. I was forced to leave a number of things behind. But not these. These I have kept in a safe deposit box in the bank. They are more precious to me than money or jewellery. These pictures are my life." She handed them to Sum Sum. "Which is why I'm giving them to you."

"By Dharmakaya heaven! They are wonderful!" She clicked her tongue just to show how wonderful.

"There's one for almost every year of Mabel's life, documenting her growth." *It's a pictorial journal of all the times you missed.* "Look, this is the first one I ever did of Mabel. A pencil sketch when she was less than three months old. I was on ship, returning from England."

Mabel and Sum Sum leaned in close, holding the portrait between them like an umbilicus.

"*Aiyo Sami!* What a funny little nose you had!"

Mabel's eyes filled with a child's delight. "Me? Look who's talking, I got it from you."

They burst out laughing, rocking each other with their giggles.

Lu See excused herself. When the ache in her stomach was bad she always wanted to be alone. She found a small, abandoned room and sat down by the narrow window in a gold rectangle of light. Clutching at her insides, drawing in gasps of breath, she felt a cold perspiration form across her forehead.

"Are you unwell?"

Lu See glanced up and saw Tormam at the door. The shy-faced nun entered the small room and placed a reassuring hand on Lu See's back. After several moments, Lu See explained her symptoms, her frustrations, her disheartening inability to find a cure.

Tormam's hand went to Lu See's abdomen; she made slow sliding motions with her palm; it felt warm and soothing. "We will sit together later and review not only the outward symptoms but the inner ones too. Let me first prepare a cooling remedy that promotes digestion. There are many herbs here that can be of use," she said, reassuringly. "Many, many herbs."

"Do you think you can help me?"

Tormam's voice was like a balm. "There are no incurable diseases, only incurable people. If your mind is willing, we will heal you." She placed a set of prayer beads in Lu See's hand.

Lu See shut her eyes.

Outside, cloud-trails marked the sky. The sun glanced off the shiny wing of an alpine bird.

Lu See opened her eyes and looked out through the narrow window and saw Sum Sum and Mabel strolling together, hand in hand, across the lawn. They were still laughing.

A long time ago, Second-aunty Doris had told Lu See that life was not made up of days or weeks or years but of moments. This was one of those moments.

Remember, keep a green tree in your heart and perhaps the trembling leaves will stay away. Lu See smiled.

The prayer beads dazzled like orbs of blackened honey. She felt an inner glow of well-being. She had no regrets.

Her eyes grew bright and moist, like sun shining through spring raindrops. Finally, after years of being half of a whole, she was complete again. Full and round and whole once more.